The Stormbirds

The Stormbirds

Anne Griffiths

PIATKUS

For more information on
other books published by
Piatkus, visit our website
at *www.piatkus.co.uk*

Copyright © 2000 by Anne Griffiths

First published in Great Britain in 2000 by
Judy Piatkus (Publishers) Ltd of
5 Windmill Street, London W1P 1HF
email: *info@piatkus.co.uk*

The moral right of the author has been asserted

A catalogue record for this book is available from the British Library

ISBN 0 7499 0516 6

Set in Times by
Phoenix Photosetting, Chatham, Kent
Printed and bound in Great Britain by
Butler and Tanner Ltd,
Frome, Somerset

Remember

During Wind And Rain

They clear the creeping moss –
Elders and juniors – aye,
Making the pathways neat
And the gardens gay;
And they build a shady seat . . .
Ah, no; the years, the years;
See, the white storm-birds wing across!

by Thomas Hardy

Part One

Chapter 1

'Why couldn't I have had a red dress?'

Susanna Lehmann stood in front of her mother's wardrobe where a garment of a strange green colour hung as limp and ugly as it was possible to be. This was a ridiculous remark, a hurtful one, and of course, it set off her mother again.

'And where would we be getting red fabric in times like these? That was given to your Buba as a sample, she made it into something nice for her granddaughter and you will wear it to the party tomorrow.' Overheated, blouse covered in thread, her mother picked at the waist and the hem of it, improving nothing.

Yet the puff sleeves were obviously wrong and the bodice too tight. Her mother didn't want to recognise how much she'd grown. She'd have to wear something underneath to keep herself in. Holding her arms around her chest at the very thought, she averted her eyes from her mother's crossness and fatigue, from the garment itself though it seemed to fill the room. And it was a room already crammed from floor to ceiling, being workshop as well as bedroom. 'If only it weren't made of the new yarn,' she said. 'It comes from wood pulp, you admitted it. I mean, a dress made of wood! It smells peculiar. Max'll notice, so will his horrible relations, and his mother.' She'd have liked to stop at this point, but a mood of contrariness was pushing her on.

'It's a beautiful shade, it brings out the colour of your eyes. When you're older, you'll have to wear a touch of green here and there, a scarf maybe, a belt, a smart little hat.'

'No one else has green eyes. I hate green and when I'm old

3

enough to buy for myself, Mama, I'll always wear red.' Susanna gazed at herself in the dressmakers' mirror trapped between wardrobe and sewing machine. Her eyes were not truly green. Sometimes they were prettily hazel – if she had on her amber-coloured blouse, say. Best of all, at the moment, with her old blue plaid on, they seemed blue, Marlene Dietrich blue. Her face, however, being plain and round, bore no resemblance to the chiselled features of the film star. As for her hair! Not only was there far too much of it standing out in a bush around her head, it was boringly dark and intractably curly. She tugged at it in a familiar, forbidden gesture and resolved to get out her mother's tongs to try straightening some into a fringe. That would pass the afternoon, and waste it. She felt like wasting time because she wasn't allowed to. At the very least, she ought to be improving herself by learning another English poem.

'When you're old enough,' her mother was saying, 'you'll wear black. A lady lawyer, a lady doctor, they never wear red. Black, it's dignified, it's sophisticated, it's elegant. I see you in black with a touch of green to bring out your eyes. And a doctor's wife wears black. Please God, you'll meet a nice boy at the university. Two doctors in the family, we'll be safe. With your father's connections, we can emigrate to England. Every country needs doctors.'

Overwhelmed with fatigue at this reminder of her future, Susanna's glance strayed round the room. Nothing revealed their present situation as much as this stuffed and cluttered place, sewing machine, dummy, the cotton and laces jumbled about on bed and chest, even on Freddy's crib. The rest of their possessions were crowded into the living area next door, kitchen and work-shop for Papa. What was the point of her mother pretending to herself there was ever again going to be a time when a Lehmann would be allowed to be a doctor? Or for that matter when she could be kept in clothes and books until she was past twenty-five? Moreover, there'd been a government decree that all women doctors be dismissed so they went back to the home where they belonged. She was also supposed to marry Max.

Shutting her mind to Mama's wild dream and other horrors, she said, without hope, 'Perhaps I should go to Max's party in my plaid? His cousin Anita will be there and she'll be in something not made of wood yarn.' Anita would also be in possession of a

4

pair of the newest brown shoes with red trim. This she wouldn't mention however. Shoes of quality leather were for people with Merkel riches.

'You think I want you at the Merkels' in something that's above your knees and you fourteen?' Her mother gathered up some flowery print material from the bed and sat down at the machine with it. 'Now go,' she said. 'Frau Hahn needs this for an outing to her son's tomorrow.'

'I shan't be able to eat at the Merkels'. There'll be pickled herring.' This was another pointless remark. Everyone served fish but she knew there'd be no herring at the Merkels'. Herring was common. And nothing but a sudden bereavement was going to prevent her being forced to their party, and in a green dress made of wood pulp.

'Herring at the Merkels'?' her mother muttered. 'I'm telling you, there'll be a feast. And smoked salmon. Smoked salmon in these terrible times and you're too grand for it? You won't be too grand, I suppose, for the spice and honey cakes or the nut cake?' Her dark brown eyes, so often unreadable, very nearly sparkled. Her hair too stood out in a mass of curl, as Buba's did.

There was no sense in getting out the tongs, Susanna decided, With a grandmother and a mother with curly hair, she was destined for it. 'You sound just like Buba,' she said, feeling a near-smile loosen the tight misery caused by the frock and other things, many others, the day itself indeed, when most of the city and half the world was enjoying itself outside for the opening day of the Berlin Olympic Games.

Her mother paused, the scissors suspended over tacking stitches. 'God forbid I should sound like Buba,' she said. And she laughed. It was a joke.

Astonished, Susanna stared at her. Was her mother going to reveal some of her own feelings that were not just a mother's?

'Please God you shan't follow us,' she went on. 'An education, that's what you're going to have. You can't lose what's in your head like Buba and Opa lost their tailoring business and me my little shop so I have to work like this at dressmaking, which isn't my favourite occupation, and on sabbath too. And still we starve.' She waved her hand with the scissors in it to indicate troubles Susanna knew too much about already.

She drew in a breath. In this moment of closeness, should she dare try and make her mother accept that her own favourite occupation was creating clothes on paper and trying to create them in cloth? That maths and physics were impenetrable languages to her and would be even if school had not become a place of misery? 'You had an education until you were seventeen,' she pointed out, as a start. 'Because Opa and Buba were rich during the war, making officers' uniforms.' That this hadn't prevented her becoming just like Buba, who'd had none, she decided to leave out.

'Ah, then I met your father . . .'

'And he was an orphan, and godless, and war-wounded and lived in a world of books and music with holes in his jacket and you had to take care of him,' Susanna recited. This story she and her sister Sophie knew by heart.

The conversation would go no further. Freddy had begun to grizzle. Half-relieved, she knew she'd keep her own dream of her future where it was, in her head. It was really sillier than her mother's because it involved being picked out by some magical chance, by someone coming upon one of her drawings for instance, and demanding she design the clothes for the next film of Marlene Dietrich. Then Marlene would demand she follow her to Hollywood, there'd be more film stars clamouring for her skills and eventually she'd be able to buy a Hollywood mansion for them all to live in. It would have a library and music room for Papa, cook, housekeeper and whole stream of maids so that Mama and her grandparents would never again have to lift a finger. Mama would continue with her singing studies and she herself would wear the most extravagant of her own designs in red or gold or any colour she chose. Filling out details of this imagined world helped her sleep on bad nights.

She watched with distaste as her mother crooned over Freddy. No one else of her age at school had a mother nursing a baby – as if she didn't have enough to bear from other children already. And there was also this to endure, the withdrawal of the loose white breasts and Freddy's greedy little sucking noises. Only women from past times kept on having children, or ones like Frau Schmidt in the ground-floor-front flat who was having hers for the Führer. Frau Schmidt was the subject of mirth. Well, mirth in the gypsy family from the ground-floor-back flat. No one else would laugh to her about the Schmidts.

'Frau Schmidt's expecting her sixth,' she announced. 'The lady from the gypsy family told me and she was laughing about it. She said their own people had babies because they loved them, not to get the Cross of Honour for Motherhood from the Führer. She's had the Bronze, you know.'

'Dear God,' her mother shouted, making her jump. 'What have I done to deserve this child? What are you thinking of, talking to that poor gypsy lady? Who else was there? Did any of the Wolters or the Mundts overhear? Doesn't she realise?' Her family may have been allowed to go selling their trinkets and laces on the streets again this summer, but we don't know how long it's going to last. What else has she been telling you? Is she crazy? She must know Herr Schmidt is Radio Warden and if he's listening for people to have their radios on when they should, he's listening for other things.' Her agitation made Freddy lose his grip and she was obliged to re-fasten him.

Susanna shrugged. 'The gypsies are really nice. They're not frightened of Radio Warden Schmidt because they can't even afford a Goebbels Snout . . .'

'A Goebbels Snout?' cried her mother. 'And what is this, tell me? Where exactly did you pick up such language?'

'It means those cheap People's Radios which only have two Nazi stations. Everyone's supposed to have one so they can listen to Herr Goebbels giving out his orders, but the gypsies haven't and they aren't afraid of Block Warden Mundt either. I've never seen them giving the Berliner Glance . . .' This was certainly where she ought to stop, she realised, for on cue, her mother shouted again.

'The Berliner Glance? Wait till I tell your father such things are being said by his own daughter . . .' She rubbed her free hand over her face in despair.

'That's when you look over your shoulder before you open your mouth, for fear of who's listening,' Susanna said. But she knew she'd gone too far and just from contrariness. There'd be a price to pay later. She began to make her way past obstacles to the door as her mother's voice rose again. 'A Berliner Mouth's what you're getting, my girl, wait till I tell Opa, he'll die of disappointment and shame, a granddaughter of his . . .'

Passing into the kitchen, she closed the door behind her, thus avoiding further reprimand. No hint of potato cake, onion or pickled fish must taint the garments of Mama's few remaining customers. She'd been foolish to admit she'd ever done more than offer polite greetings to the gypsy family. They were nice though, loud and cheerful, and they kept a funny bad-tempered goat in their living room. Her mother certainly didn't know that or she and Sophie would have to strip off their clothes and wash from head to toe in the tin bath in order to remove animal germs, fleas and bedbugs if they so much as paused in the courtyard near the gypsies' flat.

Opening the second door to the outside landing, she was met with a burst of noise from tenants' Goebbels Snouts. It was still raining. Rain for the Olympics after a month of sunshine! She was glad. Even Herr Goebbels couldn't order sunshine. But most people were obviously listening to the music and the announcements about gymnastic displays. She could hear a Viennese waltz and then something about youths as fast as greyhounds and as hard as Krupp steel. They'd put out the flags too, or some of them, the ones who were both supposed and allowed to.

Leaning over the railings of the iron staircase, she decided to make a survey. Bottom right were the gypsies who of course weren't allowed a swastika and wouldn't fly it if they were. Next to them, ground-floor-front, the Schmidts had both swastika and Olympic flags out, but they did everything to order, and the same applied to the family in the ground-floor-front-left flat, horrible Block Warden Mundt and his ugly wife and children.

Ground-floor-back and left were the elderly Benjamin couple, and her own favourite neighbour, the milliner Frau Leona, neither of whom were permitted swastikas. But Frau Leona wouldn't admit to knowing the Olympics existed. All day long, she created hats and sang the old songs of love and grief, living in her own world. And if there was a place where she herself could still feel happy, it was down there with the milliner in a glorious mess of hat shapes, veiling, silk flowers and feathers. In the last years, she'd spent hours with her, listening to the songs and her chatter about her youth when she'd had a shop in Paris and had dressed the heads of princesses and courtesans. Her only reading matter consisted of the society magazines from those lost days and the fashion trade journals showing the latest designs of the present-day celebrity couturiers, Chanel and Schiaparelli and Molyneux. With her, she was allowed to draw to her heart's content, copying some 1920 outfit by Chanel say and adding something of her own to it, or improving some heavy-looking design of Lachasse by adding a touch of Schiaparelli. Frau Leona never scolded about the waste of time or drawing paper. She was very kind to her.

It wasn't an apartment building which held many kind people. Straightening up, dizzy, she saw there were no flags on their own floor. Block Warden Mundt would have to write a report admitting he'd failed to persuade the nice old Berliner lady, Frau Hahn, to give a few pennies for a flag and had received a mouthful of coarse language instead. He'd have to add Pastor Borgmann to it, for he wasn't displaying one, not having learned during his months in the KZ prison camp that he must place the Führer on equal standing with his Jesus.

Nasty little Herr Stiller, next to him, would have put out two flags if he hadn't been on holiday. Him and his monocle. Staring at this teacher's blank window, however, made her pause in her survey. It had done her no good, apart from reminding herself that her family were not the only ones forbidden a swastika – and it was a comfort. She'd also reminded herself of school. How could she ever get away from it, with one of the worst sort of teachers living across the courtyard!

She felt very flat, and wet, and gave herself a swing on the slippery rail. At this, her father's voice called out.

She jumped down and wandered inside to her father's corner of the room, the right-hand one by the french windows giving on to the balcony and the street.

On the left was the music corner where the piano was piled with sheet music and her father's and sister's violins. Her only talents were drawing and English, whilst the others' passion for music made her feel left out. And she couldn't share her drawings with them. They weren't always nice ones.

It was books which surrounded her father at his table, books and clocks and one or two proper radios as well as their own, plus parts of radios and clocks. He earned a few marks doing repairs.

Bent over something, a tiny instrument in his fingers, his old copy of Shakespeare under one elbow as prop, he was humming his favourite French song, and the clocks ticked with their different ticks. He seemed to have become used to this noise as background to their lives, but she hadn't.

'Not "Angels Guard Thee" again, Papa,' she said, suddenly

ready to burst with irritation. 'When you sing and I can hear the ticking and then there's the music from the radios all through the flats . . .'

Glancing up with his loving smile of pleasure of the sight of her, his gentle voice in itself a reprimand for her ingratitude and selfishness, he said, 'I imagine you look quite grown-up and prettier than ever in your new green dress, my darling.'

With a rush of affection, she watched him take off his glasses and go on smiling so the shadows under the blue of his eyes appeared deeper, his strong, handsome nose and chin more pronounced. He was a handsome man, everyone said so, and if fate had decreed it properly, she would have inherited his eyes and his fair hair, as Sophie and Freddy had. 'The dress is made of wood pulp, Papa,' she said.

'Of course, the very latest cloth. I'll wager Anita Merkel will be in something quite out of date.'

She allowed herself the suggestion of a smile. 'You're a cheat,' she said, 'trying to make me laugh when it isn't funny being the worst-dressed in the flats apart from the gypsy girls. Greta Mundt and Helga are always in new blouses and skirts for their League of German Maidens things and it makes them mock me even more.'

This had come out of itself; she hadn't meant to say it. His face lost its sweetness and the hurt look came into his eyes, the look he'd had the day he'd had to admit he would no longer be permitted to work as a teacher of English. 'I'm sorry, Papa,' she said. Lethargy prevented her going round the table to give him a hug. Everything was awful, she decided, and never would be anything else. 'And just think,' she said, making an effort, 'if I were like them, I'd have a block warden for a father. But might things be going to be all right for us now, Papa? I mean, if you don't even have to hide your books that are by un-German writers. Your Shakespeare's sitting there as bold as brass, and I've put out all my favourite school stories. I used to love it when you came back from the second-hand bookshop with an English school story for me . . .'

She let her voice tail off and turned to open the french windows, gazing out into the drizzle. He didn't answer at once, taking up his instrument and resuming his song. She waited. Her father gave her a proper answer if he had one.

Here, the radio music was clearer still, magnified by the blare from the loudspeakers down on the main street. She recognised a military march from years of enduring Sunday stormtrooper parades, and with it a faint resonance of the tramp, tramp of boots. But she couldn't allow her to think, *This music makes me want to go marching myself,* though sometimes, shamefully, it almost did.

'Do you ask, Susanna, whether our Nazi government has really changed the colour of its spots instead of just covering itself in an extraordinary, detailed camouflage for the world whilst the Games are on – a camouflage which goes so far as to return foreign writers' books to the shops and removing all KEEP OUT and NOT WANTED HERE notices?'

Susanna nodded. He resumed his tinkering and began again on "Angels Guard Thee." Sometimes she thought he meant the song just for her and Sophie. But he didn't know the answer to her question. He never made false claims of belief or offered false hope. Neither of course did he have any power to guard his family from harm as he once had.

It was a strange day, she realised, because not only had she failed to ask either parent the question she'd promised her sister she would ask, she also kept having the ridiculous notion she would demand proof she no longer fill her life with worrying, and school would become normal again, and her journey to and from it.

'Papa,' she ventured instead, 'you remember Konrad, the boy from the baker's family?'

He stopped humming so she continued, gazing down at the line of shuttered shops opposite: Spiegel's shoe shop, the haberdashery, the baker's with Fine Bakery in fancy lettering over it. She didn't want to think of Konrad, but had, standing there like that. But he was the boy who'd once rushed to her defence when another had thrown insults at her, so he was important. And the evening before, she'd been on the balcony, just as she was again, and there was Konrad, striding home on his long legs, face and arms dusky in the twilight, blond hair almost white. He was wearing the black corduroy shorts, the brown shirt with its pretty little swastika armband and the belt with the dagger. 'He's joined the Hitler Youth,' she said. It shouldn't matter to her, but it did, because he'd seemed different.

It was longer than ever before her father gave his response. 'It's only to be expected, you know. If he doesn't join, he won't be allowed into university but will be sent into the Labour Service, an unpleasant fate, I imagine, for a clever lad. Didn't you meet him at the skating rink in the old days?'

'Yes,' she said casually. Of course, it had been before the KEEP OUT notices went up. She and her friend Elsa had gone in as usual and were giggling and stumbling their way round the ice, when some boy had suggested they had no right to be there and Konrad had rushed up and knocked the boy over. Not only that, he'd taken her hand and pointedly guided her round the entire rink. All the other kids gathered to watch Konrad holding the hand of a Jewish girl and there hadn't been a word muttered against him because Konrad was someone in the neighbourhood. Soon after that the notices had gone up so she and Elsa hadn't had to brave another visit. Konrad hadn't spoken to her again. She hadn't expected him to, for things got worse and he'd have had a hard task to keep on being someone and her friend. He'd remained someone to her though. She could still remember the feel of his hand, firm and male, and she wanted to cry.

'If you believe,' Papa said, 'that Konrad is not Hitler Youth in his heart and in yours there is still friendship for him, try and be patient. Separating human beings into groups and condemning most of them is for our unhappy Nazis, not for us. Remember, though, that while there are Nazis, he'll be a brave lad indeed not to gather with the other young Hitler Youth thugs who've been strutting about like fighting cocks for months and years past. I mention this in case the bad times do come back, my darling. But hold the memory of him tight. Memories are precious. The bad times do at least mean that, don't they? Never forget them and never forget what we still have, each other and the sweetness of life itself, the sky, the sun, the stars, music, our books, our wireless . . .' He waved a hand to take in all that he loved so passionately and she sighed.

She was spared from having to answer however for in the open doorway by his table her sister Sophie appeared from the bedroom they shared.

'Your Konrad went out early this morning dressed in his uniform,' Sophie announced. 'I saw him after I did peepee in the pot. You were snoring.'

'For a six-year-old, you see and hear too much,' Susanna retorted, regarding her sister with irritation. How very much

12

herself Sophie always was, planted there on her stubby legs, stomach out, her doll with its dirty bandages from her playing at doctors hanging from a fist. If her hair didn't fall in a thick straight bob instead of curls, she'd look horribly like Shirley Temple. She was also going to cause trouble.

Here it came. 'If you are going down to the parade to see if Konrad's in it, I'm coming too and you did promise to ask Papa's permission.'

'I haven't because it's still raining, silly, even Papa won't allow us out, and I don't want to see Konrad. I wouldn't be likely to, would I, with all those thousands on the streets and the runner with the torch and the limousines and everything. I just want to see a bit of it. I do, Papa, why can't I? Berlin is our city and it's special, the Olympics, they'll never be in Berlin again.' She felt she was sounding as childish as her sister, with a whining voice she was too old for. But I do, she thought, I do want to be like other people. I want to be part of things.

'The Olympics is certainly a special event, Susanna.' Her father glanced across at her. 'Shall I tell Mama I permitted you both to take a little walk in the zoo gardens, as the rain was easing off, having first made you wrap up well with rain hats and so on? If you decide to go right down to the main boulevards, be very careful indeed. Hold your sister's hand and don't expect to get too close. Wherever the Führer is to pass, the crowds become hysterical, as you know. Imagine my having to admit to Mama I wilfully sent our daughters out to be crushed half to death. I would have to leave home forever.'

'I shan't go that far, Papa,' she assured him. 'We'll stay on the edge and just be there and sort of hear it, the music and the cheering. I might hear some foreigners talking, that'll be good for my languages.' She pushed Sophie into the bedroom and manhandled her into a cardigan. 'Don't say a word,' she hissed. 'Mama's been quiet at her machine for ages. If you're good, we might get as far as the Linden. I want to see where they've dug up the linden trees to make the boulevard bigger. Frau Leona says the old song is true, the one about Berlin being destroyed if its linden trees are ever dug up. They have been and the Berliners have made such a fuss, the government's had to buy more and they could only get spindly ones from America, but they don't look right, Frau Leona says, and Berlin will one day be gone for sure.'

13

'How?' Sophie asked, allowing herself to have a straw hat jammed on her head. What made Papa think they had rain hats? 'How will Berlin be gone? Will it be burned, our apartment block and us and the railway station and our schools? Opa and Buba's flat too?'

'I don't know, it's not in the song, silly, but Frau Leona says it'll certainly happen, the old Berliners really believe it.' Jamming on her own straw hat, she took her cardigan from the back of the door.

'Have I ever been to the Linden?' Sophie sat on the bed to have her slippers changed to boots.

'You have but you were too young to remember. It must have been a few years ago, before the troubles. We went with Mama and Buba and strolled up and down looking in the store windows. Buba and Mama bought trimmings in a huge haberdashery department and we all had cakes and ice cream at Kempinski's. You dropped yours down your frock.'

The boots laced, she grabbed her sister's hand. 'Come on,' she said, 'and be as quiet as a mouse in case Mama hears something.'

Waving a silent goodbye to their father, they tiptoed past the stove where a bucket of Freddy's nappies was simmering. She was supposed to have rinsed them out but hadn't. And propped against the dresser, another duty lay in wait: writing paper and envelopes for the thank-you letters after tomorrow's party. But today, she thought, today I am actually going to join in.

Creeping down the staircase behind her sister, a sudden good humour made her reveal her foolishness in admitting to their mother she had ever spoken to the gypsy family. 'Just never admit you've done the same,' she said, 'or she'll imagine germs have leapt on you and you'll be in for it then.'

'Then I'll be in for it,' squealed Sophie, jumping the last two steps and dashing in a deliberate circle past the gypsies' door and off through the archway towards the street, her doll flying from one hand. Here she paused to stick out her tongue at Block Warden Mundt's windows.

Susanna caught up with her. 'Careful,' she hissed, 'they may be home.'

'They aren't, I saw them go out this morning. Franz was in his Youngfolk uniform and Greta and Helga in new blouses and skirts and neckerchiefs for the German Maidens.' She looked up and

Susanna looked back into her clear blue gaze. 'Susanna,' she said, 'don't tell Mama but I want to be a German Maiden.'

Horrified, understanding, Susanna said automatically, 'No you don't.' She didn't snap. How could she? Her own longings had been very close to the surface that morning and had certainly upset Papa. 'We can't afford it,' she said gently, as if that were all. 'Anyway, you're too young yet.'

'I want to join when I'm older,' Sophie persisted, her face still turned upwards, her pretty skin pink from running, her hat crooked. 'I want to have badges and some nice stomping shoes and stay in a tent in the country on Sunday like they do and sing songs, why can't I?'

Susanna hesitated around the truth and then gave it. It seemed to be that kind of morning. It was up to her. Sophie must never devastate Mama by asking for a uniform. 'You have to be Aryan to join,' she said, a surge of affection threatening to make her cry.

'Well, I want to be Aryan like Greta and Helga.'

'You don't know what it means.'

'Yes, I do.' She put her doll under her arm. 'What does it mean?'

'It means you're blonde and blue-eyed.'

'But I am. And so's Papa, and Freddy.'

'There you are then, it doesn't mean anything. It's just one of those government things at the moment. One day no one will vote for them anymore and they'll have to go away, retire or something, that man they call Fat Hermann and the nasty Goebbels one. And the Führer. All the old Berliners say he's just a little upstart Austrian corporal and he's common and who does he think he is, trying to lord it over us proper Germans. Papa says the Nazis have wicked souls and that's a great burden for them to bear. He feels sorry for them and we must too. One day we'll have a different government, he says, or maybe a king or an emperor like we used to. Meanwhile, we are going to the Olympics, come on . . .'

Breathless from this recital, she grabbed Sophie's hand and ran along the street, past the factory poster proclaiming; YOU HAVE YOUR FÜHRER TO THANK FOR WORKING HERE, across the river and into the zoo gardens. There was more than a kilometre of gardens to get through before they'd reach the boulevard where the cavalcade was to pass. They were going to watch it. They were going to be like other people.

*

15

Dizzying sound, *dizzying* colour. So much colour. There was red and white and black, and blue, and more red and white and black. Swastika flags, Olympic flags, each one ten metres square on giant green flagpoles twenty metres high both sides of the street. There was no sky left. And she had no breath left to breathe.

'*Heil, Heil, Heil!*' It was a wall of sound. It filled her lungs. Her head throbbed in time to it. And she couldn't get out, couldn't get Sophie away. They were crammed up too near the front, pushed into a crowd of screaming women and German Maidens waving little flags by kindly old Berliners who thought they wanted to see the cavalcade, when she didn't want to any more. She shouldn't have come, shouldn't have brought Sophie. They hadn't even reached the Linden, there'd been too many people everywhere, and anyway, the parade wasn't going along the Linden. She hadn't known that. It had all been a silly impulse and now she was staring into the damp brown-shirted back of a stormtrooper, and Sophie, where was Sophie?

She dragged her eyes from the brown shirt and down to her sister's tiny body crushed between two pairs of brown breeches, two pairs of shiny black boots. They were all along the road, she'd never get out and all she had of her sister was a fistful of pink cardigan. She had to stand there, deaf and breathless, her heart about to burst, and watch a stormtrooper hand reach towards her sister's hand. They were going to take her sister away, they weren't supposed to be there, they hadn't the right.

'Come on, little one, we'll make sure you don't miss seeing the Führer.' She heard these extraordinary words, saw her sister look up, smiling and flirtatious, one small hand accepting one of theirs, one plump arm wrapping itself around a stormtrooper knee. Into her hand, this stormtrooper placed a swastika that had been dropped. As if in a nightmare, she saw Sophie *wave* it as the shrieking women and German Maidens were waving theirs.

At this point, a great cry went up. 'The Führer, the Führer is coming!' The cry grew and grew and many many arms shot out in the salute, '*Heil* Hitler, *Heil, Heil, Heil!*' The women began to weep, reaching forward as if to touch the air he'd pass through. And Sophie, her sister, unwrapped her arm from the stormtrooper knee and shot it up instead, yelling, '*Heil* Hitler!' her feet stamping with the joy of it.

Head about to explode, Susanna thought, wildly, her breath

16

coming in gasps, Sophie, listen, turn around, look at me, it was stormtroopers and Hitler who hurt all the people we love, stop it, don't, it's wrong, but I won't tell Mama, *drop the flag at once*, and turn around, we're going home. But how could she get her breath in order to shout so much as, 'Sophie, we're going home,' when the terrible rhythmic chant went on and on, '*Heil, Heil, Heil,*' and she felt she was being lifted up into the sound and if it didn't stop would be compelled, obliged, *forced* to throw up her own arm and shriek it out too.

Then there he was, in a long black open limousine. The Führer. He was a little man dressed in brown. He had oily black hair and a comic moustache like Charlie Chaplin but his face wasn't comic. His face was dark and oily and not like the paintings of him on the posters. He was standing up by the front seat, one arm held out straight, the palm of his hand down, as if he were giving a blessing to the crowds shouting his name.

Searching blindly in front of her to catch hold of more of Sophie's cardigan, Susanna felt she was about to faint. What had made her come here to be included in this gesture, what treachery and foolishness had led her to allow Sophie to be blessed by this wicked man! Oh, didn't he look proud of himself, with his nasty black hair plastered down and his ugly nose! She wanted to weep. A sickness rose in her throat. She had let Sophie be tainted with Führer fever. She had let herself be tainted with it, and oh, wouldn't they be in for it with Mama now.

Somehow she dragged up some strength, grabbed Sophie by the waist and lifted her backwards, pushing herself backwards and edging through the mass. 'Sorry,' she kept shouting, 'Sorry, my sister's going to be sick.' She had to get her home.

She had to get her home as fast as she could. She'd have to bribe her with a trinket she coveted, in return for silence, but how would she silence her own memory of this day and this shame? Only Papa would be able to do it. She'd have to tell him every detail, making it into a story. He loved stories. She'd say, Papa, the Führer's a funny little brown sort of man. And he'd say, Of course he is, my darling, why else would he want to make himself into something so big?

Chapter 2

Arriving first on the landing outside the Merkel apartment, Susanna asked, 'I ring the doorbell at once, Mama?' Today, she must do things right. She'd been in enough trouble the previous evening, for of course, Sophie hadn't been able to keep the excitement of the afternoon to herself. She put down Freddy's crib and waited.

From halfway up the stairs, her mother called, 'You will stand there until I join you so we present a nice family picture to the maid. You want her employers to be ashamed of the guests?'

Jumping up the last steps, her father gave her a wink. He carried his violin and Sophie clung to his hand in her most needful, beguiling manner. She and her sister were not speaking to each other. 'Ashamed, my dear Esther?' he said. 'When I stand here with the two most beautiful girls in all Berlin?' He began to sing his French song.

Reaching the landing also, he mother had more to say. 'Remember to use your napkin properly by keeping it on your knees. Do not touch your mouth with it in case you inadvertently seem to be wiping your nose. Sophie, do not put your doll to bed in yours. Take great care please with the china and the crystal glass. The poverty of our gift is enough without our causing damage. And the grief you caused me yesterday was enough to last a mother a lifetime. All I ask is that you do not mention the incident to the Merkel guests and that you curb your tongues at the table.' She paused to adjust the neck of Sophie's frock and wipe her face with a handkerchief. In her charge was the tiny package which was their gift to Max, a grey silk tie she'd made herself.

Susanna rang the bell. Her father ruffled her curls and laughed.

A burst of voices greeted them as the maid opened the door. She took charge of Freddy, and Frau Merkel, Max's mother, appeared in the vast hall where wood panelling, rugs and carved furniture overdid richness and warmth. Susanna knew her role. She caught hold of Sophie's hand and they waited together, staring through into the salon. There was an enormous table running the length of it with food laid out in a glitter of silver and glass. Bright summer sun shone in from the balcony doors and at the far end, the usual collection of Merkel relations were making a lot of noise.

Her father had just completed his first task, kissing Frau Merkel roundly on both cheeks and passing into the salon. Here he cried, 'What lovelier sight, my dear Lottie, than such a feast laid out on a symphony of your Rosenthal.'

Frau Merkel's lavender-satin-covered bosom now collided with her mother's old-black-silk-covered one. Next the lavender satin bosom gathered Sophie to it with fake affection. Sophie followed her father and Susanna held her breath for her turn. 'Every time I see this child, my dear Esther, she has grown more beautiful.' She had the frowning ugly face of some wicked step-mother from Grimm's *Fairy Tales*, and as always, the cold dark eyes looked into hers with the silent message: You are not good enough for my son. And as always, Susanna felt her eyes flicker elsewhere for fear they reveal her own loathing. Of course, today, there was to be more, but it came sooner than she expected; Frau Merkel usually liked an audience. Fingers decorated with too many rings picked up an edge of her collar. 'Is this the new cloth, Esther, dear?'

She went on waiting, dumb and obedient, glancing past Frau Merkel's lavender satin shoulder to the mill of people in the salon and the pile of Max's presents on a sideboard. Sophie was being held in the arms of someone she barely knew, accepting titbits and simpering.

Making an exhibition of herself also, her mother called loudly, 'And where is our barmitzvah boy?'

Max emerged from the embrace of a large aunt. Ignoring her, he bowed over her mother's hand and kissed it, taking their gift as if it contained precious stones. He was dressed in his first man's suit with long trousers and seemed perfectly silly, she decided, indulging in his debonair lady's man act. He wasn't old enough, even if Papa were right and he couldn't help it, having always played the little man to his mother's not so helpless female. But he was enjoying himself. She stuck out her tongue at him from behind their mothers' backs and he winked.

'You're overdoing it,' she hissed, as the mothers merged in with the relations.

'What a strange dress,' he said, 'You've never looked so awful. Is it that new wood pulp stuff?' He stood in front of her, considering it minutely. He was the exact same height as her, though sturdier in build. He had beautifully shaped black eyebrows, thick black hair and eyes that were as nearly black as eyes could be.

'If you're supposed to have reached man's estate today and we're here to celebrate it, what about trying to do your first good deed by making me feel better instead of worse?'

She felt close to tears and thoroughly out of sorts. How he'd laugh if she told him she'd almost been caught up in Führer fever! She mustn't allow him to see she was really upset about anything, even the dress. She couldn't always rely on his support. His moods were variable, and as indecipherable as his eyes.

He grinned, put an arm around her shoulders, and they surveyed the salon party scene. 'Anita's over there by Aunt Miriam,' he said. 'She's in red silk.'

'Of course she is.' Susanna blinked and avoided searching for Anita.

'And as ugly as usual in it,' he said, 'with shoes far too heavy for the dress. Brown shoes, moreover, with red laces.'

She accepted the remark with gratitude. It was a bad choice, winter shoes with a light dress. She'd never have made it. And Anita was ugly, with jowls and big teeth. Nice clothes wouldn't alter that.

'I suppose we'd better go in and face it,' he said.

'Well, you being the barmitzvah boy, yes,' she said. 'They're only here to congratulate you on becoming a man and accepting God's covenant.'

'I believe you're jealous.'

This was a surprise. 'Perhaps I am.' She probably was, she

20

thought, acknowledging to herself the bitterness she'd felt when Freddy was born. Her mother had wanted a boy. 'I don't understand why girls shouldn't have a barmitzvah and be just as important. Papa says that if he had his way, girls would, but of course he doesn't believe in any God, so to him it's just an old ritual and an excuse for a party.'

'A woman's sole task is to produce boys to carry on the word of the Lord,' Max said.

'Oh, shut up. Why did you agree to a barmitzvah anyway? You kept skipping the classes and you mostly manage to avoid things you can't be bothered with. You've also never shown the merest bit of piety to me and we've known each other all our lives.'

'It was for Pa's sake,' he said. 'And he's promised me a personal allowance in exchange. Ma would have nagged him to death if I hadn't agreed. You know what she's like. They go to synagogue once a year for show and she wanted her only child to have a barmitzvah for show.'

'Yours is a showy family altogether,' Susanna answered companionably.

'And yours is poor and earnest,' he retorted.

'So how many prayers did you manage in the end?'

'Enough.' He grinned. 'And the beauty of my voice soaring up to the roof had Ma and all the aunts weeping in their seats. I put just a hint of a break in here and there. Anyway, come on. When your father gets out his violin and your mother starts humming a few notes, I shall say you feel sick and I'm taking you for some air. We'll get on down to the Ku'damm for a while. We'll have scoffed enough nut cake by then.'

This was more or less one of Max's orders. He would already have planned it. And she didn't mind. She felt a little better.

'Guess what makes my Uncle Oskar peculiar?' Max said, putting rather a lot of smoked salmon into his mouth.

'He's the most suntanned person here,' Susanna suggested. She cut open several more of the tiniest of bread rolls and laid a thick slice of ice-cold butter in each one. 'I thought you said your father had no cash until he sells some antique or other. He'd have had to pay for so much butter, never mind the rest.'

'Leave room for the nut cake,' Max said, unusually considerate.

Around them and along the table, the talk was the same as it

21

always was now as such gatherings: good times, bad times, and were the relatively improved recent good times going to last longer than an Olympic summer? Visas came into it, and emigration, England, New York, Belgium, Holland.

'Uncle Oskar is strange,' Max said, spooning pickled cucumber on to his plate. 'He is strange because he's *come back*, that's why. Listen.' He raised his voice and called out, 'Tell us about Palestine then, Uncle Oskar, and why you've returned home after emigrating there.'

'Too much sun, too much sand, my boy,' Uncle Oskar called back, pausing in his attack on the chopped liver. 'Too many Arab gentlemen. And dates! What food is dates for a man to live on? Pah, you can keep Palestine. I come home, I start up in business once more, I'll be all right. Things are different since I left in thirty-five, there's employment, four million men back to work, our skills are needed here, we'll be left alone again.'

'You really think so, Oskar?' Her mother's voice. 'And those poor souls trying to emigrate to Palestine should maybe reconsider? I mean, there's so little education out there and only landwork, what'll become of the children? Please God, we'll have one, two doctors in the family in a few years, then we can go to England if the bad times come back. Josef worked there several years before nineteen-fourteen, he's got connections.'

'See what I mean?' Max burped in her face and began to whisper. 'Next we'll have the bit about the Nazis being human beings really and not meaning to be quite so cruel to us, they're sorry they ruined our lives. Uncle Oskar and all these old people make me sick, going about spreading rumours and false hope to innocents like your mother.' He began to drum his fingers on the table, a sure sign there was more simmering.

She nudged his leg under the table to hint that he keep quiet for a while and served herself some pâté. She had a mouthful of chopped liver and egg when it came.

'Susanna's been asking why girls can't barmitzvah. She's wildly jealous of me and poor little Freddy.'

She hadn't expected this particular gibe, but continued eating, as was safest, risking only a glance across at her mother. though she knew every pair of eyes was directed at her and her wood pulp garment. On her mother's visiting face, there was no reaction, though shame would be churning about inside. These things were not talked about at table. I am sorry, Mama, she thought, keeping her own eyes on her plate.

Next, smug and jowly Anita Merkel spoke up. 'But Susanna dear, you know our task is to produce babies.' Her cow-like expression would certainly be aimed across the table to the youth destined to stand under the wedding canopy with her at some future date, Susanna decided, but she still didn't look up to enjoy the awfulness of it. Max hadn't finished either.

'When Freddy was born,' he said, 'she had fantasies about stifling him to death, she told me. Lucky she managed to keep herself in check, eh, Frau Lehmann, or the little chap wouldn't be grizzling away to himself in his crib over there, would he?'

She paused, her mouth ready for the 'shut up', but making herself give a sensible reply. She could sometimes manage it. 'Max is being silly,' she said, 'and it isn't true. He really ought to try some good deeds for a change instead of deliberately upsetting people. I think you're supposed to go about doing good for the rest of your life when it's your barmitzvah. I'm sure girls would be better at that than boys.'

Glancing up again towards her father's face for the comfort of his wink, she received more, his loving smile. He was pleased with her. He didn't like Max's bullying. She added pickled cucumber to her plate so she could burp back at Max and went on eating.

Max of course adored being insulted. He sat there humming to himself, planning something else.

Frau Merkel began to talk loudly to her husband, drawing in the adults at that end of the table. From the other end, far from host and hostess, Susanna heard 'Berliner Mouth' mentioned and quite clear from Max's Aunt Miriam a comment about her and Max being a good match and both so sharp they'd one day cut themselves. This she'd overheard at the last Merkel gathering.

Max squeezed her arm. 'It wasn't a bad reply, kid,' he whispered. 'You're learning.' It was the best moment for him when the mutterings started, but she felt suddenly weary. She leaned back in her chair and stared into the summer afternoon beyond the balcony. If she strained her ears, she could hear the loudspeakers blaring away on the street below, shouted Olympic results and more music. What horrible, restless noisiness filled the days now. Once, ordinary, quiet life had existed, she remembered it. It was before the troubles started. She'd been ten so there was plenty of ordinary life to remember. There was no talk of emigration. No one called her names at school. She hadn't had to sit apart at the back of the class. Papa went daily to work as a teacher of English. Her mother had her little shop selling stuffs, her grandparents their tailoring business. They didn't know they weren't supposed to belong to Berlin. There wasn't much money, but enough because white breakfast rolls were delivered every morning and there was chicken or cutlets for sabbath.

And yesterday, she'd let Sophie salute the man who'd made it disappear. She'd almost saluted him herself. All night long, that *Heil, Heil, Heil* had throbbed in her head. She hadn't slept.

'Catching flies?' Max nudged her. 'Close your mouth, you look daft. Or rather, put some of this nut cake into it, quick. Your father's eyeing his violin, and I want to be off.'

Then from her place on Herr Merkel's knees, Sophie called out. 'Yesterday, Susanna took me to the parade and a nice stormtrooper man gave me a pretty red, white and black flag to wave for the Führer.'

Max couldn't stop giggling. He giggled scoffing his nut cake, during their exit from the apartment, right through the zoo gardens and as far as the Café Kranzler on the Ku'damm boulevard. 'That Sophie,' he kept saying, 'oh, I love her, if it wasn't for her baby voice piping up like that, I'd never have known, you wouldn't have admitted it, would you! What deliciousness though, did you see their faces?'

No, Susanna kept thinking, I wouldn't have admitted it. There were other things she kept from Max too, much more than he kept from her.

'Look at my new toy,' Max said, opening his jacket to reveal a small black dagger in the inside pocket. 'Blood and Honour's engraved on it.'

Horrified, Susanna glanced about her at the other customers on Kranzler's café terrace. But every one of them was engaged with coffee and pastries, shouting to each other under the barrage of flags on the frontage. 'A Hitler Youth dagger?' she whispered. 'You haven't been mixing with that band fighting Hitler Youth gangs? Why didn't you tell me? You must stop, it's dangerous.

24

I've heard kids at school spreading rumours about who they are. They'll be caught and anyway, they can't think you're old enough.'

'If I'm old enough to be beaten up, I'm old enough to fight,' he said, revealing the edge of a second trophy. 'I've got this pretty swastika armband as well. One of these days it might come in useful as camouflage.'

'You could never pass for Hitler Youth, you're too dark!' A familiar pinch of fear lodged itself under her ribs. Why hadn't she realised the first time he'd had his nose bloodied for fun at the school gates that he wouldn't be able to bear the humiliation? She'd known then the physical hurt had hardly counted. And since that afternoon, there'd been other attacks. His upper lip bore scars to prove it. 'Surely you couldn't bring yourself to look as silly as they do in the shorts?' she said, for clothes mattered more to Max than most things.

He didn't answer, leaning back in his chair and whistling to the strains of 'O Sole Mio' drifting from the loudspeakers along the boulevard.

She didn't know everything about him, Susanna realised, searching for a suitable horror to make him listen. With a lurch of her heart, she found it. 'What about that baker's apprentice who dared to report being attacked to the police so the Hitler Youth gang found him again and threw him from a window with a swastika carved on his chest? They'd have used a dagger just like that one, and if you're taken in and one of their precious things is found on you . . .'

'Shan't be, shall I?' he snapped, his face as sulky as a small boy's. Yet he could pass for fifteen or sixteen in his man's cap and suit. 'Shan't be taken in, jeered at or knocked about. That's official now the world's come to Berlin. Orders have gone out. Nothing nasty must be seen to be happening. There aren't any NOT WELCOME notices up here, you know, and don't think you haven't been blatantly checking.'

This was true. Before she could bring herself to sit down, she'd searched Kranzler's doors and windows for notices and even the fence dividing terrace from boulevard.

'Nice here, though. Kranzler's is smart, all the Ku'damm cafés are. The Ku'damm's more our style of boulevard than the ugly old Linden.' He pulled at his new shirt cuffs and peered down at the lapels of his jacket. 'I wanted a more English cut,' he said. 'To be really swing, you have to dress English. When I get my allowance, I'm going to buy myself one of the new Potsdamer-style hats. They're soft, you put up the brim in front. Old Hermann Goering wears one but they're still swing somehow. Ma'll die when she sees me in it. Once we're married, I'll choose your outfits and we'll stroll along here on Sundays all dressed up like our parents used to do along the Linden. You'll never wear another horror like that green thing, I promise you.'

Shutting off the image of a bloody swastika carved into the smooth skin of Max's chest, Susanna said wearily, 'I'll never be good enough for your mother, as you know very well. I don't suppose I want to be.' And having a prominent part in his fantasy of an unlikely future was another burden, like her mother's. Neither would come to pass, and nor would her own. Marlene Dietrich demanding she follow her to Hollywood to design her frocks! How foolish she was, giving herself wild hopes like that. Today was awful, she decided, more worry-making than yesterday, which had been bad enough, with her compulsion to belong where she wasn't wanted dragging her into Führer-fever. Now Max with a stolen Hitler Youth dagger – something else to keep her awake at night. And what if the waiter stood at their table and because there were foreigners present *discreetly* asked them to leave?

She tried to stare into the indecipherable blackness of Max's eyes. Surely he couldn't be feeling he belonged here, or ever would again? 'The last visit we made to Kranzler's was with my father when I was ten and you nine,' she said. 'We saw a thriller with Marlene Dietrich in it at the Ufa Palace and had ice cream afterwards.'

'Well, what flavour shall I order? And don't get sentimental. This place means nothing to us, or Berlin, although we were born here and our fathers' families starved here for six generations or more. We're going to America, the land of the free. I've just got to persuade Pa to sell his stock of antiques. It's not as if he's allowed to trade normally any more. He can start up in New York, and even if your father does manage to get you lot to England, you can go out to us from there. We'll get the visas. Did I tell you we'll put Sophie through medical school? She's always playing at doctors. It'll please your mother. You can just be my wife and entertain for my deals. I'll be in films or something big.' He drummed his fingers on the table and gazed moodily at the other customers. 'We don't actually want to go on living amongst these horrible ugly Germans, do we?' he said. 'All that boiled pork and sausage they eat makes them as fat as pigs themselves, and their kids as round and pink as little piglets.'

'Don't,' Susanna whispered, glancing about for listening ears. 'Papa says if we think and talk like that, we're no better than the Nazis.' She'd once referred to the Schmidt family in their apartment block using the same terms, but she needn't admit it. In fact, she'd also done a drawing of them rolling in mud at a farm as a family of pigs not so long ago.

'Yes, well, your Pa's full of useless homilies. Much good it does him, understanding and forgiving everyone without even the excuse of doing it in the name of God. It doesn't put food in your bellies. What flavour d'you want?'

'Vanilla, please,' she said, though she'd prefer to go home. Perhaps she didn't hanker for their old life including ice cream at cafés any more, and the bewilderment at having been forbidden such public places could never be forgotten. 'And we shan't be going to America,' she said. 'You've told me scores of times your father will never sell his stock at a loss and he'd rather die.' Max was very tiring company. It'd be easy to let him get on with his boasts but she hardly ever could. He didn't like having the truth pointed out to him so he didn't answer, turning round to look for the waiter.

A tight band of expectation clutched at her waist as she saw the man making his way towards them. Oh, don't come here, she thought, we'll leave, it's easier for both sides, we want nothing. She held her breath, seeing the cloth of his apron crease into thick, starched folds as he bent towards Max. Then it came. 'I'm afraid I must ask you to leave, son.' He was being discreet. He'd whispered it. Not a single foreigner or Berliner would have heard.

But Max had. He leapt up like a wounded animal, his face gone white.

'I'm sorry, it's not allowed . . .'

'Shut up.' Max whispered too. 'We'll go.' He grabbed her arm, hurting it.

She couldn't move, darting glances everywhere, at every consumer of pastries and coffee and beer. Not one was giving her the stare back which said, yes, go, we don't want you, you don't belong as we do. So they were spared that and she still couldn't move.

'My own kids love Aschinger's, you know,' the waiter continued, as if Max had not been so rude. 'This place is a bit grown-up for you and anyway, that's the rule, no children unaccompanied are to be served here.'

'He needn't think he made it all right,' Max said.

'Of course he did, he was nice. You're just angry with yourself for making a mistake, I expect,' Susanna said. Light-hearted from relief and breathless from hurrying, she leaned against a tree far along the boulevard from Kranzler's. She hoped they were going home. Around them, everyone else seemed to be.

Leaning beside her, Max folded his arms. 'Aschinger's,' he said. 'Hot dogs and mustard . . .'

'Where you often went after school,' Susanna reminded him, 'You liked the free rolls.' She felt a little burst of joy. Everything was going to be all right. A nice waiter and no notices! Maybe her father would get a job and Herr Merkel start trading. Nothing else would matter if those wonderful things could happen as well. She'd wear any number of wood pulp frocks, and gladly – but of course wouldn't have to.

'When we're married,' Max said, 'we'll stroll along the Ku'damm on Sundays and right past Kranzler's. Not that we'll be living in this ugly old city.'

She was about to suggest they were going in the right direction for home, when he nudged her. 'Listen!' Excited, he pointed up to the nearest loudspeaker. 'Olympic results. That Jesse Owens has won a heat, the hundred metres or something, don't you see what it means?' He stopped leaning and threw his cap in the air. 'Oh, I'm so happy!' he said, laughing out loud.

Astonished at this transformation, Susanna tried to make sense of the blare of announcements. 'An American's won? Aren't they supposed to?'

'Suzy, Jesse Owens is black, he's a beautiful negro man.' He stood in front of her, grinning. 'And you're going home now. I'll take you as far as the bus stop. I'm off to see if my mate Hugo's father can get me tickets for the athletics. I want to cheer myself hoarse for Jesse.' He set off along the crowded street. 'I could kiss

28

him, you know, he's given me a perfect end to my barmitzvah.'

'Keep your voice down,' she hissed, following behind, her heart sinking. 'You mustn't mention negro people in public.'

Max paused in his flight. 'Don't dawdle,' he said. 'This is important. That Jesse has to win a medal and I have to see him do it and I have to see our dear Führer shake his hand. You do understand? This is a man's who's actually less welcome in this Nazi country than we are. He's more wrong than we are and that's why he's beautiful to me though I've never met him.' Failing to keep his voice down, he was off again, hurrying, and didn't stop until they'd reached the underground and railway area. Here he passed her some coins. 'You'll be all right. Don't tell your mother I didn't take you home though.' Offering her a wave, he left her.

She watched him swagger off towards the underground steps, cap at an angle, hands in his pockets. He was probably whistling. She felt she could see the shape he'd have when he was really grown-up instead of just thinking he was, and it wouldn't be very different. He'd always remain a boy and always need her to know him as he was and accept him. And this thought made her want to cry for his loneliness and his bravado. She wouldn't marry him of course and she wouldn't have to worry about not doing so for a very long time. On her list of worries, it had no place as yet.

All in all, she thought, it had been a muddle of a day. She'd felt happy, leaving Kranzler's. Why couldn't she always have happy Sundays, like the ordinary, happy people in the street? More kept arriving too, surging up the underground steps from some train that had brought them in from trips to allotments or the lakes and forests of Berlin. A whole stream of fathers was hurrying past laden with spades and bundles of peas and carrots. There were wives with baskets of dark juicy raspberries and early plums. A small boy staggered along with a string bag of cabbages. Lots of children carried cabbages, and daisies and sunflowers and it wasn't fair. Feasts awaited them.

She was just about managing to dismiss what her father called the meanest of emotions, envy, when she found herself surrounded by most of the Schmidt family: mother and four girls, identical more or less with their bunchy dirndl skirts, the peasant blouses, the plump limbs. They had the same pale blonde hair done up in plaits and ribbons and small eager blue eyes, presently staring at her dress.

She hadn't time to edge herself away before Frau Schmidt, a large dozing baby lodged on the fullness of a belly where the next was growing, greeted her warmly. 'What a good day we've had on the allotment, Fräulein, and doesn't our city look lovely with the flags and all, a city to be proud of, our Berlin is, and it's just one more thing we have to thank the Führer for. I wish he wasn't so hard-working and could come out and see it for himself.'

'Yes!' Susanna said politely as Frau Schmidt drew breath. Had she forgotten the Führer didn't usually include all Berliners amongst his people? Perhaps her father was right and the Schmidts were as innocent as grown-ups could possibly be and still maintain a home and family – or perhaps they too thought everything was going to be all right now.

'You'll come to the bus stop with us?' Frau Schmidt said this as if it were a normal neighbourly offer.

And it was a shock. A month or two before, she'd never have dared. Susanna realised she ought to be hopeful about this, and grateful, but she wasn't. She didn't want to sit in a bus with four Schmidt girls who were gazing at her frock and would presently ask loud questions about its peculiar appearance. 'I have to stop at my grandparents',' she said, a lie regretted as soon as it was out, because she followed it with worse. 'My grandfather's coaching me in maths for next term.' Now she'd have to keep up the pretence of maths coaching without letting her mother hear of anything so unlikely. Opa could make out his bills, which was all he'd ever needed maths for.

Frau Schmidt prodded her with a soft, fat elbow. 'You must give up that studying, Fräulein. Remember what the verse says, Take hold of kettle, broom and pan, Then you'll surely get your man.' Winking roguishly at her collection of daughters, she beat time for them to join in.

'Shop and office leave alone, Your true life's work lies at home,' they all chanted.

People were staring. The family took up so much space, they had to be walked around. Frau Schmidt was unaware of this.

'See how contented I am with my brood, Fräulein, and I've another on the way. Like the Führer says, with every child I bring into the world, I'm helping the Fatherland. And I have the Führer's gift of thirty marks a month for each of them.'

She began herding the girls together and they crossed the street, filling up most of it.

Susanna watched, imagining the recounting of the episode to her father. She could make one of her funny drawings out of it too, transforming them into the happiest of pigs with huge backsides clothed in dirndls. She mustn't though. Frau Schmidt had been nice. Maybe she'd draw them just as they were and make a nice picture she could show people.

Sudden tears pricked at her eyelids. She was very tired. She'd like to go home but at home would very shortly be her mother and reprimands and the letter of thanks to write to the Merkels with a veiled apology in it which must somehow not admit to misdemeanour at the party.

She might as well make the detour to her grandparents'. There was always comfort to be had with Opa and Buba.

'So you can see how good can come from bad, child,' her grandfather said. All in black, black silk cap, black shawl, he sat in his usual chair by the window of the living room over the empty shop, his needle and thread and his Torah on the table in front of him. 'We have just received a secret order from a captain who has obtained promotion. Only we can tailor his uniform with the perfection of fit he's used to, he says.'

'Pah!' Buba muttered from the stove where she was making tea and cinnamon pancakes. 'God forbid your Opa permits a word of doubt to pass his lips.' A tiny black-clothed whirlwind of activity who had various talismans against the evil eye secreted in her petticoats, she'd no sooner thrown a few drops of mixture on to the griddle than it was out again, done to a golden turn. 'God forbid this captain finds himself forgetting to pay us, that is all I have to say.'

Which of course it certainly wouldn't be, Susanna thought, breathing in the smell of pancake and cinnamon with underneath chicken soup and pickled cucumber. Here she'd spent some of the cosiest times of her childhood, allowed to draw to her heart's content anything Buba had a picture of or was engaged in putting together. From the age of three, she was familiar with all kinds of garments from the past, old-fashioned trousers and jackets from defunct regiments, stylised Prussian caps, even men's undergarments. Forbidden by Mama to encourage her passion for clothes or help her make little things for her dolls, Buba had nevertheless somehow taught her the skills of hand-stitching as if by osmosis, while Opa rested his calm loving gaze on both of them. Opa gave out such good feelings about people, an ideal world would be ruled by men like him, she'd always thought. A Nazi would recant his wickedness if he spent a day with Opa. Hitler would.

She went on with the tale of her Sunday, omitting only the matter of the frock and Max's dagger. 'Of course,' she said, 'if everything's going to be all right, I shall have to make myself study at school. I'll have no more excuses. Maybe I shall have to be a doctor, God forbid. That'd be bad from good!' And it would be, she knew, though so very improbable, it also had no place on her list of anxieties. 'Really, it'd be almost enough not to keep expecting something awful to happen, never knowing exactly what. That Frau Schmidt was amazingly friendly to me, yes, but when I get home, the Mundts in the ground-floor flat will be in from their Sunday outing and nasty Greta's sure to shout something rude to me . . .' Today the dress, she thought, yesterday, tomorrow, worse. 'And after Frau Schmidt being nice, I shall mind it more. Of course, if Frau Schmidt were to lean from her window on the other side of the archway and tell off Greta, imagine! She wouldn't dare though, Block Warden Mundt would report her for it and she might appear on the street list for un-German behaviour. Maybe she will anyway, if any of our neighbours saw her talking to me. Unless everything is going to be all right and there's a whole new range of regulations ordering everyone to be nice to our people or it's the KZ prison camp.'

Opa stroked his beard. 'Think first of poor Greta, child,' he said. 'You must find compassion for her in your heart. She has learned from her parents and teachers to believe Nazi slogans. And they are little people who twice in ten years have been through terrible times. They think the Nazis are saviours, the Nazis provide work with their road-building. There were once Berliners who fainted in the street from starvation. They cried for work and bread. Now they have work and they have bread.'

'He wants we starve instead,' whispered Buba, bringing tea to the table and slamming down the sugar saucer so hard the three lumps rattled. 'Then he'll tell you what's bread if we lose our soul.

32

You want to muddle the child, Leopold?' She scurried back across the room for the pancakes.

'We must be patient, my dear wife,' Opa said, picking up his glass of tea and blowing on it. 'Our people are used to persecution but the wickedness of the Nazis will be their downfall. The good German people, our dear Berliners who made no move against us when we arrived from Poland all those years ago, they will rise up and say there has been enough. This is a civilised country. There must be a place for the churches and the trade unions, and for our people. Only the other day, a neighbour greeted me most warmly in spite of the decree that no German must speak to a Jew unless it is strictly necessary. I tell you, the Nazis will soon pass into history.'

'Puh, puh, puh,' whispered Buba in Susanna's ear as she put in front of her a plate with two enticingly curled pancakes on it. This was the refrain of her days, a pretend three-times spitting against the evil eye, for she lived by superstition as firmly as Opa lived by the word of the Lord.

'Puh, puh, puh,' muttered Susanna, and groaning for the show of it at the sight of more food. 'I've just been to Max's barmitzvah, Buba.'

'Eat,' Buba commanded, waving a hand and slumping into her own chair between them where there were no pancakes, only the tea and the sugar lump, neither of which she would touch until Susanna had swallowed every crumb. 'You can be sure, child, that the civil greeting offered to Opa was without witness. What man of sense would want his name goes on the street list and he be spat upon instead of us?'

'The Berliners never have to wonder if they belong, do they?' said Susanna through a mouthful of pancake. 'Of course, I never wondered whether I did until the other children began to shout at me that I didn't. But if it's not here, where is our home?' She scraped her spoon around the plate and licked it. 'Will we be welcome in England if Papa's connections get us there?' The resurgence of this other worry made her feel light-headed and the room and its muddle of contents hazily indistinct. 'What was it like when you arrived from Poland when you were young? Tell me again. Wasn't Berlin strange to you, and foreign?'

'What time did we have to think of strangeness? We settled, the war came, we gave up our two sons to it, God rest their souls. You think we shouldn't belong when we give our sons to a country's cause?' With a familiar gesture, Buba took out a handkerchief and wiped her eyes. Huge pools of sorrow that could never be assuaged, they were always ready for tears. 'You think I shouldn't belong when I've been awarded the Cross of Honour for heroic motherhood?'

'I'm sorry, Buba, I didn't mean to remind you of your great loss, but that's just it, really, isn't it, you losing Uncle Daniel and Uncle Nathan and having the Cross of Honour, and my Papa losing half a lung and earning the Iron Cross for bravery for Germany and our still not belonging. And as if his family living here for generations wasn't enough either.' She swallowed some tea through her sugar lump. 'There'll be peculiar food in England,' she said, 'and tea with milk in it. Papa says that takes getting used to. You'll hate it.'

Neither replied to this remark. They never did. But she wouldn't press them today, or even glimpse herself at a future where Buba and Opa were left behind, too old to start a new life. Yet what if the stormtroopers came to beat Opa again without them to comfort him? Glancing at the scar running over his forehead and cheeks from the blows that had nearly blinded him in 1933, she shut her eyes, shutting off the memory of that day too, and the sound of Buba, weeping, weeping.

Half-dozing, she let them talk on, Opa's loving kindness counterpoint to Buba's simpler, sterner mind, shifting her thoughts to her own concerns, Max's dagger, the frock, and Greta Mundt's nasty little face at the window shouting something about it. It was always the same. She preferred small problems to loom largest, the big ones being too painful to contemplate for long. And if Opa was prepared to forgive stormtroopers who hurt him, who was she to keep fear and loathing in her heart? If she did, she'd have a Greta Mundt's heart, a little person's mean heart. She was actually going to walk straight past the Mundt flat with her head held high for once. Greta was such a little person, she must feel sorry for her. She must understand and forgive her. The time had come, after all. Moreover, she was going to curb her bad thoughts about people from now on, curb her tongue also and never again do a cruel drawing. Then she'd deserve for everything to be all right.

*

These resolutions were so uplifting, a surge of happiness made her hurry home along the streets, a warm imprint on her head from Opa's hand held there in blessing. She was just about to cross to the corner of Bochumer Strasse when someone called out to her. 'May I escort a young lady home?'

It was Pastor Borgmann, the nicest of their neighbours, who never looked the other way, who dared remain friends with her father, and this though he'd spent months in the KZ for refusing to swear allegiance to the Führer from the pulpit.

Accepting his arm, she smiled up at his smiling face, at his kind blue eyes which were like her father's. If he could remain as brave as he'd been before the horrors of the KZ, where he'd certainly been beaten, who was she to be afraid of taunting words?

'How very summery you are in your green dress,' he said as they set off together.

'Oh, thank you, Herr Pastor!' She laughed. 'You're the same as Papa, you know. You both try and make people feel better about themselves. This isn't a nice dress but I'm going to force myself to become fond of it.' She laughed again. She felt so confident, she was actually going to stare straight into Greta Mundt's face when the girl started shouting. That should wipe the scorn off it and put shame there instead. She'd never managed to do it, but today was different.

'You've had a happy Sunday, Fräulein?' the pastor asked, leading her to the corner of their street.

'Yes,' she said, to her astonishment. And it had been. Hope had come from it. 'A barmitzvah party, then ice cream on the Ku'damm with my friend Max, followed by cosy tea and talk at my grandparents'. They keep the old ways and I love it there, it's so comforting . . .'

'Such flags and music all over the city too,' he was saying as they reached the shoe shop opposite their apartment block, when a burst of sound reached them. Singing. Young men singing, and young men very near. Her heart leapt into her throat but she didn't falter. Nothing would happen. They were coming back from the parade. They had a right to sing. They were happy. She was too.

But the pastor paused. She paused beside him, her eyes fast to the ground. This was just habit. 'We'll allow the group to pass first,' he murmured, pressing her arm tight against his.

35

Then they were so close, she could see pairs of legs, about ten pairs, in the long socks, the black corduroy. She could see blond hairs above the knees. All the knees became still and turned their way. She lowered her eyes further. The song ended. The silence was worse.

The pastor pressed her arm again, taking her slowly past the shoe shop to the haberdashery. Here he pointed out something in the window, rows of cottons, and pretended to stare in. 'I shall have to ask your dear mother if she can spare a few hours to mend my shirt collars and cuffs,' he said.

Entire minutes seemed to pass by. She heard a sort of shuffling noise, some muttering. The old panicky, shivery feeling crept along her spine. The shoes started drumming, tramp, tramp, on the spot. 'One, two, three,' the leader shouted. A different song started up. They had good voices. Every word was as clear as could be.

'After the end of the Olympiade
We'll beat the Confessing Church
To marmalade
And we'll throw out the Jews . . .'

She thought, I shall make myself bear it, and not let myself think the torture is going to begin again and everything will never be all right. They are just little sons of little people, made big by their uniform. They want to go on hurting for a while whenever there's no one watching because they know they're not allowed to any more. They want to go on feeling big as long as they can.

The chorus of the song came round again, followed by an order: 'Turn this way, old man.'

The pastor turned. She was keeping hold of his arm so turned with him, her eyes leaving the pavement and looking up as far as the shoulders and badges and pretty swastika armbands. No further. I ought to dare, she thought, I want to dare and make them feel ashamed, I want to say they must leave us alone, it's not allowed any more. She was in fact about to dare something when her stomach seemed to leave its place and leap into her throat. For a hand came out and flicked the pastor's straw hat from his head. It rolled towards the shoes. One of them stamped on it.

She held her breath. Let this be all. But the hand reached out

36

again, she felt it brush against her hair and with a tiny sound the pastor's spectacles fell to the ground and splintered.

At once, instinctively, she knelt down to retrieve them. Only there were so many pieces of glass. She shook free the pastor's arm and got out her handkerchief. With this, she began to scrape at the glass. There was laughter. A voice said, 'Leave that.' She didn't want to leave glass on the pavement. It was dangerous. 'A dog might hurt its paw on it,' she heard herself say. And she didn't like dogs. She saw her fingers against the paving, the glitter of the pieces, her rather grubby handkerchief. She'd cut herself. There was blood.

'Well, what have we here?' The voice came again. 'Downright insolence, I think. What shall we do with her, comrades?'

Its owner leaned down into her view. He was going to spit. She wouldn't get out of his way, not this time. She'd always run before. She wanted not to now. She wanted to watch this one spit at her. She wanted to see his shame. He must feel something. She looked up. Konrad's face looked back at her.

His mouth was an ugly gash. He said, 'If it isn't Susanna Lehmann!' He folded his arms and placed one of his shoes carefully beside her fingers.

She gazed at this shoe, waiting. She mustn't stir. She knew that. He'd do worse. Her whole body felt light enough to float away. But her knees were sore. She could feel them on the rough paving. And Konrad, he was not special. He was the same.

He hadn't finished. He said, 'Here we have one of those crazy posturing churchmen the Führer scorns and a child of the chosen people – whom the Führer does not choose should belong to our Fatherland. And they are together.'

There was more laughter. The pastor knelt beside her and caught hold of the hand by Konrad's shoe. He began to scrape at the glass as well. Spots of his blood were added to the mess she'd created. Into this mess, Konrad spat.

They were lucky. It was over. They mustn't rise yet though. Side by side their fingers worked.

The shoes meanwhile were shuffling into formation. The 'one, two three' order came again and the usual Hitler Youth song started up.

37

'We'll stick in the knife
And Jewish blood will spurt out . . .'

Stealthily, she reached for the pastor's hat, glancing up at the rows of windows along the street. Who had watched, watched and turned away?

As stealthily, the pastor accepted his hat and put it on his head. He seemed suddenly at the end of his tether with weariness. His hand shook. He said, 'You were – what is the latest word? Fantastic!'

She laughed, hearing this laugh with surprise. 'I actually said something back, didn't I?' But it hadn't been much. Not enough. Her body seemed to have resumed its normal weight. She could feel the thump of her heart, a pulse beating. 'Have the boys quite gone?' She wanted to cry. The pastor was a sick man, weakened by months in the KZ. She should have dared more, for his sake.

'I believe they've gone round to the rear of the bakery.'

Leaning on each other, they got to their feet, taking a moment or two to readjust to being upright.

'We were fortunate it wasn't worse,' he said, brushing at his trousers.

'Yes!' she replied. 'They're only little people wanting to be big.'

'Made dangerously big by uniforms and togetherness, I'm afraid.'

'Yes!' She too brushed, at the dress stained with dirt. Once, Konrad hadn't wanted to be big. Then it came to her. Of course he had. All those years ago, at the skating rink, he'd used her to show off. And now he'd done it again. And an infinite number of days stretched ahead with a new fear to be overcome on every single one of them: going into the bakery for the bread. It was one of her jobs. Konrad served there in the holidays and it was holidays for weeks yet. She handed the pastor the spectacle frame she couldn't remember putting into her pocket.

He tucked it into one of his. 'I want you to promise me, Fräulein,' he said, 'that you will never cease to feel proud of what you are, even if it means you continue to be the butt of spite and malice.'

She couldn't answer. Kind words often made her cry and she was already having to hold on hard. Otherwise, she'd have liked to discuss the matter with him and tell him how strange it had been to learn she wasn't considered to be a Berliner or German. Did he have to mark 'Confessing Churchman' down on forms against 'Nationality', where her father had to write 'Jewish'?

'Come,' he said, 'let us walk proudly across the street, our heads held high and let the shame rest in the hearts of our dear neighbours who've turned away from their windows whilst a sick old man and an innocent girl are spat upon by adolescent boys.'

Standing by the cool darkness of the archway leading to the courtyard, she watched the pastor unlocking the door at the top of his staircase. The radios were still playing. She could smell cabbage and pork and coffee. Suppertime. She wanted her mother, to fuss, to scold. She didn't want to think. She'd like her father to stroll up to join her, singing his song. At least though, he hadn't been home to see her jeered at and spat upon. He'd have rushed out to protect her and the next day would have brought the knock on the door. Police. And her father led away to the KZ prison camp for being something else that was wrong, socially undesirable perhaps. They made up things. She'd been saved from losing her father. Also the pastor's presence had saved her from the taunts of Greta Mundt. The girl's face had appeared at the window, ready, and had quickly disappeared. Good out of bad. She managed to smile to herself. But she felt utterly exhausted and rather sick just the same. How to forget? How to go on walking the streets? And where was the proof now that everything was going to be all right?

Chapter 3

Passover, 1938

The preparations had been considerable and it had been a thoroughly fretful day, but worth it, Susanna decided – with some astonishment at herself, for she'd done most of the scrubbing out of the flat.

Everyone though had contributed to the feast. Cutlets and fried potatoes lay ready under a cover. Soup was keeping hot on the stove. There was gefilte fish on a huge platter and an even bigger plate with different sections to represent aspects of the Seder Night. Best of all, Buba had managed to conjure up proper *charoset* made of grated apple, crushed hazelnuts and honey. The thought of this alone was filling her mouth with saliva but she'd have to be patient, though Opa was well launched on the shortened Passover service.

There were so few of their own chairs to place around the table, the empty seat left for the prophet Elijah was the piano stool, and under several damask cloths three tables of different height had been made into a makeshift one which stretched the length of the living room. Opa was at the head by the balcony, Papa at the other end, his back to the kitchen door, with her and Sophie beside him and Freddy on his knees. None of them minded the draught.

She didn't mind any of it, she realised, not the work or the ramshackleness of the arrangements. In fact, a rare warm feeling of acceptance and affection crept over her as she looked around the room at their guests, the three Merkels and two Merkel aunts, their Uncle Oskar, the elderly Benjamin couple from the rear ground-floor flat, Frau Leona. Even Lottie Merkel had so far uttered no scornful word and she herself had curbed her usual judging thoughts as well as her tongue.

And it seemed to her it was almost as if she were five again instead of fifteen. The old childhood magic was there as it used to be, the rhythmic sound of Opa chanting and the candlelight making huge flickering shadows on the ceiling, on their walls, as if they hid unknown corners, and secrets. Opa was like nothing so much as a giant bird wheeling and dipping, the way he used to seem to her, as he prayed on in his white silk cap and shawl.

Even the empty stool looked mysterious in the candlelight. What a shock they'd have if Elijah should that night actually choose them to visit!

She smiled, just stopping herself from whispering this thought to Max, who so far was enduring the prayers quite well, with hardly a yawn. Shortly his mother was going to give one of her shivers, if her stiff face was anything to go by, though she sat in her fur cape. She had wanted the door to the staircase closed and no nonsense about leaving it open for Elijah. That the visitor could be someone less holy might also have occurred to her. The day before, the gypsy family and their goat had been dragged from their flat and pushed screaming into a truck. They were social parasites now. Whose turn next? The pastor was back in the KZ. It was a surprise that Lottie Merkel had actually ventured out in her fur, because she'd removed all her rings, having had to accept it was best not to display wealth anymore. In fact, Herr Merkel had brought with him that evening some of his most valuable miniatures to be hung on their walls for safekeeping. Not even the greedy Gestapo or SS police, who used their uniforms for robbery as much as anything, would waste time inspecting this flat for items worth stealing.

Was he regretting it, she wondered? He did so love his best pieces. He was certainly bored, and was already whispering to his wife. 'Must be near on two years since we were all together at Max's barmitzvah,' she heard him say. For a man who spoke so little, it was strange how often he chose to at the wrong moment.

She smiled at his look of surprise as his wife nudged him to be quiet. He was always surprised by his wife and always bored at the religious parts of festive meals. He wanted his cigar.

Max had not inherited his heavy features but they certainly had other characteristics in common. Already he was beginning to fiddle with the Passover text he was supposed to be following and tapping with a knife on the cloth.

'You didn't have to come,' she hissed. 'Keep still.'

'I felt the need for a decent meal,' he muttered back. 'Will there be more than one cutlet each?'

'Pray for something while you're waiting, if you can't be bothered to follow the service. I'm going to.'

There was plenty to pray for – or perhaps a single thing – more Passover nights like this one perhaps, even if the festive meal had to be scraped together, just more of them with everyone present and an end to the constant dread of what next? If the Nazis could be satisfied they'd very nearly broken their heart and their spirit, they'd be able to get on with life as best they could, not owning anything or running shops or ruling the world as the Nazis claimed they did, but keeping their heads down, grateful to be left alone. If our people ever ruled the world, she thought, it would be full of loving-kindness because men like Opa and her father would be formulating laws which forbade cruelty or persecution of any living thing from the merest animal upwards. *Fleas* would be allowed to live their lives if her father and grandfather ruled the world.

Then it was time for the best part. Everyone came to life, even Max and his father. They dipped the bitter things in the salt water and their fingers in the wine, shaking off the droplets with shouts of horror and disgust. 'Locusts!' they cried, and 'Boils!' and 'Vermin!' until each of the ten plagues was as if suffered afresh.

And shortly after that came the moment for Papa to lead them round the tables in the imaginary journey through the parted waves of an imaginary Red Sea. They rose to their feet and held hands, even Lottie Merkel, to follow his comically tiptoeing figure in and out of the bedrooms, stumbling over things and giggling wildly. It was one of her father's gifts to tell a story with mime and make it hilarious. In the end, Uncle Oskar was reduced to helpless bellowing and had to sit down.

They were all in their seats to continue with the festivities when the kitchen door flew back.

Susanna did no more than glance round once. Block Warden Mundt stood there with his dribbling Alsatian. She waited. They each waited. Sophie hiccuped. Papa's clocks ticked. Freddy crowed, 'Doggy!' Only her father moved, taking up her own and Sophie's hand in his.

The faces about the tables flickered black and grey in the candle flames. Opa seemed very tiny in his cap and shawl. He had shrunk. The dog was rudely sniffing in her lap. There'd be saliva on the white velvet frock she'd made down from one of her mother's, dark patches of it. Buba would want to wash it off.

Block Warden Mundt wasn't in a hurry. Finally he said, 'You people still have so much!'

No one replied.

Next his hand appeared near her right shoulder and an envelope landed on Papa's plate. 'Special delivery.'

The door slammed behind him and the dog.

Max said, 'Was that Elijah?'

He wasn't reprimanded. The envelope lay on her father's plate, a missive from hell.

Her father said, 'I have so enjoyed Passover First Night, Opa. Thank you. Every year you make it seem real, you know, even to my disbelieving soul. Would you mind very much if I opened this envelope? I think Esther and Buba will not eat another mouthful of our feast until they learn it contains nothing dreadful. My suitcase is packed ready if it does but I'll go nowhere until I've had my share of the *charoset*.' He was smiling. No one smiled back. Susanna saw the faces were like stone. Her heart felt like stone. It had ceased to beat.

The sound of the tearing of paper filled the room. Inside, only a slip, a note. Daring to look, she saw this. But bad news didn't need many words.

Papa's shout of pleasure was a shock. She jumped and Freddy laughed. 'I have to attend the AEG factory early on Monday morning,' Papa said. 'Esther! Everyone! I have work, I have work, there will be pay!'

Exhausted emotion meant some few minutes passed before her mother and Buba could gather themselves together in order to serve the cutlets, and they were gnawed to the bone before the matter could be discussed.

'It'll be for war production, of course,' Papa said.

Herr Merkel agreed. 'Radio parts, communications of some sort, for the war.'

'What war?' Frau Leona studied her cutlets for further crumbs of meat.

'The war the Nazis have built the new autobahn roads for,' Papa replied.

'I thought the roads were to get men back to work, Herr Lehmann.'

Max decided to be deliberately silly as only he could be. 'You haven't read Hitler's masterpiece, *Mein Kampf*, Frau Leona? Surely you have. He wrote about his desire for world domination in there. He'll need great big tanks for it, you see, and great big roads to roll them on.'

'I make hats, young man,' Frau Leona said, starting on her fried potatoes, oblivious of the sarcasm. 'You want I make your mother a nice hat, I make it. You want I read the rantings of Hitler's diseased mind, you belong in the asylum yourself.'

'But work, Josef!' Her mother spoke for the first time. 'Regular, paid work, and it means you're needed, we'll be all right.'

'I'm needed, dear Esther,' Papa said. 'And to still my bad conscience about being involved in the production of armaments that will murder innocent women and children, I shall have to consider some careful sabotage so what I do is wasted.'

Instantly, her mother cried out. 'God forbid you get yourself noticed, Josef, you'll do just what you're told to do.'

'Puh, puh, puh,' muttered Buba.

'Puh, puh, puh!' shouted everyone but Papa and they laughed.

Chapter 4

October 1938

It was Saturday morning, still cold and dark in the flat over the shop. Her grandparents must be at the railway station before seven. The police, delivering the extraordinary news, had made that clear. Yet what to pack and for how long a stay? Rumours had flown around the neighbourhood, because all the other holders of Polish passports living there had had the same police visit and instructions. But the rumours could surely have no basis in truth, so they really knew just the plain fact: Opa and Buba had to set off for Poland, that day, in a special train.

Opa said, 'I have never before travelled on sabbath.' He was sitting on the mattress of their stripped bed, a cardboard suitcase there, prayer book and Torah grasped to his heart. To Susanna he seemed very small. His feet hardly touched the floor. The long black overcoat was too big though it covered two pairs of long underpants, two vests and shirts. It would be even colder in Poland, let alone in the train.

Kneeling beside him, she was trying to roll up his prayer shawl, and Opa couldn't bear it. He wanted the shawl in its place, around his shoulders under the coat, but its light colour would stand out against the black cloth. Prayer shawls to the wickedest police, the SS, were as red rags to bulls, and SS would be at the station, herding the elderly and the slowest toddlers through the barrier. Whole families were to go. The SS liked things to move fast. They didn't like religious symbols. Or beards.

Rolling and unrolling mindlessly, she wondered why no one had dared suggest Opa actually have his beard cut off. Old men's

45

beards had been pulled right out during other SS collections. There'd been blood on pavements and the old men had had to scrub it off themselves. At this thought, a rush of absolute misery lurched from her stomach to her throat and closed it right up.

'They did say it was a simple matter of renewing passports?' Her mother knelt on the floor on the other side of the bed, folding and refolding for Buba, whilst Buba sat there muttering to herself.

Patiently Opa replied, though the question had been asked and re-asked ten times. 'Passports, dear daughter. We have to go home to Poland to have our passports reissued. It is the new regulations.'

'How long should it take, the journey each way and the filling in of forms and so on?' Susanna found her voice. They knew it wasn't straightforward. If Hitler hated any people more than their own, it was the Poles. They were sub-human so to be both Polish and Jewish was crime upon crime. She sat back on her heels and gazed at Opa's loving face gazing at his daughter. 'Why can't you and Buba not go to the station, but come and live in hiding at our flat! You can have our beds, me and Sophie'll sleep on the floor!' she cried. She kept on making this suggestion, for how was their resignation, their *letting go*, to be borne?

'If we do not leave, others may be sent in our place,' Opa said gently. 'There may be a quota. And we shall not put you all at risk.' He let his precious book rest in his lap. 'We are ready, child. It has always been our people's destiny to be moved on. Persecution is the burden of our race.'

What did this mean? That he believed the rumours and there'd be no return to Berlin? How angry her father would be to hear him! There is no excuse, he'd say, for wailing talk of a people destined to wander. These are modern times and such old myths must be rejected. Of course, Papa was still hoping modern times would return to Germany instead of Nazi ones: hadn't he been given back the right to work?

She edged the shawl into the case beside slippers and face cloth and as patiently said again, 'Papa claims we must make our own destiny if we can and you can hide in our flat. He understands you want to obey the law of the land but Nazi laws aren't fair, or just, they haven't been democratically voted for.'

Opa put on his glasses and began to murmur a prayer. She wanted to scream at him to stop, the Lord wasn't listening.

Springing to her feet, she said, 'I'll make more tea. I suppose I haven't time to run out and see if the baker is open? Perhaps we can buy some nice white rolls by the station, you can put them in your pockets for the journey. How long does it take to reach Poland?'

No one answered. A long time, she thought, hundreds of miles across the vast empty plains beyond Berlin. Then what? Polish officials were known to be incompetent and corrupt, but since Opa had nothing to use as bribes, theirs wouldn't be the first papers to be dealt with. She put the pan of water on the stove and busied herself with tea, as if she could somehow give them warmth and sustenance enough however long the journey. And what about the arrival point? Where was it? How long would they be there and how would they live?

Opa stopped praying and took off his glasses. He said, 'It is better that this has come now while we have the strength to start again, perhaps in our home village.'

'Papa,' her mother said, 'by the time you get back to Berlin with the new passports, God willing, we'll have our visas. Josef will have work in England and we'll send for you. Our good Herr Merkel will lend us enough money for the tickets and for settling in. Only the other day he told us he might be able to buy back his passport from the police chief. They confiscated it, you remember, and he can buy it back for a quarter of a million marks. He has many times that in the value of his stock. He won't see us or ours wanting if he's allowed to trade again and they'll maybe let him trade secretly to pay for the passport.'

Susanna poured the tea into four glasses. Why hadn't she worried endlessly about her grandparents being sent to Poland? Yet how could she have? It was new. The Nazis did like thinking up new miseries. They must have a special department to do it. She'd been lulled by her father being ordered to work for them because they needed his skills – and the last new lots of regulations not affecting them personally at all. The ones about having to declare property and valuables hadn't, because they had none. So that was good out of bad. The Nazis couldn't steal from you if you had nothing.

Suddenly Buba spoke. 'Our greatest sorrow,' she said, 'is to leave unvisited the graves of our dear sons, peace be on their souls. We shall also grieve to know we shan't be able to make our

47

monthly visit to our grandson in his hospital. These tasks we must trust to you, daughter.'

At this, her mother gave a wail of anguish. 'Mama, you want to break my heart? In a week or so, God willing, you'll be back here. You think there's work in Poland? Where is there work? You came to Berlin to find work. You want to go back to dirt floors and water to be brought from the water carrier without us to help you? You think our people are not being persecuted there like they are here?'

Susanna felt herself sway. A pit of misery was opening up at her feet. Opa and Buba were over seventy, and frail. They hadn't told her the full truth. They knew they were being banished from Berlin for ever. They were going to let themselves die.

It was as if one's body could go on doing things of itself. They did get themselves down the stairs of the flat and through the empty shop, locking the door behind them. On its glass front was the notice: Do Not Patronise Jewish Enterprises. The paint was flaking, it had been there so long. On the pavement was a second: Go Back to Palestine, it said.

Dizzy, Susanna stared at each one. How very mild, how very painless they were, she thought, compared to the hundreds of crueller, coarser slogans now decorating the city. Perhaps the stormtroopers who'd daubed them there all those years ago knew her grandparents personally and as a kindness had followed orders to a minimum.

As the four of them gathered themselves together, she realised the daubs no longer mattered. If the Nazis wanted it, and it satisfied them, she'd wear a label around her neck and still hold her head high. If only they'd stop at words and not send Opa and Buba away, she'd wear rags and labels and never feel a second's shame.

The Polish passport-holders were to be unaccompanied. Hadn't this been made clear? The SS men shouted and waved things. Stay back. You others this way. More SS men were grouped by the station barrier, getting everyone into order. They liked order and lines, and not disorder or emotion. There was to be no emotion. This was Jewish. Order and lines were Aryan and right.

Opa and Buba held hands and suitcases and disappeared into

the lines. The SS prodded with their whips and sticks and shouted, picking out an old man who didn't go fast enough. He had to scramble back to his feet and into his line. It wasn't Opa! The SS men laughed and clapped their hands together and stamped their boots. Their breath misted out, clouds of it.

Susanna held her mother's leaden arm as they backed away from the station area and stood sideways by a bus stop as if waiting for a bus. This must be allowed. They could thus glance casually sideways at the orderly lines shuffling through the barrier. There were children, toddlers, all ages, and the only sound was their shuffling and the SS men shouting and laughing. It was hard to keep looking sideways like that and the lines were just one mass of dark clothing. Really, only the babies in arms stood out.

'Can you see them?' These words emerged from her mother's mouth.

'No, Mama. I wish we'd asked Buba to wear a coloured headshawl.'

'Yes.'

They stood there, eyes hurting, cold riven into their bones, until there was no more chance of a glimpse. Now there wouldn't be enough days left in their lives to do enough crying.

Chapter 5

November 1938

Susanna sat up in bed with a start. There was a noise in the street outside, a truck and men, the slam of doors. Yet it was still night.

'What is it?' In the gloom, Sophie too sat up.

'Nothing,' Susanna said, 'nothing to worry about. I'll look.' Padding to the window, she pulled a centimetre of the blind. It was something. It was stormtroopers, lots of them. They had torches. 'Two trucks are out there,' she reported, 'one at each end of our street.'

'Round-up?' Sophie asked.

'I expect.'

'Stormtroopers or policemen or the SS ones?'

'I can't tell, it's too dark.'

'Poor people. I wonder who it's to be?'

'I wonder.' She didn't want to see any more, or hear the shouts. There was something so ugly about the shouts.

'I hope Papa doesn't waken and long to go down and help.'

'God forbid.' Shivering, Susanna got back into bed. 'He won't have heard it from their room. You know how soundly he sleeps and so do Mama and Freddy.'

'Can I come into your bed until it's over?'

'If you want.' She arranged the feather bedding to make space.

'Shall I bring the box?'

'Why not?'

Leaning across to the toy and book trunk which sat between their beds, Sophie scrabbled in it for the secret cardboard box their mother didn't know about, and jumped with it and her doll into

50

her sister's bed. 'We haven't had this out for ages.' She put it on her knees and leaned back against the wall. 'Can you hear anything now?'

'I thought I heard a dog, but I'm not sure.' Susanna too leaned back, pulling the eiderdown around them and fumbling under her pillow for the torch. 'We'll keep listening.'

'I wonder if Opa and Buba are lying awake like this. I don't really understand where they are.'

'They're still at the camp on the Polish border where their letter came from. The Polish government won't let them into Poland so they can't go back to their village for the moment or even start filling in the forms,' Susanna answered patiently. Often at night they discussed matters Sophie felt anxious about in order to save their parents worry about them worrying. She couldn't remember when her natural impatience had ceased to assert itself. And when had she last told Max to shut up or grumbled and fussed about household tasks!

'Why did Mama go so white when she read the letter and not be full of joy when she saw Opa's writing there at last?'

'Because if Opa asks for a food parcel and a rug, perhaps there isn't quite enough food supplied to the camp and it's a bit cold as it's winter.' Yes, she thought, but if Opa made that gentle little request for them to go to the trouble and expense of sending a parcel, he and Buba were sick with the cold, and starving, and what if the parcel didn't reach them *in time*?

'Will they come back to Berlin to be with us?'

'No one knows. Maybe the forms have to be filled in before they're allowed. There are thousands of them in the camp, it'll take months.'

'Are they living sort of like prisoners in the KZ?'

'Yes, sort of.'

'Will they have feather eiderdowns?'

'Of course not. Straw and bunks, I expect.' If they were lucky, she thought. Rumours claimed so many Polish-passport holders were massed at the Polish border, army barracks had had to be opened for them. Some had only a corner to squat in. There was diarrhoea and sickness, men had been shot. And if the stories weren't enough, the scrap of paper had arrived from Opa with the few words on it: Please send food and a rug, and how to bear that?

'What's for breakfast?' Sophie persisted. 'Is there tea

and rye bread in Poland or white rolls with butter, and coffee.'

'Tea and rye bread, of course. White bread and coffee are for the better-off everywhere. Try not to think about them too much, just pray and sort of send them love and comfort. I do.'

'How?'

'By thinking of them very intensely while keeping tight hold of the talisman Buba gave me before she left.'

'You said not to think.'

'Go to sleep instead, it's school tomorrow.'

Sophie took a deep breath. 'Susanna, sometimes I want to say to Papa I just can't go to school any more. It's no better our going to the new ones. The kids from the old school lie in wait for Magda and me at the tram stop when we get off. Yesterday Irmgard and Berthe Kunz threw horse chestnuts at us and we cried and Franz Wolters said they'd had a race lesson and he was chosen to go to the front of the class and have his skull measured as a perfect Aryan skull and he said we had smaller skulls and shouldn't be allowed a proper education . . .'

'You must try and bear it, Sophie. We all go through that sort of thing.' Anguished, Susanna put an arm around her sister's shoulders. She was only eight! 'Try and feel proud of being Jewish like they're proud of being Aryan, though it's a made-up word. It's not even a real race like we're supposed to be. I used to think we were Berliners when I was your age and Jewish was sort of like our religion like Christians have theirs. They go to church, we go to synagogue. Well, not Papa, but you know what I mean.' And I wasn't proud always then, she thought. I was sometimes ashamed, ashamed of walking beside Buba and Opa with their old-fashioned black clothes, their foreignness. They looked Polish, and poor, and she'd try and run in front to be separate. But if she could just have a glimpse of them coming down the street in their long black coats that very minute . . .!

'Well, I hate all Aryan teachers. I hate that Herr Stiller from the first-floor flat, he gives me a nasty look and kind of snorts when he sees me.'

'Yes! Listen, next time you spot him coming home and climbing the steps to his door, remind yourself what a magnificent example of the master race he is with his sweaty face and that monocle stuck in his fish eye. And his strutting little legs. And he smells!'

52

Sophie giggled. 'He smells of boiled pork and cabbage!'

'Yes, and you must be proud not to be like him but come from a people like our parents and grandparents, and always remember that one day there'll be an end to this misery, it can't go on, this is a civilized country . . .'

'You sound like Papa. What if I write another letter to Hitler and ask him please to explain why Opa and Buba are hungry and cold in a camp when they belong here and gave two sons to the Fatherland in the war? And we really do send it off?'

Susanna hesitated. 'I just don't think he'd read letters from you, Sophie. He does so hate us, and anyway, he's too lazy to read letters. Max has heard he doesn't get up until midday and soon after lunch he stops for tea and after supper he watches films or listens to horrible Wagner on the gramophone. It isn't actually true that Hitler works day and night for the Fatherland and wears himself out, it's no such thing. And what's more, Herr Merkel knows someone who was taken to the KZ for telling the truth about him. The man knew Hitler in Vienna when they were young, and he was a sort of tramp. Imagine that, the Führer was a dirty tramp, eating in soup kitchens. And he isn't even a Berliner. We are. But don't even tell Magda what I've told you, or we'll all end in the KZ, like that newsagent who's in there for repeating a Hitler joke to his customers.

'He likes dogs.'

'Who does?'

'Hitler, and he doesn't eat meat so he must have a heart.'

'Lie down and go to sleep. I'll keep watch until I hear the trucks driving away. Here, give me that box, we'll look at it in the morning.'

'No.' Sophie snatched it up. 'Put on the torch. Let's read out the letters I wrote and you wouldn't let me send, it makes me feel better, and I like your drawings.'

'All right.' Susanna shone the torch beam on the open box. 'I think it makes us both feel better.'

Sophie peered into her face. 'I'm glad I told you about my secret letters to Hitler though you wouldn't buy me any stamps. Are you glad I found your secret drawings?'

'I am, I suppose,' Susanna admitted. 'It didn't seem such a shameful habit afterwards. But I didn't like you knowing about my most wicked thoughts. When Opa comes home, you must

53

never tell him about the drawings. It would break his heart to realise his granddaughter doesn't go about turning the other cheek and loving neighbours as ourselves. I don't want Papa to know either because he says we must always search for what's good in people and feel sorry for them if there isn't much of it.'

'There's no good in Herr Stiller!' Sophie laughed and held up the sketch of the teacher. 'The best bit is the huge fishy eye you did, oh, it's the biggest fishy eye you ever saw and his mouth is all gobbly like a fish's. I bet he spits!'

Susanna gazed Herr Stiller. 'Not bad,' she said. 'Not my best though. Find Goebbels, the one I did after he heard him ranting on the radio.'

Sophie found Goebbels. He was a tiny, dejected jackal in a cage at the zoo, with a twisted foot like Goebbels and a jackal's snout and his mouth was a radio loudspeaker.

'Read out the notice on his cage.' Sophie giggled in anticipation.

'The Lower Jackal,' read Susanna. 'An inferior species which must be eliminated. Stones are provided for this purpose. A direct hit will earn the sum of five marks.'

The words were hardly out when a noise rent the air of the street, thuds and screams and smashing sounds.

Terrified, Sophie dropped the drawing. 'What's that! Are they coming for us?'

Leaping from the bed, Susanna ran to the window, edged aside the blind and flinched. There were things flying about out there, things being thrown.

Sophie cried, 'Oh, get back, where can we hide, fetch Papa!'

'It's all right, it's not us. It's the Spiegels' shoe shop, and their flat, the windows are being smashed, there's glass, I can see glass and arms and sticks and . . .' Again she flinched and ducked. She had seen something awful tumbling from a second-floor bedroom. *A body.* On her knees, heart thudding, she said, 'It's all right, Sophie, it's not us, it's the poor Spiegels!' *But them next*? 'There are stormtroopers on the rampage, they'll stop soon, they're breaking windows in the shoe shop and haberdashery too and we haven't a shop, we'll be safe, we're lucky and the police will be here soon. I couldn't really see, it's so dark out there, they've got torches and they're flashing them about, you know what they're like, showing off. Perhaps the shops have been selling to Aryans

54

when they're not allowed and the stormtroopers are teaching them a lesson . . .' She put her hands over her ears. If only the screaming would stop. The screaming was coming from the body on the ground. And she must see who it was.

Carefully, she edged herself up again and peered over the sill. The body was lying in some glass. It must have been cut. But it was too small for Norbert Spiegel, he was ten and quite tall. It was his dog. Of course. It wasn't dead.

She took a great gulp of air. 'Sophie,' she said, 'it's just Norbert's dog they've thrown out and it's screaming and Norbert is hanging from the window crying for his dog and Frau Spiegel is trying to drag him in.'

'Keep looking to see if they're coming here.' Sophie crawled from the bed and crouched by her feet. 'Don't let them come here and throw us out of the window, please fetch Papa.' She shook so much her teeth were rattling.

Susanna tried to sound soothing. 'I think it's all just another way for the stormtroopers to steal from shops and we haven't a shop so we'll be all right. They're throwing shoes out now and stamping them into the glass, the glass is like sparkling snow and they're laughing and sort of roaring and they're running up and down and pulling things out of the haberdashery and stamping them into the glass so they aren't here for stealing . . .' This was a pity. She had time to think that, for there was nothing in their flat to steal. 'They'll go off soon, they can't be here on orders. Perhaps they've been drinking too much beer.' She stopped. She couldn't speak any more, but she could see. She could see Norbert hanging from his window screaming for his dog and for his papa to help his dog. His father was downstairs, he was in the street, but he was being led away through the space where his shop door had been. Stormtroopers held his arms. He wasn't struggling. He knew not to.

The owner of the haberdashery was not being so sensible. He was protesting at his treatment. They wanted him to get into their truck with Herr Spiegel, they were beating him into it and somehow, through all the other sounds, she could hear the special thud of a stick against flesh. I must not look, will not look, I must forget it *at once*, she thought, I must not let the sound of it go into me so I can never forget it, like last time. 'Papa,' she whispered to herself, and then, 'Not Papa,' for she must somehow stop it being

55

Papa next, but how to stop it and how to move from that spot and how to bear the noise . . .

'Hide, hide, oh hide,' Sophie screamed.

'Why should I hide, my darling, when there is nothing to worry about?'

Papa stood in their doorway, funny in his nightshirt, and like a rock.

Sophie flung herself at him so hard, the lamp he held flickered and almost went out.

But it was all right. They were going to be all right and so was Mama though she looked such a spectre of horror, eyes huge and black, but somehow smiling. Freddy, in her arms, was of course giving out a great male roar of disapproval but that was all right too. It was ordinary and usual.

Susanna felt she was going to laugh with relief, but her father's gaze resting on her said: you are being brave, my darling, now help me with the others.

This was a help to her, of course. It made her move from her window vigil. It made her fly about with dressing gowns, search for her father's coat since he didn't have one, organise slippers, stir the stove – all while Papa's calm voice spoke the words of reassurance the others needed but she did not. He was right. The target was shopkeepers and they had no shop. Once it was over of course, they must go down and offer comfort.

In the end, they were almost festive, grouped about the stove, warmed through with tea and the cinnamon biscuits her mother had produced from some special source. And the candlelight helped make it seem festive. The electricity had been cut. Even Mama was still managing a smile though her hands shook.

Seeing that, Susanna doubled her efforts at making faces at Freddy until his dry sobs were no more than hiccups.

Outside, the thuds and shouts and the new sound they'd identified as boots crunching on broken glass went on and on and beyond the windows the sky had a strange red glow. They could smell smoke.

'Must be a fire in the city,' Papa said.

'Fire engines, Freddy, listen for the sirens.' Then he laughed at himself because of course Freddy mustn't listen for the noises. He

56

decided to sing instead to cover them all up and started with Freddy's favourite tune, which he'd learned whilst working in London in his youth.

'I'm Henery the Eighth, I am, I am,' he sang, they all sang, as loud as they could.

Entranced by this, Freddy demanded there be dressing-up to match the song and shortly the kitchen resembled backstage at a theatre. Papa began to transform himself into the fat Prussian king, George V, whose coronation procession he had actually watched from London pavements in 1911. He tied a cushion around his waist with string and turned his homburg hat inside out to represent the crown.

It was easy, because they'd dressed up often after festive meals in the past. For the trains they'd need as attendants to Queen Mary, Susanna and Sophie hauled out towels and bedsheets and their mother got busy making a twist of stiff muslin into a crown. As her train, she used a length of tablecloth which was her best damask. Susanna caught herself staring back at Sophie in surprise as they silently recognised their mother preparing to dirty best damask.

Shortly they were ready. Freddy sat transfixed as the four of them, suitably pompous and stately, heads held high, swept the length of the living room.

'My Queen,' declared Papa, holding out his arm. His crown fell off, followed by Mama's muslin one, and they were helpless with laughter when a face appeared at the kitchen window, three faces, four. Stormtroopers.

They didn't bother to knock but broke down the door with an axe. They had axes and there weren't four of them but five. Five stormtroopers filled a lot of space.

And the five of *them* stood together squashed up by the balcony doors, where they were like statues in their fancy dress, waiting. Papa said, 'Gentlemen, there are children present.'

One said, 'Tell the brat to shut up or it'll be the worse for him.'

Freddy went on screaming, but they got to work. Their brown shirts were spattered with stains of blood and sweat. They were there to smash everything and wasted no time, attacking the piano first and the two violins. These were easy, breaking in two with a single crack on the wall. The piano was made of harder wood and it was difficult to get an axe into it.

They were so close by now, Susanna could see the gleam of the axe blades and their wet mouths. They grunted. She could hear their grunting, and also the rattle of Sophie's teeth. Actually, none of them were statues any more. Her breath had returned and her chest heaved in and out. Papa's right arm moved too. He wanted them to edge themselves into the doorway of her and Sophie's bedroom, away from the splinters. They also had to untie the bedsheets and the damask cloth and the cushion.

This they somehow managed to do as Freddy roared on and the piano tipped over with a crash of its innards. Next Papa's table was the target. His clocks and radios tumbled off as they turned it over. His books were of particular interest. 'Foreign stuff,' one shouted, grabbing the lovely red leather of the Shakespeare, kicking his boot through the balcony doors and throwing Shakespeare into the street. The other books went after it. There was glass in their living room, and freezing outside air.

At this point, Freddy's terror was so complete, he did stop screaming. The near-silence was almost a shock as they were gestured aside. The bedroom was to have the same treatment.

Reassembling stiffly between the kitchen table and the stove, they couldn't see what was happening any more. Papa started up a comforting whisper. 'Hold on, they are not going to kill us. They mean to frighten us and to destroy our things but things do not matter, only people matter and we are together and are going to be all right . . .'

His knuckles were white as he held Freddy and Sophie against him, and their faces were white with black coals for eyes. Pressed up to her mother, Susanna had time to ask God for them not to find her secret box, because comic drawings of Nazi leaders would mean the KZ and torture and death for them all. She felt a trickle of sweat make its way down her spine and shivered.

They'd finished. They hadn't found the secret box. They stood by the door, hands on hips, ready to leave. There was fresh blood on the uniforms, their own, from the glass they'd smashed. One had his left ear cut. It was bleeding into his brown collar.

Susanna looked at the spreading stain and on up into his face. They seemed the same, in their brown shirts and black boots, red-faced and breathless, but this one had a bleeding ear and he was speaking, gazing not at her, but around the room. 'Anything else here?'

Another, a bigger one, replied. 'Pictures, there's pictures.' Sniffing, he gestured towards Herr Merkel's miniatures, hung on their walls for safekeeping, and soon ripped them off. 'Don't seem much,' he said, shining his torch, 'and these are poor Jews.' His eyes flickered on them now, defiling her mother, her father, her sister, Freddy.

And an extraordinary surge of indignation rose up from somewhere near her stomach. I want to say something, she thought, I want to tell them, order them, not to dare to glance our way. Making a small movement, she gripped the edge of the table. If she uttered a single word of surprise, much less indignation at their presence, they'd each be dragged into the trucks outside and into the KZ. This she knew, just as her father did, and that was why his knuckles were so white.

'Leave it,' the bleeding ear man said, 'and come on, we've got two more flats downstairs in this block alone to do yet.' Kicking back the door, he led the way down the staircase.

The following scream from the other side of the courtyard might have been Frau Leona's or old Frau Benjamin's. One of them would have to be first.

But in their flat, it was all over. There should be rejoicing. They were safe. They were alive. Possessions didn't matter, mustn't.

Her father moved first. He sat down in his chair. 'I am sorry, I am so sorry I could not protect you,' he said, putting his face in his hands. 'What sort of man have I become?'

And at this terrible sight, at these terrible words, Susanna felt their whole world had shifted further into something awful.

Chapter 6

Freddy put to rest in the big bed, they had a very early breakfast, rye bread, and a pat of extravagant butter her mother had luckily bought for a treat the day before. Papa also insisted they ground the coffee beans which had been a recent gift from Herr Merkel. It was a special enough day, he said.

Warmly wrapped in an assortment of clothing, they sat at the table as usual for it, in the new icy draught from the balcony doors, in the new debris, near the turned-over piano, the trail of their fancy dress.

Yet how could this be? It simply was, Susanna decided, studying her mother's face for a hint she was going to break into a wail of distress. She could read nothing there, though the circles under her mother's eyes seemed to be darkening by the minute. Unspoken between them, she realised, was the biggest fear of all: Papa not being able to bear any more. His moment of despair had shaken them as much as the stormtroopers, and had somehow helped them recover, which was truly strange.

Anyway, they remarked how wonderful the coffee was, Sophie being just old enough for coffee, and it being his favourite thing of all, and as calm as anyone could be, her mother offered a sensible suggestion.

'When you've gone to the factory, Josef, the girls and I will start clearing up. We'll have it cleared by suppertime even if we can't right the piano. And one of us will go and see Frau Leona and the poor Benjamins. They may have suffered worse than us, God forbid.' She was smiling, smiling in a grey-skinned face, her lips blue, her eyes as black as Max's.

'Yes, Papa,' Susanna joined in. 'And I was wondering if we

couldn't put the piano in front of the balcony doors to prevent the cold air coming in and shall I take the violins round to the man at the music shop, he does repairs, and there's the glass to get mended if we can afford it and our books to fetch from the street.' Exhilarated by such grown-up thinking, she went on. She couldn't stop, didn't want to, she wanted to be a tower of support, to show her grey-faced mother and her *reduced* father who sat there with the skin across his cheekbones getting tighter and tighter, that it didn't matter, she was going to make everything better. 'I'll collect our books from the street, shall I? And maybe Frau Spiegel would like me to help her bury her dog, and there's the glass to sweep up out there. I suppose the police and the street sweepers won't come. I suppose it was all just against our people and there won't be anyone to help us but each other?' Leaping from her chair, she dashed to the balcony, inched aside the door frame and leaned out.

Below her in the winter morning gloom, the street was covered in glass, tiny pieces like sprinkled snow and big frosty splinters. She could see the red of the Shakespeare lying there and her big blue English school story *Dimsie Goes to School*. And in the black hole of the shoe shop she could see Greta Mundt's nasty pinched face, in her arms a collection of shoes. Behind her were her parents, scrabbling about in the rubble. 'The Mundts are stealing shoes,' she hissed. 'If that Greta picks up my book, I shan't be able to bear it.'

About to turn away, she caught sight of Frau Schmidt emerging from the archway below and making her way carefully across the crunching glass to the shop. She was preparing to make the sight of this huge round figure dressed in her husband's overcoat and boots into something funnier than it was, when Sophie cried out.

'Such ugly men, Papa, will they break in again tonight, will they come back to kill us?'

'No, my darling, they would have done that already if their orders had instructed them to. The gang have done their worst to us and we should be glad. Nothing else can happen to us now. And our spirits have suffered hardly a dent. Isn't that so?'

'Puh, puh, puh,' Sophie cried. 'Say it for luck this once, Papa, please!'

Perhaps that extraordinary morning, he might have changed the

61

habits of a sceptical lifetime and given voice to superstition, but he had no chance. A knock sounded on the kitchen door.

They all froze, except Susanna, who had to get to her feet. It was she who first saw the caps at the window, the two grey and black SS caps with the skull and crossbones decoration on the front.

They didn't need to break down the door, a push was enough. But they hadn't been smashing anything. They were clean and smart. They were polite. They stood on the sill and bowed. One said, 'Herr Josef Lehmann, you are to accompany us to headquarters. A small suitcase is permitted.'

It had come, the summons, they'd escaped nothing, they hadn't lived through the worst. As if in a dream, Susanna gazed at the tableau far away from her down by the stove, at the three frozen figures of her family, at the two living figures inside their grey and black cloth and leather. Hair on end, she watched her father stand up to his full height, every inch of him dignity and specialness. They wouldn't want to push him into a truck, they'd ask him to get into it and he would. He said, 'My suitcase is ready, gentlemen, I shall not keep you waiting,' but he wasn't saying it for the SS, he was saying it for them, so they should see how to behave to the very end, to the SS end.

And from far away, she heard a voice speak. It said, 'I think you must have made a mistake. My father cannot be wanted at your headquarters, he's foreman at the AEG factory, and he's a war hero.'

It was her own voice, she could hear it though it seemed like someone else's, echoing out. She also heard her mother gasp, saw her put two hands to her mouth as if to cry, Stop, stop now, Susanna, it's *SS*. But she didn't stop. She said, 'My father was awarded the Iron Cross in the Great War and he has a letter from the Führer praising his bravery. It begins, Dear Comrade Lehmann, which shows it's personal, from the Führer himself. Shall I fetch the medal and the letter to show you? In the past, men who fought for the Fatherland have been exempt from questioning.' Here she did stop. She had to take her eyes from the tableau around the stove in order to point down into their rubble where the desk was lying. 'They are in a drawer.'

'That will not be necessary.' One of their voices, and then her father's. 'Susanna, my darling, it will be all right.'

She watched him take his hat from the table, get it into shape and pick up the KZ suitcase from its place between the dresser and the potato sack where it had sat so long. As it turned out, they should have called it the Prinz-Albrecht Strasse suitcase, the address of the SS headquarters. That's where he was going.

He had to go there straight away. Farewells weren't permitted. She hadn't needed to force her legs and feet across the vast stretch of the room to say goodbye. In fact, he had had to go so quickly, he must have reached the bottom of the staircase before she reached the door and Mama picked up his coffee cup and held it to her heart.

When she and her mother had stared at each other long enough with a sobbing Sophie between them refusing to go back to bed with Freddy, they got to work. They must have things tidied and cleaned for when Papa came home. This didn't need to be said.

She insisted on tackling the piano by herself, and managed to get it up at the first attempt, which pleased her. It had seemed quite desolate lodged on its keyboard, like a person splayed out front-down on their chin. Next they managed the table. They wanted that up so they could put the clocks and radios back, collecting them whilst Sophie found the pieces of violin. These she laid carefully in the centre. 'Perhaps Papa will be able to mend the violin himself when he comes home.'

'Your father can mend anything,' Mama replied stoutly from the depths of some new, changed, self, she who'd never ceased to complain at the time he spent mending other people's possessions and at the pittance he charged. 'And please God, he won't be long. They've simply made a mistake, as Susanna told them, didn't you, my darling?' Here she paused, a still-ticking clock in her hands, an extraordinary smile dredged up from somewhere. Eyes huge, encircled by black rings, she smiled.

'It was my Berliner Mouth, Mama,' Susanna said, feeling the start of a smile on her own face. 'Imagine me actually trying to put it to some use at last instead of irritating you with it or wasting it on Max.' But how did I? she wondered.

'Oh, I was so frightened!' Sophie clapped two hands to her mouth just like her mother and Buba. 'I thought, don't take Suzy too, puh, puh, puh, I couldn't breathe for pretend-spitting to myself over and over, puh, puh, puh.'

'If it had worked!' Susanna got busy wrapping up Herr Merkel's miniatures in an old towel. They'd only just been safe.

'It will, you'll see. Those SS must be human beings, and when they start filling in their forms at headquarters and have to write Foreman, AEG factory in the space for Occupation, God willing they'll send him straight to work. With full apologies to the holder of an Iron Cross for Valour in the Field of Battle, 'First Class.'

Buoyed up by this exchange, they crunched across the glass righting more things until they decided the most sensible way forward would be to collect the glass first. The broom was fetched. Mama began sweeping from the kitchen inwards. Susanna emptied the potatoes from their sack into a bucket, Sophie found all the findable gloves, and shortly they were edging the biggest splinters safely into sacking. The task was fully occupying, because Mama's eyes had to be everywhere without her fussing too much about cuts.

They hardly jumped in fact when a familiar voice said, 'You look like scavenging crows.'

Max stood in the doorway with two suitcases and his mother.

Max said,' Can you put us up?' He placed the suitcases by the dresser where Papa's used to sit. 'They've been here, have they? Us too. They tipped out our salt looking for diamonds. I suppose they didn't bother with your salt.' Vaguely, he turned his head towards the food cupboard.

As he turned, they could see his face was swollen beyond anything normal. It was red and blue and his beautiful black eyes were slits.

'You've been . . .' Susanna began.

'Don't bother.' He made as if to take off his cap, changed his mind and drew out a chair for his mother. 'Did they spot Pa's miniatures?'

He had been beaten. He hadn't kept quiet. He'd been insolent, and male. An immense pity for Max and his bravado welled up from somewhere as if she had feeling left.

Her mother opened her arms in a gesture of embrace to the two visitors. 'They have taken Herr Merkel also? Other men?'

Max nodded. It hurt him. 'And they've set fire to the

synagogues, they're still burning all over Berlin and everything else they've smashed, the Jewish shops and flats we've passed. There's looting. Spectators are standing around pointing and sniggering. They want us gone from their ugly old city.'

Like a crow herself in her fur coat, dishevelled, exhausted, Frau Merkel spoke as if in a dream. 'They've confiscated everything we own, the best pieces my husband had hidden in the flat, my jewellery, the stocks in our shop. They've sealed the doors. They pretend my husband's been trading illegally. We can never go back and we have nothing left. Whatever will become of us?'

Chapter 7

After that night, it was very nearly the end. They learned the stormtrooper attacks had been official. Over the entire country, Jewish people and Jewish businesses had suffered the same fate. Many men had been taken into custody. It was therefore clearer than ever that the Nazis intended to make life for Jewish people so uncomfortable they'd be stirred to leave. Those who had money and strength enough increased their queuing at passport and visa offices. It was a pity the message hadn't got through to the civil servants there; they didn't seem to work any faster.

Max and his mother moved into their bedroom, she and Sophie moved into the big bed with Mama. He made himself very useful whilst his mother told her story over and over. He mended their furniture with tintacks, took the violins to the music shop for repair and withdrew from his suitcase the old childhood favourites of his own that he'd chosen to save. These he seemed intent on entrusting to Freddy who had soon spread Stabilo construction pieces and marbles around the floor. He informed the bewildered toddler that toys were important and went so far as to restuff Sophie's doll with sawdust to make her last longer. These last activities surprised the mothers but not Susanna. Max had been happy as a boy and never since.

Three weeks and five days after the attack, her father came home, one of the few who did, for it had been a mistake, taking a skilled factory foreman to the Sachsenhausen KZ. That's where he'd been, not SS headquarters, but his suitcase must have gone there. He'd never seen it and returned in the same clothes he'd set out in. But something had changed. You couldn't say what, Susanna decided, endlessly gazing at him and sure her old father would never return. He couldn't, even for their sakes. Outwardly, he was almost the same, except for a tendency to stoop from the waist and the presence of a raw scar on the back of his neck which he claimed was the result of his falling from a bunk.

The day after he came home, he went back to work at the factory. His skills were required, so they might have saved themselves the trouble of his stay in the KZ and having one more mouth to feed there. It had been very crowded apparently, the only statement he ever made about it.

Max's father came home too, or his body did, in the form of ashes. They were delivered to Frau Merkel at her new address, theirs, in a pot inside a brown paper parcel with the message 'Shot While Trying to Escape' and a bill for his cremation. They didn't want him for war work, they wanted his antiques. As Max said, the Nazis were first and foremost thieves.

He also declared his father had had a very easy death just when he was most needed, fooling only a few of his relations with this statement which he also repeated to anyone who'd listen.

Some charity and welfare committees were then formed to help at least the Jewish children to leave their country even though the parents had to have work to go to if they wished to be allowed entry visas into other countries. There were visa and various difficulties continuing in Germany too. It seemed the Nazis intended to proceed with their persecution of Jewish adults but were prepared to allow a few thousand children to leave. Only Holland and Great Britain responded to the call to take in the children without the usual formalities of immigration, and travel arrangements were hurriedly started. There were to be trains at night across Holland, then boats over the Channel and temporary shelter in hostels or empty holiday centres until foster homes were found.

Passports for Jewish children were suddenly issued without problem by passport offices remaining stubborn on the subject of allowing back Polish passport-holders. Susanna and Sophie received theirs promptly once they were placed by very determined parents on the list of young hopefuls wanting to depart. They had a big red J on the front to proclaim their Jewishness, which was, Papa said, a nice surprise. It made them special, he told them, as did the pretty name Sarah added to their

67

own. They were to be proud of both these additions, he said, to Sophie's puzzlement and Max's scorn. But Susanna understood.

She'd collected the passports herself from the office and realised it was a first step towards being in charge of Sophie and herself in England. Freddy of course was too young to be parted from his mother, for which she wasn't sorry. Already she felt she was being dragged into some dark, wall-less, ground-less space where she wouldn't be able to hold on to Freddy as well.

Max wasn't on the list. His mother had left it too late. One day, he told a startled Susanna that he was going to make his way out of Germany on his own. First though, he gave her his goodbye gift, a tin of Nivea cream which she was to start using on arrival in England against the cold winds there. Think of me when you open it, he said, and keep your mouth shut until I'm well away. See you in America some time.

From the balcony, she'd watched him saunter off down the street, cap at an angle, whistling, quite grown into the shape of the man he almost was. She'd never be able to look after him now. But that world was all gone, or very nearly everything about it.

When his mother noticed her husband's miniatures had disappeared with her son, she wept. Now she really had nothing and Susanna realised why Frau Merkel's glance had so often strayed to the wall where they'd been refixed. No longer needing to keep an eye on them, it seemed, she moved to Uncle Oskar's. He'd also been sent home in a pot to his wife so the two widows would be company for each other.

For her own and Sophie's departure, there was a wait for their names to reach the top of the list. An odd limbo-like existence developed between the four of them. They talked of how soon they'd be together again, how there'd be a speed-up of forms to be processed, visas and so on, and even though Papa's connections in the coffee trade in London had long since retired, they'd take any work at all and understood that domestic and land-work permits were the only ones being offered. They'd be glad to work on the land or in kitchens, and without being too forward, Susanna was to make enquiries about such positions once she was settled at school herself.

Susanna promised them she'd study hard in order to become the doctor her mother dreamed of. Sophie did too, earnestly asking Susanna for a lesson in physics so she could begin. They both promised to write immediate thank-you letters to every English person who gave them so much as a kind word, but at the same time, they would never be a burden to anyone or ungrateful in any way whatsoever. They'd smile at every English policeman and at every English person who said sorry to them although they'd done the bumping-into themselves.

They went through each one of the saying and proverbs in Papa's book of English idioms so they'd never look silly not understanding something, they discussed whether it was better to say 'Thank you so much,' or 'Thank you very much,' deciding on this last because of Sophie's lisp, and they were very cheerful and careful with each other, hearts constricted with anguish as Papa's clocks ticked off the hours.

Chapter 8

February 1939

The strange thing about the train was that although it was crammed with hundreds of children like themselves, there wasn't the usual noise. Almost silent too were the figures behind the barriers on the platform.

Peering from the window, Susanna whispered, 'Can you pick out Mama's yellow headshawl?' It had been her idea to borrow a yellow one from Frau Leona and it had worked. Her mother stood out quite clearly and so did their father because he'd put Freddy in a white shawl. She could see that against Papa's black coat, and she could see the two ghostly masks showing no emotion. The government instruction on the arrangements for the train was marked with the order: No Emotional Farewells, and most of the parents herded into lines by the SS were doing their best.

In herself, she felt so little emotion, she didn't even lift her arm in a gesture of goodbye as the train built up steam and began to move, and was soon fully occupied by the drama being played out by the door of their carriage. A woman must have dashed out of her line and she'd thrown a bundle into the lap of a girl sitting there screaming, 'Please look after her for me!' before being dragged off.

The bundle turned out to be a baby with a label around its neck rather like their own official ones. She hadn't even woken. The chosen girl had instinctively grabbed her and was gazing at the other children with the clear question on her face: Why me? which stayed there until a charity organiser bustled in to take charge.

Well, I am glad it wasn't me, Susanna decided, as she and

Sophie gazed at each other, digesting the brief event. Sophie was enough. 'You look nice in your new coat,' she whispered, to take her mind off things. 'Just imagine Mama getting together with Frau Leona and secretly making us up outfits in Frau Leona's flat. It must have really hurt them to do without a single fitting.'

'They're almost perfect fits,' Sophie said. Installed on the opposite window seat, her face had a tinge of blue in the dim blue carriage bulb and her eyes were their darkest sapphire. 'And our hats must be the latest fashion.' She wiped her nose with the back of her knitted glove and pulled at the hem of the new coat. The boy beside her was sitting on it, trembling all over, haversack and cardboard suitcase lodged on his knees.

'The latest fashion,' Susanna repeated, glancing at her reflection in the window when she ought to be trying to be kind to the boy. He couldn't be more than six. In fact, she looked ridiculous, her face too thin under too much hair with a pixie hat balanced on top. There'd be no hats like it in England, and probably no suits like hers either, not on girls her age. Silver fox trim was for old ladies, she'd be taunted by some Greta Mundt girl. Was she to go to school in it? If not, what would she wear to school and who would ever pay for anything else? What exactly was a foster home? There'd been so many questions they hadn't liked to ask their parents, nor had they dared ask how they were going to manage in England with only the permitted ten marks they had with them. This would buy one meal. But it was all going to be all right, and wonderful, somehow. Mama believed it and so did Papa. 'Wasn't it good of Mama to cut up her silver fox for us?'

Sophie nodded, nestling her chin into her fur collar. She was going to cry. 'Why don't you see if you can spot the shapes of the buildings we know,' Susanna suggested, pointing out of the window at the city lights flashing past.

Obediently, Sophie turned her pretty head in her pretty pixie hat which sat perfectly in place on her bob. Oh, Mama, Susanna thought, red for Sophie, yes, but if I ever said I wanted red, I didn't mean for my first grown-up suit, I meant for a dress and now there are so many things I'd like to say to you about how right you always were and how I knew you loved me and I didn't wave goodbye because I couldn't.

'There's the big hospital,' Sophie said without interest.

'Yes.' She sat up and smiled across at her sister, at the

71

trembling boy beside her she really must take charge of. 'Imagine Mama actually arriving to join us in England one day, and Buba, and their not liking milk in their tea and Buba saying puh, puh, puh all over the place against any evil spirits there happen to be in England, and Papa arriving and being very grand explaining English customs because he lived there before the war.' She paused, breathless. It wasn't easy making conversation above the rattle and throb of the train, and how it rocked! Her behind hurt on the hard seats. She was going to be ill and she wouldn't be able to manage. Who'd pay for the doctor and would English doctors be allowed to treat Jewish children?

'I want to go home,' Sophie said.

'No, you don't. Remember everyone at home wants most in the world for us to be allowed to walk freely on pavements even when they're full of Aryans. In England, we won't have to get out of the way.' She nodded brightly at the boy to include him in this information, but he'd reached some stage beyond fear, eyes staring into space.

'What'll we be in England if we're not Jewish?'

'We'll just be us.'

'Puh, puh, puh,' Sophie said, burying her chin and nose in fox fur.

'Puh, puh, puh,' Susanna said mechanically, gripping Buba's talisman inside her glove. She should have forced herself to wave goodbye.

Esther hadn't been able to make a gesture of goodbye to Josef as he left her at the corner of Bochumer Strasse and turned towards the factory. They could barely speak. They were sleepwalkers.

Yet she'd climbed the stairs to the flat and here she was. She was to go on living. Placing Freddy on the floor by the stove, she knotted the shawl around his shoulders. It was colder than ever. Silently, she pointed to the Stabilo building set strewn there amongst the girls' things they left him, a puppet, a little cardboard theatre, a jumble of wooden animals. They'd treasured all their early toys and she'd hardly realised it. She'd been too busy being a good Jewish mother.

How did she get back here with such a pain in her chest? She gazed down at Freddy's curly head. She should have let him go. He wasn't too young to be given a childhood.

72

'Mama!' Freddy held up the puppet.

'Mama's busy tidying.' Sleepwalking still, she followed a trail of discarded clothing, last-minute rejections, stockings, socks, a blue jumper of Sophie's, Susanna's fourth undervest because it would soon be spring. Who'd scrimp and save for their next winter's clothing, and the next after that?

Picking up the jumper, she put it to her face and wandered with it into their bedroom.

'Mama!'

'Mama's coming. Try and build a train for me like the girls went away on.' Lowering herself on the Susanna's bed, she found she was hugging the pillow and breathing deep the scent of her daughter's skin and hair, rocking to and fro. Here she would have to stay. She was stripped bare.

She must have dozed for a minute or two. Freddy had tottered into the room and had somehow managed to lift the lid of the girls' trunk.

'Books,' he was muttering to himself, flinging them about. 'Box!'

His nose was running. She wiped it with a corner of eiderdown and took hold of the cardboard box he was trying to lever out. 'Mama's,' she said and he tottered off again with a spinning top.

'Charlotte's Summer Clothes' was inscribed on the box. She smiled to herself. Here was something she could do to occupy a little time. She'd sew something special for the doll. She had lace scraps and ribbon ends galore. She could make up a parcel.

But there were no dolls' clothes in the box. There were drawings, and letters, her daughters' terrible secret fears turned into pictures and pleas. Frantic, she laid them out on Susanna's bed, letter after letter in Sophie's crooked writing, Dear Herr Hitler, I know you are a very nice man, Frau Schmidt says so, she says you wouldn't want wicked things to happen to people, so please could you order them to be stopped . . .'

And the drawings! There was Goebbels as a jackal in a cage, Hitler as a giant brown hamster with a devil's horns and madly staring marbles for eyes.

I must make myself take this in, she thought, wheezing for breath, and then I must burn every scrap, for Josef will not be able to bear this evidence of our daughters' pain. And I must bury it deep in my heart so I can go on living long enough to tell them how I yearned to sit with them and weep but dared not.

'What are you doing with a violin of this value? You are not permitted to remove such items from the Fatherland.'

It wasn't over yet. They were near the Dutch border. Dawn was rising over flat fields that reached to Holland but it wasn't over. A troop of SS men had boarded the train and one of them was standing by their seats. He was pretending to be a customs official. SS made themselves into whatever they chose.

Her doll held tight, the cloth parcel open on her knees, someone else's violin exposed there, Sophie couldn't answer. In her chalk-white face, her lower lip trembled.

Susanna said carefully, 'The violin isn't valuable, it's a half-size instrument.' Her heart was going to burst. It wasn't a child's instrument. How had it got into the parcel they'd carried all the way from home with their haversack each and one suitcase each? She'd carried it, and it had been awkward because the original case had been smashed on the night no one referred to any more and it had been wrapped in cloth and string. Max had brought it back from the music repair shop all tied up and he'd said it was best to leave it like that, for the journey. She gripped Buba's lucky charm until it hurt and stared across at Sophie, willing her strength.

A black glove appeared and picked up the bow that was someone else's, an adult's bow. The violin was an adult's too. How had it got there?

'You Sarah, play it.'

Susanna held her breath, the whole carriage seemed to, she'd heard a sort of gasp. Sophie lodged her doll between herself and the trembling boy, removed her new gloves and held out her hands to take the bow. Eyes getting bigger and bigger, she stared back at Susanna and was very sick all over everywhere.

This did not seem to trouble the SS man. He removed the violin from Sophie's knees and propped it up in the corridor. The black gloved hand reappeared with a little dagger in it, snatched up the doll and ripped open her stomach. The new sawdust, packed in there by Max, began to dribble to the floor and Sophie set up the loudest scream of her life.

*

An older boy kindly reported that the SS had actually left the train, carrying with them the violin and assorted other valuables, and he was the one who threw the cloth parcel from the window with the sick in it. There was a lot of laughter in the carriage because most of them had escaped trouble. Sophie was congratulated for having endured hers, and another girl offered her a piece of crystallised ginger to settle her stomach.

The older boy was much interested in the matter of the violin. 'And was there anything in that doll?' he said.

'What sort of things?' Susanna said, occupied with tying up Charlotte's stomach in a handkerchief.

'Diamonds? Gold coins?' He grinned. 'One kid was led away just before you were checked. You should have seen her face. Pity she couldn't do the sick bit. Can your sister manage it any time?'

Susanna shook her head. Nothing much mattered at the moment. The boy reminded her of Max. Max had made the mistake with the violin. He wouldn't be very pleased to hear they'd lost it if it were valuable. Why hadn't she and Sophie been taken away? She was going to be sick herself.

'Hey, everyone!' The cocky boy again. 'We're there, it's Holland, we're free.'

A mass of children began running up and down, peering from the windows. In a daze, Susanna took her eyes from her sister's face and turned to the window too. A pale sun was rising over more icy flat fields. Dutch fields. And a Dutch station was coming into view.

This station held the most extraordinary sight. Ladies, ladies with smiling faces, lined up along the platform with tables. The tables were stacked with food. The food was for them. It was to welcome them into the free world.

'God bless Queen Wilhelmina!'

As the train sped off, it was the cocky boy who cried those thanks to the Dutch, which they all echoed between mouthfuls of white bread so sweet and soft it was like cake.

Susanna laid out the remainder of her collection of offerings on her knees so that Sophie could pick out anything she wanted. Two sandwiches were left and an apple and some sort of biscuit they weren't sure they'd like. Sophie had gone a little green over the

75

cup of hot chocolate but it had settled and she'd managed half a cream cheese sandwich.

'Look at Holland for a bit,' Susanna suggested. 'We're in another country, imagine. And what a lot we'll have to write home about already. The violin for a start. Papa will get straight down to that repair shop, won't he, in case they're worried about what happened to the valuable one they must have given Max by mistake for yours. They'll never get it back of course, but it wasn't our fault.'

'Holland seems nice,' Sophie said, her first words since the SS man.

'Yes!' Susanna laughed, gazing out at the most beautiful flat fields she'd ever seen. 'I wonder if England will seem as nice.'

England might well seem nice, she thought, but it wouldn't be nice. It would be terrifying, a place of terror because she and Sophie were going to be alone in it and she wouldn't be able to make anything right for either of them.

Chapter 9

Dovercourt Holiday Camp, Essex

'Whatever do you mean, you want to become a doctor?' The charity organiser lady stared across the office desk at her. 'Oh, I can't write that on the form, dear, you're a refugee.'

Susanna stared back at the lady's spectacles. She couldn't see her eyes. She began again, sitting up straight on the chair, eager to make it plain. 'My mother longed for me to become a doctor one day but our not being allowed in the state schools meant I missed a lot of education. I promised her I'd try to become a doctor in England.'

'Haven't you understood, dear? I can't put "doctor" on these forms' She tapped a finger on a pile of paper. 'My job is to start you older ones on the way to some settled future.'

'Yes, and I realise my maths and physics aren't good, but I'll study hard because I know I must. Nothing could make my mother happier, you see, and once she and my father join us . . .'

'Have you been helping your mother at home?'

'Of course, we helped each other.'

'Well, that's good news. I'll put "kitchen work" here, shall I? If you're very fortunate, you'll be taken on by an employer who'll train you properly and you'll always have employment.'

Kitchen work? How then, was she to offer her mother the greatest gift of all, a safe future? 'I'm not to be sent to school? But I must be, please.'

'You're over fourteen, dear. Higher education has to be paid for.'

'But if I'm to work, will I have a foster home? If not, where will

77

I live?' Her breakfast porridge sat like a lump in her stomach. She could smell the kippers again. Some kids actually ate those things. Oh, horrible England. She wanted to go home.

'You'll live in a hostel, I expect. Head office will see to it all.' She smiled, leaning across the desk. 'The main thing is we'll keep an eye on you until you're settled well enough to fend for yourself. Now, I think that one of our big shops, Marks and Spencer, has sent us a huge stock of clothes, shoes, all sorts. Why don't you pop over and get yourself something so you can keep that nice red suit for best? Goodbye, dear. Good luck.'

'Thank you very much,' Susanna said.

'Will it be the same school as me?' Sophie, waiting outside the office, reached up for her hand. Together they plunged back into the hubbub of the great hall of the camp where hundreds of children like themselves had to spend the days until their future was decided.

'I'm not to go to school.' She stood still, gazing from the group who were learning a dance to the one being taught an English song about chestnut trees. 'Remember how I decided I'd really start studying hard at physics and maths so I could be a doctor for Mama?'

'Yes, and I said I would too when I was old enough so Mama could have two doctors to help her feel safe.'

'Well, it'll just have to be you now, Sophie.' There were some kids in a far corner listening to a lesson on English customs. She didn't need such a thing. She should be allowed to go to school. She couldn't think for the noise. 'Remember how we used to wonder who'd pay for our keep?'

'Because we only had ten marks, yes.'

'I think actually no one will.' She was trying to make herself understand. She was on her own. She must work herself as well as finding work for her parents. 'Shall we go back to our chalet for a while?'

'If you hold on to me.'

Hats pulled down to their eyes, they manoeuvred themselves out of the main doors of the hall and into the wind which had howled around the holiday camp since their arrival. They were getting used to it. England so far was wind and a grey foaming sea and windows rattling in the strange little houses and sleepless nights under peculiar bedding called blankets that froze over them as they lay. They hadn't yet undressed properly and Susanna could foresee no time when they would. Most of the pipes were frozen. It was one less thing to have to bother about.

Struggling along their pathway and up to their door with the number 11 written on it, they fell inside and slammed it behind them. Recovering their breath first, they huddled shivering on the bed they had to share for warmth.

'Shall we have our last sweet from home but one?' Sophie asked.

'If you want.' Susanna reached under the bed for her haversack. 'Sure? There'll be no more.'

Sophie nodded. 'I'm hungry.'

'You'll have to start getting down some of the breakfast porridge.'

'It looks like sick.'

'No, it doesn't, and I love it now. It fills me up and the syrup stuff is as sweet as any sweet, you must try it.' She gazed down at her sister's face, paler than ever, the shadows under her eyes almost as blue as her eyes. 'How can I write home and say you're not eating? What stream of worries will that set up in Mama? You want her to suffer?' She held out a square of flattened marzipan. 'Eat!' she commanded.

Sophie didn't manage a smile. She grabbed the marzipan with her chilblained fingers. 'What are English sweets like?'

'Don't know. Papa never described them.' She put her own marzipan into her pocket. 'I'm going to warm mine and shan't care about the fluff.'

'Susanna, I want to go home.' Sophie's face began to crumple.

Anguished, Susanna hugged her tighter. 'Don't cry, you'll make your cheeks colder.' She took off a glove and wiped away the trickle of tears with her hand. 'Listen, I'm going to tell Mama you've been the bravest kid here, you've hardly let yourself cry or complain and I shan't tell her about your not eating if you promise to try the porridge, and when I get my first wages, I'll come and see you with all the sweets I can carry.'

'But where will I be, Susanna?' She wiped her nose with her sleeve.

'Living with some wonderful foster family where you'll be warm, and they'll be so nice they'll buy you white rolls for breakfast and liver sausage for lunch. Listen, it's Sunday tomorrow, the foster couples come round at dinnertime. Why don't we smarten you up in the morning and when they stroll up and down the aisles looking for a nice child to take home, you can put on your most beguiling smile and they'll say, We'll have that dear little one, please . . .'

'And what'll you do?' Sophie took a bite of marzipan and sucked it.

'I'll look grown-up and capable and one of them will say, That's the sort of girl we're searching for, we'll pay her a good wage . . .' Oh, Papa, she thought, I have to work. I must make the best of it, mustn't I? And there'll be money for things like stamps so we can write home at last. 'Just think,' she said, 'I'm saved from having to be a doctor for Mama. That's good out of bad. I'll be glad when it's sunk in.' But she couldn't get it to sink in. Her head hurt. She was going to be a maid in a kitchen, peeling potatoes and carrots. Her hands would get sore. She'd never see the sky. Kitchens were often basements. She'd spend the rest of her life in a basement and how would Mama bear that? 'Lucky we haven't any money for stamps yet,' she said. 'I shan't have to admit to Mama I'm not going to school. When I can write, I'll tell them English people are nice though, and we're always saying thank you though we haven't been anywhere to walk on pavements so haven't bumped into to anyone yet to hear them say sorry.'

'I don't like it.'

'What don't you like?'

'England.'

'Yes, you do, or you will when Mama and Papa get here, you'll see. Puh, puh, puh?'

'Puh, puh, puh,' repeated Sophie and began to cry in earnest.

Part Two

Part Two

Chapter 10

Downlands, Dorset, England, February 1939

Setting his mare, Meg, to a furious gallop, David Montgomery thundered along the ridge and down the hillside. Cold air whipped at his face. He could barely see, didn't want to see, and anyway knew every inch of all that lay before him, the sweep of the downs, the valley with the great house so perfectly nestled in it as to seem to have grown there. And once to be his. But this would be the last day he rode down to tea.

Patch was in the stables, rubbing off her pony. 'Hey,' she called. 'Georgie's come to visit, she's just gone up to Ma. Want me to do Meg for you?'

'No need, thanks,' he replied, leading the mare into her stall and getting off the tack. He had no wish to talk to Georgiana. How many times, he wondered, how many hundreds of times had he and Patch worked side by side on their mounts whilst shouting bits of family information to each other!

Horse brush in hand, he moved round the stall to peer at her, plump and sturdy, pretty as ever with the high colour in her cheeks, the brown curls she hated sticking out from her cap. As my sister, I suppose I am fond of her, he thought, I suppose I'm sodding well going to weep. 'You can finish Meg for me if you don't mind,' he said, 'I'll get on in. I probably will spend a few minutes with Georgie later, but you know it's no good.'

Leaving the stables, he crossed the yard to the kitchen door. An unholy mess of ivy had crept along the wall in his absence. He'd have to speak to the new land agent about cutting it down, or rather, not do anything of the kind. The ivy was no longer his concern and nor were the loose flagstones by the well that would sooner or later cause an accident.

Installed in the comfort of the kitchen with Flo, he scoffed more than his share of the scones. Still hot, the butter soaked straight in. He added spoonfuls of plum jam, his favourite, and cream so thick it sat there as round and satisfying as a bantam's egg. Bizarre to be hungry after news like he'd had that day. Where would he sleep tonight? He'd have to go to his club. 'Better than the officers' mess, this tea, Flo,' he said.

'You want a slice of my caraway seed cake?' Flo's gentle Dorset voice emerged from the pantry.

'I do, Flo, please, and will you send Mary to see if Miss Georgiana's down from my mother's yet.'

'Why no, Mr David, of course she ent. They're doing the crossword same as always and Mary's taken Miss Georgiana a tray up. You know what a healthy appetite that lovely girl do have.' She arrived beside him at the table with one of her vast cakes and cut him a piece of it. She'd put on a fresh apron, it stood out from the roundness of her breasts and hips. It occurred to him he'd like to rest his head there and breathe in the clean smell of Robin starch as he used to do after trouble with his father or falls from ponies. The man isn't anything to me after all, Flo. He'd liked to tell her. He'd have to some time and she'd be glad for him. Or perhaps not. She'd realise the repercussions at once.

He took a mouthful of cake and coughed out some crumbs. 'Went the wrong way,' he said, pushing in more. 'My mother eat anything for tea?'

'A morsel what wouldn't keep a flea alive.' Flo drew up a chair and put two plump arms on the table with the ease of one who'd ruled over it for forty years. 'She do seem to have settled into that bedroom of hers and I'm fearing she won't never come out, not with you in the Army, Mr Henry gone sheep farming in Australia and Mr Will over in Ireland with his father running that place. And if war is coming, there won't even be the staff here. Whatever will me and Bert do rattling around with only Madam to see to? Times is changing, Mr Davey, and me and Bert thinks we shan't be staying on much longer, though we did hope as we'd be here for the day you takes over ...' She took hold of his wrist and squeezed it. 'You will understand, darling boy?'

He looked back into the familiar, loving face, all plump cheeks and softness. His heart lurched. 'We'll talk about it again, Flo, don't do anything daft until you get my permission, right?' He wiped his mouth with his hand and stood up. 'Got a newspaper of some sort, have you? I think I'll sit by the fire for a bit, if you don't mind. Can't be bothered with anyone for the moment and I might not be staying the night.'

'I thought you had a week's leave? Now what'll I do with my extra baking? Even Miss Patch won't take all of it back to London with her and I do hate that lazy tyke Sidney stuffing himself silly.'

'I'll take some of it, Flo. Will you make me up a hamper? Don't forget the seed cake and I'll need something hearty, ham or sausages. Who shares Patch's flat with her, d'you remember?'

'Why, Miss Georgiana, Mr David, however could you forget that?'

'Of course. My mind must be going, Flo. It's the bloody Army regulations, they stunt the mind. Anyway, don't bother about a hamper.' He slumped into the rocking chair with the *Herald* on his knees and wondered if opening up the London house would be an answer. But what would he do with himself without a decent ride and how long did the tenants' lease have to run?

'You be minding my chair, rockin' like that,' Flo said. 'You bought it me for my sixtieth and I ent aiming for it not to see me out.'

'Sorry, Flo. Call me when Miss Georgiana's left, will you? I'll go up to my mother then.' Yawning for the show of it, he closed his eyes. She was creeping about like a mouse to let him sleep. I shan't sleep, he thought, and in this house, I shall never sleep again.

'Mother, I may get off to London tonight.'

'So soon, darling? But you said a week. I was looking forward to seeing you five more days.' Propped on her pillows, she seemed brighter, with some of her old prettiness and coquetry. She'd tied a ribbon around her hair and wore a blue shawl to bring out the colour of her eyes. She'd made an effort for him. And in the lamp-light, resting, her fine pale skin flushed and unlined, you'd think her no more than forty.

'Shall I draw the curtains?'

'No, let me see the stars.'

'You eaten some of that supper?'

'Certainly. Half the egg, three bread and butter soldiers, a cream caramel. Will you pour the coffee?'

'Won't it stop you sleeping, Ma?' He stood in the middle of the scented cosiness, ill at ease, avoiding the daft bedroom chairs he was too big for. The last time he'd sat in one, that very morning, she'd dropped her bombshell and turned the world upside down.

'Oh, this boy of mine! You used to have a good memory. You know I can take coffee at night, how often have you poured it for me?'

'Sorry, Ma.' He clattered about with the supper tray, found space for it by the door, put it outside and returned to settle the coffee things on the hospital table contraption she used. 'I do remember half coffee and half cream.'

Finally forcing his behind into a chair, he watched her lift her cup with that slight tremor of the hand which filled him with pity and fury in turn. 'It's the Army making me absent-minded, Ma.'

'Is it very dreadful at the camp? I do wish you hadn't been so eager to join up, especially since war hasn't actually been declared and might well never be. If you'd waited a bit, that last row between you and your father would have been forgotten.' She was gazing at him, the lamplight making her seem more delicate than ever. She'd been a very pretty mother. He'd been proud of her when she managed the visits to school. 'It isn't the Army, though, is it, David, it's what I told you this morning.'

He got himself to his feet and walked to the window. 'It was a shock, Ma. I mean, all this.' He waved a hand towards the starry night and the roll of the downs, the farmland, the cottages, the wood, pheasants and foxes, the courtyard below, the great warm house itself. 'Since I can remember, as the eldest boy, I assumed it would be mine, my inheritance, and now I've learned it's not.'

'Whatever do you mean, darling?' She struggled to sit up.

'Careful.' He went to her bedside and managed to do something not very clever with the pillows. 'It'll be Will's, not mine.'

'Will's? You're not going to leave me? You are the eldest, David.'

'But not Father's ... dammit, what shall I call him, your husband? I'm not your husband's eldest, Ma. There. I cannot even feel this is my home any more. I haven't one. I intend to leave tonight for my club in town.'

'David! You wish to reveal to the world what I told you this morning, for your father to know the truth after all these years, Patch and the boys too? What does it matter? Only mothers count really. The fathers could be anyone!' She laughed. She seemed ten years younger. She didn't understand. She ought to!

'My actual father was anyone,' he said.

'He wasn't, I told you, he was a very nice, charming and handsome young man. You're the spit-image of him actually. Seeing you standing there sometimes brings it back to me. You've got the same long, slender face with lovely high cheekbones and a really fierce frown when you're displeased, as you are now. Your eyebrows are the same too, black and silky, like your hair and there's the same surprise of the blue eyes and black hair together. It's a bit of luck I have it too but then I'm a Celt. What is amazing is that you have a scar in very nearly the same place as he did.' She reached up and ran a finger under his left eye. 'D'you remember when that wicked horse, Prince, threw you? You had concussion. I nearly died.'

Impatient, he turned away. 'What made you, Ma, so early in the marriage?'

'What made me?' she asked, her gaiety gone. 'I was married two years to your father, that's what made me.'

'Better call him by his name, Ma, we'll get muddled.'

'Arthur, then, I was married to Arthur Montgomery, landowner and brute, and he wanted an heir and would come to my bed to force an heir upon me and nothing happened. He blamed me. He said he'd got a bad bargain and I couldn't even run his house and if he wanted, he'd send me back to my father. So at some shooting weekend in Northamptonshire when he was full enough of port to snore through the night, I crept along the passageway for an assignation with this very sweet chap. And yes, I did do it on purpose. I never could think I was infertile. I assumed it was his fault, and the drink. What would I be for if I couldn't have children? I planned it. I chose him, from the discreet offers one gets at those horrible weekends. I also needed someone to be nice to me.'

'After the brute, yes,' he said, with fresh rage. 'I suppose I'm glad not to be of his blood. There is at least than in this mess.'

'You should be, darling, and if you'd waited long enough this morning, I'd have explained more, but please don't do anything proud and silly.'

'It was a shock, Ma, truly. I'm just trying to get used to it.'
Feeling stifled, he opened the window. He could see the gleam of
the Humber in the drive, the dark silhouette of the carved stone
beasts guarding the entrance to the terrace. As a boy, if the wind
howled and whistled along the valley, he used to see monsters
there, and devils, and feared that when his father died, he'd be
turned to stone and would sit there forever, watching him. 'This is
not mine now, you see.'

'It is yours. To Arthur, you are the eldest son, he raised you to
follow him and that's what you must do. David, you hear me? I
couldn't bear it if I'd struggled to live on and then had to die
knowing you wouldn't inherit and one day be happy, as I haven't
managed to be for long. You made me happy though, and the
others. What else did I have? I'm so glad that girls nowadays can
choose and don't have to sell themselves to some creature for
life.'

'The others,' David repeated. 'And the father of Henry and Will
and Patch is who?'

'They're Arthur's, darling,' she said, almost indignant.
'Somehow, once I'd produced his heir, he was nicer to me in bed,
you know, kinder, and I wasn't so miserable and tense. I had you.
His taunts and nastiness didn't weigh so heavy. I didn't get such
awful migraines and depressions, and he was away a lot. He
adores the round of house parties, then there's the estate in
Ireland, ghastly, sinister place. He's got that barmaid there, as you
know, and she's got two brats I assume are his.'

'But the London house, Ma, that's from your side of the family,
isn't it? May I have it now, will you make it over to me?'

'Of course, but whatever for?'

He shrugged. 'To have something that's mine. I'd rather.' He
shut the window and returned to the chair.

'What if there's war and bombing? I wouldn't be able to stand
you being up there.'

'If there's war, I'll be in it,' he reminded her. 'That's why I
made so much fuss about taking on a new land agent, so I can be
away without worrying. It's not as if Pa, Arthur, wants to be here
for more than a few weeks a year by the time he's done his fishing
in Scotland and interfered for months on end with Will's running
of the Irish place, just as he used to interfere with any decision I
tried to make for Downlands.'

'Patch is the one he adores. I suppose those two Irish brats are girls.'

'Everyone adores Patch.'

'I wish you adored Georgiana.'

'I'm sorry Ma, I don't, not in that way, she's like Patch to me, I'm fond of her, we rode together as kids. If she were in trouble, I'd help her. But I can't marry her.'

'She's so beautiful though. Everyone says what a lovely pair you'd make, you so tall and dark, Georgie tall and blonde. She's keen, you know.'

'She's not my type.'

'Oh, I hope you'll marry soon. I'd truly love a grandchild. It'd give me something to look after. Please be sure you choose a nice wife who'll let me interfere and spoil it. Georgie would. Daughters-in-law are even more important than people realise. I was always nice to Arthur's mother, poor old dear. Gone now. I'm lonely, David.'

'I know you are.'

'It's what makes me low. I try and escape from life in this room, don't I? With my tots of gin and my aspirins, the wireless, the magazines which tell me all about other people's lives. Mary and the cats come and go, and you when I'm lucky, and the doctor. But I'm going to stir myself. I've made up my mind. It was the doctor, last week, who started me off. He said I ought to start thinking about war work. You, a lady of the manor, he said, letting the vicar's wife organise the local women to do their bit. There's billeting lists, fund-raising lists and plans for replacing the men on the land, all sorts going on, and the villagers expect something, he said. I bet they don't, I said, but my heart sank. I do hate groups of women being cheerful and busy, they overwhelm me, I can barely organise the staff, can I? If it wasn't for Flo . . .'

David sat up. 'Now don't talk yourself out of it before you've begun. It's only Arthur that's knocked the confidence from you. You can do anything you choose to do. Let's have a think about something not involving Women's Institute sort of women, they'll get on with things without you. You're capable of different stuff.'

'I've had a think actually.' She too sat up, suddenly eager pushing away her cup. 'And I think refugees. There's been a wireless programme about young people driven out of Nazi Germany by those Hitler thugs, and how foster homes and sponsors are desperately wanted, and jobs for the older ones. Children don't frighten me like grown-ups but I feel so weak sometimes, it's all in my head, I know, but if I took in a child to fuss over, it'd give me a reason to go on until you produce my grandchildren. Help me get started, David.'

'Trust you to find something different, Ma. Foreign kids in deepest Dorset, Germans, just when we're likely to go to war with Germany!' He found he was smiling. 'That'll stir up the natives a bit, and as for Arthur, harbouring the children of the Hun in his house, heavens, he'll be thrilled. Still, they won't be Huns, will they, not in Hitler's evil eye. Jewish refugees, at Downlands, eh? Dammit, I feel like a refugee myself.'

Restless, his glance flickered round the room. All her things were so familiar, the fancy armchairs which were no more than beds for the cats, the knick-knacks, the photographs of the four of them in various stages of childhood, too many tables for them to be stacked on, the watercolours from her painting period, the casket of jewellery she never wore, embroideries begun and never finished. Had he actually formed the thought this bedroom would one day be his wife's? Well, no, but nevertheless, it would have been.

He began to pace to and fro from window to door. He must take over the London house once the tenants' lease was at an end, get his few personal possessions installed there. He wanted to simply walk away from Downlands, in fact. He had no moral right to it, and from the moment he learned the truth, he was living with deception.

'And what with our connection to Germany,' his mother said.

'What connection?'

'Yours and my secret connection, darling.'

'With Germany?' Startled, he turned round.

'Yes! Don't make that face. I'd have told you this morning, but you wouldn't wait. Your father was attached to the German Embassy in London. His name was Otto Freyhan. I decided you ought to know, now you might one day be facing your own half-brothers in battle.'

His mouth was still open. A Nazi. He had Nazi blood in his veins. 'A Nazi, mother?' he said. Worse, this, than the brute? Almost certainly worse.

'There weren't any Nazis in nineteen-ten as far as I know, darling,' she said mildly. 'Don't be silly. And he's probably dead anyway, killed in the Great War like so many of our officers. What does it matter, politics, heavens, but people of that class wouldn't follow nasty little Hitler, would they?'

'I'm afraid some of them are most enthusiastic about him, but never mind.' His head throbbed. Worse and worse, he thought, and yes, he was sodding well going to weep sooner or later. Nazi blood. How was that for an inheritance, and how was it to be borne?

'If you want to choose to believe he's not dead and has become a Nazi, all the more reason to help a refugee from Nazi Germany,' she said. 'Do stop fretting. Fathers don't really count, only mothers, and it's the one area where we do have the upper hand. We're the ones to know whose seed we bear inside us. Oh, I did love hugging to myself what I knew about you when I felt you kicking. Such sweet revenge. Was it bad of me?' She laughed and patted the bed. 'Come and sit here.'

'Fathers don't count, Ma?' he said. 'Yes, they do, dammit.'

'I hope I've made you think twice about actually going into the thick of things anyway. Get a desk job, darling, will you? Please. I'm sorry I've given you such a shock, but you do see there are moral issues involved here?'

'Yes, Ma,' he said. 'I do see.'

Chapter 11

Dovercourt Holiday Camp

Through the open office door, David could make out the long rows of dining tables where hundreds of children sat over English messes. He could smell boarding-school dinners, boiled vegetables, and something from breakfast. Kippers. Good Lord. What could these Continental kids think of kippers and lumpy porridge and the mind-numbing cold of a holiday camp built for summer visitors where every pipe was frozen!

He searched for a sight of his mother's fur coat and hat amongst the other fosterers making their way along the aisles picking out nice clean pretty children to take home. It was no more than a cattle-market for kids, he decided, and wanted it to be over. He felt pity, standing there, and shame and a great disturbing turmoil of feeling he wished he could be rid of. He was like them, uprooted from his place in the world and he wanted most of all to stop thinking about himself. He might as well volunteer for overseas duty, and displace himself further.

'Here we are, dear!' His mother's voice sounded across the hall. She was waving with one hand and with the other held on to a small child in red. He waved back, embarrassed, as they made their way towards him. 'This is Sophie, David, isn't she sweet? We've chosen each other.' She couldn't wait to call this out before arriving breathless and radiant in the doorway. 'Oh, she was so sick, a horrible fat woman tapped her on the shoulder and she threw up all over the woman's suit. I've used up my hankies, lend me yours, please.'

He passed her one of Flo's best starched creations and waited in amusement as she licked it and wiped the small face.

'I used to be sick constantly when I was your age, Sophie,' she told her, 'but when I grew up I had headaches instead, much less troublesome, especially in public. Now, this is my big son, David. We live in the country with lots of lovely animals. D'you like animals?'

The girl shook her head, suffering the wiping. She looked tired and very pale and her eyes were filling with tears.

'Well, there's lots of lovely places to play in and always scones for tea, and cake.' She stuffed the handkerchief into her bag and straightened up. 'Shall we leave the official bits for David to fuss about and go and sit in the nice warm car to talk about things?'

Well, whatever came of it, he thought, the effort she'd had to make had done his mother good, but the girl's tears hung like pools ready to spill over. The red cloth of her coat was grubby, her fingers chilblained, as his always were at school, and heavens, she must be terrified. He wanted to say something welcoming and searched for a suitable phrase while his mother bustled about with gloves and a red hat. He willed the girl to glance at him with those tear-filled eyes but they finally tipped out and two words burst from her. 'My sister.'

'You have a sister? Of course, why didn't I think there might be more than one of you? I am thoughtless, aren't I? David, we can take two, can't we? Do fetch the organisers, darling, and see to it for us.'

He hadn't time to get on with practical matters, which he was more than prepared to do, for the child flew back into the dining hall and returned in half a minute with the sister, an older girl clothed in the same red material. He decided their mother was a seamstress, for her suit, like her sister's coat, had been made a little too big to allow for growth. She was also so very slender it seemed to weight her down. He noticed that at once and the shy, tentative way she stood there, arm around the shoulder of the younger one.

As his mother fussed anew, his eyes settled on her, and he saw the most startling eyes, green or gold they were, he couldn't tell, and she had a lovely pale still face framed in a lot of dark hair.

Good heavens, he thought, and his heart turned over.

Chapter 12

Downlands
Piddlehinton, Dorset

13 March 1939

Dear Mama and Papa,
Yes, it is true. We are not dreaming and we are here, in our
own rooms on the first floor of the west wing of a manor
house and we are not only not a burden on Mrs Montgomery,
she really wants us. She has four children of her own, but they
are grown-up and she's lonely. She does suffer from
headaches and dizziness but there are staff to do all the work,
so you are not to worry we are overtiring her though we have
a bedroom just for us, a sitting room which was the children's
schoolroom and the splendour of a whole bathroom with
entire tablets of scented soap in it and enough towels for a
shop. Mama, we have a whole wardrobe for our clothes and a
whole set of new clothes with chests to put them in. Our old
clothes are washed and folded and put away. Mrs Montgomery
says they are the most special and we must keep them for
special occasions. You see how nice she is? She says she has
had the most fun for years deciding on our outfits and the
colours that suit best but they'll take too long to describe
today. I'll just tell you, Mama, so you can picture us, that
Sophie is wearing a pretty blue and pink plaid dress with blue
velvet collar and cuffs, pink and blue being decided on for her,
and for me the autumn shades so that I can more or less keep
to brown accessories for winter and beige for summer. She's
worked it all out. Today I'm in a brown jumper with collar,

brown lace-up shoes and a brown and cream speckled skirt with back pleat. Our own boots have been repaired at the cobblers, polished by Sidney (more of him later) and put away in the bootroom. This is one of a series of workrooms and storerooms and pantries leading off the kitchen.

We're in the kitchen now. Try and imagine us, sitting side by side at a huge wooden table in the centre. All around there are shelves and beams holding pots and pans of every size and shape – several fish-shaped for poaching fish! An enormous dresser similar to our little one is covered in blue and white striped china – the staff's and ours. There's much finer house china but it's only used for Mrs Montgomery's trays. She has minute meals upstairs in her bedroom. She thinks food is a fuss and can't be bothered with it and Mr Montgomery lives mostly on the estate in Ireland with one of the sons, Mr Will. Mr Henry, the youngest son, is in Australia learning sheep-farming, and Mr David, the eldest, no longer runs this estate and has gone into the Army. The daughter, Miss Patch, works at a film studios in London.

So the staff just look after Mrs Montgomery, and us and themselves. They follow the day in an exact routine, congregating here at precise times to eat mountains of Flo's food. She's the cook and the gentlest person you can imagine, very plump and sort of floury from constant cooking. Straight after lunch most days, she makes the bread, huge cakes, biscuits and things called scones you put butter and jam on and cream so thick it just sits there. Are your mouths watering? Hurry up the visa papers, Papa, so you can be here to try them. Mrs M. says you'll stay in the house with us until you get your bearings and there may be a cottage vacant on the estate for us to live in later. You'll easily be taken on to work on the land because so many men have joined the Army. Mama, you're to be in charge of linen and upholstery in Downlands itself. 'If your mother would consider such a post,' Mrs M. said to me. I could hardly speak for answering you would and quite missed out how much you disliked always to be sitting at your machine. Her last lady died and there's stacks of linen waiting to be mended and every curtain and chair cover to be washed this spring. She's been on the telephone to the Home Office saying she'll act as guarantors to you both – that's where the work permits are issued.

Naturally, this'll seem *too good* to be possible, our all being together and you being able to work and our being actually wanted. I feel I ought to be thanking Mrs M. all the time but I can't of course so I just try to be helpful and not in the way. When she goes for her rest and in the evenings, Sophie and I go up to our sitting room – the old schoolroom where there are lots of books to be read – school stories, Papa, reminding me of you and how you used to bring second-hand ones home. Just the covers and the titles make me feel I'm home again, and picking one up, I get the same little lift of pleasure as I used to. It's in this room we stand by the window every night as we promised to do. We put your photographs on the windowsill and gaze down at the dark shapes of the terrace and the trees outside. The ground slopes upwards into hills where cottages and farmhouses are hidden and a village. But we're really watching the hand of the clock tick round to the hour and we talk about you until it's time. We know that over there it's ten o'clock and cold and quiet in the flats and the street and you're side by side talking about us. Freddy is in bed and you are both soon to go because Papa has to rise early. When it's exactly the hour, we stop talking and think about you most intensely in our own minds and stare at the self-same sky and the same bit of moon and stars as you are. We send our love up there and will it to go flying on and on until it drops down to you in Berlin. Sometimes we say Opa's prayers there together but sometimes we say them over and over in bed until Sophie falls asleep.

We rise early too. Mary, the maid, knocks on our door at seven thirty, calling 'Wakey, wakey,' which we like. We don't care for Mary much though we're trying to find the good in her, Papa. Besides her and Flo, there's Flo's husband Bert, who's as round and plump as she is and the 'butler', and Sidney who does the heavy work. There are gardeners too and stable boys but we don't see much of them.

Anyway, I must stop now. It's Flo and Bert's afternoon off and Mary's made the outside workers have their tea early so she can have hers with Sidney in one of the pantries or store-rooms where she'll giggle a lot. She's putting our tea things on the table. After tea, Sidney collects the letters, sticks on the

stamps and takes them up to the village post office on his
bicycle. He reminds us of the Mundt boy, he's pimply and has
no chin, but of course he's not like him really and there aren't
any Hitler Youth or stormtroopers or SS or Gestapo in this
whole country and the policemen don't have guns – and they
do smile! So please hurry up the papers and come here soon.

By the way, did you notice my casualness in mentioning our
bathroom? It has hot water, as much as you like. Sophie keeps
turning on the taps to make sure it's true, and yes, I do make
sure she washes behind her ears. Her nails are as clean as a
baby's.

'There you are then, you two Miss Red Riding Hoods. Tea. Not
that it's tea, eh, you funny pair, fancy having coffee at teatime.'

Mary finished slamming down the crockery, snatched up the
envelope Susanna had sealed, and flounced off with it towards the
pantry corridor and her rendezvous with Sidney. 'That Flo do
spoil, you, heaven knows why. Here, and by the way.' She paused
in the doorway and glanced back. Her face wasn't unlike Greta
Mundt's, mean, dark and pinched. 'You really ought to know your
place and call Madam madam, not Mrs Montgomery like as if you
was equal. And I might as well warn you now, the master's to be
called sir, double sir, to you, and Mr David will be sir to you as
well, and Mr Henry and Mr Will when they get back. And it's
Miss Patch to you, right?' She was gone, having launched what
might or might not be her last arrow of the day.

Susanna sat regarding their own feast. She always had the same
shock, that such extravagant heaps should appear at such short
intervals. Without realising it, she must always have been hungry
at home if people were supposed to eat so much so often. She
lifted the lid of the pretty blue pot and considered. 'It's very dark,'
she said, 'but it's not black cherries. We'll taste it later.'

She placed two bread and butter triangles on Sophie's plate and
a small pile of them on her own. 'Eat!' she commanded. This was
her joke. She did a few hand-waving gestures in further imitation
of Buba though they didn't make Sophie any more willing to
obey. She'd hardly eat and wouldn't speak a single word to
anyone but her when they were alone, except 'Thank you very
much,' for Mama's sake. But how to weigh down Mama with a
worry of such a scale? She'd have to cope with it herself until their

97

parents arrived, an event which would render their lives in Dorset so near perfection, she daren't allow herself to dwell on it for long in case it should take on the quality of a dream and thus never happen. For the moment also, there were too many other matters on her list of anxieties. 'I should like Mrs Montgomery not to have such headaches,' she said. 'I mean, we're supposed to be going to visit our schools soon. How shall we manage if she can't come with us?'

'I don't want to go to school,' Sophie pointed out, finishing her portion in big bites.

'Yes, you do,' Susanna said mechanically, savouring the deliciousness of white bread with her mind already on the scones. Mary had warmed them and their scent made her mouth water. 'If we don't go to school, we might get in the way here and we mustn't do that.'

Sophie kicked her new boots against the rungs of her chair. 'They all laugh at us for our red clothes though we don't wear them any more.'

Susanna took three scones and cut them in half, letting the butter melt in before spooning up the sweet stuff made of berries she didn't recognise. Then she added the cream that was thick enough to sit there in little round blobs. In a confusion of spoons and dishes, she shortly had her fingers covered as well as her mouth.

'And for being foreign they laugh at us,' Sophie said, licking jam and cream off her two halves. 'It's blackberries,' she added.

'We are foreign.'

'We're German,' Sophie announced, kicking harder, 'and we're refugees. We're Huns and refugees and Jewish, Mary and and Sidney keep whispering it to me.'

'I thought you couldn't understand their English because it's not like Mama's and Papa's.'

'Mary says I'm like a dumb animal with my great big eyes staring at her.'

'Don't stare at her. And you really must expect them to think you're odd since you don't speak though they know you can.' Susanna recognised her old edge of impatience. 'Sophie,' she said firmly, 'whatever will Mama and Papa say to you when they get here to this glorious house and find you're being so rude as not to answer people, not even Mrs Montgomery although she's constantly kind, patient and generous to you and has even restuffed your doll Charlotte and wants us to call her Aunt Daphne? She'll get cross in the end and you won't like that.'

Sophie declared herself to be ready for cake.

'Mama wouldn't let you have any cake.' Susanna cut and sniffed two generous slices. 'Vanilla,' she said. 'Buba's favourite.'

'Mama wouldn't let you sniff food.' Sophie arranged her doll so that she sat up against the oil lamp in the centre of the table. 'Charlotte's got a silk-stocking tummy,' she announced, as if she were six again instead of nine, and reminding Susanna of another problem she'd rather not have.

'I only sniff food to make sure we'll like it.' She put her elbows on the table and set to demolishing her sponge. 'I think it's sensible and we mustn't waste anything. Waste is wicked because of so many starving people in the world and because of Opa and Buba having to send for a food parcel.' She stopped. 'Listen. What's that? Is it boots?'

It was boots, the sound of boots thudding in the front hall, familiar, awful.

Sophie squealed and shot under the table. Carefully, Susanna herself swallowed the cake and made herself get to her feet. Here, they had come here, to Downlands. And she'd always known they would. 'Who's there?' she breathed.

'Who were you expecting?' The owner of the voice emerged from the shadows of the doorway leading to the front hall. He was a man in a uniform, a brown uniform, she saw that at once, a brown British stormtrooper uniform. What to do? Where to run with her hands sticky with forbidden butter? Her head reeled.

'Have I frightened you? I'm so sorry. Please sit down again. Where's the little one?'

She should have recognised Mr David's voice. She wiped her mouth with the back of her hand, dumb as could be and looking as foolish as could be, trying to manoeuvre Sophie from under the table and back into her chair. 'My sister is rather nervous.'

He was so nice about their silliness and so like his mother, he pretended not to notice their clattering about and clattered with a chair himself, drawing it up to the table and sitting in it with a blue cup he'd grabbed from the dresser. 'Must be Flo's day off if the rest of them aren't here for tea,' he said, helping himself to bread and butter and reaching across for the jam pot. He pretended not

99

to notice the stickiness and in fact made himself a number of sticky sandwiches.

She suddenly knew she wanted to be the same as him and his mother, to have such perfect manners you'd put people at their ease no matter what strange activities they indulged in. She wanted to wipe her fingers clean. Why hadn't Mary thrown down their napkins, today of all days? She pulled out the drawer where they were kept, surreptitiously licked a corner and wiped everything.

Now she must say something polite. She glanced across at him, longing to express proper thanks for the day at the camp and their later drive along the seashore in the Humber Snipe – and more. Without him, Mrs Montgomery wouldn't have been able to sort out the matter of their foster care, being a ditherer, she'd told them, and moreover weak in the head.

'We have a lot in common,' he said, sparing her. 'We prefer coffee to tea and like to sit here at this table scoffing Flo's wonders. I spent hours here when I was a boy. A great comfort, Flo's kitchen is when you're miserable and I was mostly miserable.' Pausing long enough to finish his sandwiches, he cut into several scones and began the three-tier process.

Every inch of him was clean and smart, from his dark hair to the buttons and braid on his jacket that had nothing to do with stormtroopers. She searched for the words to say something about the English army in order to soothe Sophie's fears indirectly as it were, but he kept talking through his mouthfuls. 'I've only called in for a few belongings. I've got a new posting and won't be back for a while. I wanted to say goodbye to my mother, of course, and I wanted to see you.' Here he paused again to tackle the cake, cutting three slices of it and reaching across to put a piece on each of theirs amongst the mess of their last. 'And I wanted to tell you how grateful I am to you for making my mother so busy and happy. You've given her a new lease of life.' He stopped, leaned across again and cut Sophie's cake into small squares. From the corner of her eye, Susanna saw Sophie's hand pick one up.

He grinned at her and winked and she wanted to cry. He was so nice. His eyes were very blue, bluer than her father's. There was a tiny scar under the left one and if anything he was handsomer than her father, with a long, slender face and wide mouth, and darker too, for his hair and eyebrows were almost black, like Max's, and

100

his chin seemed to need shaving, as Max's always did. The most unusual thing, she decided, was the fact that the rather deep frown between his eyes did not make him appear ill-tempered but rather gave a concerned quality to his gaze, as if he cared very much about you, the way her father's different, more smiling gaze did.

'Listen,' he said, licking his fingers like a little boy. 'I have to be off now but I did want to say to you that if every you're in trouble and my mother has one of her heads, turn to Flo, won't you, because she's like a rock in this house. She claims she wants to retire but I've persuaded her to stay on until the war begins, and then until it's over because the east wing will have to be opened up for evacuees. My mother needs her, and I do, and you, and the evacuees will.

'Also, I want you to remember that when my father gets back from Ireland, his bark's worse than his bite and he never stays here for long. You will remember, Susanna?'

It was the first time he'd said her name, awkwardly, as if he'd never known anyone called Susanna before and it was the nicest way she'd ever heard. Dumb still, she nodded.

'Got a napkin, have you?'

She passed him hers and he wiped his hands vigorously before passing it back and getting to his feet. With one or two strides, he'd disappeared back into the shadows.

'He's nice,' Sophie said.

'Yes.' Susanna put her elbows on the table, changed her mind and picked up a fork. She was going to eat like a lady and the next time he sat at tea with them, he'd be able to behave like a gentleman, because that's what he was.

'Why will Mr Montgomery bark like a dog?'

'I think it's another of those English sayings like Papa tried to teach us before we left.'

A bell rang in one of the pantries and Mary hurried through the room with a pile of clean laundry which must be Mr David's, followed by Sidney with a pair of shoes.

After this flurry, the silence fell again. Outside in the yard, the stable boy was leading a horse back into its stall. The hoofs clattered on the cobbles and a blackbird flew off with a shriek. These might be the last sounds of the day. Dusk was falling with a smoky pink glow over the stable roof. Soon a mist would settle on the vegetable garden and its row of cabbage stalks and the cow pastures beyond would grow darker and darker.

She shivered. 'We must remember there are no stormtroopers in England, so you don't need to be frightened like that again. We're safe here.'

Sophie kicked her boots against the rung of the chair. 'How d'you know?' she said.

Chapter 13

July, 1939

'Today I learned, "Sticks and stones may break my bones but words can never hurt me," ' Sophie announced. 'And Vera Brown asked if she could be my friend.'

'And you said yes?' Taking her hand at the village school gates, Susanna noted her sister's smile and the fresh open-ness of her face.

Sophie nodded and skipped as far as the street. 'We're going to walk home?' She turned to wave at a small girl in a blue dress.

'We are,' Susanna replied, taking a deep breath of contentment and relief. Sophie had not only begun to speak, she had a friend. There'd be chatter and giggling and playing chase. She'd be ordinary, and happy, and it was a miracle. 'Bert's sent the Humber into the garage for repairs and Flo suggested we walk back by way of the little copse to see if we can find any of those wild orchids. Aunt Daphne does so love them and since she's poorly again . . .'

Sophie set off skipping along the grass verge. 'Is it war yet?' she called.

'Not quite, but something called Public Information Leaflet Number One arrived this morning telling us what to do in air raids and about the sirens, and how we must all have a label, a made-to-last label with our names and addresses on it which we must wear at all times. What about asking after my day or have you forgotten?'

'Did they say you could go to the college or not?' Sophie stopped and waited for her to catch up. 'I was trying to guess from your face and I decided the answer was yes.'

'It's yes, really, yes, and in September I shall catch the train to Bournemouth every morning very early and in Bournemouth I shall start learning how to be a dress designer. So. What do'you think?'

'I'm very glad. And was Aunt Daphne glad too?'

'She was! And she was so brave, with her headache and all and facing the principal of the college and being so nice about me, and laying out the drawings I've done since I got here, the cats on the chairs, and the trees on the top of our hill, and the ones of Flo and the stable boy and Bert. He said it was quite clear I had artistic talent and was I sure it was designing I wanted to concentrate on and I said it was. And Aunt Daphne signed some papers and very regally we swept out and went to have several cups of coffee in a café, weak at the knees. Aunt Daphne wanted me to do the course as much I as did. I think that's what's brought on the headache. But imagine, Sophie, my drawing's going to come in useful at last, and I'm going to be a dress designer. I can't wait to write home and ask Mama to tell Frau Leona.'

'No more wicked drawings,' Sophie shouted, skipping off again. 'Nice ones, pretty ones . . .'

Susanna laughed, setting off behind her. No more Goebbels, no more Hitler hamsters with mad marble eyes! It wouldn't even matter if Mama found the secret box when she packed up to come to England. Soon she'd be strolling sedately along this very lane in her black velvet coat and hat and best kid gloves, her only kid gloves, breathing clean, free air and staring with astonishment at the layers of fat Dorset hills and the dizzying space. And Papa would have to keep pausing, speechless at the sight of so many treasures for him to explore and savour, hidden flowers and little surprises of plants and fungus in hollows and great stretches of woodland carpeted with flowers. He'd be too happy to sing. He need never sing "Angels Guard Thee" ever again.

'Puh, puh, puh,' she cried, her heart ready to burst.

It had seemed a day for everything being right, so they did things right at the house in order that it shouldn't be marred by scoldings. They scraped the dirt from their shoes on the scraper outside the kitchen door. They washed their hands in the scullery and found the tiniest glass amongst the array in the flower room for their gift to Aunt Daphne, a solitary orchid. And after tea Susanna carried it on a small tray to avoid drips across into the spendour of the front hall, where they lingered to enjoy the glow of firelight on the warm chestnut colour of the polished oak floor and panelling. It was cold for July. The old spotted hound, Pox, slumped by the hearth, raised his head and dropped it again. They'd learned to accept each other.

Towards dusk, the lamps would be lit along the walls and then the portraits ranged there would seem to come to life. There were generations of Montgomery relations looking mostly fierce and unpleasant, and Mr Montgomery himself in a riding outfit with whip, a horse in the background. The four Montgomery children were featured in a dream-like country scene when they were all under the age of twelve or so, and their favourite, Aunt Daphne, was young and misty-eyed in a white dress with a blue sash, pearls and diamonds decorating her ears and neck.

Inspection of these familiars over, they climbed the stairs, a hand on the satisfying roundness of the banister and inspecting another favourite as they climbed, the intricate pattern of the ancient rose-pinks and browns of the carpet, following it along the corridor at the top. Sophie always counted out the doors: Mr Montgomery's dressing room, his bedroom, Aunt Daphne's dressing room, her bedroom. Here Aunt Daphne's teatray sat untouched on its stool.

'She must be feeling worse,' she whispered.

'Yes. I'll put the vase on the tray. Mary will take it in with her supper. We won't disturb her now.'

They'd reached their own doors past the others, when Aunt Daphne's door opened. Bert the butler appeared, followed by the doctor and Flo. They paused at the top of the stairs and the doctor spoke. 'I'll send a nurse. She can't be left. Meanwhile, you must contact the master. Tell him it's urgent though there'll be little he can do. With strokes you can never tell. I shall expect paralysis certainly, if she survives, but she could be gone before he gets here.'

Standing there unseen, they heard every word of this, which was a pity. They might have had a bit more time.

Chapter 14

They'd let in her favourite cat, little black Billy, and he'd paused at the end of Aunt Daphne's bed, contemplating her stillness. Nurse was downstairs at tea. They were to call her if Madam moved or made any sound.

Settled into chairs on each side of the bed, Sophie held her hand whilst Susanna laid out the silk ribbons she'd taken from the dressing-table drawer. 'The deep pink one will give colour to her cheeks,' she whispered, cautiously easing it around Aunt Daphne's hair and tying it with a bow. 'Nurse doesn't understand she'll be wanting to look nice however ill she is and never seems to consider she might prefer to listen to something other than, "Can you hear me, dear?' I'm positive she can hear. Silence must frighten her just as much as the paralysis. Have we told her everything that's happened today so far?'

Sophie nodded. 'And how much we love our life here in case we haven't been able to say enough before. Shall we do another story about Opa and Buba to show how sweet and funny they are?'

Susanna hesitated. 'That might start her worrying that she's not able to keep writing letters and telephoning the Home Office about the work permits. I'll read her something from one of her magazines. There was an article that made her laugh the other day, and a pattern offer for one of the new seventeen-inch-leg frocks I was going to make up for her. You were having your music lesson. We could hear you scraping away on the new violin and we had a lovely time discussing whether we'd try Gould's in Dorchester for the material, or Beale's in Bournemouth. She had a fancy for some silk in a design of bands of small flowers going round horizontally. It'd be quite a challenge for me to make the pieces match up, she said, and we'd more or less decided to try Beale's on Saturday because they have a bigger stock . . .' Her voice tailed off.

They stared dumbly at each other until Susanna made an effort and reached for the magazines in the bedside cupboard where Aunt Daphne's treats and pleasures had been tidied away by Nurse. 'Here it is,' she said, turning the pages until she found an article headed 'Portrait of a Lady.' 'Listen. "A lady likes clear, candid eyes. She knows all the tricks to make hers worth gazing into. A lady likes a low-pitched appealing voice. She takes lessons, not because she wants to sing, but because she longs to have a voice as resonant and romantic as Claudette Colbert . . ." Aunt Daphie laughed at that part, and forbade me ever to let my eyes be gazed into until I'm really sure it's a prince doing the gazing and not a frog. That's why she wants us to be independent, like Miss Patch is, working in films, and you're to be a doctor and me a dress designer. Still, according to this, even if it's a prince I suppose, we've got to have a variety of hair styles because men like variety. And listen, "There was a time when a lady thought the pale look of destiny was stunning, but now she prefers to personify a rosy future." You'll be all right for that, Sophie. I won't but I must tell Flo it's my pale look of destiny every time she claims I'm poorly. We must also try not to startle but to please, apparently, according to this article.'

'We're not to wear our red outfits then?'

'No. And of course, Mama was right, a lady doesn't wear red. She only bought that cloth for my sake. It was against everything she knew about clothes. She'll practically faint with pleasure seeing what a choice of fabrics she has here though, I bet she'll be tempted with those pretty prints in Beale's.'

'When I grow up,' Sophie said, 'I want to be an English lady so no one call me the things they do call me.'

'No, you don't,' Susanna said lamely, glancing at her sister with understanding. 'And it'll all seem different when Mama and Papa get here.' Please God, let it be soon, she thought. Once or twice, she'd shocked herself with a sudden guilty longing to be Aunt Daphne's real daughter. And yet, often, making her way up the great oak staircase in the glow of the lamps, she'd be overwhelmed by the need to be back in the cluttered cold-water flat, with the fear and the dread – and most of all, her father and mother. 'We'd better do the prayers, Nurse'll be up soon.'

'You are sure Jewish prayers will work for Aunt Daphne?' Sophie began to suck the thumb of her free hand. Mention of their parents sometimes made her revert to this habit but Susanna chose never to scold or point out the risk of germs or crooked front teeth. She'd caught herself at it.

'They are the only prayers we know,' she said. 'And Papa says if there is a God, there'll one for the whole world. Do a verse of "Angels Guard Thee" first, she loves the tune.'

Sophie took her thumb from her mouth and began to sing, as Billy made up his mind and set off along the counterpane, reaching Aunt Daphne's left shoulder and settling his behind on it before minutely inspecting her mouth and eyelids with his nose. Finally, with a round-eyed stare at nothing, he arranged his body on her head and flicked his tail so the long silky fur of it lay on her neck like a scarf.

Aunt Daphne's eyes opened for a second and a tear rolled out.

Halfway through the line *All sorrows seem to rest*, Sophie stopped and cried, 'Don't die, Aunt Daphne, please don't die.'

The eyelids flickered and another tear trembled on her cheek.

'Say some more,' Susanna whispered.

'We love you,' Sophie cried, 'and little Billy does and we all need you.'

They were so completely absorbed in gazing at the cold white skin of her face that Bert the butler was in the room before they saw him.

'Master's come,' he said, and put a finger to his lips.

Bert shouldn't have worried they'd make a noise in the presence of Mr Montgomery. His personality was part of the house, its only dark element except for Sidney and Mary. Susanna had sometimes thought she'd rather have done with the meeting of him, and here he was, standing at the foot of Aunt Daphne's bed, puffing for breath and glaring.

'Daphne!' he shouted. 'Can you hear me?'

He was far less handsome than his portrait suggested, even allowing for age. He was purple about the face and hands and very stout. His neck spilled over his shirt collar and on to the green tweed of his jacket. She had an instant picture of him as a cross old boar flinging piglets out of his way.

Sophie was actually transfixed with horror at the sight of the vast intruder and her small hand still gripped Aunt Daphne's though he was thundering around to her side of the bed. She just had time to duck under his arm and run to the window as he leaned over his wife's pillows.

'Bloody cat,' he shouted. Billy slipped under the sheet and he lifted his wife's lids one by one. 'Daphne?' he yelled again, snorting with exasperation and turning his glare to Susanna. 'Bloody refugees, I suppose,' he said, and he stamped off, slamming the door behind him.

Matters then moved rather fast. They were having their tea in the kitchen with a worried Flo, when Mr Montgomery stalked in and threw some money on the table in front of Susanna. 'Get yourself and your sister back to the refugee camp first thing in the morning,' he said. 'My wife is not expected to recover and there's nothing for you here. I don't want Jewish brats in my house.'

Chapter 15

'Whatever next,' Flo muttered, lifting Sophie on to her knees and enfolding her in plump arms. 'And whatever will Madam say to it?'

She'd been very tearful. They hadn't. Susanna sat stiffly before the remains of tea. She could still eat. She'd eaten three scones and two slices of currant cake. Tomorrow afternoon, they'd be at Dovercourt Holiday Camp where teatimes didn't exist and the wind would still be howling. Sophie hadn't eaten of course and certainly hadn't spoken. Her face was as white and glassy as Aunt Daphne's.

'Can it be true, Aunt Daphne will never get better, Flo?' she asked. 'Or was he just saying that to be rid of us? Is it our fault, her stroke? We've been too much of a burden to her?' And Flo, she thought, help me with the letter home. How to tell them?

'Oh, my dears,' Flo said. 'You was the best thing that happened to Madam in many a year. She wouldn't hardly get out of bed when her own didn't need her any more. You give her purpose, that's what Mr David said, and she loves you.' Flo's eyes filled with fresh tears. 'She knows you need her and that'll help her get well. She won't want you going back to that camp and you aren't going back to it, so what we got to do is have a good think and find a way out until Mr David arrives from wherever he's been sent. Before he left, he says I should look after you if there was any trouble and trouble we got, ent we?'

'Yes, and Mr David said I should come to you, Flo, if I had to, but if he's in France or somewhere with the Army, he won't get here very quickly. And we'll certainly be a burden on him because he'll be worried enough about his mother.'

Mary appeared from the pantry corridor and trotted past with a pile of clothes. 'This is them red garments they come in, Flo,' she said, 'and their boots. I'll put 'em up in the nursery, ready for packing, shall I? I don't suppose they'll be taking their new stuff, not to some refugee camp, eh?'

'You mind your mouth, Mary Smith,' Flo said sharply. 'And put them things back. They'll be leaving with their new clothes, same as Madam would want. Why don't you unpick that pretty frock what Susanna sewed for you if it comes to that?'

Pretending not to hear, Mary dropped her collection on the stool near the stove where the haversacks and the two cardboard suitcases had been laid to air.

'It's Miss Patch we wants here as well,' Flo said. 'If she'd left an address for that hotel where she and Miss Georgiana's staying, she'd be back home by now. She can twist her father round her little finger. She could tell him you're essential to Madam's recovery and you're as good as unpaid nurses, which is the plain truth. Then Mr Will can drive the master back to the place in Ireland where he can get on with his fishing and shooting and interfering with Mr Will's a-running of it, and we'll be nice and cosy again.'

Dear Mama and Papa, thought Susanna, absently picking a currant from her plate, there is a little bad news but on reflection we feel that Downlands would really be too quiet for you . . . Dear Mama and Papa, Aunt Daphne is dying, God rest her soul . . .

This was so occupying, she barely noticed Sophie scramble down from Flo's lap. It wasn't until Flo gave a cry of distress that she looked up and saw her sister flying in from the pantries, followed by a furious Mary. Mary was shouting, 'Give them here, you little devil, them's ours!'

Evading her grasp, Sophie went straight to the stove and knelt on the floor there. Horrified, Susanna watched as she dug a giant pair of scissors into one of the haversacks. Within seconds, the two carrying straps were off and she'd turned to the other. It too she stripped of its usefulness before getting to her feet, levering the cover from the stove and tipping the straps into the fire. Blue and yellow flames flickered up and a puff of black smoke. 'There!' she said, wiping her nose with the back of her hand.

Mary rushed to replace the cover and stared in disbelief as Sophie turned to her next task, which was apparently to drag the

111

suitcases into a space on the flagstones. It was clear she intended to damage them also but somehow none of them could move to stop her, and the sudden appearance of Sidney in the courtyard doorway didn't stop her either.

Sidney said, 'Blimey!' just as Sophie made her first run and landed on Susanna's case. Jumping up and down, wilder and wilder, she didn't pause until with a satisfying crump, it gave way.

Extracting her feet, she was soon leaping on the other and still no one moved. Only she did, and she'd destroyed her own suitcase and declared, 'Now we can't go anywhere,' before a baffled Sidney reached the table. Throwing down the mail, he muttered, 'Just as you got a letter from Germany,' as if that had anything to do with it. 'Violent, they are, them Jews, they killed Jesus, didn't they,' he said.

'I'll tan your hide, Sidney, if you says another word,' Flo shouted.

Grumbling, Mary began to sweep up. 'I'll get them old school cases of Miss Patch's out, shall I, Flo?'

Flo didn't answer, and a breathless, triumphant Sophie leaned her head against the comfort of the white-aproned bosom.

Susanna finally made herself move and reached out for the letter from home.

'What do Mama and Papa say?' Sophie asked, accepting a piece of bread and butter sprinkled with brown sugar from Flo.

'Oh, the usual,' Susanna replied vaguely. 'That they can hardly wait to see us, why haven't we sent the photographs we promised, how much have we actually grown, and so on. There's no news yet from Opa and Buba and Max's mother has no news of him. Papa claims he's probably got himself to America by now . . .'

Half-blind, she forced herself to read the letter properly. 'Briefly, my darlings,' Papa had written, 'Mama doesn't yet have her exit visa because they now say she must have a certificate of exemption from war work (Germany being under threat from Poland as you know), but since Jewish women have been excluded from war work, there has been yet another mistake to be sorted out, which means more time must pass before the visa is issued. So, those photos please, to help us bear it. Sometimes we feel you will be strangers to us and Freddy. He can say two whole

112

sentences in English now and is quite the little man, with the gift of total absorption in what he does.

Whatever else, though, don't waste a minute worrying about us, and even if Mama does have to come alone with Freddy as I warned, that's not a problem for you to dwell on either. They say my skills are vital to the factory, but I am to teach another man to take over from me. Once that's done, my exit visa will go through. Of course, we are upset ourselves by any hold-up that keeps us away from you but we feel truly fortunate to have been spared the distress of your being unsettled and unhappy without us.

'In an hour or two, we shall be gazing at the moon and sending our love across the Channel, but write more letters, please. We thirst to know every detail of your lives. Frau Leona asks after the fashions in England also, Susanna, and believe it or not, how hats are being worn. I have promised to pass this message on to you, so my duty is done. Are you to be accepted by the art college for next term and is Sophie practising regularly? We dare not think what dear Mrs Montgomery had to pay for the instrument, but she has written often that you have become cherished companions and lighten her days, so we are grateful you found each other at the holiday camp and such good developed from such bad . . .'

'Doesn't Papa send me a message of my own?' Sophie broke in on her reading.

'Of course he does, that you practise every day and he longs to hear your progress. He actually does mention war with Poland this time, which must mean it's allowed to be spoken of in Germany, as long as it's Poland who's the aggressor, of course, instead of the other way around. Probably there is going to be one then, Flo. He wouldn't risk saying it otherwise, in case his letter gets opened. It's a clue for us, I think.' Dazed, she replaced the letter in its envelope. 'Still, they'll be with us soon.'

'God willing,' Flo whispered, making Sophie laugh.

'That's one of our sayings, Flo,' she said.

'So it is, my lovely. Well, to my mind, there's only one God for us all, else there'd be gods squabbling amongst themselves up there like peoples does down here and that'd do no one any good.'

'It's more or less what our papa says, Flo. You will get on well together . . .' Susanna came to a stop, stifled by a surge of anguish that took away her breath. Hurry, she thought, oh, Mama, queue up all night at the visa office and hurry, hurry.

113

'Eat!' Flo commanded with her most loving smile, passing Sophie another piece of bread and butter.

'You've got to wave a hand about when you say that, Flo. When our Buba gets here, she'll show you how to do it properly and she'll like you so much, she'll give you one of her lucky charms.' Giggling, Sophie spat grains of sugar.

'Make some fresh coffee, Mary,' Flo said, 'and another pot of tea. And fetch that lemon tart. This mite'll have a bit now she's in the mood for eating. Then have a glance at my roast. After that, rinse them trout I got brought up this morning. I'll do one for the master's first course, the others is for these girls. Sidney, stop gawping, get that rubbish out to the gardeners' tip afore anyone else sees it and then get off upstairs to see if Bert's anywhere near finished with the master's unpacking. We wants him down here.'

Susanna stood up with dizzying suddenness. 'How much is the train fare to London, Flo? I shan't go back to the refugee camp. I shall go to London to that Home Office where they do the permits. Aunt Daphne won't be able to keep telephoning now, will she? And Flo, how much is it to stay in a lodging house, and how much are wages for a dressmaker in a workshop? Really, I'm meant to be a dressmaker, it's in my blood, I get it from my grandmother, I don't have to go to art school at all, so I won't . . .'

'You give me a fright,' Flo said. 'That Hitler! If I had my way, we'd be sending a few bombs across to kill him off, making a girl of sixteen have such worries.'

Mary opened the oven door. 'Your roast's catching, Flo, the master won't have it overdone and you can't expect me to see to it, I ain't no cook.'

'No, you ent, Mary Smith. Bring it here to the table and check the master's gooseberry fool is set. He might have to have some of this tart for his supper. He don't care for a slopping pudding.'

'Mr Montgomery! Send a bomb to kill him!' Giggling louder, on the verge of tears, Sophie began on the lemon tart with a spoon.

'Little devil, did you hear, Flo?' Mary slammed the roast as near Sophie as she could get it.

'Sticks and stones break my bones, Mary,' Sophie said, 'meat smells can't hurt.'

Susanna tried to catch her eye but failed. There were bright red spots on her cheeks. Soon there'd be tears. Everything was slipping away. They were to be moved on. It was their destiny.

Only she mustn't sit there wailing about it inside. Papa would be furious. Destiny, it was what you made yourself. And she must make it for all four of them and then for Opa and Buba.

In a blur, she listened to the familiar bickering. They couldn't know. It wasn't their fault. 'Sometimes,' she said, 'sometimes, in Berlin, they tell you you must have a certain form in order to have another certificate form issued to you, and when you take it to the office they say, Why haven't you brought your dog licence, or some such. You say you haven't a dog so they tell you to go away and come back with a certificate proving you haven't a dog, or whatever . . .'

Mary turned to stare at her from the pantry corridor. Sidney dropped the pieces of suitcase in the doorway. 'Listen to her,' he said, 'don't she go on?'

Poor Flo's eyes filled with more tears. 'You mustn't dwell on it, my lovely,' she said.

'It's a kind of slow torture, you see, and they've started on my mother, they say she must have a certain form it doesn't make sense for her to have, that she couldn't possibly possess . . .' She stopped. The red spots had vanished from Sophie's cheeks. 'So it may mean a bit of a hold-up again,' she finished lamely.

'We'll sort things out between us,' Flo said.

'Of course we will.' Susanna smiled at her. Flo had never heard of a KZ. She'd lived sixty years without a second's real fear, her only suffering the loss of a miscarried baby.

Through the open doorway, the air drifted in, damp and scented, manure in it, honeysuckle. A horse clattered across the cobbles, the stable boy whistled, blackbirds sang from their perch on the stable roof. I sit here for the last time, she thought, and Mama and Papa will never sit here.

And somehow that has to be borne.

Chapter 16

Sunnyside Cottage, Piddletrenthide, Dorset

'You poor things, how ghastly, it's simply too terrible for words. I can't think how you survived it, I couldn't have.'

Over the supper table in her old nanny's parlour, Patch's blue eyes glowed in turn with sympathy and tears. 'The extraordinary brutality of those Nazi thugs, smashing every bit of someone's home and as a finishing touch throwing a pet dog into the street! You mean, you and Sophie had to listen to the screams of the dog whilst waiting for your turn? Incredible. And you knew not a soul would raise a finger or protest in any way about this treatment though they were witnesses to *crimes*?' She shook her head in disbelief.

Exhilarated by her centre-stage story telling, Susanna nodded, arranging spoon and fork on her empty plate. She'd only ever revealed the details of that November night to Aunt Daphne but Patch had somehow drawn them from her. 'It was the beginning of the end really. We didn't know what might happen next. We could all have ended up in the KZ just like that, and not just the rich people the Nazis wanted to steal from. Some of those had already disappeared, including a family friend. Anyway, the charity organisations decided the younger ones should be got out of Germany even if the adults were held up by problems with exit visas and work permits. Not many countries are prepared to offer work, it's only Britain actually as far as I know, and they'll only issue permits for domestic or land work.'

'And you and Sophie were two of the younger ones, and picked

116

by my ma.' Patch beamed, peering into the pudding basin. 'Shall I finish this up, Nan? Had enough, Suzy?'

Susanna nodded again, as full of clove-scented apple sponge as it was possible to be. She watched the rest of it, covered in custard, slip into Patch's generous red mouth. Aunt Daphne's daughter had the bounciest of curls, quite unlike her own dense mass, and the skin of her bare arms and face seemed to glow with a sort of golden colour. Her voice was so clear it practically vibrated through the cottage. Sophie could probably hear it upstairs in bed. 'Sophie and I were lucky to get on the list,' she said, 'and especially lucky to be picked out by your mother. We have been worried, though. Could we have caused the stroke by being too much of a burden?'

'Golly no, don't go upsetting yourself on that score. Ma's always been a sufferer, from headaches mainly. It was possibly brewing for years. But she'll rally. Until she does and can sort out Pa's silliness, you've got this temporary home with my old nan. Pa's not as bad as he seems, he can usually be got round. But nannies always come up trumps.' She abandoned her spoon with a satisfied sigh and winked at the straight-backed old lady seated beside her. 'Smashing pud Flo sent down, Nan.'

'I'm not sure you should have allowed yourself that third helping, Penelope.' Nanny pursed her lips and poured herself a glass of water.

Penelope! Susana smiled to herself. That was the real name of the girl who resembled every head prefect in every school featured in the stories her father used to buy her from second-hand bookshops before the troubles. And it was true that girls like her had nicknames and gave themselves names they decided suited them better than their own. Patch had referred to herself as Edwina throughout her childhood, after the society beauty she longed to look like, and everyone else had called her Patch, except sour little Nanny.

'I believe I can hear your sister shouting for you, Susanna,' Nanny said.

'I'm sorry,' she cried, leaping from her chair. 'Please excuse me. I'll go up to her. Thank you, Patch, for coming to talk to us and for bringing us the wonderful supper from Flo. If you leave the dishes, Nanny, I'll clear and wash them later.'

Closing the parlour door behind her and making her way up the staircase, she added a few words to the imaginary letter home that was a perpetual refrain in her head. Mama, you will be proud of me when you see how polite and grateful I am and how prompt to offer thanks and how I never shirk household tasks, doing them in advance if I can . . .

Perhaps she could also admit to the disaster of Aunt Daphne's stroke in the next one she sat down to put into writing, now that Patch had arrived to sort matters out. Yes, she thought, pausing on a stair, I shall make light of it by saying it's only temporary but we're in a dear little cottage with an outside toilet full of spiders and a nanny who was Mr Montgomery's before the children's. Nannies always come up trumps, I shall say, and they'd soon see that as another bit of good against the bad.

'It is kind of you to have taken them in at such short notice, Nan. Ma would be devastated if we didn't try to continue her work. Frankly though, I haven't an earthly what to do with them. I mean, two German kids stick out like sore thumbs in the depths of Dorset at the best of times, never mind with war more certain now than ever. Only my Ma could be so daft and so brave as to make foreign refugees her personal bit of war effort. I'm just relieved you took this cottage when you retired and didn't go and live in Wales with your sister. Flo would have had to hide 'em in the cellar if it weren't for you. She's grown fond of 'em, she says, and it shocked her no end watching Sophie smash that luggage. Must have been desperate, mustn't she, poor kid? Still, I can't deny they're something of a burden on us, what with Ma and everything.'

Crouched halfway back up the stairs with the pail of water and cloth to deal with Sophie's sick, Susanna heard these words coming through the parlour door and each one was like a stab at her heart. German, Patch? Didn't you understand?

Why had she told her the story? She'd almost given up more, about Herr Merkel's ashes being sent home in a pot, and that she'd never revealed to Aunt Daphne. Patch's sympathy had seemed so real, it had warmed her right through. Nanny, of course, had merely tut-tutted her disapproval, as if being the target of Nazi cruelty was one's own fault.

'I don't mind Sophie,' came her sour answer to Patch. And how to bear even that? 'But I've only the one spare bed and they can't

118

go on sleeping head to toe night after night, it isn't healthy. And have you considered the cost of Susanna's travel to and fro from here to the college? You won't be able to pay for it.'

'I won't, Nan. I'm always skint. I get through my allowance as well as my salary before the end of the month. London's pricey, and so's Paris, where my film company's working at the moment. Georgie's come over to Paris for a while with the excuse of keeping me company, so of course, we trail round the cafés night after night, buying drinks for a pack of no-goods who follow that ghastly painter chappie Georgie's got a fancy for, though she's still mad for you know who, same as always. I did cook up this wild scheme I'd forge Ma's signature on a cheque but the bank might query it with Pa. Oh, gosh, what a mess to be saddled with.'

'To my mind, Penelope, you'll do best for the elder girl by cancelling her place at the art college and asking for a refund of the fees. Then you should think about finding her a job with lodgings included.'

Cautiously, Susanna balanced the bucket on the narrow stair and sat down beside it. Dear Mama and Papa, she thought, I didn't tell you that Aunt Daphne has become unwell, so as not to worry you, but it's all right, we are to be taken charge of by her daughter who is very pretty and much loved by everybody but not nearly as nice as those head prefects in the school stories I loved so much . . .

'Well, David might come up trumps with some cash when he gets here, Nan, but meanwhile I suppose a job's the thing. If we let her go to the college, there'll be books and so on to pay for as well, won't there?'

'It's a responsibility I'm not sure you're ready for, Penelope.'

'A job's the thing, then, you think? Flo says she's a wonder at dressmaking. Perhaps Georgie could get her an apprenticeship up in London. Since she's been a mannequin, she seems to know half the fashion world and the kid could camp down on the floor till we get her settled somewhere else. Georgie wouldn't mind. You sure you can't have both girls here though, Nan? Flo'll send their food and see to their laundry.'

'There doesn't seem enough space. The little one now, she's quiet. She likes to play down by the stream with the ducks or sit by the hearth with me listening to the wireless. I'm teaching her to knit clothes for her doll, but I'll have no nonsense, mind.

Wantonly destroying the luggage did her no good whatsoever and she must learn a lesson from it. Susanna's another matter. She's somehow in the way, she's forever offering to make me a winter suit or a new nightie but at my age, I don't know as I need anything. And where would she do the cutting out? I feel I must be making conversation with her too and she does with me, so careful and polite she is, trying to help me every which way, and I got my routine . . .'

Always trying to help, yes, Susanna thought, a trickle of very hot tears setting off down her cheeks, always trying to be grateful, always trying not to be a burden.

'Course you have, Nan, and I do see the little one sort of fits in with it better. I wish David would hurry. We'll have to get in touch with the refugee committee in London. Ma signed fostering papers, I think, but she can't act as guardian lying in bed. She's only said one word so far. We decided it was "Help", which was awful, and I shan't let her down. She won't want to find the girls disappeared entirely when she wakes up. Flo says they really got her out of her depressions. She hasn't been low since they came, not in the depths. If only Pa weren't such a silly old bigot. He's practically a Nazi himself, of course.'

'That's another thing, Penelope. If we are going to war with Germany, what'll the locals says if I'm harbouring two little Germans? They won't be making the distinction between Nazi and German, or Jewish. They could start breaking windows and shouting insults same as was done in the last war. Sophie told me she'd been called a nasty Nazi at the village school and down at the house that Sidney kept whispering all sorts. Then there's the matter of their religion. Where would I be able to find Jewish instruction, even in Dorchester?'

'Flo said they didn't seem specially religious, Nan, though the grandparents were, she thought . . .'

Susanna wiped her nose with the back of her hand. Her mouth was open in an ugly gash, she could feel it, but it didn't seem to matter. Dragging the bucket with her, she managed to move herself backwards, stair by stair, until she reached the landing, where it was easier to sit down properly, lean against the wall and let out all the tears, years and years' worth.

Chapter 17

The cool damp air was scented with earth, flowers and the musty thatch of the roof. Hidden in every bush and tree in every cottage garden, the birds sang about territory. It was dawn, their time.

Kneeling at the tiny open window, Susanna watched the ribbon of the road grow paler and paler. The birds would soon get on with their rustling about in the eaves and diving for worms and she'd get off to where she was going. She was ready, emptied of tears, packed, resolute, and very frightened. But she was never going to be a burden to anyone ever again and somehow she must see that her parents never were either. She had nothing to lose. Downlands was already lost to her, and Aunt Daphne whispering 'Help' with no one to listen.

Behind her, Sophie's regular little puffing snore faltered and ceased. 'What are you doing?'

Susanna got to her feet and sat down on the end of the bed. 'Waiting for day,' she said. 'I couldn't sleep for thinking. Over supper last night, Patch gave me a vital job to do on my own.'

'Without me?' Sophie sat up.

'Yes, but you've got your job, here. Patch can't do either as she must get back to work on the film in Paris. It's our papers, our refugee papers and the papers for Mama and Papa to come to England. We can't make any mistakes, of course, so first of all, I have to go to that refugee committee office.'

Gazing at her sister's innocent, trusting face, she went on embroidering her big lie. 'That's where the lady came from to sort of inspect Downlands and Aunt Daphne to make sure we were being cared for properly. We laughed then, didn't we, but she gave us the address, just in case, and I put it in my shoulder bag

121

and Patch said that's really lucky as it happens, Aunt Daphne's bureau being locked and she not being able to find the key. The Home Office papers are in there too, which means I must go to the Home Office myself as well to make sure the work permits for Mama and Papa are going ahead as they're supposed to. Patch says we can pretend Aunt Daphne is in hospital for a few days and the work will still be available for them at Downlands. She says she'll forge her mother's signature on the documents if she has to.'

Sophie digested this information. 'What if I'm sick? Nanny'll be cross.'

'You won't be sick, you'll be too busy doing your job. It's the most vital one, really. You're to make sure Nanny sends the letters from home on to me in London. I'll have got lodgings, which Mr Montgomery's money will pay for, and I'll send the address to you here. Without their letters to know exactly what their position is, day to day, I can't get on with anything. You do see?'

'Tell them to come quickly.'

'Yes. But I shall still say nothing about Aunt Daphne's stroke, that's why we must keep up the pretence of our living at Downlands and why your staying here is so important.'

'They'd worry.'

'Yes. And even not come so as not to be a burden on the Montgomerys.'

Sophie hesitated. 'Shall I go down and see Flo if I get muddled?'

'Only if you hear Mr Montgomery's gone back to Ireland. Then you can perhaps creep down secretly to sit with Aunt Daphne. You must really be here to do that, in fact, no one else will, will they? You can sing to her and play the violin and say the prayers and tell her how much we need her to be well.'

'I don't want you to go on a train.'

'I'll be all right. It's not the same. We're not being thrown out of Dorset like we were from Berlin.'

'Sidney says when the war starts, Hitler'll send bombs over specially to kill off Jewish people.'

'Even Hitler's not clever enough for that, no one is, and anyway, Britain's going to fight him off, that's what going to war means.'

'Puh, puh, puh?'

'We haven't said that for a long time.'

'Buba and Opa seem very far away.'

'Yes. But they aren't really. Only because of papers.'

'Which you're going to see to.'

'Yes. And every night I'll stand by my window sending love across to Berlin and Poland, and prayers, and you must do the same from this very window. Don't forget. It'll help remind you why you need to be brave.'

'Shall I send you love too? In London?'

'Yes, and I'll do the same to you. Where's Buba's talisman?'

'Under my pillow. Where's your one?'

'In my hand, look.' Susanna held out the little gold scissors.

'We need them again now.'

'Yes.'

Chapter 18

London, August 1939

David could hardly stay in his chair. Outside the window, the blasted rain kept on falling as if it would never cease. He was damp and irritated, he wanted to get up and pace to and fro. 'I'm sorry about what's happened,' he said to the wretched woman behind the desk, 'but my mother would hardly have wished a stroke upon herself. Now, I have a few days' leave to see her again and I'm spending one of them here in order to sort out the matter of the two Lehmann girls' fostering, as she'd want me to do. Naturally, I'm prepared to take over the responsibility until she's well. I'm only sorry I didn't have time to visit them on my first flying trip to my mother's sickbed. I do have a little longer this leave, but I'd be most grateful if you'd realise I have to return to my posting abroad.'

The official regarded him from behind her glasses. 'I feel most strongly, Captain Montgomery, and the refugee committee will agree with me, that a single Army man is hardly a suitable fosterer for two young girls.'

'You are right,' he said, 'but as I've already pointed out, my sister Penelope will shortly be returning home from Paris to London. She will oversee their care, helped by our cook and our old family nanny, with whom the little one is presently lodged. Of course, they'll need a woman to turn to, but I shall be the one to settle all costs for their keep, clothing, education and so on until my mother is well enough. I should have thought you'd require some sort of signature from me. It seems you don't, and neither will you accept my bank draft so that Susanna's expenses can be properly met by you whilst I'm away. As part of the fighting forces, I may never return and I do want to ensure she knows she'll be looked after. I've been most concerned for her welfare since hearing that she ran off as she did.'

'As indeed we've been, Captain. Why d'you think Susanna did run off, as you put it? And may I see your identification, please? A Mr Montgomery was mentioned in her explanation to us when she arrived here in a very distressed state. Would that be you or your father?'

He blinked at the woman, horrified. 'You mean? Dammit, madam . . .' He fumbled in his jacket. 'My father is many things but he is not whatever you are thinking.'

The hair pricked at the back of his neck. He put his Army pass carefully on the table in front of her. 'My father is a bigot,' he muttered, 'he loathes foreigners, he is a bully, whatever you want, but that's all.' And that's too much, he thought, a sudden pain around his heart. What's more, the man preferred fat, middle-aged women, barmaids in fact, Irish ones. 'Susanna left Downlands because he demanded she did. I don't know why she decided to leave the village and set up on her own instead of going back to the holiday camp, but I should like to. My cook has recounted the entire sorry tale of getting the girls relodged. She felt Susanna had accepted the move.' But she had had enough hurt in her life, he thought, and how had she borne this second banishment and where was she now?

The woman peered at his pass and slowly wrote something down in the manner of all civil servants. Not that she was one. She was a charity worker, unpaid. He should be ashamed of himself. He was.

After an age, she held out the pass to him and he breathed a sigh of relief. There'd be time to take Susanna to tea somewhere glamorous, Claridges, that's where the smart women had tea. She could study their frocks and their hats, as girls did, and he, well, he'd be content to gaze on her lovely pale skin flushing with embarrassment at her own keen appetite and her clumsiness with spoons and knives. He was hungry himself, and full to bursting with the wish to see her and show her how much they had in common, displaced as they were, belonging nowhere. I shall tell her what I've never revealed to a soul, he thought, that I am not of the same blood as my supposed father and she will feel sorry for me and that will be better than nothing. Would she need a hat, for Claridges? Yes, and gloves. They'd stop somewhere, to buy them. And an umbrella. Was she too young for it to be incorrect to offer her clothes? Well, he was her guardian. And anyway, she wouldn't know about such daft customs.

He smiled across at the woman. She was going through Susanna's file, for her address. Hurry, he thought, getting to his feet and putting his cap under his arm. The uniform would get him extra deferential treatment at Claridges. She'd like that, girls did.

The woman looked up and smiled in return. 'The committee will appreciate your offer of a bank draft, Captain, but I'm afraid Susanna has expressed the desire that she no longer need have any contact with your family, except through her sister, unless or until Mrs Montgomery recovers enough to want to see her again. She has a little money. It's paying for the room we found and her keep until she receives the first wages. She's been taken on by a refugee lady from Vienna, a dressmaker with a small established concern, and she's determined to become independent in every way. If she's in dire need of shoes or a winter coat, she must come to us, but she asks of us only that we allow her to use the office as her correspondence address for her sister to send on letters from their parents. She's most anxious they learn nothing of the break with Downlands and I believe she spends her spare hours at the Aliens department of the Home Office. The sad thing is, she's heard her father's exit permit is being held up on the German side still because they want his skills in one of their war factories. Ironic, isn't it? The Nazis say get out, we don't want you, but we shan't let you go until we've finished with you. Apart from that, of course, the unemployment problem here means that very few work permits are being issued in case refugees getting jobs will turn the British public against them. And it's astonishing how few professionals are prepared to help each other across the boundaries of country. Doctors for instance don't want a lot of clever German Jewish chaps coming over. One wonders if they fully understand it may be a matter of life or death, and that time is running out.'

She had a big red mouth with a mole on her upper lip and her eyes were as round and as bright as a schoolmistress's. All this he noticed, staring at her, the truth sinking in. Susanna would not want to see him. Why should she? And there was worse. 'You mean to tell me that not only have you placed Susanna in a sordid lodging room, you also expect her to beg you for shoes? She is seventeen years old yet you blithely accept that her few shillings a week will not stretch far enough to clothe her?'

'Captain Montgomery.' She was being patient. 'Many English girls not fortunate enough to be born into the moneyed classes are in the same position. We cannot offer our refugees higher education or luxury homes. Every penny we have been given has to go towards bringing in more children from Germany and Austria where they daily suffer increasing persecution. Susanna understands that, I assure you.'

'I understand it, madam. Why d'you think I'm offering you a bank draft for Susanna's expenses? I ask for her address also to see for myself if there is anything else she needs, other than a sordid lodging room, of course.'

'If you'd care to sit down again, Captain, and write a note for Susanna explaining that, I shall make sure it reaches her.'

He sat down, accepted paper and envelope and wrote as much as he dared.

Half-blinded by rain, he stood on the pavement thinking about his mother's own family house in Mayfair where she'd spent her childhood and which was currently let to a milliner. She'd forgotten about making it over to him, naturally, wanted to forget, wanted him to go on managing Downlands and be near her. But Downlands didn't need his managing. The new agent did it better. And the war would keep him often enough absent from it to satisfy even himself. It would also settle many other matters, his own future, his sense of being in some limbo, disengaged from his past life yet seeing no other. Of course if Downlands and the Mayfair house were flattened to dust by Nazi bombing, or worse were *occupied* by them as conquerors . . .

Why was he standing here, rain running down his face, soaked, disappointed, angry? I have no right, he thought, setting off again past a lorry disgorging more sandbags, no right to expect to take charge of Susanna's life. She wants to be in charge of her own. What courage she must have, what pride! He didn't blame her. He just wanted, oh Lord, he wanted to bear gifts, to see her face light up at the spread in Claridges, to take away all the hurts, to help her feel safe. How could she feel safe in a foreign city about to become part of a war zone?

He paused suddenly, halfway across the street. How would she feel tonight when the practice blackout cut every light in London and she realised time was running out?

He began to hurry. He'd wasted half an hour. He had to get to Westminster and the Aliens office. She might be there, or on her way. It was Friday, late afternoon. She might have begged an hour or two off in order to do some more standing in offices so po-faced civil servants could go on saying No to her.

Shortly he'd found a taxi in the Tottenham Court Road and inside it, dripping rain and wiping the windows with his sleeve, he scanned every single scurrying passer-by for a slender figure in red. She liked red, he knew, and he knew other things about her, how she'd hate the blackout all alone in that room and how, when she learned the Nazis might really turn for England, and she and her parents had nowhere else to run, dread would reach into her heart, and terror.

Susanna, he thought, wait, wait, I can sign papers, I'll guarantee them work, I'll get rid of the tenants and have a whole London house for them to pretend to work in, and you will live there, and the little one, and you will be happy, and safe.

Chapter 19

Soho, London, August 1939

'Milko-o-o!'

The milkman's call echoed along the street and up the three storeys to her open window. Susanna, waking with a start, thought at once, It's Madame Lola's wedding day, will she remember it's also my payday, what was that word Sophie was worried about and is it still raining?

She lay listening to the clatter of the milkman's cart and the rumble of traffic along the Charing Cross Road and Shaftesbury Avenue. What was missing? The sound of wind and rain! Flinging aside the blankets which still smelled of someone else's body, she crawled on her knees to the window at the foot of the bed. She unhooked the blackout curtain she was absolutely not going to be able to bear – another thing! and glanced up at a rainless sky. Almost blue it was with ordinary white clouds in it. Not a single swollen menacing one sat there waiting to tip water over her head as soon as she put a toe outside.

Good, she thought, stepping on to the linoleum and padding across to the hearth. I don't actually care if rain shrinks the skirt of Madame Lola's wedding frock or spoils her new fancy silk parasol copied from Queen Elizabeth, but I do care whether it falls on me. I have had enough of it. It was supposed to be summer.

Allowing herself a brief surge of self-pity and the solitary tear it brought, she fingered the underclothes she'd draped to dry over newspapers on the wooden chair the night before. She'd given them an hour of the gas fire but they'd done no more than drip. How did other tenants manage to deal with their rain-soaked

129

clothes, much less the washing of them? She used the tiny basin under the gas water heater by the door for a minute all-over wash every evening, and rinsed out her cups and jug in it, but it would hold no more than knickers and stockings, certainly not a blouse or a frock. Each day she told herself she would have to resolve the problem but never did.

Moving to the second, upholstered armchair she used for reading, as side table and for spreading out those items just damp, she sat on the bed, wriggled into her girdle, tied round the loops of her brassière, both still unwashed, and held several pairs of knickers to her face to test for dryness.

Settling on a peach-coloured silk pair she'd sewn herself at Aunt Daphne's, she pulled on dryish stockings, reached for her keys under the pillow and more or less made the bed, padding back across the room for the frock she had hanging on a hook behind the corner curtain which served as wardrobe. It was the beige and navy blue printed silk with a butterfly pattern she'd also made herself at Aunt Daphne's and it had shaken out quite well in spite of having been crammed into a suitcase.

It would do nicely for the wedding as long as it didn't crease too much during the morning's work. And Madame Lola had promised to create a hat for it. She was a genius at hats but sometimes forgot promises. It was certainly a smart frock anyway, even if it didn't have the new shorter hem. It was soon buttoned and she was stepping into the beige court shoes she'd laid ready. She'd been right to keep her sandals for walking to and from the salon, in spite of the rain, for they were as good as new.

Right also to have developed a routine so she was never late and need never hurry though she relied for the time on the milkman and the boom of Big Ben if the wind was in the right direction. The saucepan of water on the gas ring on the table was ready too, with matches beside it, coffee jug, milk jug, teaspoon, cup, biscuit tin, halfpenny for her quarter-pint of milk, and the penny for the gas meter in case the gas should run out. All in order.

She lit the flame under the saucepan, turned it to its lowest and unlocked the door, peering out on to the landing. No one there. Good. Now for the relocking of the door behind her and the feel of the keys safely back in her hand. They were rather too much part of her life, these keys, and the source of unwelcome anxiety. Frightened to be shut in or out, frightened to leave the door unlocked in case the strange silent man from the room next door should take it upon himself to creep in and lie in wait for her, she longed to stop fussing about them but couldn't, even when she had a lot on her mind, which was always.

Down on the ground floor, she passed the open kitchen door of the Italian tenants whose front room was a shop selling Italian foods. She recognised the usual morning sound of the Bertoni family squabbling – or being happy, she couldn't tell – and was soon out into the street. Still on time, for there were several customers left by the milkcart – Greek women, French seamstresses, more Italian housewives unfortunately. The entire street was filled with foreigners in rooms like hers in lodging houses like hers with little shops offering foreign goods, but what she needed was one of those sensible middle-aged English women. Then it would be perfectly easy to come straight out with it: Excuse me, please, but we haven't been in England long, and my little sister keeps being asked if she'd had a movement and we don't know what it means though we've been brought up to speak English and know most of the words, even old sayings and proverbs . . .

It was her turn. Passing over her halfpenny, she briefly considered asking the milkman for help. He seemed like a sensible middle-aged English husband, but what if the word 'movement' concerned a female matter? It probably did, yet Sophie was far too young to start her periods.

She'd better not ask the milkman, she decided, accepting her quarter-pint from the churn and walking back to the flats where Mr Bertoni was opening the shutters for business in order to catch any early customers. One of the Bertoni toddlers was peeping round the kitchen door at her, and Mrs Bertoni herself, nodding a lot and smiling, as people speaking different languages tend to do. She had full red lips and wore a bright green scarf around her hair with matching wrap-round overall over embarrassingly big breasts. They were shy with each other though she'd helped Mrs Bertoni sew up her blackout curtains and had received two packets of coffee in exchange. Hesitating, she nevertheless found herself hurrying back up the stairs. She certainly couldn't ask Mrs Bertoni what the word meant because they'd never get to the end of half-explanations and little worried frowning smiles.

Hot at the very thought, she recited Sophie's letter to herself to try and find some meaning in it somehow. 'Nanny keeps asking

131

me if I've had a movement and I always say yes. I have moved out of bed, haven't I? So I say yes straight away but what if it's the wrong answer and she finds out and gets cross? And have you remembered I need new sandals?'

Clark's sandals were five shillings a pair. Hastily unlocking her door in case the strange neighbour appeared, she relocked it behind her. The water on the gas ring was bubbling nicely, a comforting sound.

Shortly, in fact, the coffee was made and she was sitting back on her bed with her cup and four Nice biscuits, a double breakfast ration in case Madame Lola's wedding preparations might prevent her producing their usual lunch of soup and some delicate Viennese pastry or other. She could never quite be relied on, Madame Lola. But at the wedding tea that afternoon she herself could eat a lot and thus save the sixpence halfpenny she usually paid for her supper of poached egg on toast in Lyons Corner House on the Strand. If she did without ten suppers, she'd have the five shillings for Sophie's sandals and threepence over towards a pair of socks, but she couldn't sleep if she was hungry. She'd tried it.

Finishing the last biscuit, she got up to refill her cup with the rest of the coffee and the milk and spread out the contents of her purse on the table, three shillings and elevenpence. One penny she put beside the gas ring for the next day's coffee and another two she collected up to replace the emergency stock she always kept on the gas meter itself. She'd used them last night for the fire and hadn't replaced them, a bad slip. On her knees, she crawled under the table and lodged them on top of the grey metal box with its dials and needles that went ticking round too fast. You could kill yourself with gas if you had enough pennies to put in and turned on the tap and stopped up your draughts. Once she very nearly had.

Crawling back out again, she replaced coins and purse. There wasn't really any point in that counting until she knew whether Madame Lola was going to remember her pay. If she didn't there'd be nothing to give to the rent man unless she used the five-pound note and using it had presented another problem she'd rather not have to face again. Perhaps Madame Lola's new husband would be able to help with it.

Of course. She should have considered him already. During the

132

jollity of the wedding tea, she'd find some moment in a corner with him and just come out with it: Excuse me, but I wonder if you'd be so kind as to change this five-pound note? I've tried to change it in two shops and they asked me where I got hold of such a large sum and did my parents know I had it? They think I've stolen it, but honestly, it was a gift and it is mine! She'd laugh and he'd laugh. He'd get out his wallet in a flash. Will pound notes do, my dear? he'd say. Anything will do, thank you, she'd reply, stowing the money in her bag and quite casually asking about the word 'movement' as they stood there. He'd solve that problem too, and they'd feel like conspirators. Afterwards when they met he'd wink at her to show they had a little secret.

And she was standing there with her coffee gone cold, another dream as real as could be. But she felt better. Diving under the bed, she dragged out the suitcase Patch had given her and unravelled a number of items of clothing until she reached the hidden centre: the big white five-pound note folded into the letter from Mr David which had been delivered by the refugee committee lady calling to see if she were all right. She hadn't been all right. She'd been in her very deepest pit of misery, an absolute burden to *herself* and contemplating gas taps and how many pennies she'd need for the meter. Mr David's letter had saved her. For one thing, she'd had to write the thank-you letter for it straight away and send it off to some man's club place which was his address.

And it had also taught her there were two perfect men in the world, even if one of them was quite agonisingly unreachable.

Chapter 20

Grey frizz of hair tied up in a scarf, uncorseted under her wrap, Madame Lola's vast bulk was occupied in concocting something at the worktable under the window. Filling most of one side of the salon, the table held both their sewing machines, back to back, and they were still covered – so the concoction was possibly the promised hat, Susanna decided, pushing the door closed behind her.

'Not quite finished?' she ventured, picking up Fritzi and kissing his flat Pekinese nose. This was a morning familiarity permitted by Madame Lola's little spoilt prince of a dog. They'd grown attached to each other and she'd almost forgotten she was raised to believe the most pernicious of germs lurked on the private parts of animals.

She sat down at her place opposite her employer. Nothing lay waiting for her to complete in a rush, she was glad to note. Nor was any length of cloth spread on the cutting section of the table. Both facts spoke well for an unrushed morning in spite of the wedding to come – and for Madame Lola to remember without prompt that seventeen shillings and sixpence must be wrenched from the purse she preferred to keep closed.

'Near finished,' her employer replied, pointing to a tiny pillbox covered in navy blue shot silk and veiling. 'What else I got to do all night? I sit here behind nasty black blinds like the government tell me, I wait for this blackout thing, lots of lights in street, I wait for police to come shouting at people, they don't come, you think I could sleep?' She clapped one plump hand to her breasts and waved the other towards the Tottenham Court Road beyond the window to indicate the trials sent her by the outside world.

134

'Well, at least it did take place last night,' Susanna said, trying to compare the navy of the hat with the navy butterflies on her frock. 'The newsagent downstairs told me on my way out last night that the blackout practice might be cancelled again since it had been another horrible stormy day. The clouds must have cleared in time. But the police wouldn't be able to check everyone had actually put out their lights or blacked-out. There aren't enough, policemen, I mean.'

She often found herself explaining matters to Madame Lola, though her employer had left her home in Vienna six years before and was at least forty years old. She knew she often sounded arrogant about it and pleased with herself and that Madame Lola knew it too but chose to allow it for reasons of her own.

'You not run up to tell me might be cancelled?' Reproachful, Madame Lola fixed on her the greatest of her weapons, huge black eyes encircled with dark rings, eyes like her dog's, eyes like Buba's, pools of sorrow that could never be assuaged.

'I'm sorry, I didn't think and just as well, because the clouds cleared.' Susanna dragged her own eyes away and down to the dog snuffling at her feet. 'Shall I take Fritzi for his walk first? That's if Miss Simmons' suit is ready. She'll be calling for the final fit at nine, won't she?'

Taking advantage of the lack of a reply, she turned to gaze round the room, still a source of fascination. More cluttered than Frau Leona's ever was, not only did it hold the usual dressmaking tools – the two gas-heated irons giving out their hissing warmth on the big board attached to the wall, the dummy next to it beside the hearth, and the fitting cubicle with the cheval mirror often clouded with a haze of steam – there were also ranged along the walls, boxes of trimmings, braids and buttons, rolls of cloth needing to be turned weekly against moth and piles of *Vogue* from years past and *Harpers Bazaar* and all the trade magazines British and French. From these at some point had been taken the cuttings which Madame Lola had pinned to every inch of remaining wall space.

There was Madame Lola's absolute personal favourite, Queen Elizabeth, in a pink satin crinoline dress with pink flowers and bows, Queen Elizabeth in mourning after the death of her mother, clothed for an official visit to Paris in pretty mourning white, all white tulle froth and broderie anglaise, white tulle wheel hat, long white gloves. She was pictured in white in New York also, where the white parasol lined with green silk she'd worn had been copied and sold seven million times. Madame Lola had copied it herself for her wedding, but the strange thing was, she never seemed to want to persuade her clients into the Queen Elizabeth style, being far more likely to sell them the slender, understated look of elegance and taste favoured by Princess Marina, who was also featured on the walls. She considered her to be the highest class of lady, as the daughter of a king, albeit a Greek one. She adored royalty and had a big patch of pictures of debutante girls queuing up to be presented at Buckingham Palace. It was her ambition to create evening frocks for debutantes and their mothers and to this end, the plaque on her door stated: MADAME LOLA, COURT DRESSMAKER, although she wasn't yet one. FRENCH COUTURE was also engraved on it, meaning she could copy French garments and often did, with astonishing skill.

'Fetch me bow, feather, something for this hat,' Madame Lola said suddenly. 'You think I got all day?'

Dragging her gaze away from the startling drawings of the 1939 Paris fashions where hour-glass figures seemed to be encased in corsets and tight-fitting jackets curved out over flared skirts in plum and purple velvet and hair was piled up high over fussy little tilted hats, Susanna hurried across the room with Fritzi at her heels and began to rummage in the boxes of trimmings. Settling on a long navy blue feather with a full floating end, she held it up for approval.

Levering herself from her chair, Madame Lola waddled across on her swollen legs and gave one of her lugubrious moans of distaste. 'You want to look like mad blue hen? You too young to stand and walk right for big feather, small feather maybe, big navy flower maybe, but what about bringing the eye *in* to the outfit and not let it have nothing to settle on. Stop the eye going all over, I told you.'

'The eye?' Susanna asked, twisting the feather around Fritzi's neck.

'Match something up,' Madame Lola said patiently. 'And don't buy no more navy. It not suit you. Brown OK, amber OK, gold OK, black when you get older, green best for you.'

With this dart, she swept through the inside door to her living room and Susanna was left with a flash of memory so vivid, she couldn't get up. Dear Mama, she thought, in the perpetual silent message home, dear Mama, don't imagine you and Madame Lola will become friends exactly, she's far too Viennese, but you do have things in common and there'll be plenty for you to discuss . . .

She was so slow realising Madame Lola meant her to find a navy butterfly trim to match the butterfly shape in the pattern of her frock, that her employer had changed into a working outfit before she joined her. This consisted of a flowing black crepe frock with ivory lace collar and dressmakers' cuffs and a black turban with a brooch pinned to it. She had an eye for accessories and the half of the room containing iron bedstead, wardrobe and dressing-table was draped and cluttered with silks, muslins, tulles and antique laces, plus belts, combs and elaborate paste jewellery.

She was skilled at cooking also and was already occupied on the kitchen side of the room by the morning ritual of making soup for the lunch she shared with Susanna. It was the only concession Madame Lola made to her refugee status. After the interview for the job had established the main facts of the past, she asked no more questions about Susanna's family or life in Berlin, gave no information herself about her home in Vienna, and never let a word of German pass her lips.

Susanna just guessed that within the confines of her flat, she had recreated the routines of her own past, and that this, the making of the soup, was part of it. A little heap of carrots, leeks and potatoes was being thoroughly scoured and chopped and thrown into the pan which sat on the stove beside the coffee pot bubbling there. The room smelled like a Viennese café in fact – and sometimes, gloriously, like a Viennese bakery.

The bakery smell meant it was one of the two or three pastry days of the week, depending on Madame Lola's appetite. These were filled with the scents of vanilla, chocolate and cinnamon. Apple strudel was lovingly created, and Sachertorte and delicate puffed-up confections of mille feuille. As the perfumes followed each other, she'd find herself in a state of exquisite impatience, watching the clock tick its way to teatime.

In spite of her resolution not to, she realised she was awaiting next orders with her eyes fixed in fascination on the bed rather than the kitchen table. Unmade as ever, the huge corset thrown on it, a tangle of stockings, nightgown, wrap and unknown hidden items, there was also Fritzi's nestbed of petticoats up by the pillows. Usurped he'd be that night, by some snoring male body who'd moreover want meat for his dinner and would smoke. There wouldn't be marital intimacies, of course, not at their age, but goodness she was going to feel awkward being sent in there on errands and finding him still asleep in the talcum-powdered mess smelling of Yardley's lavender, green liniment and Eno's Fruit Salts.

She actually wished the marriage was not going to happen, that she and Madame Lola and Fritzi could go on together in their enclosed, very nearly silent world.

'A lady no stare with her mouth open,' Madame Lola observed. 'You too tired to walk Fritzi?'

'Of course not.' Susanna jumped into action, taking the lead from the back of a chair, fixing it to Fritzi's collar and assuming a ready position, at which point the ring of the doorbell made them all jump.

'She early,' Madame Lola announced, instantly as always, beginning the process of transformation Susanna didn't dare pause to watch.

Scuttling as far as the door with her, Fritzi took up his waiting position by it as Miss Simmons flew in for her final fitting and Madame Lola appeared from the kitchen, the transformation complete. She was now French and somehow a different shape from the Martha Bock she really was, taller, more imposing, the drooping weariness gone, eyes no longer pools of unknown sorrows but glowing with life and more, optimism.

Susanna fixed a pincushion to her wrist, drew back the curtain of the fitting cubicle and saw the blonde and pretty Miss Simmons take in the full glory of her newly created summer suit, an exact copy in air-force blue and primrose of something Princess Marina had worn to Ascot in a different colour combination.

'Oh, Madame Lo-o-la,' Miss Simmons cried, drawing out the exotic sound of the name as many clients liked to do. 'You're so-o-o clever!'

Madame Lola waved a nonchalant hand. At this moment, she rarely spoke, waiting instead until the client was clothed in the garment and thus able to appreciate its perfection, how it flattered the figure and how the shades she'd recommended brought out the true beauty of eyes and hair.

138

As Miss Simmons emerged looking far prettier and slimmer than in the lumpy maroon suit she'd arrived in, she was ready to mutter, 'Oh, là, là,' more or less the extent of her French, except for 'Belle dame,' which she murmured next with an inward gasp as if to suggest somehow that the suit was the pinnacle of her achievement and the body it clothed, God's.

Part of this scene many times already, Susanna went on standing there in her role of plain, sensible assistant, gravely prepared to appreciate the colluding glance Miss Simmons threw her in order to imply that the two them, ordinary mortals, must only wonder at Madame Lola's genius.

Next to the vegetables on the table now lay an envelope: final payment for Miss Simmons' suit. Resuming her usual self, Madame Lola ignored it and went through the entire ritual of retrieving her handbag from its hiding place in the jumble of her kitchen cupboards and finding her purse in it. Susanna was to go shopping on her walk with Fritzi.

'Fetch us two fresh brioches with the loaf at the baker's,' she said. 'Don't let him try you with yesterday's. We'll have a piece of that cheese from Antonio's and a quarter of butter, the cream like always. Bring two ripe tomatoes.' A half-crown appeared and the purse closed with a click.

Fritzi under one arm, shopping bag under the other, Susanna hesitated too long. In a flash, the handbag was back in some other hiding place and her employer was picking over the leeks. All right, she thought, but I shall simply have to come out with it later: Madame Lola, I need my seventeen and sixpence or I can't pay the rent man. She stared deliberately at the pleating on her turban, willing her to remember and thus avoid the humiliation. And as if she had felt it, Madame Lola looked up with a roguish smile.

'Be quick. Mrs Waddington come at ten to discuss winter dress and coat. She very high-class lady. You talk for me?'

'Of course.' Susanna slipped the half-crown into her palm.

'And you talk this afternoon at wedding for me? You remember?'

'Yes. I have to stand near you at the register office, ready to tell the registrar that through our family correspondence, I've sort of known you all my life and for several years you've been mentioning a widower, Mr Ketley. You didn't want to marry him

139

until your business was established, which it is now. He also had a child at school but now he's free, he's lonely and needs a wife. I am to say this because lots of refugees are trying to get married to English people so they can never be sent home and sometimes the officials ask lots of questions.'

Listening intently, her head cocked to one side, Madame Lola kept nodding. 'Is nice,' she said. 'Is right. But you no say nothing unless man asks. OK?'

'OK,' Susanna replied, dimly aware that bits of pretence were part of this new life of hers but they didn't matter and somehow more important lies wouldn't matter either.

Madame Lola pushed across Miss Simmons' envelope. 'Wages,' she said.

Susanna took it with thanks, not knowing whether to laugh or cry. Each would be appropriate, and the envelope certainly contained more than seventeen and sixpence. Final payment for the suit would. So Madame Lola had come up trumps in the end.

She felt she'd like to say something about the difference in their lives Mr Ketley's presence would mean and how she'd regret it, how the routine of their days together had been a comfort. Of course, she couldn't get out anything of the kind, so trailed from the flat and down the stairs instead.

Pausing at the foot, she opened the envelope. Inside was one guinea and a ten-shilling note: thirteen shillings and sixpence extra. Enough for the sandals and a pair of winter boots for Sophie. And payment for the lies.

Standing there, Fritzi squirming to get out, she searched for good in the bad of the lies and found it straight off: it would mean Madame Lola would become a British citizen and never be sent back to Austria where she would very quickly find herself travelling to the KZ. I am saving one person from the KZ, she thought, so yes, Opa, it is all right, isn't it?

Aunt Daphne would think it all right too. 'Lie through your teeth if it's in a good cause, darling,' she'd say, 'I do all the time.'

This reminder however made her long for Aunt Daphne's laughter so intensely, to be telling her that very second all about her new operetta life, she almost couldn't open the door. She managed it, of course, and a blast of noisy air from the street hit her, and the real world.

Chapter 21

At the corner of the street, past the register office, Susanna stood beside Madame Lola watching the new husband, Albert Ketley, accept the package offered by his bride.

'Ta,' he said. 'Bit hot in there, weren't it? Still, all's well that ends well.' Stowing the package in his jacket, he removed his bowler hat, wiped his head with a handkerchief and replaced it. A thin, tiny man, he wore a suit which didn't seem quite to fit him. In fact, he was so thin and tiny there'd be plenty of space for him and Fritzi on the bed.

She'd no sooner decided Madame Lola would shortly be measuring him for something smarter in the way of suits, than he held out his hand. 'You did good, kid,' he said, shaking it hard. And he winked.

'You can always see me in that pub in Covent Garden,' he then said to his bride. 'That's if there's any trouble, like.' With that, he kissed her hand, winked again, scurried across the road and disappeared behind the two witnesses who were friends of his.

And the solution to the meaning of the word 'movement' somehow seemed to recede with him. Susanna felt there was something she didn't understand. 'But where . . .' she began.

'You did good,' Madame Lola said, setting off in the other direction, her wedding frock billowing out like the sails of a ship, cartwheel hat, parasol billowing out too. She hadn't trained herself to manage them with the delicate charm of Queen Elizabeth. People were staring. They had to get out of the way of this vast area of white silk crepe and tulle and having blinked at her passing, had to turn around to make sure she was true.

Seeing this, Susanna felt her eyes fill with tears in the silliest way. Forcing herself not to pretend they weren't together, she snapped open her own parasol, a last-minute handmade gift from her employer in beige with a navy blue lining to match her dress, and in which she looked the daftest possible. She was too tall and thin for a parasol, it wasn't sunny enough, they weren't at the races, and she also had too much hair for the hat to sit properly. Could it really be an English wedding custom for the husband to go off by himself, and to some public house?

Tottering on swollen flesh pressed into high heels, Madame Lola finally paused by the square at the end of the road, an oasis of railed-in grass and trees. Eye lighting on the nearest seat, she sank into it, exhausted. 'You did good,' she said. 'All right now.' Lodging the parasol against her shoulder, she took the marriage document from her bag and began to read it to herself, mouthing the words.

Exhausted also, Susanna sank next to her with a sense of incomprehension she couldn't be bothered with. She'd just like to stay here a long time, gazing at the Saturday afternoon scene. Laughing with glee, a toddler on a red tricycle was chasing pigeons, an old lady lectured his mother. Two men read newspapers, three girls were giggling over some new shoes. Ordinary people, ordinary life, she thought, without envy, only with the familiar stifling pain in her throat. It wasn't their fault they didn't have to live on two levels, this ordinary one and another underlying one, where a state beyond fear lurked because your parents and grandparents were trapped in faraway countries where terror ruled and you couldn't get to them and they couldn't get to you and no matter what you did, you couldn't make anything better, or different.

Madame Lola replaced the marriage certificate and closed her bag with a sigh of satisfaction.

'Well,' Susanna said, stirring herself. 'At least you won't be sent back to Austria now, even if war is declared.'

'I not worried I be sent back, I worried I be sent to KZ.'

'Yes, that's what I meant.' She turned to look at the drooping face in its inappropriate surround of white, which actually did suit her. She was right about colours. 'I suppose scores of KZs exist in Austria by now. It's months since Hitler marched in.'

'English KZ.'

142

'But there aren't any English KZs, what an idea!' Susanna laughed.

'You think?' The huge black eyes narrowed. 'You wait till you sent in one when war come,' Madame Lola said. 'You want be safe, you got to get married. You find boy. I pay him, you pay me back shilling a week. Then we both be all right. Divorce later. Now, run get taxi. We be late for tea. You want we keep my friends waiting?'

Sometimes, Susanna thought, making her way back to the street, sometimes I have to be grateful that Mama and Papa will not hear of certain things. But after all, it wasn't much different from the matchmakers of the old days, except that this husband was never to be seen again. The three of them could continue their cosy routine, with the world shut out.

It wouldn't be quite the same though. A few words from Madame Lola had changed everything, had changed this English street for her, these English strollers looking rather shabby in the sunshine, the big red buses, the taxis, the bobbies in their comic-opera helmets. Her head swam. Behind all this were English KZs. When war started, some of the policemen, smiling now, would knock down her door and drag her away to a camp.

Chapter 22

'And so it has come, Esther,' Josef said, splashing his face and hands at the kitchen sink. 'The tanks have finally moved on poor Poland.'

She handed him a towel. 'Tell me again what good there is to be found in the suffering of the Poles. I cannot remember.'

'It means Britain and France will be forced to help Poland drive out the tanks because they are allies,' he said. 'And the war will begin and we will be nearer the end and therefore nearer our release from the Nazis.'

She watched him rub some colour into his cheeks, but his eyes remained as pale as they'd turned at some point she couldn't remember either. She only remembered they'd once been as blue as the summer sky and it felt like a betrayal that she couldn't remember noticing the change – for this brought a terrible possibility: she had not. 'And we are to endure getting nearer to the end with no letters from our girls,' she said. 'Mail doesn't cross frontiers in war. We shall be quite cut off.'

He kissed the top of Freddy's head, admired the tower the boy was in the process of constructing on one half of the table and stood at the other end. 'They are cut off from us already. Those precious pieces of paper they send us are not our girls. Every day they grow and learn a little more without us. The tanks actually represent the sole chance of our being together again. That's the awful truth.' He looked at her with his steadiest smile which always gave her such a piercing pain in her heart, she wished he'd weep instead.

'Sabbath's in,' he said, 'I can see a star in the sky. Come and sit by me, Freddy, and Esther, light the candles. I'm hungry and you've produced a feast as always, my darling.'

Freddy clambered into his place and she waved a hand at the poverty of her sabbath table where the wine glasses held no more than a few drops of cordial she'd got from the chemist, with water added, and the soup was chickenless. *I am still clinging on too much*, she thought, covering her head with the scarf, lighting the candles and reciting the benedictine. *I am still trying to pretend.*

As always, the special hush and subdued excitement seemed to fill the room as the candle flame flickered over the silken threads of the challah cloth and Josef, the very tone of his voice conveying love, asked for the Lord's blessing for their children. Yes, Esther thought, I am still trying to pretend, but it is all so deep in me.

'Now sabbath prayer,' Freddy whispered, his eye on the cordial he'd been waiting all day for. 'Then a surprise, Papa.'

The surprise was her poor little attempt at baking an eggless challah. Lifting the cloth from it, she laughed at the dried-up thing, her laughter turning to tears as Josef broke it into pieces as if it were the golden scented dough of all the past sabbaths of her life before these Nazi times brought so many restrictions, so many terrors.

Clinging on in this way, Josef began describing his day at the war armaments factory. 'In the canteen,' he said, 'I overheard that terrifying Nazi, Bleicher, claiming Poland is to become a sort of slave colony with the sub-human Poles trained to be slaves for the German master race.'

'Josef! Not in front of Freddy, please.' But their son wasn't listening. He'd reached out to gather a few pieces of his building things towards his plate and was busy constructing, his mouth open to receive some soup-soaked bread. She pushed a spoonful in it. 'Please tell me Britain is not to become a slave colony, that's all I ask. I need to know we haven't sent the girls away from us into something worse.'

'I cannot, my darling.' Done with his soup, he served himself fish. 'I can just say God forbid. And that it's most unlikely. America won't let Britain be lost. They're supposed to stand for democratic freedom. Once they learn what Nazi brutality is really like, and they will, reports will stream out of Poland, they'll wake up and realise Hitler's boast that Germans will one day rule the world might be more than the rantings of a madman. And they will put all they have into stopping him.' He swallowed his fish in a minute and sighed. 'What I would do for American freedom to feed myself coffee the day long! I suppose my continuing desire for coffee is a wicked one, but smother it I can't.'

She lodged another spoonful into Freddy's mouth and felt her eyes fill with tears, when of course she was beyond tears.

'Esther,' he said, 'I can see you giving your own bread to Freddy. You think that's useful? You starve yourself, we have to go on without you, it wouldn't be fair. If Freddy could understand, he'd agree. What we have, the three of us divide up.' He took the spoon from her fingers.

'They mean to starve us anyway,' she said suddenly. 'I forgot. The ration books have come. Seven of them, different colours, pink for flour, rice and acorn coffee, white for sugar and jam and so on. We are to have smaller amounts of each, of course.'

'Of course. And we must go to the shops for these smaller rations only in the late afternoon when all good Germans have bought their fill and there is nothing? You didn't forget, you just can't bear not to feed us, can you? But we will survive, the three of us. The British are coming, the Americans, you'll see. Aren't I rearly always right?' He put a hand gently on her head as Opa used to do and the feel of it was beyond bearing. Today is a bad one, she thought, for I have taken another step and accepted there will be no more letters from the girls and I have given them up absolutely.

Josef scraped the last of the crumbs from Freddy's bowl and slipped them into his mouth. 'Some fish, darling boy? Rice?'

Freddy shook his head fiercely and considered his tower.

'You know that most days I curse myself for not dragging you to the visa office and yelling at them that you wished to leave without me?' He sat back in his chair and sighed again.

'Yes, but for that you must keep pretending to yourself they wouldn't have kept finding different excuses for not letting me leave. And they would have beaten you for your impertinence.'

'As you say, my darling. Sometimes I fool myself. It's good to mull things over and blame yourself entirely so you can feel that next time you will have the power to alter events, if you're just quick and clever enough. Did Block Warden Mundt come up with his orders today?'

She nodded. 'You are to meet him in the cellar at eight in order to continue with your share of the digging for the air-raid shelter.'

'Well, it'll be a dark, miserable place when we tenants have finished it, my darling, and you need not fear we and Freddy won't be just as safe in our allotted shelter under the stairs. We'll be safer, we'll be able to get out if anything collapses, whereas down there, if the water pipes burst in the bombing, they'll drown, poor souls. For myself, I shall enjoy being in our cramped permitted-for-Jews place because I shall cuddle up to those big, beautiful breasts belonging to our dear Frau Leona. I hope she won't be wanting to take a stock of hats down. Hats are prickly, with all those feathers and bits. You, my darling, will sit comforting the bony little Benjamins. We shall be very cosy together, anyway, we'll sing the old songs – and if they are British or American bombs crashing down, rejoice.' He reached out and took her hands in his. 'But you mustn't start worrying about air attack on Berlin yet, your list of worries is long enough. How was your nephew, Jacob, this visit? Are proper arrangements being made to protect the sick in case of bombing in that area?'

'Yes,' she said, 'And Jacob wasn't much changed.'

'He just lay on the bed staring into space as usual?'

She nodded. Lies, she thought, lies are all I can offer you, Josef.

'Best he knows nothing of what's to come.' He kissed her cheek, took his jacket and cap and was gone.

She couldn't see the last edge of the cap disappearing down the staircase because of the blackout paper over the window. This seemed the most ridiculous loss.

'My cousin Jacob very poorly,' Freddy announced.

'Very poorly, darling,' she agreed. In fact, her dead brother's son, moaning like an animal, had lain on a rubber sheet with an open wound to his head and his hands tied to the bedstead.

'Nurse lady tell us go away,' Freddy said.

'She did.' The nurse had shaken her head, finger to her lips. Please forget what you have seen, dear lady, she'd whispered, and do not come again or ever, ever speak of this place.

And she wouldn't speak of it. I know, she thought, that Jacob has somehow been used for a purpose I cannot fathom, and this is because he is both Jewish and mentally sick and so disposable. I

147

know too that I am grateful Opa and Buba will never learn of his suffering, being dead, God rest their souls. I know also the time will come for Josef and me to follow them east to a work camp from which we shan't return and that I must savour every moment with Freddy until very nearly the last, when I shall give him up.

Gazing at his thin little flushed face in the candlelight, she felt her eyes grow heavier and heavier and her body lighter, as if only the watching over him mattered until then.

'In street by hospital, poor man chased,' Freddy said, reconsidering his tower.

'Yes. Poor man.'

'Yes.'

'Nasty people laughing.'

'Yes.'

'What did paper round neck say?'

'I didn't read it, darling. We had to hurry for our train, didn't we?'

The label had read: I am a Jew. And what had she done? She'd scurried past, searching all the faces of the watchers. She'd found two, a middle-aged woman's and an elderly man's – not laughing, turning away, ashamed.

I need only one face though, she thought, and one good brave heart, to help me. For the rest, I must help myself by letting go a little more each day and each day becoming a little stronger.

Chapter 23

Installed in her chair by the bed, Susanna laid some paper on her tray, the tray on her knees and began to write:

Dear Sophie,
I hope you are not worrying too much about the war news. Yes, war does seem inevitable: I am thinking of it as good out of bad, though, because this very minute, thousands and thousands of soldiers are setting off for their barracks to begin the fight against the Nazis. I know many of them will be wounded or will die, but it is a just war. All the newspapers are saying it is and that finally the 'Nazi hordes' must be stopped from taking over another country which isn't theirs. They've already gobbled up Czechoslovakia, swallowed Austria, murdering hundreds of thousands in both, they've been murdering hundreds of thousands in the KZs for years, not only our people either, and finally it's occurring to everyone they do mean it when they rant about world domination. I only wish well-meaning politicians here and in France had realised it long since, as our people always have.

What we have to hope is that it won't last long. A few months, people are saying, and when it's over, Mama and Papa will be able to come here on a visit, even if the visa papers aren't through. I am not having much luck getting seen at the Home Office, things have become rather frantic there, a lot of desperate relatives are queuing up, but I will be seen – and heard if I can, even though I know an actual declaration of war will mean no more visas go through until it's all over. To me, the beginning of this war brings its end nearer, and the end of the Nazi rule and the suffering of our people and all the others. Meanwhile, I'm preparing for the future by working at the salon, learning my trade and saving what I can towards Mama and Papa's arrival. I've put the five pounds Mr David gave me in the Post Office (and no one asked me where I got it!), and I add whatever I can each week to a little pile of sixpences. When I have a pound, I shall put that in. I don't want you to be too mean with the sixpence Flo gives you every week though. Will you spend some on sweets? I don't think Nanny's very generous with her portions, is she? Save perhaps tuppences and collect them to give to me when we meet next. You could think of those tuppences going towards Papa's first packet of coffee. Imagine his face when he smells it bubbling away in whatever flat I've been able to find them by then. I hope coffee won't be one of things in short supply if the war goes on more than a few months.

You do understand, don't you, that any bombing won't come as far as Dorset, even if they are taking air-raid precautions down there? I suppose they have to, just in case, but there's nothing important to war in Dorset, no airfields, ports, big oil depots. It's the very best thing for me to know you're safe down there, you know, and I want you to think of me being safe up here for the simple reason that London is so well protected. Did I tell you about the barrage balloons? They are sort of giant silver porpoises like the ones in your *Treasures of the Sea*, and they're fixed to the ground on huge chains all over the city, in my favourite parks, everywhere. No air pilot, even a horrible Nazi one, could possibly see his way through to bomb anything down here, and that's without the searchlights which sweep the sky. And if any bomber did dare get too close he'd be shot down straight off by the anti-aircraft guns – they're monsters. Gun isn't quite the right word for them.

It's a nice feeling having all that around me – I feel safer than at home, of course, anyway – and when it gets dark, I sit looking out of my window at the balloons already up there and the pretty beams of the searchlights practising away, hoping my intensest thoughts about you and Mama and Papa and Opa and Buba still get through!

I'm sorry the village children are beginning to say a few things to you now it's plain the country is going to war against Germany and they think of you as German. If you can, darling, be brave and try and make it clear we're not German, though I know it's hard. Try saying with great dignity: I am a refugee, or I am Jewish even. I don't think Dorset country people have any particular hatred for our people. They've never known any. Sidney and Mary didn't before us. I feel we can't expect them to understand the difference really. They've only known their own kind, and Dorset, where they've always felt safe and never afraid and have never had to wonder who they were. They've never been waiting for the knock on the door like us and have never been outcasts. I expect some of them may have been called 'Foureyes', or 'Skinny', or 'Fatty', perhaps which we'd find rather mild. You could try laughing about Hitler like they do. Remember how funny I used to think he was in the early days? Well, I do, you were probably too young.

Whatever else, do what they do as far as you can. Wear your label and carry your gas mask and march up and down with your finger under your nose for a moustache and fall about giggling, then you won't stand out.

Madame Lola won't carry a label or her gas mask. She simply refuses to accept that having once had to leave her home in Vienna, she'll be picked on by fate a second time, which is a very un-Jewish thing for her to think, isn't it? Papa would be delighted to meet her, he does so hate talk of our always being persecuted. And when you think about it, there can't be a bomb clever enough to land just on us.

She's clever though, even if she does pretend to be a slightly mad genius too lost in creation of works of art to bother with practicalities. She's been buying in warm tweed and fur strips, claiming war always means fuel shortages, and as for her dressmaking skills – she just throws a piece of cloth on the cutting table and skims the scissors straight up it. It makes my hair stand on end – yet I'm planning to learn how. Then Mama and I will be able to start a little business together. We'll be so successful, we'll be able to keep Opa and Buba in comfort and put you through medical school. Estanna Modes is a name I thought up for us the other day.

What d'you think? Or Bestanna Modes? This has the word 'best' in it, very appropriate. Let me know which is your favourite.

The other day, I was idly drawing a sketch of the dog, Fritzi, on a spare bit of pattern paper, when Madame Lola spotted it and was most impressed. Far from being cross at my wasting time, she wants me to start drawing if a client describes something she particularly fancies, as well as doing the talking for her. I can hardly believe my sole talent's going to be useful after all. Perhaps my dream of becoming a designer might one day come true – and I'll design for Princess Marina herself, or Queen Elizabeth, and put her into the slim, understated lines I like myself. (Actually, I think she's a little too plump!)

I don't do wicked drawings any more, but it has occurred to me that if I did, I'd do Madame Lola as a truly enormous Pekinese, the same breed as Fritzi, sort of slumped somewhere and immensely sad but covered with frills and bows. Then I began to wonder how I'd do her 'husband' and instantly pictured him as one of those worried-looking dogs Dorset men keep for catching rats. I've only seen him once though. I do hope Aunt Daphne was able to laugh inside when you told her the story of the wedding, even if her face couldn't show it properly. But if there's more and more movement in the stiff limbs, surely that's hopeful?

What does that nurse say? I bet Aunt Daphne absolutely hates her and would knock the spoon from her hand if she could. I can't think of anything she'd loathe more than that woman poking food into her mouth. Keep reading out bits of my letters when you go down on Saturdays, take your school problems to her as well, anything to make her feel she's still useful. Ask her which salon name she prefers.

In fact, if Mr Montgomery does decide to stay at the place in Ireland for the war, I'd feel things were improving all round. And I'm glad the East Wing's going to be taken over for the evacuated orphan babies, he'd never be able to stand the constant crying, or the smell of nappies.

I must stop, darling, my hand's tired. I do miss you and I know you miss me – but don't worry about me for a single second. I can worry about you, because I'm the eldest and

Mama told me to look after you, but I am very happy and comfortable here, and safe, and beginning to earn for the future. Soon you'll be up in London with me and Mama and Papa and none of us will be a burden to anyone, we'll all look after each other. I can hardly wait, can you?

Exhausted, Susanna rubbed her wrist and got to her feet. Dusk had fallen, she could barely see. So it was time.

Checking the key was turned in the lock, she manhandled her armchair, her suitcase, the wooden chair with its quota of damp knickers as far as the door, jammed the back of the armchair against its knob and arranged the rest on top. As always, she pretended to herself she'd forgotten to run down to spend a penny on the first floor and checked the bucket from Woolworth's was in its place behind the corner curtain. Since buying it, she hardly ever used the lavatory in the evenings, in order to avoid the strange man in the next room.

It was when she'd completed this new ritual that her heart would begin to thump, which was the silliest thing, for it mostly behaved quite well during the day. Nonetheless, as always, she went to the open window and leaned out. The city noise was beginning to quieten. Tonight there'd be no horns, no rumble of traffic, no friendly lamplighters wandering along the streets with their poles. There were to be no lamps any more, no red glow to remind her she was in London – only this blackening sky with the sweep of the searchlights and the ghostly floating balloons that certainly wouldn't stop Nazis getting through. Nothing would. And she should know.

All of London was waiting for Nazi bombs to fall and she was waiting for unsmiling London bobbies to come shouting up the stairs to break down her door and drag her to the KZ.

Chapter 24

Berlin, 3 September 1939

'It seems the British warmongers can no longer keep their hands off poor little Germany,' Josef said, emerging from the eiderdown which had covered his head and shoulders whilst he sat at his desk listening to the wireless. He stood up, replaced the cover on their bed and joined her in the kitchen.

'War is announced?' Esther looked up from the table where she was chopping carrots.

'It is. Our Austrian corporal is very cross indeed about Britain and France daring to protest over his rape of Poland and they will have to pay with all-out war. And millions of Germans will believe this messiah of theirs. They will for evermore assure themselves Britain is the aggressor.'

'You listened to the BBC as well?' she asked, before she could prevent herself. 'And turned the dial . . .?'

'And turned the dial back to Berlin, I promise, though I imagine our neighbours will not have their ears to our wall to check on my treasonable activities this morning. I even wonder whether we might be left alone for a while. There'll many excitements to come, battle news, triumphs in the field, Polish aircraft lost: uncountable numbers, German aircraft lost: nil.'

'You have explained the good of the matter to me many times, Josef,' she said, gathering carrot pieces and dropping them into the pot. 'But the truth is that if anyone hears you listening to foreign stations, you will be executed by axe. God forbid.' She put her head in her hands, suddenly exhausted. 'Not only will I be alone to protect Freddy from English bombing, I shall be alone

154

and helpless here knowing our girls are subject to German attack. And there's more. The Nazis will presumably invade England, England's on their list, isn't it? Our girls will be on their list also. In fact, it's probably a Nazi joke to have allowed our children to get to safety, to let them feel briefly safe, and then storm over to round them up. One day, there'll be an announcement, "England has ceased to exist," just as they boasted about poor little Czechoslovakia. "Czechoslovakia has ceased to exist thanks to the greatness and special qualities of the German people." D'you remember? And we'll learn that our girls have ceased to exist, thanks to the greatness ...' She stopped, unable to go further, because deep in her heart, she knew that outside of their own city of terror, soon, there would only be a Nazi world.

'The Nazis will be beaten back in Poland, my darling,' he said, pacing to and fro in the space between stove and sink. 'They'll never cross the Channel. All their mad dreams of world domination will start getting further and further out of their reach, from today. It was the British Prime Minister I heard speak on the BBC just now. Britain was going to fight against brute force, oppression and persecution, he said – those were the very words he used, so it seems to me they've finally recognised the Nazis for what they are, and this is the beginning of the end.'

His skin flushed with some of his old excitement, he leaned down to press his face against hers. She could feel the bones of it and his thin arm on her shoulder, and wanted to weep.

'I have just spotted that Herr Stiller has put out a flag to celebrate war against the English,' she said instead. 'What do they call the English? I have forgotten.'

'Devils. It's one of their rantings, that no race is more diabolical than the English,' he said, looking through the open window to their neighbour's window opposite. 'Now there's a teacher who'll enjoy spreading war fever amongst his pupils. How did Suzy draw him?'

'With a fish eye and a gobbling fish mouth.'

'Yes! I still find it fills me with sadness to think of her drawing out her pain and bewilderment and our little Sophie writing out hers. I wonder if they do it still. I hope not.'

'I didn't mean to show you those secrets, you know, but I couldn't keep them to myself. You realise they will be the enemy's children in England?'

'Yes, but in that lovely Dorset countryside, I imagine the locals will hardly realise where Germany is or much care.'

How he too managed to free some of his pain – with word-pictures! 'Go and play with Freddy on the balcony and let me get on with this soup,' she said.

He kissed her and took himself across the room with his post-KZ walk, half-stooped, slow, his old man's walk that she could not bear. 'You did turn back the dial, Josef?' she called.

'I did, my darling,' he said, getting down on his knees beside Freddy and the Stabilo. You are fussing.'

I am fussing, she thought. I am glad there is something left in me to fuss with and something left to me to fuss over. Eyes blurred, she tried to make out the shape of them against the morning light, having their male conversation. This I must hold on to, she thought, the familiar anguish a sharp pain under her heart, only it isn't easy, because every day, I feel them slipping further away, and every day, little by little, I feel myself letting go.

She was so deep in her reverie that she barely heard the gentle knock at the door and first noticed that Josef had got to his feet, having properly heard, and was coming across the room with a careful, set look on his face which told her something was about to happen.

But the man who stood in the doorway was an ordinary policeman, an old-style neighbourhood policeman who would once have passed the time of day with them. He was also the son of their neighbour in the first-floor-back flat, Frau Hahn, and it was therefore not surprising that he had an air of embarrassment as he stated his business.

'Herr and Frau Lehmann?' he asked, as if he did not know well enough. Once, in the early days of the troubles, she'd mended a tear in a new jacket for him because he'd been afraid to face his mother with it.

'You are in possession of a wireless set which is against regulations,' he said.

She could feel Josef hesitating.

'New regulations,' the Hahn boy said, flushing. He was barely more than a boy. 'I have to remove it.'

'Ah.' Josef could say no more. He led her away to stand by the

156

balcony as his precious possession, his link to the outside world and to hope, was carried across the room.

Stumbling under its weight, Alfred Hahn placed it on the table, opened the door to the staircase and hesitated himself. 'I think you may be receiving another visit this morning,' he said, not turning round to look at them. 'But it's nothing to worry about, only the Hitler Youth collecting for Winter Aid. They'll expect fifty pfennig.'

Then he was gone and the wireless was gone. Josef said, 'At his age, I wonder they haven't recruited him for the SS.'

'His mother wouldn't allow it, not the SS.'

'No. Well, I suppose he isn't tall enough, or blond or handsome enough.' Josef went to sit at his desk with the awful space on it and she returned to her carrots because this loss he would not be able to make into something positive, even for her sake.

She picked up her knife before she discovered the little collection of coins sitting amongst the carrot tops. 'Josef,' she said, 'Prepare yourself for me to tell you a most astonishing fact. Fifty pfenning have appeared on this table and only the Hahn boy could have left them. Can he have worried we might not be able to pay the Winter Aid demand?'

He raised his head from his hands and she felt they looked at each other for a long time, digesting this. At last he spoke. 'Esther,' he said, 'I think he has decided we are his good Jews. You know every German family has one or two. And now we have our very own good German.'

Yes, she thought, her heart thumping, and what a very long time she had been looking for just such a brave and wonderful thing.

Chapter 25

'Hadn't you better have the wireless on?' Susanna said, standing aimlessly in the middle of the salon. 'The Prime Minister's supposed to be going to make an announcement about whether Britain's going to war or not.'

'What I care?' Madame Lola cried, waving a pair of scissors. Still in her wrap, she claimed to have been at work since dawn. 'I got five frocks, two winter coats, three suits to get finished because clients is worried, you think I got time to be?'

'Well, I just thought I'd come and fetch Fritzi and take him for a walk as far as Downing Street. There's people waiting for news outside Number Ten. I went and saw them last night. Some of them are refugees like us.'

'I no refugee,' Madame Lola said. 'You refugee. You go. It no matter to me. My clients wants to run to country to escape but I tell them, Hitler, he'll go east, he want all Poland, Russia, terrible cold countries, let him, we can't do nothing to stop him.'

'I thought you'd like Fritzi to be out for a bit. It's a lovely day, but I'll help if you'd rather.'

'Go,' Madame Lola said. 'You think I need you?'

I think I don't know what to do with myself, Susanna decided, gazing blankly down at the little dog. Making up her mind, she grabbed him and his lead, and was halfway to the door when Madame Lola cried, 'Don't be sad, maybe Mama and Papa on way here already.'

Susanna waited for more, but there wasn't to be any. 'All right then,' she said, a lump in her throat. 'I'll bring Fritzi home this afternoon.'

Shortly she was back in the eeriness of the street which seemed more than Sunday-quiet. She couldn't see a single Italian off to his café in his best suit or anyone hurrying to church in theirs. Most Sundays so far she'd spent wandering around the streets and parks. There were always plenty of others doing the same – and they were a feast for her eyes because she had so much to study in their clothes: fabric, cut, fit, even age. She'd spot styles from the twenties and the frumpy long skirts and diagonal stripes of the early thirties. Veering in her own personal taste now between the clean, fluid lines of Chanel and the starkness of Schiaparelli where a touch of surprise was allowed in a charming little hat or buttons that were shaped like animals instead of being merely round, she permitted herself a silent commentary that was mostly scornful. If there was one word to describe what she saw it was messy. Englishwomen tended to choose wildly patterned and shapeless outfits with braided edging, they flung ends of fur around their necks, often two, so two tails and two heads hung down, they added two-tone shoes and a hat with awful trimmings and veils which must feel as if they were about fall to off.

Yet they must be delighted with their image in the glass and pick out a pair of contrasting gloves with a buttoned wrist whilst failing to ask themselves: what brings in the eye here?

Delighted to have learned to ask herself this question with every female she came across, she had occupation and interest for hours, but if people were to leave the pavements and parks empty, how would she ever get through war-Sundays? If she weren't behind barbed wire, of course.

Gas-mask case thudding disagreeably against her back, she scurried along a very nearly empty Charing Cross Road where the only sign of human activity was a man painting white lines on kerbs and lampposts so they wouldn't be bumped into or tripped over in the blackout, and another one putting yellow patches on pillar boxes, a yellow that would magically turn a dirty green on contact with poison gas. Well, she needn't worry about such problems. She'd be safe from them behind her barbed wire. She should be grateful, actually. How's that for finding good out of bad, Opa? she thought, turning into Trafalgar Square where Nelson's Column was sandbagged up against bombs, the flower

159

sellers were gone and no children were feeding the pigeons. The children had been sent to the country and the pigeons would starve. They'd be war casualties.

Along Horse Guards Parade, the guards weren't glorious in red jackets and furry black bearskins, they wore khaki and steel helmets and were ordinary and so were the policemen. No more comic-opera things on their heads but flat steel helmets against bombs. There were going to be bombs, German ones, and she'd be an enemy whilst these policemen turned into SS and rounded her up.

I am angry, she thought, practically running down Whitehall and getting hotter and hotter, angry for letting myself feel safe and for always searching for good in something that can't have good in it. War. I want to start crying and then someone will feel sorry for me and take me in hand and if I can't stop, which I won't be able to do, they will see I couldn't possibly be a spy and will put me in a lunatic asylum instead, where I'll be absolutely safe and can lie quietly in a cell until the war is over. Christmas, that'll be. Not long. And I am so tired. Also hot beyond being hot.

Pausing to pick up a panting Fritzi, she sat herself down with him in the shade beside some other people on steps opposite the end of Downing Street, and stared resentfully at the crowd waiting there. It was people like them with their solemn earnestness and patience who stopped anyone else enjoying the last few days. Some were refugees. She could pick out the men by the continental cut of their suits and the women by their grooming and the sober taste Englishwomen rarely had unless they were rich or actresses and dressed in couture. She'd be meeting them again probably. They'd be gathered up into the KZ as potential spies for certain. She wasn't a spy. She was too young to be a spy. Any old-style British policeman would recognise that, but perhaps the KZ-collector ones had had special training in brutality and hard-heartedness, like the SS.

Every inch of her skin was damp with sweat. Reaching into a pocket for a handkerchief, she wiped her neck and forehead with it.

'Scorching day, ain't it?' her neighbour on the steps said.

'Yes,' she replied, and looked round at the hot, flushed face of Aunt Daphne's daughter, Patch.

*

With Patch was her childhood friend and flat-mate, Georgiana. They too had been wandering about the city that morning – dressed in riding outfits, having been thwarted in their desire for a last ride from their favourite stables. 'Stable doors all shut,' Patch said, once introductions were done with. 'Horses flown, evacuated, and daft fools, we never thought.'

'Which we should have. Millions of kids were being sent off to the country all day yesterday, why not horses?' A vision of blonde Englishness, Georgiana unfolded herself from the steps, yawned, and stretched to her considerable height. 'Why don't we all go and get ourselves a last feast of something wicked in that café near the Strand, instead of sitting about feeling gloomy?' she said.

Without waiting for an answer, she picked up Fritzi, kissed him thoroughly and nestled him under one long and slender arm. Everything about her was long and slender and her eyes were as blue as Patch's, but sleepier, and smiling rather than laughing.

She hadn't been looking gloomy, Susanna decided, scrambling to her feet, she'd been looking happy and absolutely at ease with herself and very much the mannequin she apparently was, whereas she herself was hot, grubby and ungroomed, from the dusty socks in her sandals upwards.

'Bags the éclairs,' Patch said, scrambling up and linking her arm in Susanna's. 'Hope it's not too early for the cake trolley to be laid out, we don't want stale stuff, especially not if it's our last feast ever for tomorrow we die.'

Caught up by Georgiana on her other side, Susanna realised that neither of them had the smallest fear they were about to die under a hail of German bombs, and that they were taking charge of her because they realised she was alone.

And she let herself be taken charge of. She felt better, infected by their pleasure in the sunshine and the clear blue sky, in life itself. She forgave Patch for her betrayal that evening at Nanny's and decided that Geogiana, the girl so hopelessly in love with Mr David, was the most beautiful she'd ever seen.

Installed at a table in the café, the only customers, Susanna thought they were probably the only three people telling each other funny stories on the day war was to be declared.

She started on her second apple strudel, delighted with the success of her recital of Madame Lola's wedding.

161

'You mean Madame Lola wore a white silk crepe crinoline dress like the Queen's?' Patch wiped her eyes, wet from laughing. 'Golly, George, imagine it, a ship in full sail floating down the street and that tiny man scurrying off in his bowler hat.'

'We'll have to meet this divine eccentric of yours, Suzy. We'll wander along that way later. Got nothing else to do. It's a weird sort of day somehow.' Georgiana blew cigarette smoke into the air with the utmost elegance and leaned back in her seat as if she were at home. 'But you aren't worried about your refugee status, I hope?'

'Not really,' Susanna replied, because of course, sitting there with them, she wasn't. I should like to learn to ride, she thought, and wear riding outfits like theirs, black velvet caps and trousers with a special name I've forgotten, and I should like to learn to be totally at ease everywhere as they are, and blow smoke about.

'You mustn't worry.' Georgiana sat up and fixed the huge blue eyes on her, eyes that made you think you were the only person who mattered. 'You're too young to be classified as an enemy alien, you know.'

Hypnotised, Susanna nodded. I should like, she thought, I should like to have a gold sheen to my skin and straight blonde hair tied back with a bow, and yawn in public and laugh with Georgiana's nonchalance and I should like never to have been a refugee, classified or not. *I want, in fact, to be other than I am.*

'What about that bloke you met from the Home Office, George?' Or the high-up police chappie? One of them'll surely have learned something about the new position of refugees now war is certain?' Patch fed éclair pastry crumbs to a happy Fritzi lodged on her knee.

'You're right. We'll go back to the flat at some point, so's I can telephone. Meanwhile, I suppose we might as well wait here until the dreaded announcement's made. We'll ask the café man to bring in the wireless, I can hear they've got it on in the back.' Georgiana stubbed out her cigarette, inspected the coffee-pots and turned her blue gaze on the waiter who hurried off for more.

Susanna took a deep breath. Recounting the story of the wedding reminded her a problem she hadn't been able to solve. 'My sister's worried about a word she doesn't understand, and I can't find the meaning of. I seem to be surrounded by foreigners but I know you'll know, Patch. It's one of Nanny's things. Every

162

morning she says to Sophie, Have you had a movement? And Sophie . . .'

Patch stopped her with a howl of joyous laughter. 'Oh, George,' she shrieked, 'hear that? You explain, I can't . . .' She put her head in her hands and shook.

Georgie couldn't speak either. She was laughing so much she'd slipped out of her chair and was sitting on floor holding her knees for support.

Eventually Patch managed to gasp, 'Lav, old thing, lav,' and Georgiana, dragging herself to her feet via the table leg, got out, 'Have you *been*?' which made Patch howl the more.

'Have you been?' she repeated. 'Golly, Suze, you've taken us back a bit. That's been every nanny's and every school matron's obsession for centuries and if there's one thing to make a kid constipated, it's that.'

Not quite caught up in this laughter, Susanna took a few seconds to make 'lav' into lavatory and reach an understanding, but she hardly managed a smile. She'd spotted the café proprietor setting up the wireless on a table. Suddenly, horribly, it was time. And war was certain.

'We shall be fighting against brute force, bad faith, injustice, oppression, persecution . . .' the Prime Minister said.

Yes, she thought, at last, so you have understood, at last, at last, and there will be an end to it. Heart thudding, she stared at her plate until the speech was over, seeing Papa crouched under the eiderdown in the bedroom at home listening to the words crackling across, his heart thudding with the same feeling: at last. He'll rush into the kitchen to tell Mama and they'll hug and kiss each other. At last, they'll say, and rejoice.

'That's it, then,' Patch said, as the strains of 'God Save The King' faded away. 'What shall we do now? Bit of an anti-climax, ain't it? And are we going to join up to do our bit, George, or shall we volunteer to drive ambulances like we talked about?'

'First thing,' Georgiana said, 'is a slap-up lunch at the Ritz. Might be months before we can do that again. Come on, Suzy, we'll wander back to our flat and get some glad rags on.'

'I can't come,' Susanna said, 'I haven't a hat and this isn't my best silk dress, it's only rayon and it's crumpled.'

163

'You can choose one of mine, and a hat.' Georgiana considered her figure. 'I may be a bit taller but something'll fit.'

Before she could protest further, they'd linked arms again and were practically carrying her out into the sunshine.

'What a glorious day . . .' Patch was saying when they caught sight of them – a whole row of extra barrage balloons floating gently up into the perfect summer blue of the sky. 'Blimey.' She grabbed Fritzi. 'Adolf must be on his way already. D'you think?'

'Don't be daft,' Georgiana said, shading her eyes to stare up. 'If he was, we'd hear the planes. Wouldn't we?'

They were listening for planes, standing stock-still and squinting at the ominous silver shapes when they did hear something – the wail of the air-raid siren.

'Run!' Patch shouted. 'Where's the nearest bloody shelter?'

Emerging from the café cellar after a dark and embarrassing half-hour of fear-filled imaginings – how much of the city would be left? how many bodies would be lying out there, how much blood? – the first thing they saw in the otherwise empty and unchanged street was a policeman on a bicycle. He had a placard around his neck.

Instantly, Susanna knew what it said: I am a Jew. What else could it be? She should have known how quick the Nazis would be, how many spies they had ready in London to help them, all those pretending to be anxious: for news outside Downing Street, for some. They'd been waiting for the signal to start rounding up the ones on their lists. Jewish people. This policeman with his blank face is Jewish and actually terrified, she thought, and soon it will be me having a label strung around my neck. I shall never see Sophie again, or Mama and Papa, and this is my end.

'Oh God,' Patch said, giggling so much she had to sit on the kerb.

'Should have known,' cried Georgiana, collapsing beside her.

They are having hysterics, Susanna thought, I ought to slap them or something, but I should be the one with hysterics. They'll be all right, especially Georgiana, because she's a perfect example of Aryan-ness. I shall not be all right. I am going to die.

'Here, Suze, see what the label says?' Patch tugged at her skirt.

Susanna forced her eyes back to the doomed policeman. The

164

words on his placard were: RAIDERS PASSED. 'Can it mean the street's clear for Nazi tanks?'

'Don't be daft,' Georgiana replied. 'It means the air raid's over, we haven't even got all-clear signals organised yet and we'll probably be standing up to the enemy tanks with policemen on bikes.'

'But we'll still win, somehow, you'll see,' Patch said.

'And absolutely no brooding, shut in here on your own at night. OK?'

Arms akimbo, Georgiana stood in the middle of her room, having tipped on to her bed the parcel of clothing she'd given her: two frocks, some blouses, a tweed skirt, and the books and diary notebook given by Patch.

'OK,' Susanna replied, putting her gas mask in its place on the door handle. 'And thank you very much for all the clothes, they'll be such a help, and for the diary, Patch. You are right, it's going to be nearly as good, pouring everything about my war into it, and my parents'll have a lovely time reading it through when they get here after it's all over. I mean, even if I could still write home, I wouldn't be able to mention air raids or anything, would I, because of the censor.'

'Not that this morning's was one. Remember that, Suzy, if you start getting scared, there were no German planes over England, nothing . . .'

'Only a very English bungle job,' Patch said. 'We'll bungle lots of things in this war, I expect, and then suddenly, we'll get it right and finish off that little Adolf for good, won't we George?'

''Course we will,' Georgiana said. 'And you did understand what my Home Office mate told me? You will be called to the police station now war's started, just to be checked on as it were, but you won't be sent to any camp. You're not old enough to be a spy.'

'They'll only send possible spies to camps,' Patch put in.

'Yes, but if Adolf does invade, they might call you in again and if they do, you'll still be all right. You'll have us to speak for you.'

'And we'll probably be second lieutenants if we've joined up then, so we'll carry a bit of weight,' Patch added.

'You've been so kind to me,' Susanna said. 'I never thought I'd spent the first day of the war laughing. I'll make that the first thing

I write in the diary, because it's hardly believable. I'll make a list of what I've eaten too. I mean, we didn't even stop at the five courses at the Ritz, we went on to Madame Lola's and had coffee and Viennese pastries there, plus soup for supper we stayed so long. I'd better mention my terror when I saw the policeman and thought he'd been captured by the Nazis, that'll even things up . . .'

'And you could put about how we all blubbed at Madame Lola's when the King spoke on the wireless. I mean, "Now I call to my people at home and my peoples overseas, I ask them to stand calm and firm!" Makes you want 'em to come roaring over in their tanks so we can man the barricades, shoulder to shoulder . . .'

'Madame Lola thought you were very high-class ladies,' Susanna said. 'Very 'orses, she told me when we were making coffee. She'll be boasting about her assistant's high-class friends I expect.'

'Well, I intend to have a winter suit made up, just to see her again.' Yawning, Georgiana strolled to the doorway. 'But for the moment, I'm whacked. Cheerio, old thing.' She turned her sleepy blue gaze in Susanna's direction, waved and was gone.

About to follow, Patch came back into the room. 'Suze,' she said, 'don't forget there's my brother, David, to speak for you as well, if ever it should come to that. He's abroad somewhere now doing something important, heaven knows what, but he has been worried about you on your own in London. In fact, he was furious with me for not seeing you had no reason to leave Downlands and he made me promise to try and find out where you were. You sent him a note to his club but didn't put an address, so I'll be sending it to him now. Actually, listen, he's a wonderful sort of bloke, my brother. He doesn't say much, he's the strong silent type. Loads of girls at home were mad about him, but he never somehow got . . . he was always, I dunno, not happy, or settled, as if he didn't want to take over Downlands, and he and Pa were always in a fury with each other. In a way, this war might settle his future, give him another way of life. Of course, some people are getting married in a hurry and I think Georgie was hoping he might suddenly see her as his life's mate but I know he won't. If it's not there, it isn't. Anyway, I know he is terribly fond of you so remember he's someone to rely on, won't you.'

166

Hands in her pockets, hat lodged by its elastic at the back of her neck, Patch hurried out.

I am exhausted, Susanna thought, lying on her bed dressed in Georgiana's flowered silk frock. I have eaten too much and laughed too much, but I needn't worry about being taken to the KZ or the war lasting more than a few months because everyone here is going to stand shoulder to shoulder to see off little Adolf for good. Only he wasn't really little Adolf. They still didn't understand.

She could hear the last dong sound of Big Ben striking the eleventh hour of the first night of the war. And she could hear the geese honking over the lakes of St James's Park. Imagine that, she told herself, London is so very much more than quiet, it has the densest silence possible, perfect for sending silent messages. Dear Mama and Papa, she thought, I have spent the first day of the war laughing. I hope you have done the same, and can find the good in it, as I am trying to do.

One week later, in a London police station

'Here you are, miss,' the policeman said, 'you just sit down there at that bench and have a proper read of this paper that's called Emergency Orders. Then you can ask me if there's anything you don't understand, but it's quite simple, really. Now war's been declared, you got to try and not stand out or seem not British in any way so as not to stir up public trouble, like. I mean, don't speak any German in the streets and so on, then you'll be all right, a nice girl you are.' He smiled at her. He was nice himself, pink and earnest. Susanna took the paper and sat down on the bench.

''Course,' he said, 'you can see why you mustn't own maps, a camera or a motorbike or a boat, can't you? I mean, if you was a spy, you could soon go around on the bike photographing our war defences and when you got enough information, setting off in the boat to take 'em to Adolf.'

She wasn't sure he was joking, and sat there vaguely staring into space as other refugees went to the desk for their turn. I am an enemy alien, she thought, I am to be different again, I am not to belong. A nasty surge of self-pity was threatening somewhere in the pit of her stomach and she was fully occupied in trying to keep

167

it back when a voice said, 'You look daft with your mouth open like that.'

This didn't really sink in until the same voice spoke again. 'I've been searching for you,' it said. 'And where's Sophie? I hope she's been taking proper care of that violin.'

She glanced up and Max was standing in front of her, nearly the same, grinning all over his face.

Chapter 26

Max's Foster Home, Stepney, London

'And she's got a bloke she calls Mr David hanging round her all the time,' Max said, wiping egg yolk from his plate with a piece of bread. 'He must be the one who wrote a letter to the Tribunal last week and had her labelled Category C Enemy Alien instead of Category B like me, Ma. Still, I had a poor hard-working tailor to speak up for me, not a country landowner's son.'

'If this really is a girl with connections!' cried Mrs Lipinski, Max's foster mother. She ladled him another egg from the frying pan and peered down at Susanna from her position by the stove. Her plump moon face lost its good humour, growing sharper behind her glasses. 'Then she's got to get our boy put in Category C, else he'll be taken away from us come an invasion, and we don't want that, do we, Pa?'

Thin little Pa Lipinski, a man much resembling Madame Lola's husband, winked at her in a kindly, familiar fashion. He did not apparently have much of a habit of joining in so far as speech went, but then between his fat and voluble wife and two daughters of sixteen and seventeen already showing signs of growing into versions of their mother, he hadn't much chance to be heard.

From her seat beside him at the kitchen table, Susanna smiled back. 'I'm sorry,' she said, for his sake, 'but Mr David isn't actually what you could call a connection. I really couldn't get in touch with him and ask him to do such a thing, and I'm sure he wouldn't lie and pretend he's known Max for ages when he hasn't met him – and Max has only been in England a couple of months.' The wonder of it, she thought, is that Max can call Ma a woman who spent her days in this kitchen dressed in pinafore, slippers and hair curlers. Warily, she swallowed a piece of her own breakfast egg. It tasted of kippers. In fact the entire house, crammed somehow with a family of the parents, two huge and noisy daughters and Max, smelled of fish and the chicken from the day before. 'Anyway, Mr David's with the Army in France,' she said. 'He pays for my sister's lodgings and last Sunday he came to London on his way back from his mother to see if I needed anything. I told him I didn't of course, because I have my wages. He wanted to know how I spent them and he took me to Lyons Corner House in the Strand for supper, where I've been going since I came to London because the prices are always listed and you don't need to be afraid you can't pay.' Or that you look too poor to be there, she thought. 'He brought me a copy of French *Vogue* as well. He knows I want to be a proper dressmaker with a salon like Madame Lola's.'

'A Corner House,' Max scoffed. 'Hear that, Pa? One of those places we went in together when you and the girls showed me round the city. What d'you have? The cheapest, beans on toast, like us?'

'God forbid one of my girls gets taken to a Corner House by a gent what's rolling in lovely money,' said Mrs Lipinski. 'But this boy here's going to make us some, ain't he? There won't be no holding him in a year or two. Savile Row's where he'll be, and not working there, mind, owning half the street, that's what. He won't be staying no presser for long.' She ruffled Max's hair with a greasy hand. 'Oh, he's a Jack-the-Lad, he is, but he won't forget his Ma Lipinski when he's got his name up in nice gold letters.'

Susanna watched the intimacy with distaste. How had Max fitted himself so quickly into this family's life as if he were born to poverty in tiny rooms full of too many chairs and too many people, all imbued with the smell of frying, when he certainly wasn't. 'Yes,' she said, avoiding Max's satisfied wink, 'he is a Jack-the-Lad, so I can't ask Mr David to write a letter saying he's of good character.' She took another piece of bread from the loaf in the centre of the table. She was hungry, and it was a long way to Downlands. She wished she hadn't agreed to make this Sunday train trip with him. And why was he suddenly so interested in the country when he couldn't bear fresh air? 'But the whole family has been very kind to me,' she said.

'Except the father, he threw her out.' Max grinned and poured himself another cup of tea.

'You get thrown out of anywhere again, Suzy, you come straight here to Pa, we got place for one more.' The little man wiped his mouth with the back of his hand, stood up and went off to tend his strip of a garden at the rear of the house.

Mrs Lipinski shuffled behind him into the scullery where they could hear her pouring water into the copper.

'Haven't you nearly finished?' Susanna said. 'The Lipinskis very kindly put me up on the sofa last night so we could catch the early train to Dorchester. Let's not miss it if you don't mind. I sent a postcard to Sophie telling her we'd be on that one and she'll be running down the lane to wait for us by the Puddletown road, though why you want to go there, I still don't understand. But since you've paid my fare, I'm very happy to be visiting my sister and Aunt Daphne, and I'll be saved the postage on the winter pyjamas I bought Sophie. They're a make called Viyella, very good quality. I hope she doesn't grow too much, they might last another winter . . .'

'Oh, shut up,' Max said, spreading margarine on a thick slice of bread and dipping it into his tea.

He hadn't changed in any way, she decided, although he had somehow made the hazardous journey out of Germany on his own. He still exhausted her. She'd also had a bad night on the parlour sofa after a argumentative supper and a long evening when she was jostled and stared at by the two Lipinski daughters. They already seemed to have the habit of sharing Max between them as new brother and something else she didn't care to think about. There'd been dominoes, Richard Tauber on the gramophone and talk of films she'd never seen, and she'd longed for her quiet room. If Max hadn't persuaded her into this trip, she'd be retracing every step of her walk with Mr David today. Last Sunday, she'd taken him on her most usual one along the streets of Soho, Piccadilly and the Strand. They'd sat in Green Park and St James's and fed the geese she heard honking on her war-quiet nights. Only her father would take the same interest as Mr David in the things that interested her.

'Finish your bread,' Max said suddenly, getting to his feet. 'We're going, Ma!'

'Go! You think I need you?' Mrs Lipinski emerged from the

171

scullery, her arms covered in suds. 'Mind you're not late coming home. If the cops stop you because you got your torch on in the blackout, you'll end up in them cells for going more than five miles from Stepney. Still, maybe your girl can get you made Category C like she is then we won't have no more worries.'

He blew her a kiss and moved to the doorway, calling up the stairs for his foster sisters who hadn't joined them for breakfast. 'Fanny! Rosie!'

If his mother could see the familiarity of it all, Susanna thought sourly, as the two girls rushed on to the landing barefoot, busts spilling from their wraps, hair in little screws of curling papers – and fully lipsticked. 'Don't do anything we wouldn't do, Maxie,' the elder and heavier Fanny cried.

Rosie merely shot a hard look down the stairs at her, but Susanna didn't care. Shortly she was following Max along the pavement with a feeling of sameness which she supposed might have been a comfort to her, but wasn't. Yet each on her own side had lived through extraordinary experiences since they'd walked together along Berlin streets! Still, it did seem she would no longer feel obliged to look after him; three Lipinski females were prepared to do that.

'You won't like Downlands,' she said, catching him up.

'I will,' he said, 'because that's where my doll is.'

'Sophie's doll, you mean?'

'Mine. I restuffed it. You think it's not enough you let the bloody SS have my violin?'

Susanna didn't answer. She was aware there was something she didn't understand, but Max liked riddles and he'd like her to try and find the answer to this one. She wouldn't. 'How much was the violin worth?' she asked instead, feeling rather over-heated in the brown tweed suit and beret Aunt Daphne had bought her. They'd hurried along the Stepney streets so fast they'd already reached the underground station for Waterloo and then Dorchester.

'Enough,' he said, pulling her down the underground steps. 'Anyway, you obviously didn't lose the tin of Nivea I gave you. Your skin doesn't seem too bad.'

'What tin of Nivea?' she asked, to a gain a minute. Of course, she'd never touched it.

'The one I gave you back home in Berlin to use against the

English winds.' They'd reached the platform, so he was forced to stand still.

'Oh, yes,' she said. 'I must have used it up before I came to London.'

The train swished in with its dirt and noise and by the time he'd chosen their seats, she'd found a diversion.

'If you'd warned me we weren't carrying Sophie's half-size violin out of Berlin, I'd have been more careful and hidden the valuable one.'

'If I'd told you how much it was worth, you'd have been shaking with fright. That violin was actually our future. You surely don't think my Pa wouldn't have had the foresight to try and get something out of the country? That violin would have given us our start. I sold his miniatures to buy it, just as he'd have wanted me to. Can't you work anything out?'

'The ones your father brought round to our flat?'

He didn't bother to answer, pretending to watch the bricks and girders speeding past. 'You got to the end of the Nivea, did you? What did you do with the tin?' His fingers drummed on his knee.

'All right,' she said. 'I left it untouched on the shelf at Downlands. I'm sorry, it was a gift, but I don't like greasy skin.' In her mind's eye, she could see the round blue shape of it on the glass shelf. Mary, the maid, would probably have used it. Yet surely a Nivea tin couldn't be made valuable? She felt nevertheless that she was reaching a glimmer of understanding. 'Is Sophie's doll worth something too and that's why you restuffed it?'

'I wish you'd bothered with the Nivea.' The fingers drummed faster and his right foot began to tap far too close to her left shoe. 'Restuffing a doll would reduce the value of a doll straight away, daft,' he said. 'And it's a cheap, ordinary doll. Even you must have noticed that. The diamonds in it were worth a bit, though.'

Susanna felt her glance dart round the carriage. Had anyone overheard this remark? No. The few other passengers were absorbed in their newspapers. THIRTEENTH NAZI BOMBER SHOT DOWN OVER SCOTLAND, she read from the big-lettered headlines, and GERMAN WARSHIP SUNK OFF NORWAY. She could point them out to Max, but he wouldn't care. And it wouldn't do her any good. Once he'd taken the doll from Sophie, he'd find nothing but Aunt Daphne's cut-up silk stockings inside. The diamonds of course

173

must have been trodden into the sawdust on the railway carriage floor when the SS dagger had done its work. The cleaner would have swept them up as glass.

She waited several minutes, enough for a stop at a station and the entrance of another passenger, before taking a deep breath. 'Max,' she said. 'In the train from Berlin, the SS officer who stole the violin had one of those daggers ... The stones must have dribbled out with the sawdust.' She didn't dare look at him, but she saw his fingers had stopped tapping, and his right ankle perched itself on his left knee. This wasn't usually a bad sign, but dread didn't leave her heart. 'Max,' she said again, 'the doll's stomach ...'

'You think I wouldn't realise they'd suspect everything? I stuffed the diamonds in its arms, daft. Only small ones, I couldn't risk their being heavy enough to be felt. But they'll bring us in a bit, later. Any war makes gold and precious stone prices go up, so I'll wait. We're not going to be slaving away for other people all our lives, we have to get a start somehow. You almost ruined us by not hiding that violin on your own initiative, but never mind, we've still got a chance, thanks to my foresight. You think I'm going to be a presser in a miserable tailoring factory in the poorer streets of London all my life? You want to be like Ma Lipinski, do you, never out of an overall and curlers, hardly out of the house for that matter, and our kids always sickening for something and rats in the scullery and damp everywhere?'

Susanna didn't answer. Her dreams certainly did not include curlers or rats or anything to do with the East End of London. For quite a long time now they'd involved a dressmaking business called Bestanna Modes and its address was Mayfair.

Chapter 27

'Too much wind,' Max yelled. 'Where does it come from? If it wasn't for all these dear little green fields, I'd think I was back in ugly bleak old Berlin, God forbid.'

Beside him on the curve of the hill leading up to Downlands, Sophie held his hand. 'It comes from the sea, Max,' she said. 'Can't you smell it?'

Holding Sophie's other hand, Susanna breathed in deep. The trees of all the copses she knew so well were russet-coloured and orange and gold, and the cows were black-and-white picture-book pretty.

She was back, and it was all familiar, but somehow familiar like a repeated dream.

'I can smell cow mess.' Max dropped Sophie's hand. 'Anyway, where's this Downlands, Sophie? I'm starving and your sister's been going on about the wonders of the cook.' He put an arm around her shoulders. 'You look nice in your new tweed coat. Aunt Daphne buy it for you, and those boots?'

'Susanna bought the boots, Max.' Sophie put out one foot to admire the polished brown leather. 'Mr David pays for me to stay with Nanny but there isn't much over, Nanny says, and anyway, we have to put some aside for war saving certificates, and I like our doing that. I think of the tanks we can build, and the aeroplanes.'

'Well, you are grown-up. The last time I saw you, you were trailing that doll of yours everywhere. I restuffed it for you, d'you remember?'

175

'No, I don't.'

Susanna watched in astonishment as Sophie snatched away her hand and went running off up the hill towards the turning for Downlands. 'You've upset her talking about home, I expect. She's probably got the doll propped up in bed at Nanny's. We'll call in there on our way back to the station this evening.'

They set off behind her and had reached the lane leading to the front of the house, when Sophie stopped and faced them. 'If you want to know,' she shouted, 'Charlotte is gone. Nanny made me give her up for the war effort. Charlotte's been *sold*.'

As soon as they put a foot in the Downlands kitchen, Max's silent rage was gone, replaced by charm, too much charm, Susanna thought, as they, Flo, Bert and the other servants made their way through a lunch of chicken soup, baked fish and crème caramel. In fact, at the Downlands kitchen table, Max stood out like a sore thumb, darker than everyone else, foreign-looking, city-looking, Jewish – and trying too hard to please, when no one else there need to. A surge of the old pity for him made her eyes fill with tears as she watched him wipe his mouth with his napkin and replace his spoon in the right position on the dish holding the caramel pot.

Sophie left her chair to go and lean against Flo's shoulder, because Flo was talking about her.

'And that Nanny,' Flo said, 'fair broke her heart, she did, dragging her doll off her like it wasn't her best love in the world and her comfort.'

Sophie beamed. 'I was brave about it though.'

'You was. Two good days of sobbing and you was over it,' Flo said. 'But I'd never have dreamt that doll had any value.'

'It was very old indeed.' Susanna let this lie slip out because her pity for Max still sat like a lump in her throat. He seemed so wrong there. Where was Max's place in the world now? Where was hers?

'Very old,' Max repeated, giving her a glance of rare warmth. 'But never mind, let's hope the war charity put a good price on it, or maybe it isn't sold yet. I wonder if the same charity came here collecting toys, Bert? I've a feeling a man in your job might have a memory for such things.'

176

Susanna found her sister staring at her with the silent question on her face, the one she was asking herself: what did Max know about butlering? It would be easier, she thought, to just come out with it and confess that Max had hidden diamonds in the doll, but Sidney and Mary's mouths would drop open and they'd get things muddled and decide Max was a foreign thief, an enemy alien thief, and report him to the local police, he who wasn't supposed to travel more than five miles from Stepney.

Bert considered the question carefully before shaking his head. 'They didn't,' he said. 'Maybe they telephoned, all the charities telephone the big houses for their jumble sales, but we cleared the children's things out of the east wing when we had to set it up for our allocation of evacuees. Orphan babies, we were given.'

'Too many orphan babies,' Mary said in her spiteful voice. 'Must be able to hear them, we can, night and day we hears 'em.'

'But it do keep the master away, that crying, and them nurses playing their gramophone.' Flo beamed her loveliest smile across the table and ordered Mary to make coffee for Madam and Susanna who was going to spend the afternoon with her in the morning room.

Everyone got to their feet and began to clear the table. Aunt Daphne's nurse appeared with her luncheon tray and informed Susanna that Madam was looking forward to another nice long chat but she mustn't be tired.

Susanna was vaguely aware of Max asking Bert for permission to see around the house, but she soon forgot all of them and was settled back in an armchair by Aunt Daphne's fire in the place where Aunt Daphne now slept and ate. Constantly searching for tiny improvements in her movements and the glint of laughter in her good eye, she was shortly launched on recounting every detail of her own life with Madame Lola, her walking Sundays and the dark, silent evenings she'd grown to savour. To her surprise, she was able to remember every detail of every garment she'd helped make or seen made, and they were briefly happy again, just being together as they used to be.

But when it was time for her to leave for the return to London, she thought she saw in Aunt Daphne's eyes the same regret she felt herself, for what was lost to them both, and she knew that their separate loneliness was probably the worst of all to bear.

*

'Perhaps we'll have a grand house like that Downlands some day,' Max said, his steps sounding very loud on the Charing Cross pavement.

'So you've told me several times,' Susanna replied. 'And don't walk so fast, I can hardly see.'

'It was well worth the journey, anyway, and of course you can see, it's full moon, daft.'

Barely avoiding a lamp-post, Susanna didn't care to argue. The moonlight couldn't show up everything. For some reason, he'd decided he had the eyes of a cat and the blackout had never troubled him, although she knew he'd once walked straight into a brick wall and hurt his face, as she had. 'Forty people a day are killed in the blackout,' she said, for the sake of it. 'And why was it worth it? You didn't get the doll or the diamonds.'

He stopped, pulled her into a shop doorway and held out a handkerchief. 'I got this,' he said.

'A handkerchief?'

'Don't be daft.' Whistling quietly to himself, he took his torch from a pocket and switched it on. 'I got the sapphire.'

She gazed at the dark stone. It was almost black against the white fabric. 'Where from? Max, you haven't stolen it?'

'It's my sapphire, Suzy. My Pa worked hard to give me a life the same as he'd earned for himself – and this is all that's left. I'm not blaming you and Sophie. I took a chance on the instrument and the doll, and I lost. But I haven't lost the sapphire.'

He was grinning at her, waiting for her to guess the answer to this other riddle. A solitary bus rumbled past like a great noisy ghost, lightless and lampless in the blackout. 'I give up,' she said.

'The maid's room,' he crowed. 'Sophie led me over every inch of that west wing. They've got some pictures that must be worth a bit, haven't they? And some good eighteenth-century silver. I was only interested in the maid's room though.' Lovingly, he rewrapped the stone and slipped it into his inside pocket. 'Maids clear the bedrooms and bathrooms of departing guests. They take anything left behind for themselves long as it won't be asked for – or if the guest is a nobody Jewish refugee.'

And suddenly, from nowhere, came the image of the round blue tin on the bathroom shelf. 'The sapphire was pressed into the Nivea?'

'Of course it was.' He pulled her back on to the pavement. 'And

178

it'll have to do as our start. I shan't try and sell it yet, stone prices go up in a war as I told you, but one day, we'll have a house like that Downlands. You can be a sort of Aunt Daphne, you've got her grand ways already. You'll be all right from here, won't you? That awful lodging house of yours is only around the corner and the moon's making it seem like day.'

He kissed her on both cheeks, setting off towards the underground station with a few dancing steps and a daring flash of his torch because the street was clear of air-raid wardens and policemen.

'Mind you're not stopped and have to show your papers,' she called.

'Oh, shut up,' he called back. 'We'll go to the pictures on Saturday afternoon if you like. You can choose the film. There's one with Joan Crawford.'

Our own Downlands! Susanna thought, seeing him disappear. Max's new dream, his latest dream. Why did she feel they'd all turn to dust? She knew it, as well as felt it, and knew she'd still be watching over him when they did.

Part Three

Part Three

Chapter 28

London, May 1940

'The newsagent downstairs says it's the end of the Phoney War,' Susanna announced, picking up Fritzi and sitting with him in her chair at the worktable by the window. 'He says there can be no more messing about, letting Hitler march into Poland and Denmark and Norway with hardly a gun aimed in return. Now the Nazis have bombed two more neutral countries in the middle of the night and poor little Holland lasted four days, this government's got to start getting serious. Belgium's barely holding on, he says, even with the British and French Armies moving up to support it. If they don't succeed in breaking the Nazi advance, it'll be goodbye Belgium, goodbye France and goodbye Great Britain, great no longer but a tiny part of the German empire instead . . .'

Pausing for breath, she spread out the newspaper and eased aside the folds of the jacket she must tack up that morning. 'And the newsagent says we'll have to have our gas masks checked and the new smoke filters fitted and begin carrying them as we used to. Well, I used to. You never did. I'd better take yours in with mine. Though I don't suppose the Dutch people fast asleep in their beds had time to put on theirs. It was dawn when the Nazi planes roared over and it wasn't gas they dropped but bombs. And parachutists. So there are German troops strolling the streets of Holland now as well as the others, and millions more being terrorised by new rulers, the SS! There'll be Dutch KZs by now I expect, full of Dutch gypsies, Catholics and Jews. I hope none of the Dutch ladies who welcomed our train last year have been rounded up.

They made us feel like children again, it was such a wonderful shock . . .'

And I have had an awful new shock this week, she thought, a shock of fear which she supposed she would rationalise. She was going to have to say to herself, all right, SS parachutists may well be sent to take over London, but they can't float down like silent black birds of doom on every single street, there were too many streets. That's how she'd make the fear bearable for herself.

Madame Lola remained perched over some hand-sewing and made no response, though Susanna knew this fresh daily routine of hers of arriving early and reciting the war news was listened to. Her employer found the reading of English difficult and her wireless needed repair. In fact, this morning, although it was only half past seven, she was already in her summer working outfit of grey silk frock with white lace collar, and grey silk bandeau tied with a bow at the side of her head. Perhaps she too wanted to be in control of herself when the SS came for her. But she hadn't seemed to want to talk about what they'd do, the two of them, if it should happen. Yet she must know they'd float down ready armed with lists of the ones who'd escaped the Nazi regime, and that included them both. And *Sophie*, Susanna thought, a band of pain gripping her chest.

'I no like Dutch people,' Madame said suddenly, making her jump. 'They build no planes nor no proper army. You think they wants to fight Nazis? They is Nazis. They looks the same.'

'Well, there's a nice piece here about the Dutch Queen, Wilhelmina. She's so anti-Nazi, she can't bear to stay in her country with Nazis in it and has daringly escaped by boat. She's just arrived here travel-stained and weary, the paper says, and has been welcomed by King George. She's a refugee like us, a royal one. I don't suppose they'll be threatening her with Category papers though . . .' But is she terrified, as I am, Susanna thought, that England is the Nazis' very next target? Probably. But she'd be able to get to America if there was nowhere else to run, as she and Sophie and Madame Lola would not.

'Take Fritzi and get bread,' Madame Lola said, shaking out the silk chiffon flounces on Mrs Potter's blouse.

'It's a bit early. Antonio won't be open. We've had our butter ration but we do need cheese today. I hope the troops are getting the food we're being deprived of. There's a huge battle taking place somewhere near the Belgian-French border, the paper says, two thousand tanks are involved and the BEF, that's the British Army, is moving up to help the French with a stream of artillery. The French are trying to help the Belgians save Belgium from the Nazis. I hope that's not what's called the front line. Patch and Georgie might be there if it is. That ambulance unit they volunteered to drive for was to go to the front line to pick up French wounded as the French are without ambulances for themselves, I don't know why. Not ready for war, like the others, I suppose. They should have taken Hitler seriously.' As we did, she thought, because we Jewish people were amongst his first targets. But there are going to be many more, millions more. With Poland, he has only just begun and his target is anyone who isn't likely to choose to be a Nazi slave. In Poland, babies had been bayoneted to doors to show how fearless the SS were and how easily the whole world was going to be ruled by them. 'Still,' she said, to keep talking, 'now that my friends Patch and Georgie are out there so all the men can fight, if it has to be women, why not French women?'

'French women not put their fancy shoes near no war.' For the first time that morning, Madame Lola glanced at her across the table, the dark pools of her eyes more sorrowful than ever. 'They got no heart.'

'Patch and Georgie have heart.' Susanna dreamed for a moment, remembering the first day of the war eight months before when the two friends had helped her spend it laughing instead of brooding. That's how she imagined them now, dressed as if for riding, caps pulled down against the glare of the sun, crouched over a driving wheel, edging their vehicle and their war-wounded round tanks and guns, and giggling over English jokes. Were they already injured themselves though? Captured? Dead?

And what of Mr David? He was in France with the BEF. The band of pain gripped her chest again as she thought of him smiling across the kitchen table at Downlands, the frown between his eyebrows coming and going, but smiling always a concerned, attentive smile like her father's which made her feel she mattered very much. I have known two perfect men, she thought, and they are both suffering in some place where I cannot offer a word of comfort, where they cannot comfort me though now, today, I have begun to be really frightened. 'Well,' she said, 'I'd better go for the bread.'

Gathering herself together, fetching purse, shopping list and the lead for a very impatient dog, she soon found herself standing with him by a lamppost on the pavement. The street and the shops had the Phoney War normality everyone had become used to over the last months: sandbags piled up in doorways, windows criss-crossed with tape against splintering, arrows pointing to air-raid shelters. Perhaps the usual people going about their usual morning tasks were also feeling the eerie strangeness of the routine they might very shortly find quite gone. For another might be forced upon them by loudspeaker commands, marching boots and their babies being snatched away to be nailed to doors so the proper amount of fear at SS savagery stops their heart.

Can it be all right to pray for Nazi deaths? she wondered, trying to picture Opa's face pondering the matter. It must be. Because if the Allies kill enough Nazis, Belgium will be saved, and the other countries, and England and all the babies therein.

Chapter 29

Near the Belgian-French Border

And so this is the end, David thought, sitting on a hill in a field of peas from which every swelling pod had been stripped. He watched the messenger reach the lane and begin to weave his motorcycle in and out of the troops trailing along with their walking wounded. There were some with the soles of their boots flapping, a strange sound, so unfamiliar he felt he could hear it over the others, cannon and shell fire in the distance and nearer, the tramp of these long lines of exhausted men making the lanes and roads dark. Miles of countryside he could see from this vantage point, villages with pink and white garden blossom, church spires, clutches of barns, farmhouses, trees in pale bud – and everywhere the black threads, thin far off and getting wider and wider and more poignant as they came nearer with their flapping sound. Some of course made no sound, their blistered feet bleeding into rags. Each one had been burned by the sun, tortured by insects, half starved. They had licked up the dawn dew for water. They had been so seriously let down, he felt that at the first sight of top brass they would find the strength to transform themselves into a raging mob.

Only there'd be no top brass coming their way. Top brass were somewhere other than in this line of retreat. They were sending telegrams.

A few cheers rose as the motorcycle messenger passed them but they were too weary for more. They'd suffered two weeks of moving back so far and no sign of relief but what was written on the slip of paper in his hand – and for too many days before that had had to take pot-shots with rifles at tanks speeding towards them at forty miles an hour.

He took off his cap and wiped his burned and swollen face with his sleeve. 'Any luck, Lambert?' he called to his driver, finished, apparently, with the car that had brought the two of them this far and would surely go no further.

Lambert clambered up the slope between the rows of peas. 'Radiator's holed and I can't find anything that'd stick. Much less any water, sir.'

'No. Sit down, man. The message is that the port of Boulogne is also in enemy hands. A full retreat is therefore ordered to the coast along this narrow corridor. The enemy's north, south and east of us, and we have to make for that column of black smoke. . .' He paused and pointed north-east. 'That is apparently the port of Dunkirk, burning. There'll be no more action for us.' Stupidly, he felt his throat close.

'I see, sir. Anyway, easy objective, that smoke, sir.' Awkwardly, Lambert did decide to sit beside him but he need not have bothered. There was nothing to discuss.

'So,' David went on, 'as I warned our unit when I sent them on ahead yesterday, it'll be every man for himself.'

'Yes, sir.'

'Off you go, then.'

Lambert got to his feet and held out his arm. 'I'll come with you, sir. You'll not manage it alone with that leg.'

'Make for the black smoke, Lambert. I don't need you.'

'Very well, sir.' He brushed down his filthy uniform, wiped his burned and sweating skin, offered a salute and took a few steps down the hillside. 'It's a last stand at this Dunkirk, is it, sir?' He turned and glanced back at him. 'Only the men would fight on if they had food in their bellies and something decent to fight with.'

'Let's hope it's being organised this very minute. Good luck to you, Lambert. See you back at barracks, if not before.'

'If not before, sir. Good luck.'

He watched Lambert stumble off to pick up his backpack from the car, a nice eager fellow from a village in Norfolk, mother a housewife, father an office worker, two sisters, younger brother – and who else to start worrying about? A girl, probably, cousins, grandparents, aunts and uncles. He'd start worrying about them very shortly, once he understood what the order the messenger had brought actually meant. It meant disaster, most of the BEF trapped and useless on the French coast, its equipment, transport, arms and ammunition destroyed to keep it from enemy hands – and the enemy free to turn for an England without defences. How long would it take them to finish off France? A few days longer than Holland, a week or two? No more, because the French Army was cut off, as they were, and travelling down the very same roads.

All right then, he thought, frowning towards the black column of smoke and the hypnotic glare of the setting sun, a couple of weeks more to set up bombing bases and an invasion fleet along the coasts of captured Europe, and there the enemy would very triumphantly be, plunging their nasty little arrows of attack along every road in Britain. Britain would be lost, because its Army was here, trailing along this valley, starving, filthy, thirsty, *finished*, the soles of its boots flapping. Britain would have concentration camps in it. It'd be nothing but a vast larder and playground for Nazi leaders and any British citizens not murdered would be forced labourers, every single refugee it had ever offered refuge to routed out. Susanna, he thought, Susanna with terror reaching right into her.

How soon before the BBC was allowed to release the news that the Army was walking its way to the French coast, trapped, cornered, and helpless with only the sea to aim for? And Susanna began her wait . . .

Already the entire nation was praying – for all the good prayers would do. He took his eyes away from the egg-yolk sun and gazed down at the ball of paper in his hand – the last message he'd receive in this war, he realised, for high command was no more as far as he could tell. But if it still *was*, it needn't have bothered with this last instruction. He'd only had a driver to pass on the first part of it, and he simply wouldn't dare to edge his way down to that lane to try and pass it on to those lines of men with their flapping soles. He could. He could get himself back to the vehicle and somehow prop himself up and yell out the good news: Men, His Majesty the King has sent you a message. He particularly wants you to know that last Sunday was declared a day of prayer and the hearts of the nation are reaching out to you . . .

But that would make then realise their desperate position better than anything else.

Smoothing out the ball and tearing the paper into tiny pieces, he ground it into the earth with his left boot and stamped some torn-off tendrils of pea after it for good measure. It had been pleasant sitting here amongst all this growth, he realised. He had smelt the dry soil and the fresh green-ness of a field as yet undamaged except by the first few stragglers of the retreat. How soon before tank and cannon got here and churned it up?

He must hurry; he could hear them not far off beyond the blossom and the neat red roofs and the black threads of the men. When would they come to an end, when would a break in the threads show him the enemy had got far enough to be taking prisoners?

He must hurry. He edged his left boot right up against his left thigh to get some leverage and began the inch-by-inch task of easing his right heel nice and firm into the ground. The devil of it was to force himself upright on to it and then somehow set off, dragging the stiffened thing that was his right leg into first one step and then another. He had to make for the column of black smoke that was the port of Dunkirk, burning, and it was thirty miles away. And he had to get home.

Chapter 30

London

'Any news of that boy Max?' Madame Lola enquired gently. This morning, she was making an effort at conversation when it was obvious she wanted to keep her mind on her creations as she usually did.

'None,' Susanna replied, laying out the pieces of Mrs Macpherson's silk crepe blouse on the ironing table. 'And no letters from us are allowed, in case we pass on war information to him, or he passes us some which we send to Germany, but if it was thought either I or his foster family would do that, surely we'd have been arrested too, so I don't understand . . .' Her voice tailed off. 'I don't know what they think any of us could get up to, but the rule is, no letters either way. We assume he's in some KZ, and I try and convince myself it's not like a Nazi one. His foster mother, Mrs Lipinski, has been going to the police to demand why he was arrested although he's so young, but the rule is Category B Enemy Alien males between sixteen and sixty had to be rounded up once Belgium fell to the Nazis because that means England might fall now. And I suppose we aliens will rush out with open arms to welcome the parachutists and tank drivers and cook them a boiled pork and cabbage supper to help them feel at home – which can only make you wonder what the English authorities believe we had to come here for.' Yes, she thought bitterly, why does no one bother to ask themselves that?

She began to edge the iron along the seams of the bodice. 'If this new Emergency Powers Act is going to include an order Category C females be rounded up, Max will find that the best of

191

all jokes.' Except that he may never hear of it, she thought; he is somewhere unreachable in a prison camp, behind barbed wire, and perhaps this very minute a camp for female aliens is being prepared and I shall be in it when the most feared, the most unthinkable thing actually does come to pass.

She draped the bodice on the dummy for the sake of neatness and started on the cuffs and the long strip of fabric which was to form an unnecessary and useless flounce. One's body did go on doing things as if of itself. She learned that the first day she and her mother had helped Opa and Buba leave their home for ever and walk off into the darkness. I am of good stock, she thought. I will go on working, as if for the future, although the official warning has been given out by the government, and I now know it wasn't some silly imagined fear of my own, which I probably believed it safely was. The official warning had simply and baldly stated the very words of her personal nightmare: 'parachute descents on England are now extremely likely'.

Shortly she was back in her chair, one knee propped on the rung, launched on the task of hand-sewing the hem of the flounce Mrs Macpherson wanted for the neck of her blouse, although no one with her waist and chest measurements should choose a flounce – or indeed the tiny flower design in the crepe. Of course, parachute descents on Soho would mean this particular garment would never clothe Mrs Macpherson's barrel-like body, because the dressmaker's assistant would never finish it.

A light summer breeze was blowing in from the open windows, enough to cool the skin without disturbing anything. She could hear a bus rattling past the corner of the street. There was vanilla tart for tea and all was Phoney War normal, except that the BEF and the French Army were losing their rearguard action in France. The Nazis had taken Holland and Belgium and were pushing both armies right into the sea at a French port called Dunkirk.

In and our flew her needle, in and out flew Madame Lola's needle, the iron hissed, the clock over the mantelpiece ticked the minutes forward . . .

Where were Patch and Georgie now? Captured by the Nazis with their ambulance and their wounded, shackled and used the way troops used women, then thrown aside to die the way Nazis threw away people? And Mr David, he must be lying dead on

192

some canal bank – the BEF had been defending various canals for weeks past – lying dead, then, body pierced by shell wounds, a bloody swastika carved into his chest.

'I forgot to tell you about Hitler's speech reported in the newspapers yesterday,' she said, biting off her silk and rethreading her needle. 'He actually addressed it to the poor struggling French, if you can believe the cheek of such a thing. 'People of France, cease thinking the world is with you, the world is overwhelmingly ours.' Jackal Goebbels will be shrieking that out endlessly on Berlin radio, can you imagine!'

I can imagine Papa repeating that to Mama, she thought, and their both searching for the good out of such evident bad and being unable to find a glimmer.

Madame Lola got to her feet and made her way to the kitchen, followed by Fritzi. Good. It was time for the vanilla tart and perhaps one or two of the little choux puffs from yesterday. She could still eat. She must eat as much here as she could get down, because she wouldn't be able to go as far as the Strand or Marble Arch Corner House any more. She'd have to have supper in Soho where nearly everyone was a foreigner if not a refugee. The worst would be for someone to point at her in the street, but no one pointed in Soho.

Eyes blurred, she gazed at the kitchen doorway, listening to the clatter of the cups. She had failed to find the courage to read out the headlines she'd seen splashed across certain newspapers that morning. There was no need for her to know yet, and anyway she was no longer an enemy alien. She was a British subject, Mrs Albert Ketley, and as always, she'd been cleverer than she seemed.

'NEVER MIND CATEGORY THIS AND CATEGORY THAT' the headlines shouted, 'THEY'RE THE ENEMY, AREN'T THEY? DON'T WAIT FOR THE INVASION, LOCK 'EM ALL UP!'

And the only good to be scraped out of those was that her parents would never feel the shock of them and never learn their daughter was creeping along the streets of London just as she'd had to do in Berlin.

Chapter 31

Dunkirk, on the French Coast

Behind him, the rest of Dunkirk town was more or less rubble, and beyond this beach where he lay with most of the British Army and some of the French, the sea was on fire.

He had somehow stumbled thirty miles and now, his body scorched by the sun, swollen and throbbing, David lay in filthy sand, watching the sea burn.

The sea was a shelled and bombed salt-water graveyard of the craft that had been crossing the Channel to ferry the troops to England. Flames licked along its oily surface, in and out of the broken vessels, and roared up into columns of fire hundreds of feet high. There were spirals of boiling water from the ships' burst geysers throwing up sailors and sailors screaming as they were scalded and thrown back to drown.

I am witness to hell on earth, he thought in a fever of thirst and pain, his head against something, the wheel of a truck that had got that far. Under its upturned carriage was the body of a major from the artillery who had half-crawled the last few thousand yards with him and whose chest had been pierced by a fragment of shrapnel.

Around him were propped many more dead and dying and a whole messy litter of defeat, every truck and tank smashed, every cannon and machine gun destroyed to prevent the enemy's gleeful, triumphant use of them.

Packed along the beach and far out into the dirty sea, the defeated were queuing in uncountable numbers, thousands and thousands. Half the fighting men of England, the walking

wounded, the survivors, the ones not yet gone mad with thirst and
fear, were queuing for a miracle, for one of the ships to churn its
way into the bay, around the lost vessels and their lost companions
and somehow zig-zag under the shell for long enough to send in
the tugs to lift them out.

But here they came again. The ten-minute respite was up. You
could hear their high-pitched whine over the screams of the dying
and the man who thought he was a Red Indian and the horses
ridden down to the beach to die. He felt his body tense and
wondered how, in its misery, it could have this left, this remnant
of will urging him: run, run.

He could not run, and if he could, there was nowhere to run.
This was the farthest edge of French soil.

Behind him, a young lad cried for his mother and down by his
feet, a corporal from the gunners raised his voice to repeat to the
boy he'd pushed there in a wheelbarrow. 'I told your old mum I'd
get you home, didn't I, Tom, didn't I, well, take an eyeful of that
bloody great destroyer out there, Tom, it's going to pick us up
soon as this next lot's gone over, let's just block your ears up.'
Tenderly, he reached into the wheelberrow to put his hands over
the dead ears and an artillery sergeant perched on top of a half-
buried truck yelled, 'Come on down, you buggers, you bloody
cowards, come on down and fight fair and square!'

Suddenly the high whine became a roar, the black shapes were
fouling the sky to the east, the smoky light was cut and the black
shapes spread out into fighters, bombers, dozens and dozens, and
the hail of shell and machine-gun fire spattered along the beach.

David recognised a swelling of sorrow. He realised he was
about to weep, that he was weeping, and dimly, realised his last
sight of the world would be these massed lines of dirty, defeated
men, their only weapon a sand-and-waterlogged rifle held up in
rage and helplessness.

Chapter 32

Berlin, July 1940

'Victory! Victory! Victory!'

Standing well back in the crowd, Esther heard the cheers and the music of death and the tramp, tramp of the boots. She could just see, through the clouds of confetti and the waving flags, the tanned young faces under the caps, the ever-onward flash of rifles.

Some mothers are happy today, she thought, and some mothers bereft, their sons buried on the battlefields of foreign countries. No, German countries. She corrected herself. Not Holland now, or Belgium, but more German Protectorates. And France, beautiful France captured by these young men, a Nazi commandant ruling Paris.

The boasting and the years of ranting had finally come to this, a triumphal march, more flags, more cheers, and champagne in Berlin, and scented soap. Of all the wonders the market women's gossip claimed had been brought back from France, scented soap, or just soap, was what she most missed and craved. Chanel No. 5, they could splash it on themselves, those soldiers, or give it to their mothers or their sisters – silk stockings too.

I should not care to covet silk stockings again, she thought, sun beating on her hat, the throb of the music and the marching boots in her ears, especially not silk stockings stolen from the women of France, but a little edge of soap stolen from them maybe. I would keep it on the side of the kitchen sink, just to remember such things did and do exist, just to feel that even for us they might one day exist again. This would mean of course that there would be no more of these triumphal processions in Berlin. I must not wish that more German women will be grieving for their sons and husbands, God forbid, but that is what I must see as a possibility in order that my girls, and my son, will be able to go into a Berlin store and buy a scented tablet of soap for themselves. It will be possible. It will be permitted.

'Mama!' Freddy tugged at her skirt.

'Yes, my darling?'

'Can I stamp my feet, please, to the music?'

'Yes.'

He blinked up at her, his blue eyes like Josef's, like Sophie's. 'I am not allowed.'

'We won't tell Papa.'

Tentative, his eyes sparkling, he lifted one foot and then the other in the too-big boots that had been Sophie's, girls' boots, and did boys' things, pretend-marching, making a noise. 'It's for victory?'

'No, for the sunshine and the music.'

From behind her came Frau Hahn's voice suddenly, startling her. 'I have what we've been talking about, Frau Lehmann.'

'You are so kind.' Quietly, Esther made an ordinary reply to this ordinary remark. She edged herself backwards a few centimetres, away from Freddy, and let her eyes glance about. People were moving off now the parade was nearer its end. If only Suzy could see me giving my Berliner glance, she thought, how she would laugh, and how she would kiss me, and how proud I shall be, recounting all this to her when we meet again.

There, it was done. She felt the merest of movements in the region of her waist.

'I have slipped it into your shopping bag.'

'Thank you, dear lady. Be careful, for yourself.'

'As you must be. And when I sell you something at my market stall, don't be silly and thank me if I slip a miserable turnip or carrot or two in with it. I don't want thanks. I'm am old Berliner, I have to make my gesture against that lot out there defiling our streets.'

She was gone. Trembling, Esther forced herself not to look back and watch her old neighbour and new friend scurry off home. Their friendship was begun in the laundry cellar of the flats when Frau Hahn had dared ask her if she might share the laundry day permitted to her. This in itself was an act of defiance. Since then,

197

it had grown from whispers and more daring. God keep you, dear Frau Hahn, she thought, tears of weakness and relief and fear ready to spill out. And God keep your son who brought to you the paper in my bag. To think that the boy whose new jacket she'd mended because he was afraid of his mother's wrath should be the instrument of *so much*. In the widow Hahn and her son, she realised, she had found what she'd been searching for: goodness. How very much they risked, the two of them!

And how far forward she was now in her plans. But she must deny herself the merest glance at the precious piece of paper until she was safely home. She must be vigilant with herself, more vigilant than ever.

Chapter 33

Green Park, London, August 1940

'My father would be passionately interested in the battle for London,' Susanna said, 'and I try to take it all in, so I'll be able to describe it to him later. He loves skies, you know, the way they're constantly changing, and I think he'd like to follow the pattern of the smoke trails left by the fighters trying to shoot each other down.'

She raised her arm and pointed towards the south-east. 'Day after day, you can watch them over there, and hold your breath, and try to imagine the poor pilots.'

From his chair beside her, David gazed at the slim beauty of the raised arm, at the tender skin of it, at the profile thus revealed to him, strong, and lovely, at the independent hair curling around her hat. She was fond of hats, he knew, she had spent happy hours at home with a milliner. He noticed the hat, it was a gold sort of colour and lodged on her forehead in the jauntiest manner possible. It had a flower, silk, and this flower was the same shape as the flowers in her dress, a swirl of a thing, gold too, and amber.

'Of course, I'm silly enough to keep on listening to the BBC reports on Madame Lola's new wireless. They sort of give the scores, don't they, thirty-five RAF planes lost to seventy-three enemy fighters, and I feel a surge of gladness and hope for the RAF being able to save the city, and therefore England, and us. Then I have to ask myself what my father and grandfather would think about my rejoicing over deaths.'

She looked down at the grass at their feet where sparrows pecked for the breadcrumbs she'd brought with her. 'I also wonder if I actually went to school with any of the Messerschmitt pilots or gunners I long to be brought down, because those aircraft come from my home. Or what was my home. I'm sure I'll never return there even if the Nazis are driven out, yet here I'm Category C Enemy Alien and don't belong at all. I sometimes feel I'm suspended somewhere, or nowhere. And quite by myself. It's just self-pity, isn't it?'

His heart turned over. She needs me, he thought, oh, God. I just have to open my mouth and begin. It doesn't matter that I'm not Jewish, that she is so young, she isn't young in experience or in strength. Susanna. He was forming her name, to begin, when she shouted, 'Fritzi!' and shot off towards the pond behind the dog who'd spotted some other canine. *Susanna, you belong with me. Will you feel you belong if you're with me*? Begin straight off, with something like that for heaven's sake.

Yes! It was so simple. Gazing helplessly after her, he tried to get his old man's stiff leg to move. She was going to notice all over again what a pitiful wreck he was. Blasted dog, he thought, searching for some less dramatic approach, a less bald one. It would have been all right if he'd said it straight off, if the dog hadn't been a dog.

'You're to have another operation on your knee?' She had noticed his old man's struggle and was trying not to show it, re-establishing the animal under her chair with a murmuring of love he'd dreamed of for himself far too often.

'Yes,' he muttered, 'they're to have a go at removing the splinters of shrapnel. It was too much of a mess before. I've only been allowed my freedom to attend to some family matters and make this trip to London for a new uniform.' And to see you, he thought, and to tell you how it was for me, lying in that filthy sand on Dunkirk beach, all shot about, near to death, and realising the last ships were turning about to leave without me and the SS would be after you because we'd lost the war and I'd never be able to save you. Mrs David Montgomery of Downlands, Dorset, he thought. You'd belong then, my darling girl. For her, he'd reclaim what in his mind he'd given up the right to.

'The uniform's very smart. And a perfect cut and fit.' Finally done with giving the dog the fuss he deserved himself, she sat down beside him and spared the jacket a glance. 'Madame Lola admired it, I could tell, when you called for me.'

200

'I could have had it sent on, of course, but one feels awkward in the country without a uniform. The locals tend to speculate on why you're not engaged in their defence.' He should have kept the bloody shreds of the last one, the one they cut off him after Dunkirk. She'd spare him more than a glance of pity then.

'But you're war-wounded! That dreadful wound to your face . . .'

'Yes,' he said. She'd hardly glanced at that either, and didn't now, couldn't. He drew down his cap as if to hide what couldn't be hidden.

'You're not too hot?' she asked, nurse-like. 'Shall I help you move under the trees?'

I want more than a nurse, he thought, a sudden gloom redescending on him. And I shall never have it. But me, looking after her, that is what I can have, still. He said, 'I hope you aren't worrying too much about the Category C business, because you will be able to apply for British citizenship, eventually, your entire family will, and you'll settle as refugees have always done.'

'Yes. Jewish refugees are always having to settle somewhere, we've been wanderers with no land of our own except Palestine and we're not wanted there. It's a bit special though, here, now, because not only have Sophie and I been driven out of a place we assumed was our own, we are being pursued. From the skies.' She pointed up at the sky again and laughed. 'I expect you were too ill at the time, but after Dunkirk, the news broadcasts gave out the awful words: "Invasion is imminent," and once, the warning not to leave our homes and take to the roads like the French and Belgians had done because we would also be machine-gunned from the air.' She laughed again and turned towards him with her lovely eyes full of tears. 'I'm not very brave.'

'I think you are brave,' he said, 'I think you needed tremendous courage to come here with your sister to care for and your way to find, Susanna, if only you had not left the village as you did! If you'd waited there for me to get home, I'd have found you somewhere better than Nanny's in the village and you'd be safer in Dorset today.' This is the beginning, he thought, a great well of feeling rising in him. He sat up and leaned towards her.

'You had enough to do,' she said, blinking away the tears and pretending to shade her eyes from the sun, which didn't fool him. 'I knew I had to try and deal with the visa papers for my parents since Aunt Daphne could not and time was running out. I hide a lot of problems from myself, but I did realise time was running out last August. And I was right. I never did get the papers through.'

'Susanna, if you had given me time!' Surely she could see, could guess, how he felt? Give me one word, he thought, one simple gesture.

'Well, time's running out now,' she said, getting up so quickly she'd almost brushed him aside. 'Your watch says twenty to two and my friend'll be furious if I'm late. We only have Saturday afternoons together.' She began to busy herself with brushing off her skirt and brushing off the dog who was stuck about with grass and burrs.

Yes, he thought sourly, and Susanna, you are bored by a cripple and sitting in a chair with the guardian you think of as a father-figure and you want to be off for a light-hearted afternoon with your friend. He watched her little thank-goodness-I-can-be-off movements, and with as much strength as he could muster got himself out of his chair and picked up the stick, blackest depression lodging itself somewhere in his chest.

'Saturday's the day we've always had to meet,' she was saying, as if she hadn't made it clear enough. 'If you could call any other day in future, I'm sure Madame Lola will give me a few hours off. Or another Sunday would be nice perhaps, because Max would be furious if I didn't see him on Saturdays.'

Max. He'd assumed a girl, and he was a fool, and a cripple to boot, a scarred cripple.

'He was the same in Berlin.'

Worse. A friend from home, a past in common, the miseries of the last years there, Jewishness in common.

'And we have to meet somewhere smart like Piccadilly as we used to at home. The Ku'damm boulevard was his favourite. He's someone with grand dreams, Max, and I've been part of them since we were nine and ten or so because it's sort of been assumed we'll marry.'

Somehow he got himself up to the path and limped along it at a snail's pace, dragging his leg like an old man, bent over a stick, whilst she forced her whole and healthy legs to a snail's pace to match, and then he'd shaken the hand of the boy she was destined to marry.

*

'That's the famous Mr David, is it?' Max said, leading her to a table in their favourite Corner House in the Strand. 'You didn't say he was a cripple.'

'He isn't a cripple,' Susanna said. 'He's war-wounded, how could you?'

'Easily.' Max slumped himself down in the seat opposite. 'I bet you've given him a nicer welcome back from his battlefield than you ever did me from my KZ. What did he do? Just arrive at the salon door? Must have given you and La Lola a shock, an ugly scar like that on his face and clutching a stick. A real war hero!' He picked up a menu. 'I'm starving. I hope you have some money with you. I haven't been able to earn any yet, I don't start work again until next week, and you weren't sent to a KZ, were you?

'No, but as it happens, it was more like a holiday camp than a prison and anyway you were let out pretty quickly.' She wished she'd been able hold Mr David's arm. It hurt him to take a single step, yet he'd come to see her. He'd set himself to take his mother's place, and he had. If there was anyone else she'd be able to spill out all those girlish fears to, it was Aunt Daphne.

'What money have you got with you?' Max said.

'Enough for a fruit bun and coffee each, that's eightpence, ninepence each for the cinema, so don't bother with the menu.' Everyone is suffering the same fears, she thought, it is nothing to be ashamed of, to fear being machine-gunned from the air, but that's precisely why there's no need to go on about it. It's almost bad taste, in fact. And it isn't English. They just talk about how they're not going to give in. 'I'm surprised you haven't wormed a few shillings from the Lipinskis. They were desperate about getting you released. I hope you've thanked them properly.' I have never thanked Mr David enough for anything he has done, she thought. He doesn't let me. He just draws other things from me I hardly knew were there. He does it with the way he gazes straight at me, as if I mattered very much.

'They love me like their own son,' Max said, launching into a long tale about Mrs Lipinski's miscarriages.

She could have told Mr David how often in the Dunkirk days she'd run across Waterloo Bridge and hung around the station to see if he were one of the men brought back across the Channel. She'd lived then with a tight band around her chest, caused by willing him not to be one of those left behind to die alone in some Nazi hell, and dread that he would be.

Waiting for news of him had brought back all the misery of waiting for news of Opa and Buba when they had disappeared into the darkness of Poland, and it had seemed to her time might drift on until months of it had gone by and he was going to vanish into the darkness, as they had.

'What film d'you want to see?'

'You choose.' She had no desire to sit in a cinema. Most in the world, she'd like still to be sitting with Mr David in the park, to be sitting there until the sun turned into a red ball over by Victoria.

'I wish you wouldn't bring that dog with you.'

She put a protective hand on Fritzi's head. He was looking forward to currants and a lap of coffee. 'He's a help in the blackout,' she said. He's my "wear something white so you can be seen".'

'You just like there being no notices. You think, Here I am, allowed in a café like I was someone wanted and I am bringing in a dog . . .'

'I certainly don't.' She didn't give him the satisfaction of receiving the full spite of the glance he shot at her across the table. He was at his most restlessly angry. The KZ had hurt his feelings, or the fact of his having taken there.

But they wouldn't be talking about it, or about the old days of DOGS AND JEWS NOT ADMITTED notices, or the great blank wall between them and her parents and his mother.

Or the rumour that Jewish people were being sent to work camps to labour for the Nazi war, because they never did.

She thought: If I could sit with Mr David in the park until the sun went down, I could tell him all about my foolish fear that my parents will never be able to come here, and that the Nazi darkness is going to cover us all.

In fact, the very best thing to help her go on enduring what had to be endured would be to see him limping along the pavement outside the café that very minute and coming inside and calling her name.

'What are you crying for now?'

'I'm not crying.'

'Yes you are.'

Chapter 34

Berlin, 7 September 1940

'It's a repeat of Hitler's speech of the other day,' Josef whispered. 'Listen.' On his knees, half-in, half-out of the wardrobe, he increased the volume of the wireless he had cobbled together from spare parts left from his repairing days, 'The speech he made when Nazi bombs went beyond their usual oil depot targets, attacking London itself, and the RAF came to Berlin.'

Sitting on the bed, Esther leaned forward. The man's voice came far too loud, making her heart thump with loathing and dread.

'In England they are filled with curiosity and keep asking: why doesn't he come? Be calm. He's coming! For three months I didn't answer because I believed such madness as this war would be stopped. Mr Churchill took this for a sign of weakness but we will raze their cities to the ground, we will stop these night pirates. When the British air force drop three or four thousand kilos of bombs, we will in one night drop two hundred thousand, three hundred, four hundred thousand kilos of bombs . . .'

By now, the fist would be thumping the podium, the veins in his face standing out as if they would burst. 'It's to start this very minute?'

Josef nodded. 'Goering's going to speak. He's apparently standing on the French coast watching waves of bombers go over.' He increased the sound a fraction more and the words of the chief of the Nazi armed forces crackled through.

'I have come to take personal charge of the battle. The target is London, a stroke straight to the enemy's heart . . .'

He shut off the sound with a snap and covered up his most precious possession with hers, the eiderdown her mother had sewn for her dowry, a delight of embroidered linen with panels of Brussels lace.

'And this is in retaliation for the RAF reply to the Nazis' first bomb on London?'

'Yes, but RAF bombers can barely reach Berlin whereas the Nazis planes are only twenty miles or so across the sea from England. That's one of the triumphs of their capture of France.' He got stiffly to his feet, closed the wardrobe door and dragged the dressmaking dummy across to its place.

'You are sure, Josef?'

'I am sure, my darling, that only a radio expert would spot my collection of wires might be able to pick up radio waves. I promise.' He sat beside her on the bed and put an arm around her waist. 'I know what's in your heart now, but what you must remember is that our girls are safe in a manor house hidden in a valley many miles from the city of London.'

'Yes,' she said, 'but you cannot promise me, can you, Josef, that once they have razed London to the ground with their twenty-mile-away bombers, they won't be lining up all those barges you say they'll need, barges stolen from the Dutch, Belgians and French, jumping into them in their thousands and cruising across that little strip of sea called the Channel?'

She leaned her head on his shoulder. 'There's nothing to suggest an invasion is imminent,' he said. 'Or indeed that the English will be completely helpless under this rain of bombs. I shall find out. Sometimes, I can get a word or two of the BBC on that clever thing of mine and I'll learn the truth of the Nazi losses, and there will be some, you'll see . . .'

She could hear the vibration of his voice. Give in, my darling, she thought, give in and accept as I do, there is no more hope. 'Are we going to sit here imagining the great battles? Will there be anti-aircraft bringing down the Nazi planes? How long will it all last? They occupied Holland in four days.'

'Esther.' He hugged her closer. 'We shall imagine our girls going to the cinema this Saturday afternoon in that market town of theirs. The sun is shining. They are happily adapted to their new life. The Red Cross letter we had last month told us so. What a treasure that Red Cross is to try and maintain a system of messages between the two countries at war, however short they have to be.'

'I am grateful to the Red Cross, Josef, for those few pitiful words from our girls. But is there any reason to suppose they contain the truth, any more than our our reply did? You think Susanna would worry us with a cry for help fitted into the twenty-five words?'

'No.' He kissed her cheek and got to his feet. 'But I'm sure she'd have put something guarded which we'd recognise. I'm going to take Freddy for a stroll. If the Berliners in the streets seem subdued about this big-scale bombing of London, they'll have understood too.'

'Understood what, Josef?'

'That if London is destroyed, America will certainly stir itself to help Britain. They won't want one the greatest cities in the world destroyed, and if American power is turned on them, the Nazis will be beaten back and swept out of every country they've conquered. I actually feel this the beginning of the end, this decision to try and raze London to the ground. History books will mark it as the day the Nazis began their descent, you'll see.'

He had left her. She could hear him talking to Freddy and both of them waved at her and were gone.

Shall I see? she wondered. May I live that long! She felt along her waist for her mother's talisman against the evil eye, a tiny gold elephant she sewed into her dresses and skirts as she wore them. Mama, she thought, twenty-three months since you and Opa had to leave me, twenty months since I had to let go of my girls.

She closed her eyes and allowed her mind to drift. Where was the Red Cross office Susanna stood in to fill out the form? What was she wearing, how long was her hair, did she let it stand out in a bush? Or was it nicely trimmed at the nape of her neck? And Sophie's? Another woman had paid for their hair to be cut, for the dresses that clothed them that very minute. Sophie will have grown by twenty months, she'll have longer legs, a longer body, she'll be anxious about her breasts, and need her Mama and only her Mama to explain about periods.

She wanted Susanna to do the explaining and not this other woman whose pretty smiling blondeness was set in the black and white of the photograph Susanna had forwarded of Daphne Montgomery. Daphne Montgomery is having the pleasure of helping my girls grow into young women, she thought, and I must thank God for it every day.

Sometimes a sour bitterness overcame her instead of thanks, and yet, but for Daphne and women like her, she'd now have three still to let go, agonising hour by hour.

Sometimes she could barely remember the scent of their skin, the feel of it, and yet often, Sophie's face would come, in all its young glory, chin pressed over the violin, her short fingers flat on the strings. She could remember the exact sound then of the first few bars of the Bruch and Susanna's voice calling from the bedroom about the irritation of all that practising, poor tone-deaf darling. How much had she had to bear since, how many hurdles had she had to face?

My dear hearts, she thought, I have already found great good in today's bad news: you precious ones are far away from poor suffering London.

Chapter 35

'And I hate the underground,' Susanna said, stumbling up the last step of the station and taking a breath of air. 'It's not only stifling down there, the noise is unbearable, and the rattling.'

'You're terrified of the walls collapsing on you, admit it,' Max said, jumping up behind her and setting off along the Whitechapel Road.

'I don't mind admitting it. Claustrophobia's nothing to be ashamed of, and nor is not wanting to spend a lovely summer evening trapped in the Lipinskis' front room, mocked and stared at by those two girls.'

'It's because you refuse to join in. They think you've gone goy, and all grand, as if you weren't poor and Jewish, same as them.'

'They just don't like me. Don't bother to make excuses.' She was having to hurry to keep up with him, a familiar irritation. 'And don't make it seem my fault. You've done that since I can remember.'

She gazed around her with distaste at the tiny packed-together houses, nothing brighter about them than the scrubbed and whitened front steps and the geraniums in pots. The sound of the wireless came from the open doorways and women sat knitting outside in their overalls and slippers. 'These are what's called the mean streets of the East End, are they?' she said. Sometimes, she thought, I do feel a wave of longing not to be Jewish, to be magically other than I was born to be, and like Georgiana instead, languidly, effortlessly at ease in the world, belonging in it *unlabelled*. But then at night I remember this treachery and see

209

Papa's face smiling at me with understanding and pity, and Opa sitting on the bed in his black coat with his Torah that day he was sent back to Poland and I have to give way to great floods of tears.

Max waited for her to catch up. 'We needn't stay the evening,' he said, making an effort to be nicer than usual. 'And there's a good supper, gefilte fish balls, pickled cucumber, stuff from the old days. A sort of sabbath meal, she knows you never have one.' He gave her one of his rare intimate looks, as if the old days were often brought up between them, which they weren't.

Susanna refused to share the moment. He never chose to share hers. 'If you think back,' she said, 'I don't eat much of anything pickled, and I've got used to Madame Lola's Viennese cooking, she doesn't do poor food from the old days.'

'You'd better not show you don't want pickled cucumber,' he said, 'you'll hurt Ma Lipinski's feelings. She's made a special effort for you.'

'She'll just pretend she made it for me, that I'm this honoured guest, when none of them like me and I'd prefer not to be there.'

'You must. You're my girl. Fanny's chap'll be invited next Saturday.' He paused at the door of a tiny pub as a crowd of customers surged from it, singing. 'You have to admit these East Enders know how to enjoy themselves on a Saturday afternoon when they've got money in their pockets.'

'They know how to get drunk.' She watched a Chinese woman in a tight satin skirt wobble along the street behind a soldier with his jacket undone.

'Better than being crouched in that room of yours mooning over a pile of old letters. You won't be any good if the RAF haven't shot down enough Messerschmitts and the SS float down in the night over London like they did over Rotterdam.' He paused and caught hold of her elbow. 'Hear that singing and those raised voices? Crammed with people these little houses are, from kids that didn't want to be evacuated to ancient grannies sitting on the doorsteps. They're full of life, these poor, and they've got something you haven't. Guts, that's what and they won't stand for Nazi jackboots marching on their roads. Resistance'll grow up in no time. It'll be quite exciting.'

'You won't find it exciting,' she said. 'You'll be in a KZ, a real Nazi KZ. Or dead. And why imagine all that when you believe the RAF will keep them off?'

210

'Want to believe it, I suppose.'

She sensed one of his sudden glooms descending on him as they turned another corner. She was far too hot in the dark-green linen dress and wished she'd worn her blue silk and no stockings. A hot uncomfortable evening lay ahead, for Max wouldn't leave early whatever he claimed now. There'd be songs, silly ones like 'Yiddle with his Fiddle', and sentimental ones, 'I saw the old Homestead and the Faces I Loved'. Mrs Lipinski would get loud and tearful and she herself would find it impossible to say a single word, much less sing one. I don't belong anywhere anymore, she thought, I am a recluse. I like the sanctuary of my room in the evenings. Or did, until last Saturday when some Nazi aircraft got through the RAF and ack-ack gun defences and hit Croydon. Croydon wasn't far enough away.

'Remember you promised to take me right to my door tonight, Max,' she said. 'Whatever moonlight you say there'll be. Max.' She pulled at his sleeve. 'I want you to promise to take me to my door, or I won't take another step.'

'I have promised.' He was staring down at his feet to show her his gloom hadn't lifted.

'Promise me on your mother's life,' she demanded, surprising herself with this expression from the past. But that was how uneasy she felt in the blackout. She'd even begun to abandon her suppers at the Corner House and had bought a saucepan to heat her own baked beans, toasting bread on a fork by the fire and saving tuppence.

'Where did you drag—' Max said, and stopped.

The air-raid siren was wailing. The old lady dozing over her knitting in her chair just near them woke up, two girls skipping in the road let their rope go slack, the wirelesses were switched off. Faces appeared at windows and all eyes turned upwards to the sky where an ordinary summer blue was marred with nothing but a few flecks of cloud.

'Here,' the old lady said, 'it's daylight, can't be no raid now, can there, son?'

'Well, if there is, Ma, it'll be on the docks, not us, don't worry.'

Susanna smiled. Women had always referred to Max since he was a boy. 'I expect it's a false alarm anyway,' she said, through the banshee wail of the thing.

'We'll still make for the shelter.' Max, suddenly masterful, took her arm. 'And you'd better, Ma.'

Around them, people were tumbling from their doors, men in vests, yawning, a girl with her hair in a towel, a woman trying to push her cat into a shopping basket. A policeman appeared too, shouting instructions.

'Make for the shelter in the next street, ladies and gentlemen, and hurry along please. You girls, find your mother, quick, and you, Ma, leave your knitting, and don't go hunting for shoes, them slippers is all right for a shelter.'

She and Max began to run then because everyone else who could was running. The wail had died down and a new, fainter noise took its place, a buzz like a giant insect, and with it, a throb that was more a feeling in the air than sound.

'Mum, Mum,' someone shouted, 'they're coming, quick!'

Susanna looked up, everyone looked up, and where the flecks of cloud had been, there were black shapes, the black arrow-shapes of aeroplanes.

'There's hundreds of them,' someone shouted, 'hundreds!'

A long second seemed to pass as everyone stumbled on and just as the sky was very nearly black, the buzzing noise turned into a shriek, the shriek of a very fast train, of hundreds of fast trains.

Trying to drown his disappointment with a drink at his club, David considered the wastes of the afternoon. He should have written, or sent a telegram: Released hospital, calling to see you around three for tea and the park and dinner. He had actually stood in the post office by the hospital and thought, dammit, I can be with her nearly as soon, and, yes, if I just arrive, even if she's going out with that boy, I shall have had something of her, one of our walks perhaps, something. Now, even if he called the next day, her Madame Lola had warned him Susanna sometimes stayed the night at the boy's foster home. And the address, please? Stepney. She thought. Which was hardly helpful.

Susanna! He looked up at the eastern sky and foolishly sent off a plea. Have pity on me. On Monday at eight, I have to report back to camp, and I must know you need nothing I can give you. At least that.

He was still her guardian. He still had that left to him. But what to do now in his misery? He'd telephoned his mother. She wasn't longing for his presence. In fact, her new worries since the war began in earnest had seemed to give her the strength to force herself to get about with a stick, and to write letters again. Apart from himself, there was Will risking death every day as a Spitfire pilot, Henry in the artillery, Patch and Georgie somewhere in France. If there wasn't someone for her to write to, there was someone for her to write about. The Foreign Office must be very familiar with her handwriting and her demand that two English girls be wrenched from the hands of the Nazis.

He hadn't actually a home to go to either, or not one he felt entitled to, and the trouble with hospitals was that they left you too much time for reflection. His only visitors had been Army men, though his brother Will had dashed in once between his sorties. Hospital had reminded him he wanted a wife. He wanted for his wife a girl he could never have. As his wife, she'd have visited, she'd have visited every hour allowed, she'd have sent a stream of loving letters and parcels full of things lovingly collected, and photographs of herself to prop on the bedside table.

Abruptly, he left his whisky on the bar and made his way to the front entrance to stare out into the street. I have let so much time slip by, he thought, waiting for this war to force change upon me, the end, or the beginning of something. But it has brought me no great change other than several wounds which must fill a girl with distaste, and a stiff knee that obliges me to walk like an old man.

He would have liked a few hours with her, though, a few awkward hours to drink her in, as it were, her frail shyness, her delicate voice with its hint of accent, the worries revealed to him bit by bit.

He was just about to slope off in the direction of Green Park to do the walk on his own, when the wail of the air-raid siren started up. A daylight raid on the city? Surely not.

Limping down the steps, he joined the other people on the pavement asking themselves: false alarm – or shelter? He didn't give a damn, he realised, didn't want male conversation about the last war in the club cellar and certainly wouldn't go and sit in some cold, damp street one.

A thick, tangible misery settled in his chest. He was the loneliest man in the world.

*

Susanna stared down at two black arms, two dirty black arms. They were hers. She had fallen somewhere, and Max had fallen with her. One of his black hands rested beside hers and the sleeves of his good suit were covered in dirt.

'Max.' She might have said this one word though her mouth was full of grit. She tried to spit some out.

Max groaned and turned his black face towards her. His eyes were circles of white and red. 'Get up,' he muttered. 'They're coming again.'

'Who?' Her ears were full of noise. They hadn't shut off the sirens. She remembered. The bombers. She'd seen them making the sky black and then a great swoosh of air had lifted her up, moving, breaking up air. We've been bombed, she thought, this is what it's like, moving air and dirt all over you and grit in your mouth.

They'd been lying here a long time because night had fallen, but she was quite comfortable. Cupping her hand over the nice roundness of a cobblestone and easing herself further against the wall of one of the little houses, she decided to go to sleep. At some point an ambulance would arrive, or something would, a policeman. She closed her eyes. She felt wonderful. She felt as if she were cradled in sleep.

And there you are, David thought, emerging from a cinema where he'd dozed off. The damn all clear had of course sounded and not a solitary fighter had appeared, much less a bomber. The air-raid officials would cry wolf too many times. Londoners would cease taking any notice and would be out in the streets when the Nazis finally made their move as only they knew how to do.

Misery and depression well established, he limped back to the club. He'd dine alone and go to bed.

'See that smoke, Captain?' The club doorman was out on the steps. 'And see them black specks?'

'What smoke?'

'Over in the east, Captain.' The man pointed. 'Seems the East End's getting it good and proper. Them specks is bombers.'

David stood beside him gazing into the eastern sky. Piles of ominous grey and black clouds sat there. 'That's *smoke*,' he murmured. 'And it's the docks getting it?'

214

'Docks and half the East End. That's the news coming in so far, Captain. Jerry's changed his tactics.'

He got himself back down the steps and put out a hand for a taxi. 'Take me to Stepney, please,' he said, manoeuvring himself into the back seat.

'Don't know as I can, sir, lot of trouble over that way,' the driver answered. 'There's been deaths, that's the word out to us drivers, whole streets is razed to the ground. Old Adolf boasted he'd do that, didn't he, sir, and that's what he's done, we reckon, near enough. Anyway, the whole bloody East End's going up in flames.'

'Take me as far as you can will you? I have family there.' He'd go by tube if he had to. The tube system wouldn't be on fire. Then he'd find her.

A stifled voice, Max's, through the whistling in her ears and the thud, thud of more bombs landing. Susanna forced her eyes open. His hands were dragging at hers. She mustn't sleep. He needed her. She opened her mouth to answer and choked on smoke. Rolls of smoke and dust were moving gently along the cobbles towards them. The cobbles had turned black.

Taking her hands away from Max's, she used them to edge herself on to her knees, and rested there. 'They've gone,' she said. Her tongue had swelled to twice its normal size.

Max got to his knees beside her, a spectre of grittiness, everything about him tattered, his hair in a gritty fringe, and using each other as support, they stumbled to their feet to discover their feet were encased in black things, and her legs were black.

'Shelter,' Max muttered. 'Round corner.'

Which corner? He was trying to flap away some smoke. He couldn't see across the street. It was filled with smoke and dust, making the day seem like night, making the rooftops disappear.

She reached for her shoulder bag, its grittiness already familiar, and let herself register the fact that her stockings had disappeared too. Her silk ones. Where had they gone when her shoes were whole?

'This way,' Max decided, reaching an arm around her waist and holding her close.

Half tottering, managing to run a few steps, sobbing or laughing, afterwards she couldn't remember which, they found

215

themselves hanging on the door of the little brick street shelter now harbouring whole families, the lady who'd been knitting, the one with her cat and the Lipinskis, just as the hundred-train shriek started up again and a hundred bombers were coming their way.

'Oh, my boy's safe,' wailed Mrs Lipinski as the two of them fell in. The air-raid warden slammed the door. The shriek reached its highest point of torture, the thud, thud of the bombs could be heard, and the following shudder as the floor beneath their feet took the shock.

'Pa, that's our house going,' Mrs Lipinski sobbed, 'what have we done to deserve it, I ask you, oh, I'll die in here I will, my heart can't stand it . . .'

The good thing was that when the all clear rang and they stumbled out again, the nearest row of houses was still more or less whole. Windows were shattered, chimneys down, and a dirty layer of smoke, dust and soot covered everything, as it did them, and they had to peer through drifts of smoke to gain their bearings.

Everyone agreed, though, that the docks were what Jerry had been aiming for and he'd got 'em fair and square – because, to the south, great black towers of smoke were rising and a nasty, oily, crimson glow of fire.

After reaching this conclusion together, dream-like, they made their separate ways home.

Dreamily, trembling, as weak as kittens were supposed to be, Susanna sat on the Lipinskis' scullery doorstep. Beside her was Max and their third or fourth bucket of water drawn from the scullery tap. They'd been taking it in turns to wash parts of themselves.

Wailing, giggling and silent at intervals, washed and changed, the two Lipinski girls, Fanny and Rosie, ran up and down the stairs to peer from windows and report on street damage. The pall of smoke was clearing in the neighbourhood, but over by the docks the sky was red and black.

Susanna realised she and Max had ceased to wonder at the fact of her stockings being stripped off by some extraordinary movement of air that had left her shoes on, they had ceased to wonder at anything, being at the point of needing silence and inner digestion.

216

But they still had to eat, it seemed, and once the worst of the sooty stuff was off, they realised it was probably suppertime, and supper was already prepared, so they wasted no time tucking in. Mrs Lipinski kept repeating that the war was killing her to which her husband responded that it hadn't yet, which would start off the youngest replica of Mrs Lipinski, Rosie. 'They're not coming back for us, are they, Pa, are they?' Wild-eyed, she'd stare round the table, her mouth full of ludkie.

This Max couldn't resist. '' Course they're coming back, they know Smithy Street's still standing. You think they want Smithy Street left?' Yet his heart wasn't in it.

Unable to decide whether she was starving or couldn't eat a crumb, Susanna served herself potato cakes and ate several. She wanted to go home, be somehow flown back, and find herself in her room, safe, the geyser busily boiling water for a proper wash. She wanted hot water and plenty of it, half a dozen chocolate biscuits from the patisserie, and to be lying on her bed with them watching her personal square of clean sky.

'Wonder how far they've gone into the centre of London, Pa,' Max said, as if he had guessed.

'Isn't it just the docks hit?' She put down her fork, the ludkie suddenly disgusting.

Max shrugged. 'Can't really know, and the radio'll tell us nothing until the damage news has been suitably doctored for Nazi consumption.'

'I wish it wasn't so smoky, I can't taste that fish, Ma,' Mr Lipinski said.

Mrs Lipinski laughed. 'Should do, Pa, it's smoked as well as pickled.' She was beginning to enjoy the feel of a disaster overcome, Susanna decided, picturing a hail of bombs ripping through Soho, blowing Madame Lola flat as she strolled to her friends for Saturday tea, and shaking the windows out of all the houses in her own little street, and her own window.

Mr Lipinski got to his feet. 'We'll have a drop of that brandy you keeps for accidents, Ma. It ain't as if we've not had the shock of our lives.' He'd taken it from the cupboard and was holding up the bottle to judge the level of the contents, when the air-raid siren wailed afresh, as if more of it was going to be bearable. This was instantly joined by the wail of Mrs Lipinski and her daughters.

Susanna stood up, surprised by the weakness of her knees. Max snuffed the candles and grasped her own and Rosie's hands. 'I'll take these two, Pa.' He was trying to be strong, and male. His face though had gone as white as the tablecloth. 'Don't forget to tell your mother I did my best for you when this is all over,' he hissed, pulling her and Rosie to the doorway.

Out in the street, she didn't need to look up, because the noise was back, the hundred-train noise which meant hundreds of planes would shortly be making the sky blacker and blacker, machine-black instead of smoke-black.

'They're coming for us again, Pa,' yelled Mrs Lipinski, 'whatever shall we do?'

'Run, you silly old woman,' shouted her husband, dragging her along faster than her feet could go.

Dread in his heart, David realised he could read the posters displayed outside the underground station. FRY'S COCOA, RICH IN NERVE FOOD, he read over and over, and DO YOU PUT CHICKEN IN YOUR SOUP, HEINZ DO. Then he looked at his watch and read the time. Five to ten, and blackout hour long past – blackout kept to, as well. Not a glimmer of light came from the underground or the passing buses. Instead, there was a nightmare of light in the sky, it was orange and red because the East End was on fire, and somewhere out there, choking on smoke, terrified, burned, needing him, was Susanna.

'It is just the docks they've hit? he asked the patrolling air-raid warden.

'They got the docks, Captain,' he replied, 'they got half the streets, that's the word coming out. And when they'd set the factories on fire this afternoon, they could see their way nicely this evening. Quarter past eight they started and they're still at it. If you got good hearing, you can hear 'em, a sort of roar they're making.'

'And I'm not allowed to travel in that direction?'

'You're not allowed to, Captain, sorry. People are getting out by tube, it's bedlam down there, you wouldn't credit it, whole families is dragging their bits and pieces into the trains, bedding, the lot, grannies, kids . . .'

'East End's being evacuated then?'

'Evacuating itself, it is, and the poor devils don't know where they're going, there's no one for 'em to go to, the planning's been done for dead bodies, not this kicking, screaming lot.' The man swung on his heels and pointed up at the painter's sky. '*And* the order's gone out, Captain.' He lowered his voice and leaned towards him. ' "Invasion expected". Yes. So maybe it's the para-troopers floating down tonight. Never did think we'd see that here, did we, but we'll cope somehow. Got my special issue, anyway, and I wouldn't mind catching a few myself, and using it on 'em.'

'Hope you do,' David said, his heart thumping. Her very worst fear, he thought. She'd laughed about it, telling him.

'Good luck to you,' he said, shaking the man's hand. I must get back up west somehow, he thought, I must get through to camp for orders. Invasion! The church bells were going to be rung! Dear God, the awful eerie sound across the fields in the dead of night, the Home Guard out with pitchforks, old ladies fetching the fire irons, Bert ready, and Flo, wheeling his mother down to the cellars, she spitting fury, the little pistol he'd bought her got out ready.

'Come on, you lot, call yourselves East Enders.' The street warden began to pace up and down between the rows of benches placed in the shelter at some past time when air raids were being planned for, but not seriously enough. 'Come on, *Run Rabbit*, you want to let Jerry get you down?' He clapped his hands in front of Max and Susanna, 'Run, rabbit, run, rabbit, run, run, run,' he sang.

Another crash drowned out his words. That was closer than ever, Susanna thought. They were getting nearer and nearer, and this brick construction with its thirty or forty Lipinski neighbours, the Lipinskis themselves, her and Max, wouldn't survive a direct hit, or be able to suffer much more shaking about. She didn't feel safe. She had to try forcing herself not to take gasping breaths.

She edged herself further along the bench towards Max. 'I want to go outside,' she whispered.

'Don't be daft, they're getting nearer.'

'That's why.'

' "Underneath the Arches," ' announced the warden, 'and give it all you've got!'

'Here comes another one,' a woman shouted.

The very earth seemed to roll with an explosion of noise beyond bearing, louder than the last, more powerful. Yes, Susanna thought, Mama and Papa, Opa, Buba, these are to be my last moments. I send you my love for the last time. At least you are spared this drawn-out waiting-to-die death, and I am glad of that.

'We're going to die, aren't we?' shrieked Mrs Lipinski.

'Listen, isn't that our guns answering back?' a young lad cried. 'They've brought in more ack-ack, them bombers'll soon be shot down.'

'Brought in more ack-ack?' a man replied. 'How may I ask? Under them bombs tipping out like confetti, like confetti, I say, and them with hundreds more to tip out and hundreds of planes to tip 'em out from. And who's getting the lot, us East Enders, that's who, and our docks, that's what, and when we wakes up in the morning, we'll all be dead!'

'Logic in there, somewhere,' Max said, reaching an arm around Susanna's shoulders. 'Lean on me. Our mothers would like us to be together, you know. Close your eyes.'

'Yours wouldn't.' The warmth of him was a comfort.

'You weren't good enough, no, but she liked you.'

'Of course, she didn't realise you'd end up as a presser in a trouser factory.' She closed her eyes. She could feel her pulse beating, or maybe it was Max's, maybe their pulses were throbbing as one.

'What's the time? And I won't end up a presser.'

'Midnight. We've been here four hours.'

'Oh, what a night,' a voice wailed, as the same giant force shook their shelter and everyone in it all over again.

In fact, the most astonishing sound of that night was the all clear; they had simply ceased to expect any end to their torment. But it had come to an end. It was four thirty in the morning.

Groaning, rubbing eyes and limbs, they got themselves out into the smoke-filled dawn where a strange red light revealed to them that the street had been bombed to rubble. Over the rubble rolled drifts of sooty smoke. Was everything gone, everyone dead but them? It seemed so, yet some of the little houses had half a kitchen wall left, a copper boiler where the scullery had been, a solitary door-frame. At one of the street, an entire house still stood. Someone had been lucky.

'Shan't need put up the blackout tonight,' a wit remarked.

'Our old Thames is burning,' someone else announced, for the weird red light was coming from there.

Susanna stared dumbly at the lady trying to edge her slippered feet into the mess of brick dust splintered wood and glass where the street she knew had been. 'Oh, my poor puss, whyever did I leave you, puss, puss . . .'

A son held her by the arm, someone else offered theirs and somehow several people set off into the smoky ruins.

'Look out for the glass,' Susanna said. She could see it glinting. I ought to tell them how it can get into your clothes, she thought, and how quite unexpectedly you can have a little river of blood on your skin, which is frightening but not serious. She was an expert on glass.

'Our house is gone, Pa, I know it is, get on and see!' Mrs Lipinski's voice echoed out, muffled by smoke. Pa didn't reply, and he and the other Lipinskis, the other night-survivors, she and Max watched, dumb, as the braver ones, hunched together, shuffling, edged their way further into the unknown with muffled exclamations and slow, climbing movements as they negotiated broken beams and someone's fireside chairs and bed-frames.

Suddenly into this tableau an ambulance came rocking over the rubble, a ghostly grey moving shape proving the world existed yet. A lady driver put her head from the window. 'Anyone hurt?'

None of them answered.

'Righto,' she called. 'Better get yourselves a cup of tea before you start cleaning up.' And with a nasty crashing of gears, she rattled off.

'Make a cup of tea, she says,' cried Mrs Lipinski. 'We won't have no kitchen left, will we, nor no kettle . . .'

Some time later, cut about the legs and hands, the Lipinskis, Susanna and Max had made their way to the street where the Lipinski house had been. She and the Lipinskis then stood and watched as Max, king of the castle of rubble, dug. He had found a coal shovel, but mostly he used his hands, throwing up the bits and pieces of the Lipinskis' past life, the one they knew they'd lost that very night.

'The Rosenthal's in the parlour cupboard, Maxie.' Mrs Lipinski could barely shout now for smoke had crept into their throats and lungs, and soot had formed a fringe of black around their mouth and eyes.

221

'Ma, ain't that our parlour sofa?' A subdued, dirty Rosie held her sister's arm. I must look like them, Susanna thought, standing beside the two girls in the companionship born of that night, and my hair must be grey with dirt and my skin and however shall I get home and will my home be standing, my little room, or the salon?

Max threw up a saucepan, a slipper, a chamber pot, the lid off the boiler.

'Don't bother with that stuff, Maxie, find my Rosenthal.' Mrs Lipinskin couldn't shout it loud enough, and Rosie couldn't, croaking, 'Find my jewellery box, Max.'

'Jewellery box, she says,' croaked Fanny. 'A glass necklace and a paste hat pin's all you got.'

That's more'n you got, our Fan.'

'Find the jampot we keep the gas and electric in, boy.' Mr Lipinski's voice was the hoarsest of all. Thin arm around his wife's plump waist, he seemed to think he was directing operations, but Max never glanced up for orders.

Susanna kept her eyes on the filthy, digging shape of him and away from the giant hole at the end of the street where the nearest bomb had exploded, away from the crimson sky behind them. The Thames was burning. How soon before the flames reached these piles of house, licking and swirling across the rubble and turning it into a wasteland for the landing of the SS with daggers in their belts inscribed 'Blood and Honour'?

Max dug on. They could hear him grunting. Everything had to be moved, a rag of damask that had been the sabbath cloth, a wardrobe door. Suddenly, Susanna realised why; he hadn't found what he wanted. He wasn't looking for china or the gas money, he was looking for the sapphire.

In the end, David thought, what a pointless, fruitless day, spent walking the streets that she might be walking on, lurking around the underground stations she might be coming in from Stepney on – as if some miracle of chance would put her in his path, as if she could not be one of those killed in that night of horror, because he could not bear it if she were. As if, by heaven, chance wasn't at work, but design, and Susanna should be saved from death because she had suffered enough, and deserved therefore to be saved, and he deserved not to have the love of his life snatched from him.

222

As if, he thought, even as he climbed into the taxi for his return to camp, she were not destined from birth to marry the boy Max. The salon lady, Madame Lola, had confirmed that point to him. He had sat in her kitchen with her over coffee, listening for a ring at the doorbell, Susanna's steps up the stairs, her call to her employer: You can't imagine what a night we've had!

He'd actually asked the woman outright, if Susanna's family expected the marriage, and if it was the custom for young Jewish people to marry each other even in these difficult times.

She had nodded, occupied with rolling out pastry. Yet he knew she hadn't married a Jew, Susanna had told him so, and could only imagine she'd chosen a man not likely to interfere in her business, as a Jewish one would expect to do.

Gazing vaguely from the window, he realised the taxi driver had had to slow for a diversion around the entrance to the tube station. A mass of people was emerging from it and streaming across the street.

'East Enders, Captain,' the driver remarked. 'Coming up the West End shelters to bed down for the night. They ain't got enough of their own and they're expecting Jerry tonight, same time and place, like. Shockin' night they had, there's four, five hundred dead, did you hear? Got their belongings with 'em, look, pitiful . . .'

'They are. But will you draw in by that kerb for me? I've just remembered something . . .'

Slamming the door behind him, he stood scanning every figure stumbling up the steps. There were entire families, ancient old men, toddlers, dogs on string leads, all with a dazed look as if they didn't know what they were doing here, in this wide street with proper pavements and an ordinary sky.

He was a fool because, of course, Susanna wasn't going to be amongst them, things didn't happen like that.

Then he saw her. She was holding on to a rail in order to drag herself up. He thought, oh, the darling girl. Her face was white, her eyes were huge and blank, her pretty dress was grimed with dirt, and her hair, her shoes. She had been in it, all right. But she was whole. Whole, with her slender legs black with dirt!

Glued to the tarmac, he realised he mustn't rush across and startle her, he must stroll over and say: Susanna, what a surprise,

223

what luck to come upon you like this, my mother will be so relieved, she's been listening to the awful news . . .

Before he could move, a familiar figure appeared on the steps by her side. The boy. And the boy put an arm around her waist. She smiled at him and together they stood blinking in the sunlight.

Shortly he was back in the taxi and on the way to the railway station, his new camp, his new batman running him a bath, dinner in the mess, whiskey, longing.

He had what he wanted though. He'd seen she had not suffered burns or a lost limb. She wasn't one of the five hundred dead. And the invasion hadn't started, there were no barges massed in the French and Dutch ports. The Nazis weren't ready. Razing London to the ground was their present plan.

Not yet then, my darling, he thought, staring into the red and black eastern sky as his vehicle crossed Westminster Bridge, not the SS coming for you, only bombs, and bombs are random. But when the sirens sound, please go down into the big shelters as I have often asked you to do, and stay there, safe.

Chapter 36

The Cellar of Susanna's Apartment Building, November 1940

At last, Carlotta Bertoni appeared to be asleep. Susanna edged the shawl around the toddler's face to shade it from the glow of the hurricane lamp on the floor beside them. She tried to lean back in her deckchair. She was exhausted, the weight of the child, as always, more difficult to bear as the evening progressed. And soon she was going to run out of the stories she remembered from her own childhood.

Another series of planes was going over, she could hear the distant whine. And here it was, the crump, crump, crump of the bombs and the cellar shaking itself like a wet dog.

'Ever think it might be someone you know throwing down them things,' remarked the first-floor-back tenant from his camp bed in the corner.

She didn't answer. The man expected no answer. Too unfit to be called up because of a patch of TB on his lung and flat feet, he usually managed something of the kind. She felt it like a stab to the heart each time. Any one of those pilots might indeed be someone she knew, yes, someone who'd jeered, spat, laughed at her, or sung 'We'll stick in the knife and Jewish blood will spurt out' during years of Sunday parades.

She smiled across at Mrs Bertoni who sat in her makeshift bed with her son Marco clasped in her arms. She hadn't closed her eyes at all, her husband having just been lost at sea in the torpedoed ship taking Italian enemy alien males to a KZ in Canada. Well, he and the thousand or so other shopkeepers and chefs could do no harm to England now, being dead.

Restless, the office girl from the first-floor-front groaned, turning over on her mattress next to Susanna's. 'Oh, God,' she whispered, trying to drag the blanket around her ears. 'These cellars are as cold and damp as the grave. I think I'll try one of the tube shelters tomorrow night. At least they're warm. You ever tried one?'

'Only in a daylight raid once.' Susanna, too, whispered. 'I was on an errand for my employer and I'd just got to Marble Arch tube station when the sirens went and this warden ordered me down into it. I felt absolute panic about being trapped. I wanted to claw my way out and if the warden hadn't been standing by the doors, I would have. I think it was the next day a bomb got down there, in that very station, caught between two girders it was, did you hear about it?'

'Yes, that was that blast thing, wasn't it? The dead had every stitch of clothing whipped off them. I suppose it's the air going at the most fantastic speed.'

'It whipped the tiles off the tunnels too,' Susanna murmured, shifting Carlotta's weight to the other arm. 'And the tiles sliced into people. I can't forget that somehow, a day later, it might have been me.'

'Caused rivers of blood, I expect,' the girl whispered, 'like glass does. My friend was in her office over Holborn way when every window in her office block was shattered by a near-miss. Everyone was cut all over with little cuts, there was so much blood, the ambulance men slipped going up the stairs.'

'Why don't you two shut up,' the flat-feet tenant muttered. 'I got to work in the morning.' He stopped.

Something had changed in the muffled cacophony that reached them from the outside drama of ack-ack gun and bomber and bomb. They all sat up and gazed at each other in the glow of the lamp. It was the eerie pause that might mean this one was headed their way.

But it wasn't. It had landed elsewhere, not far off. The cellar shook itself again. Someone said, 'Bit close, that,' and with a few sighs, they settled themselves. If they were lucky, it would be their near-miss of the night.

'You been in the Dickins and Jones shelter?' The girl resumed their conversation. 'I've heard it's the cleanest and best run with tea served and everyone having to behave themselves.'

226

'I'd try it if I didn't have to work until six. It's full by then, queuing starts at four, and only seven hundred are allowed in.'

Cautiously, she eased Carlotta off her lap and laid her beside Mrs Bertoni, who nodded and whispered her thanks. 'You go bed.'

'Yes.' Rubbing her stiff arms, she edged herself in, shoes and all, tweed slacks, old brown jumper from Aunt Daphne's, brown hat she'd knitted to match. She couldn't be one of those who slept in nightwear in a public place. At this point, she invariably failed to stop herself glancing up at the water pipes running across the cellar ceiling. If your building had a direct hit when you were in a cellar and the water pipes fractured, you drowned.

'My worst fear is being buried by rubble,' her neighbour whispered.

'Yes,' Susanna replied, yawning, her eyelids heavy. 'But you have a chance of being rescued from rubble.'

'Long as there's a pocket of air. And you can keep tapping. If you got a hand free and something loose to tap with. The rescue teams can start digging then. They got some sort of new expert, did you hear? Body sniffers. They can put their nose into the mess and scent out fresh blood. If it's stale, they shout, "Only a stiff!" '

'No,' muttered Susanna, instantly finding more good in being buried by rubble. She wouldn't have to lie there knowing that Papa, frantic to help digging, wouldn't be allowed to, that Mama, her eyes growing hollower and blacker by the minute, would be beyond uttering a sound, waiting for a glimpse of a leg, a finger.

She ought, in fact, to be grateful, she was, that she had grand-parents safe from bombs in an army barracks on the Polish border, parents safe in their flat with nothing for the SS to steal in it, Freddy safe with them. More, she'd never have to stand around a pile of rubble, praying not to hear those three short and terrible words, Only a stiff.

'Did you hear about that street shelter in the suburbs where everyone died as they sat on their benches? Their spines cracked, from the tremor, imagine. They don't put those things in the newspapers, do they, people'd go mad. Mind you, I'd rather that than burning, there's been such fires, the bodies look like little black tree trunks, how those rescue teams sleep, I don't know.'

'And how can I sleep?' shouted Flat-Feet.

Susanna closed her eyes. So very many different ways I might

227

meet my end this very night, or tomorrow night she thought, and upstairs in my room I have all that unanswered correspondence. Mr David is unthanked for his gift to Sophie, and Aunt Daphne, Max. Worse, the Red Cross form for home has hardly been thought about, because I have been unable to think about it.

If, in fact, she were to die within the next hours, her parents would remain in their terrible silence, the great blank of letterless days and wonderings going on and on. What kind of good Jewish daughter was she? As soon as the all clear sounded, she must fill in that form and get it into the Citizens Advice office *by hand* so it could begin its long twisting journey through various Red Cross departments and Switzerland and finally her parents. She could picture their receiving it, their faces, their tears, and now she was wide awake.

Settled back in her room, the gas fire lit, blankets around her knees, coffee and shortbread from Flo on the floor beside her, she lodged her other correspondence on the arm of the chair and her pad on a teatray and began. It was only five fifteen a.m. She had two hours and no excuses to offer herself.

SOPHIE GOES TO SCHOOL, she wrote. Four words. But would her parents understand this to mean that Sophie was to be sent to a private boarding school by Mr David and Aunt Daphne? Rubbing out the full stop, she added two more. SOPHIE GOES TO SCHOOL LIKE DIMSIE. They'd remember, or Papa would, that this resembled the title of her own favourite English school story, about a poor girl who attends a rich girls' school and proves herself their equal. He'd probably fetch it from the trunk to reread to Mama and she'd lap up every word. Would she realise Sophie would make connections at such a school, meeting girls' brothers, boys with a future, budding doctors, businessmen, good Jewish mothers' sons even? Yes, and she'd dream and dream. She'd dream as far as the wedding and beyond, and acquire five grandchildren before she got to bed.

BOTH WELL AND HAPPY, she wrote next. Ten words. LOVE AND MISS YOU. Fourteen. DOWNLANDS GLORIOUS AND SAFE. Twenty. ONLY WANT YOU BE HERE. Twenty-five words. Done.

Eyes full of tears, she copied them at once on the Red Cross form itself. It was as well the message had a word limit. She might otherwise have descended into a recital of self-pity, and how, though she often felt it would be easier to die quickly under a hail of bombs than endure this nightly fear of death, she was keeping herself as safe as she could for their sakes, so they'd never receive the briefest message of all: REGRET SUSANNA KILLED IN AIR RAID.

Mr David was next on her list, because her non-acknowledgement of his latest kindness was more unfinished business. What shame would lodge in her mother's heart if she were ever to learn her daughter had left him unthanked before dying!

Dear Mr David, she began,
I cannot tell you how happy I was to hear from Sophie that you and Aunt Daphne are to establish a trust fund for her to attend that wonderful school until she is eighteen. A good education was what our parents always meant us to have, and I have tried to let them know that Sophie will after all with a few coded words in the Red Cross form we can now send home. They will be overwhelmed with gratitude to you both when they read it. It will put their minds at rest for her future and I see that as the greatest gift they could possibly receive in the present circumstances. My thanks are really quite inadequate but I feel you know you have them.

I hope your hospital days are over for good and you are enjoying your new camp.
Yours sincerely,
Susanna Lehmann

Now, Aunt Daphne. She was beginning to feel better. She must remember how satisfying it always was to get on with tasks instead of letting them weigh on you.

Dear Aunt Daphne,
I have never had such a joyous letter from Sophie. You are such a darling and so thoughtful. I can't imagine any of those refugee kids on the transport trains are being indulged by a more generous and loving foster mother than you. You know what my first thought was? I thought, Have I been complaining too much in my letters to Aunt Daphne or my occasional talks with Mr David about Sophie's life with Nanny? Yes, at once, Jewish self-blame! Trust me! But I have, haven't I? I never considered any change for her though until

229

the war was over at least, or even these air-raid attacks on London. I decided she might be able to come up here to me then – and deprive you of her, Aunt Daphne, you're thinking that straight away, aren't you? Well, Nanny is *careful* – may I say that one more time? I mean, we've lived with carefulness most of our lives, but poor Sophie has been forever saving for the war effort until she could hardly allow herself to put a toast finger into her mouth, and I'm sure she's been a bit of a nuisance, running about the village reminding the women to take their saucepans to the collection point. It may not have gone down very well from a newcomer – and a girl probably still considered to be the enemy, German. It's not as if the villagers can be expected to understand we're keener on more Spitfires being built than anyone else. Anyway, now she's going to school, an English boarding school, and I'm happier than I can describe. I can imagine just how it's going to be for her from all those books I read at home. I hope I shan't be disappointed and there will be midnight feasts and secret trysts and the poor girl (Sophie!) winning through.

I've written a few coded words in the Red Cross form I told you about, and I know they'll be desperate to be able to thank you themselves.

And you know how I appreciate your nagging me to come back to Dorset and lodge with Flo's sister in the village while the air attacks are trying to finish off poor London – and me. I would, honestly, if I were really terrified, but I'm not. I feel I'm living through a tremendous adventure. Daft, isn't it? London has this sort of pulling-together atmosphere, everyone's suffering the same (not just this poor self-pitying refugee), and really, the damage has the most extraordinary beauty. I ought to try and draw some of the sights I see. John Lewis's is the most stunning, it's a black, smoking skeleton, like a burned-out liner. Its mannequins are still sprawled out in the street as if they are bloodless corpses. In fact, there are great black skeletons of buildings all along the streets, and huge craters the buses have to trundle round. The Londoners say things like, 'Terrible night, wasn't it, the Savoy's copped it again, did you see,' then they stick out their Union Jacks and scrawl up chalk notices: *Send us another one, Adolf*, or, *Go on, we can take it*. And they can, and so can I, I'm finding every bit of good in the bad, just like my father would. He used to exasperate my mother no end, so I hope I'm not exasperating you, Aunt Daphne.

I think of you often, and Flo, it's a great comfort to me to know you are both in my life. Are Mr David, Mr Will and Mr Henry not doing anything dangerous? I don't want you to have too many of us to worry about!
With fondest love,
    Susanna

Dear Max,
I'm glad to hear you and the Lipinskis have moved out of the temporary lodging and in with Mrs Lipinski's mother. It's very kind of them to invite me to stay one Saturday night, and will you thank them for me? I'd rather not stay even if this mother does keep chickens in the yard and there'll be a fresh chicken soup. I don't know that I fancy eating something that's practically family. I don't find your telling them that I'm just a shy Jewish girl waiting to stand under the wedding canopy with you and not peculiar at all very funny. I don't care if the Lipinskis do find me peculiar either. I think they are, but I'm glad you're happy with them.

Still, imagine your mother's face when she meets them for the first time. Actually, I think it's amazing you ask me to come when I endured *that Saturday* in the East End itself. That's what people up my end call it.

If you are feeling lonely though, come up on Saturday afternoon, same time and place. We can have an early supper and you can get back before blackout.

Have you had a Red Cross form from home yet? Sophie and I have had our first.

If you do come, bring me some eggs, please, for Madame Lola's cake-making. And don't be late. I shan't wait long, I have other things to do. Aunt Daphne has been asking me to go back to Dorset until the air raids cease, if they ever do, but of course, I won't. I know how much you need me.
Susanna

Yawning, skin itching from fatigue, Susanna sealed and stamped the three envelopes. There was no reason why she didn't release

231

herself from the new city terrors at least for an occasional weekend because she could take work down with her – except that Patch actually had referred to her as a burden. She'd also spend the time waiting for Mr Montgomery to stamp up to her with money in his hand.

I don't want Jewish brats in my house. The only difference from the other thousands of world examples of Jews being chased out was that he was prepared to pay for them to be gone, rather than depriving them of their possessions first. How the words had cut to her heart though, and how foolish she'd been to suppose only the servants were sneering at her and Sophie at Downlands! Servants of course had the excuse of ignorance. The upper classes were supposed to put a veneer of politeness on every statement emerging from their tight little mouths – and it would have been easy for him to pretend. *I'm afraid my wife is too ill to care for you.* Simple. He should take a glance at himself, ugly fat purple and pink man, despising good, loving people like her parents and grandparents!

After that day, it hadn't mattered how fond of her Aunt Daphne was, or Flo, or how achingly polite, charming and sensitive Mr David was. Would the creature rather have Kraut brats in his house, with their cruelty and their arrogance, was he looking forward to Kraut pilots bombing his house that mustn't be sullied by two Jewish girls?

Sometimes, she thought, it is easy to fill one's soul with hatred and turn Nazi oneself. Tears welling up, she made herself finally edge out the Red Cross letter from home, from Berlin, or rather Berlin via Switzerland and a number of Red Cross offices. Read and reread, its half-page, its pitiful quarter-page folded and unfolded, she read it once more.

It said, PAPA WORKING, MAMA COOKING LESSONS FREDDY CHATTERBOX LONGING FOR ARRIVAL KEEP SAFE FOR US UNTIL THEN OUR DARLING GIRLS WE BOTH WELL AND HAPPY.

This was their gift to their daughters, she knew, their lie, and they needn't think it fooled her.

The burden of correspondence dealt with, she felt quite cheerful fitting her key in the downstairs salon door, and planning the morning. She'd deliver the Red Cross form on Fritzi's walk, do the shopping, have coffee, then start on the linings for Mrs

232

Hamble's coat and the broaching of the matter of salon-designed slacks for the house of Madame Lola. She'd already done a drawing of some with a narrower leg. Full trouser legs flapped and got wet in rain and snow. The fact was, however much Madame Lola was against the very idea of girls in slacks, they were beginning to wear them. This was wartime. Girls were working in factories, they had to work sometimes all night, or go straight on duty after spending it in a shelter. She couldn't be the only one finding a pair of trousers easier to be running up and down stairs to shelters in either.

Running up the stairs now with the cold reaching the gap at her stocking tops, she had her casual subject-broaching sentence prepared. But when she opened the second door, she had a surprise. The room was dark and cold – no fire blazing in the hearth, no whirr of the sewing machine, no Fritzi, no scent of coffee.

A strange other smell though. Something had happened.

She snapped on the light. The smell was soot. Soot covered the machines, the three tables and the dummy. The new wireless was black with soot, the wall cuttings. A dark rim of it sat on the mirror and little dots of it on the sequins of Miss Campbell's remodelled evening gown hanging by the fitting cubicle. The cubicle had big soft heaps of it and it had been blown in wave-shapes across the carpet like a sea-tide on sand.

And the mound of soot by the hearth was Madame Lola in her wrap, fur coat and turban. Fritzi was a tiny, sooty shape beside her.

The dog's little whimper told her he was alive. But Madame Lola was dead.

Chapter 37

Susanna watched the ambulance men preparing to take Madame Lola's body to the hospital morgue, St Thomas's, they said. She must inform the next-of-kin that's where she was in case they should wish to make a last visit, and the undertaker would want to know. Soot had stifled her to death, they said, soot blown down the chimney by bomb blast, and people didn't realise. You should never sit by your hearth in a raid, and if there hadn't been enough soot blown down to put out the fire, she might have been burned to a cinder as well, and the dog and the salon with everything in it.

Then they were gone, and Madame Lola was gone. They had quite a struggle to get her down the stairs.

Anyway, that was that. A film of soot all over herself, she closed the door behind them.

She knew you could get yourself moving if you had to, so, making a mental list of where to start with the cleaning, she brushed some soot from Fritzi's fur, put on his lead, checked for money and the Red Cross form in her bag. She'd sensibly get several other things done on her trip to Covent Garden to find Madame Lola's husband.

By blackout, she had a lot done and was perched on her work chair cuddling Fritzi, chilled to the bone, starving and sooty.

On her return from Covent Garden, she'd visited the undertaker whose name was given her by the newsagent, the undertaker had telephoned the rabbi of a synagogue, and the rabbi was to call and discuss a funeral with her the next afternoon.

The undertaker also had a list of solicitors, suggesting she pick

234

one with an office near the salon, to make things easier for herself. He was most sympathetic. There were many deaths these days with no surviving next-of-kin, but she wasn't to worry, the solicitor would take all the necessary steps to do with official forms and so on. 'The deceased's husband was long deceased?' he'd asked. She'd shaken her head. 'That Saturday, I think,' she'd replied, because it was what some manager person had told her at the Garden. 'That Saturday was a raid and a half,' he'd said, 'but we can take it, can't we? Pity about poor Albert.'

She had an appointment with the solicitor for ten in the morning, but meanwhile, she had other things on her mind. Supper, for instance, and breakfast, and lunch – for her, and Fritzi, and an awful lot of cleaning. And where to sleep. And what to do with Fritzi. How to pay her rent. Would it be acceptable morally and legally for her to pay herself from Madame Lola's purse? She must ask the solicitor. If the answer was no, she'd have to draw out some savings from the Post Office, where she'd deposited Mr David's five pounds and the ten-shilling notes Aunt Daphne had been sending.

Tomorrow, she'd telephone Aunt Daphne, News of a death, of two deaths, justified the expense of a long-distance telephone call.

By the time the sirens and the guns started up, she'd stopped creeping across the soot and doing pointless things like blow some off Miss Campbell's sequins, and she'd shut herself and Fritzi in the kitchen with two gas rings lit and the oven. She'd feel quite safe keeping them on all night. The building wouldn't be touched twice, none ever was, or hardly ever. The newsagent was delighted he'd only had his back windows out and his back kitchen ceiling down. Adolf could do what he liked now.

Madame Lola wouldn't have to pay for the extra gas on the bill either. Who would?

Frowning over the matter of gas bills, electricity bills, bills to clients and her own wages, warmed through enough to remove her beret, scarf and the fur jacket she'd bought in Berwick Street and Madame Lola had remodelled, she sat down at the table. Here she'd laid out a pot of coffee, a jug of hot milk and yesterday's bread to dunk in it. Fritzi had had his tin of sardines and his bread and milk and was making himself a nest for the night in Madame Lola's corsets.

235

His mistress must have eased herself out of that armour a mere twenty-four hours ago, dropped her silk bloomers, her stockings on the floor and with a great sigh of relief, put on her nightgown, her wrap.

Who'd pick it all up, clear her wardrobes? Who'd look after Fritzi? She must. And she must tackle the cleaning. It would take days. But she'd bought two new buckets, mop, dustpan and brush in Soho market, also washing soda, household soap and three floor cloths. The worst part might be actually carrying the soot down into the dustbins in the rear courtyard, then burning the cuttings of Madame Lola's heroines, the Queen Mother, the Duchess of Kent.

She was going to be well occupied. There were clients to explain matters to, the bare walls alone were going to give them a shock, never mind the empty chair and the covered-up machine.

Furiously dunking bread, she gazed at Madame Lola's bedside table holding the two Milk of Magnesia tablets, her glasses, a box of peppermint creams, the Eno's Fruit Salts and the green liniment for her rheumatism. She could smell the liniment, its sharp herbiness, and her lavender-scented talcum powder. A film of it lay on the dressing-table collection of paste jewellery and belts and scarves.

What would Madame Lola want done with it all?

What she herself wanted was to dress again in her jacket and beret and go out for a bus to St Thomas's hospital morgue. She wanted to make sure Madame Lola was absolutely dead and wouldn't wake up there on some marble slab amongst a lot of corpses.

If she didn't know the buses would be lined up in eerie, shadowy rows waiting for the end of the raid, that's what she would do.

Meanwhile, she must sit here until she did remember the prayers for the dead.

'But I'm only nineteen,' Susanna said, gazing blankly over the desk at the face of the solicitor. The office was as cold as ice though a gas fire popped and fizzed near her chair.

'Well, there you are,' the solicitor answered. He resembled Mr Montgomery, with folds of loose skin spilling over his high collar. But he was jolly and pink-cheeked like an English Father Christmas. 'Your employer obviously had faith in your common sense and maturity, and I can see why, if I may say so. I might have advised her against it had I known your present age, yet . . .' He shrugged. 'It was what she wanted.'

'Madame Lola must have had a premonition she was going to die,' she said. 'Or why did she come here to make her will several weeks ago?'

He shrugged again. 'Call it premonition if you wish, my dear, but you know, with civilians as war targets, most adults are doing the same because they have faced the fact the next bomb might have their name on it. Interesting, isn't it, how a whole new range of phrases emerges from the Blitz? What I will say is that lucky chance made you pick out my firm from the list you were given, it means things are easier all round. I remember your Madame Lola calling here very well, a fine figure of a woman . . .'

Susanna took off her gloves and glanced down at Fritzi's face with the same dumb question on it he'd had since the day before. 'She never picked up any war words,' she said. 'I used to read her the news every day, but I suppose she had begun to listen to the wireless I persuaded her to buy. Hers was past repair I think. I told her about *ITMA* on Wednesday evening and *Saturday Night Music Hall.* Air raids make the evenings so long, don't they? I thought she'd hear her favourite singer, Richard Tauber, sometimes, he's Viennese. The wireless was still on when I found her, full of soot it was, the sound was all muffled, I didn't hear it until I went to pick it up. She must have been listening that night by the fire. I wish now she'd decided to have it in the kitchen but she maintained clients might like a little music while looking through the magazines. She could copy anything.'

'A skilled woman obviously, and a sharp one. She wanted me to tie things up so her husband could make no claim on her estate, and I had a statement drawn to the effect that she had paid Mr Ketley to marry her in return for British citizenship. I'm delighted to hear of his death, as a matter of fact, since it means we should have no trouble from that side, especially if, as you believe, he was a childless widower. You will need someone other than me to act for you, your former foster mother, perhaps, another solicitor. Meanwhile, if you are able to cope with the salon's day-to-day expenses, using these few pounds from the cash box that you most sensibly brought with you, and you can continue with the orders in hand please do. If I were you, I'd give notice for that room of

237

yours and as long as you won't feel too lonely, move in with the little dog. I really don't expect any probate difficulties. but as she had bequeathed her pet to you and as it is his home . . .'

She could feel him smiling. He liked her. 'I send you the big bills, the gas, electricity and so on?'

'I'll deal with everything, and the funeral expenses. In six weeks or so, probate will be granted and you'll find yourself the owner of a nice solvent little business with a tidy sum in the bank. You must consider investing some of it so you can draw interest, because once you have enough in your current account for the purchase of cloth . . .'

She put up her head and watched the wet pink mouth going on and on.

'. . . the rent of the salon is quarterly, due in December, I expect, so I'll settle it, then I advise you to engage an accountant, there's a very good man down the street . . .'

Oh, Mama, she thought. Susanna Lehmann, dressmaker. My daughter has her own salon. You'll be able to say that. So young? So young, and so talented.

If only I could let you know, if only you could tell Frau Merkel and Frau Leona and boast about what you and Papa are coming over to. Estanna Modes.

She had suddenly decided on the name.

She wanted to begin on one of her big weeps.

Chapter 38

Late December, 1940

The all clear. Waking with a start, Susanna tried to sit up, banged her head, and remembered where she was – lying under her own version of an air-raid shelter, Madame Lola's iron bedstead.

'Time, Fritzi,' she muttered, edging him off her shoulder and disentangling them both from the mess of spare blankets they slept in. Side by side, they crawled out, yawning, she with the retrieved torch so she could see to switch on the light. Next, shivering, she lit the four gas rings to heat water and milk and to warm the room.

Anxious eyes fixed on her as always, Fritzi stood by the door into the bathroom where she now kept an old tin tray filled with soil. 'Peepee?' It was as if he nodded. He was a very clever dog. He even seemed to know that her furtive digging up of earth in Soho Square with a spoon and slipping it into a bag was somehow to be helped. He therefore acted dog-busy. She loved him. And what a relief not to have to dress and take him out on to the slippery pavements on winter mornings.

'Finished?' He trotted back into the room and jumped up to his chair. His bread and hot milk next, her coffee, their new routine, with the slight variation that it was a holiday one, the post-Christmas lull. There'd be no clients calling. She had nothing to do but work.

Soon she was sitting beside him at the table, holding his saucer with one hand, dipping biscuits in her coffee with the other. It must have been an easy night. It was only four forty-five in the

239

morning. But today she wouldn't settle herself in the armchair she'd dragged in from the salon, though it looked enticing up by the stove with its quota of blanket, shawls and hot water bottle. Often, she did settle in it with Fritzi after the all clear and they'd doze off very cosily until day, but she'd had enough rest, nearly a week's worth, since Christmas Eve, though she'd also got many tasks out of the way.

'Bed or armchair for your nap, Fritzi?' she said, getting up and clearing the table.

He was waiting to see where she was going to be, so she washed both table and her hands, fetched the pillowcase from the end of the bed and installed herself back in her place. 'Miss Campbell's aunt's black velvet evening jacket to unpick,' she told him.

He chose comfort by the stove so she was left with a blank of a bed to gaze at as she worked. In a way, she'd like to throw something of Madame Lola's on it, a scarf, a pair of her stockings, the peach-coloured corsets, all bone stays and laces. For a fortnight after her death she'd lived in this room with the poignancy of those corsets on the bed where Madame Lola had thrown them. The peach-coloured silk bloomers with lace insets and matching petticoat had been dropped on the floor. Madame Lola was an untidy woman in non-work matters yet she'd turned down the sheets ready for the night, plumped up the pillows, put out two Milk of Magnesia tablets.

But the problem had been what to do with all those things she'd left behind, how to set about the strange, indecent gathering-up of them, touching garments only she had touched, only the most intimate parts of her body had felt, folding and listing them for the laundry: Item 7, cotton and silk brassière, size forty-four inches.

And what to do with the gratitude due for such a gift as a solvent little business. Where to send the thank-you letter.

Me with an accountant, Susanna thought. And never again to be a burden, to have a finger pointed, to have money thrown down to get you away the faster.

She laid out the black velvet jacket Miss Campbell's aunt had apparently once worn. It had extraordinary full sleeves of a very intricate design almost like wings, but its greedy use of fabric meant no woman would want to be seen in it in wartime. She'd certainly get a plain-sleeved jacket from it, and the waistcoat and beret Miss Campbell wanted.

240

How though to get out of this longing to have someone come back to life?

The sole sound was the prick of her little blade snipping off the seam stitches. Shortly, she'd have a rest from this close work, go into the bathroom, turn on the geyser and actually remove her air-raid outfit, bathe and dress in clean air-raid outfit, including clean knitted hat. It wasn't as if she hadn't knitted herself two.

Not that anyone was coming to call. There wasn't a soul in the street, not a bus, hadn't been for days, and she'd had plenty of time to notice, having only her work to do and Fritzi to walk.

She'd sorted out Madame Lola's clothes too, the fur stoles, the full-length mink, the crepe dresses, the bandeaux, the scarves, shoes, underwear, stockings. It had been quite a task. Now they were hanging in sections, or boxed with labels. They filled the wardrobe almost entirely and she was keeping them there for any next-of-kin who might arrive in England after the war.

If it meant she couldn't use the wardrobe herself, that didn't matter. She hung her own clothes behind the bathroom door.

What did matter was that she couldn't manage to step into the washed and laundered bed because it felt to her as if she were stepping into a liniment and lavender-scented grave.

Furious over finding herself staring at it again, she stuffed the black velvet into its pillowcase, got up, threw her hat on the Brussels lace counterpane, also the jumper she hadn't removed for three days and nights. 'Bath, Fritzi,' she said, 'and a brush for you, then a very long walk, all three parks.'

The real problem of course was that the bed seemed to become more and more her parents' bed.

Another problem was that she felt the loneliest girl in the world.

She had a hand over the bath tap when the doorbell gave its most piercing shriek, yet was quickly downstairs to answer it, armed with a pencil and fully expecting it to be the postman with a package from Flo to be signed for. She'd have liked one.

But it was Max, parcel-less, cap-less, in a tramp's clothes, bleeding about the head, and somehow better than a parcel because he needed her, and she needed him. It was the first time she'd ever realised it.

*

241

'Well, I think we can say you look more comical in that pink dressing gown of mine than I do in my air-raid outfit.' She sat at the kitchen table with him, pouring coffee. It was Max who'd had the bath and now, contrary as always, she couldn't wait to have her own.

'I can't believe you decided that bedstead would protect you in an air raid.' He surveyed the spread she had put out for him, the rest of the baking Flo had sent for Christmas.

'I can't believe the Lipinskis left that huge shelter where you've been sleeping all these months just because Mrs Lipinski's mother refused to go there any more.'

'She made up her mind she couldn't stand it, she wanted to take her chance under her own stairs, she hated sleeping with hundreds of strangers, and if her name was on it . . .'

'So that meant Mrs Lipinski decided to stay at home with her?'

He nodded. 'Then Pa said he couldn't stand another night in the Tilbury either, and there was nothing to prove the Tilbury could withstand a direct hit, and if your name's on it, and the girls started wailing it was New Year coming up, the place would be full of drunks. Anyway, before the sirens started, they got panicky, rushed upstairs for blankets and pillows, rushed down again to install themselves in the cellar with Pa's mushrooms and the rats. I knew I wouldn't be able to stand a rat running over my face in the night so I made my bed up in the scullery. Freezing, it was.'

Elbows on the table, Susanna scrutinised the cuts and swellings on his face and neck, wondering if she should call a doctor. 'And it was the incendiaries that saved you?'

'Yes, I did sleep, I suppose, through the usual racket, but something woke me and I saw the little blue and white flashes coming down. I was outside in a second with the sand bucket and shovel to put them out when something hit me. I was thrown several metres into the alleyway.'

'Blast,' she suggested.

'I suppose. But I knew straight away I must get up and look for the shovel because there were all these little burning balls flying around the yard. Incendiaries, I thought, damn them, but they weren't, Suzy, they were little burning chickens.' He tried to put his head in his hands, and winced.

242

'You're not going to be able to eat yet, are you?' she asked, indicating his untouched plate. 'Why don't you get into bed?'

'Am I supposed to sleep with that hairy Pekinese creature?'

'If he likes you enough.' She began collecting her outdoor clothes, Fritzi's lead, her purse. 'I'm going to the shops for the things you need, but I don't expect any complaints if they're not right. I'll try and get a shirt in the market, otherwise you'll have to stay in your rest-centre outfit until you can go to the shops yourself.'

'I'd like one of those Viyella ones,' he said, making his way to the bed. 'My skin's so sore.' He drew back the sheet and slipped into it as if it were a perfectly ordinary bed, which it was, nicer than most, with its best linen and drop-stitch edging and the Brussels lace cover. Suddenly, contrary, she wanted him to step right out of it again; it was her parents' bed, she was keeping it for them. He looked wrong in it too, and about twelve, a boy with a boxer's swollen face and one of the smiles that used to melt his mother's stone of a heart.

'I can't promise,' she said, reflecting that her own heart had a mere shrivelled core left. 'I've only got about two pounds in cash and there's extra food to be got. I expect you'll be wanting plenty of chocolate and there's a toothbrush to be found, socks, yours were caked with blood from the cuts on your legs, and you'll need shaving things.'

'Leave out the shaving things, you won't choose the proper sort. I may forget shaving for a while. Don't you think I'll be handsome with a dark chin?'

'You'll look like a gangster,' she said, pulling on her jacket.

He watched her. 'What have you done with the old lady's furs? They'll be worth something.'

'I've put everything of hers neatly in the wardrobe in case any next of kin arrive after the war. Of course, if my parents get here first, I shall put it in store, I don't want to yet, this building's already suffered once and if I trust a warehouse that could be destroyed. The newsagent claims hardly anywhere's touched twice, except the buildings along the Thames, the Savoy's been bombed several times.'

He was almost asleep, his boxer's red and blue face sunk into Madame Lola's linen. She'd seen it like that before, at home.

'Suzy.'

243

'What?'

'Did I tell you the chickens went dashing round the yard like little burning balls?'

'You did.'

'Little burning balls,' he repeated. 'I couldn't hear them screaming for the other noises.'

'I expect they did scream.'

'Yes.'

She put on her gloves and reached down for Fritzi. He'd jumped from his chair and had been eagerly waiting for minutes past.

Max opened his eyes and sat up. 'Of course, nobody screams from blast, do they? I mean, blast just gets you, strips off some clothes or kills you stone dead. Blast's quick, you don't see it coming. Why don't you point out the good of it?'

'Good out of what?' She tucked Fritzi under one arm and took the string bag from the door handle.

'Good out of my foster family dying by blast.' He looked up at her with black, over-bright eyes. A cut near the right one seemed as if it were going to bleed again.

'I must remember the Elastoplast,' she said.

'A good way to die, Suzy, and I couldn't have saved them, could I, they were already dead when I found them, lying there as if they were asleep.'

By the time she'd reached the door, he'd put his hands to his sore face to hide the fact he was going to cry. 'I'd better get a room here in Soho,' he said, 'and a job. And we'd better get married as soon as we're old enough.'

He was feeling lonelier than ever, lonelier than she was and she was struck suddenly with a terrible anguish, a yearning for someone else to be ringing her doorbell, someone from home to come up the stairs, Max's mother, she'd do, anyone, to cry out with suitable horror at the state the two of them had reached.

Chapter 39

A Party in Patch and Georgiana's Flat, May 1941

'. . . and this,' Patch shouted, 'is Susanna Lehmann, the dress designer who'll one day take London by storm. Already has her own salon, no less.'

'And so young, ma'am.' The American officer bowed over her hand and Patch led him on around the room where two or three other Americans, a Polish pilot and a dozen or so Free French men and girls were crammed into the room, all in their various uniforms.

'And this is her boyfriend, Max. I'm trying to get the two of them to dance, but they won't, so I'm relying on you, Hank, to persuade Susuanna on to the floor instead of propping up the mantelpiece . . .'

Outside, the usual air-raid din of ack-ack and bomber went on and on, and the whistle and whine of someone else's bombs. Lights in the flat had been switched off, the curtains were open and the sky was a greeny-blue backdrop to the flash of searchlight and flare.

Susanna watched as a giant chandelier of incendiaries hung there, spitting like fireworks. Someone was getting it, someone not far off. But inside this first-floor flat with its fug of cigarette smoke and scent, there was laughter, music and dancing.

'Must be one of Adolf's worst spite nights,' Patch called from the kitchen doorway, 'and he's chosen my birthday, for it. Never mind, let's eat, drink and be merry for tomorrow we may certainly cop it. I've got the last of the whisky here, so anyone who wants a drop, please hold out your glass. After this, unless my brother gets to my party like he promised he would, you'll have to settle for warm beer.'

'*Parlez-moi d'amour,*' sang Georgie at the piano.

'*Dites-moi les choses douces . . .*' Lodged on the piano stool beside her, an arm about her waist, Georgiana's new Free French boyfriend crooned into her ear.

Patch edged round the dancers in the middle of the room, interrupted Max's conversation with Hank and led him to Susanna. 'Look, I'd like to see you two dance, and it is my birthday. Then I want Suzy to dance with Hank. I might never have another birthday, everyone has to be happy, please, and get together.'

'Aren't she and that George girl supposed to be recovering from months in a Paris prison and a treacherous journey through Nazi France?' Max leaned against the mantelpiece near her and blew out American cigarette smoke.

'They recovered from all that long ago. They're ambulance drivers here in London now, dashing about gathering up dead and wounded, which you wouldn't be able to do, so don't make some other sarcastic remark. They might be saving your life one of these nights. You don't even want to join the Pioneer Corps as some refugee men are doing.'

'Was going to make no comment whatsoever. They're your connections, not mine.' He flinched as another bomb whistled down. 'Don't any of them use the shelters?'

'Friends, not connections,' she muttered, watching Patch's Free French boyfriend lead her towards the dancing. Eyes half closed, he removed the cigarette from his mouth, placed it in hers, and together, entwined, they began to move.

Max said, 'They give you good business, they're connections, and connections are what I need.'

'*Je vous aime,*' sang Georgiana.

'You're still only beginning to make your way, though I admit being taken on as a messenger and trouser-maker in a one-room outwork tailor is a step up from a presser, but I've been learning for years, I began at my Buba's knee.'

'Just because I didn't spend my childhood playing with ribbons and copying drawings from ancient tailors' books and fashion magazines doesn't mean I now need years of training. You let me have that second machine at the salon, I'll train myself, I'll pay

246

you for it as soon as I start making enough, or I'll pay you with work.' He threw his cigarette into the hearth and opened a packet of Camels, apparently just acquired from Hank.

'Don't blow any more smoke on me, please.'

'You want me to go on struggling to survive on twenty-five shillings a week? That room I rent's got mouldy walls, I wouldn't eat if you didn't feed me. My own business, ours, is our only hope, we have to build up that salon, and we should change the name, it sounds French, she made a mistake there, La Lola, Viennese dressmakers are known to be the best. To my mind, Estanna Modes sounds English, whereas Maxanna . . .'

One day, Susanna thought, I am going to have to tell Max nicely that the business is for my parents and me, and for Sophie's future at university. She wished she hadn't come, but Patch and Georgie were right, she had spent an entire winter of evenings crouched over hand-sewing in the kitchen with Fritzi and it was now spring, nearly summer, even if another spate of air raids was spoiling it.

'It's not as if I wouldn't have given you a secure future. How easy d'you think it was getting that stuff bought for you to bring out? Losing the sapphire wasn't my fault.'

'No. I'm sorry. When the war's over, everything will seem different and if you can get a job with a jacket outworker next, you'll learn a lot there. Someone might take you on, think of all those backrooms in Soho, you must be making some connections for yourself already.'

'We must get out of Soho, Mayfair where's we have to be.' He left the cigarette to hang on his lip, Humphrey Bogart style. 'You don't want to dance, do you?'

'As far as I know, we can't dance,' she replied, turning her glance to the lit-up sky beyond the window. 'There are lots of fires out there. We'll never get home tonight, we'll end up on the floor with a blanket each.'

'I'm going to talk to that American,' he said. 'I bet he knows how to get more of these Camels. You want some nylons? Bet I can get you some.'

'Max, no black market meddling, please.' He wasn't listening; he was already across the room and sitting on the floor beside the American. I don't like Hank's face, she thought, it has something of a Berliner boy about it, very set and stiff, tight-lipped and yet weak, blond of course, small blue eyes, a lock of damp hair on the forehead.

Georgiana left the piano stool and wandered across to the gramophone. Soon the strains of 'I've Got you Under my Skin' drifted up and the dancers shuffled on.

Outside, a stream of flares dropped by a bomber turned the sky yellow and white.

'Wow.' A second American officer got to his feet and threw up the window. 'Free fireworks, folks, and something big coming down.' He leaned out. 'The east's getting it again, City, Holborn, lots of fires, great fat sparks, very pretty.'

Georgie linked her arm with her boyfriend's and strolled across the room, dragging up Max by the arm and bringing him over to Susanna. 'I want this dance with little Maxie and you, André, my love, are to dance with this gorgeous creature. She's the designer of the future, *chéri*, got her own salon no less.'

Susanna looked into a pair of smiling brown eyes and her heart sank. She certainly couldn't dance.

Max grabbed her arm, hurting it. 'Suzy and I were just going to join the others, thank you,' he said.

'You want to be embarrassed by not being able to dance with a Frenchman?' hissed Max. 'Your mother'd expect me to save you.'

'Oh, you mean you didn't want to be embarrassed by not being able to dance with Georgiana? I did wonder.'

But it was pleasant being held by him, and familiar, although they'd only ever play-danced together as children, at festive meals. They were still the same height and she could see the true blackness of his eyes. He smelled nice, of the lavender soap she'd given him, and tobacco. She closed her eyes, lulled by the shuffling round and round movement. Dancing was easy.

'David's here,' shrieked Patch. 'Thank heaven. Hey, everyone, my brother, David, and more of the good stuff.'

Susanna turned her head towards the doorway. Mr David was framed in it, looking suntanned and more handsome than ever, the scar on his face adding somehow to the interest of his face, the long slenderness of it, with the silky black eyebrows and his frown.

Patch, beside him, seemed even prettier, having something of

248

his face in hers. 'Wow, real string?' she cried. 'We got some real string, Georgie, don't let me put it away in such a safe place we can never find it.'

They'd hardly moved away from the door when something terrible exploded so close, the window blew in, and the curtains, and a cloud of green dust.

Susanna watched this green stuff creep over two Free French girls sitting on the floor and roll towards her and Max. She heard a strange noise like hailstones and the gramophone stopped.

Everyone was giggling and spitting out bits of plaster. The hailstones had been the ceiling coming down.

'God, have we died? You look like a ghoul, Georgie.' Patch's voice.

'So d'you, love.' Georgiana.

They all looked ghoulish. The green dust had stuck to their skin over the little dribbles of blood from cuts and had formed an indoor, foul-smelling fog. They were just shapes in it, stumbling and spitting in slow motion, skin green, eyes and mouth shockingly red and white. They had green-powdered wigs for hair and the piano had gone green.

'Susanna.' David's voice, and his hand, reaching for hers.

'We must get out fast!' An American. He had crawled to where the door had been. 'I'll go and see if there's any staircase to get out by.'

'Suzy.' Max touched her leg. He'd been knocked over and knelt on a carpet which had turned into a shingly beach with glass in it.

David reached down to help him up and Susanna used her free hand to try and brush plaster off his face.

'There's half a staircase out here,' the American shouted. 'You guys bring the girls out, quick.'

'You are trembling,' David said.

'I'm all right.' They were on the landing in rubble and fog. Max had got himself down on his behind, and now she must.

'Come.' David released her hand but before she could feel the loss of it, both his arms went around her and she was lifted up against the gritty-rough cloth of his jacket.

'Rest,' he said.

She laid her head on his shoulder and closed her eyes. She felt beyond reason joyously happy. 'Our name wasn't on it,' she said.

All the men but Max had run off to help dig people out. Whatever it was had exploded at the end of the street and brought down several buildings. Max was instructed to escort the ladies to the nearest tube station, where they were to wait until the all clear. The Free French girls were going to their lodgings after that but Patch and Georgiana were returning with Susanna to the salon to bathe and change into something of hers before making for the rehousing offices in the morning. Meanwhile, they stood on the pavement trying to brush off dust, though Max kept demanding they start for the shelter. Couldn't they see they were surrounded by flames?

'I suppose a clean, empty street would be the most astonishing sight of all,' murmured Georgie.

'Yep.' Patch coughed.

At their feet were wet black snakes of hose. Firemen slapped it about amongst the rubble. Dribbles of their water had turned the rubble to mud and pink fountains of it played on the church opposite where fire licked the steeple and crept in and out of the gravestones.

Huddled together they watched the nurses and the rescue men stumbling round the hoses, black capes shining, torches flashing. There were three fire engines spilling out the hose and two ambulances screeching up, bells jangling.

'Sometimes, it's just the noise of it,' Patch muttered.

'And the lights when it should be dark.' A Free French girl.

No torches were needed. It was as bright as day, a tropically flame-pink hot and hazy day. Fires reached right up to the mountain of rubble blocking one end of the street. They could see the digging shapes dark against it and the first of the stretchers being lifted up.

'Look at the sky,' the Free French girl said. 'All London is burning.'

Yes, Susanna thought, eyes so full of smoke she couldn't begin to search for Mr David's digging shape against the flames, and there is never going to be any end to it, and one day, soon, when the entire city is a smouldering ruin, the parachutists will float down on us, and glory in their ruins, and laugh as only the SS know how. It has taken them five-and-a-half months so far.

None of the women wanted to bother with a proper shelter. The French girls decided to risk trying to reach their lodgings and Georgiana made up her mind the rest of them should wend their way to a mobile canteen because she was dying for tea, and what's more, there'd been no bombers aiming north, as far as she could tell, and she was an expert, so if they kept to a northerly direction, they'd be safe enough. Still, it had been quite a night while they were dancing!

Outvoted, not knowing the roads well enough, Max could only follow her and Patch as they crossed this way and that around fires and craters, his hand gripping Susanna's as his sole expression of male authority left.

There were many craters and countless fires, mounds of masonry, heaps of rafters that had once supported people's roofs. And tipped anyhow in it all, people's front doors, their lavatory seats, their bits of blue and white china, their teapots, great jagged splinters of shot-down bombers' wings, and little piles of spent shell casings, still warm to the touch, from the ack-ack guns.

Eventually, Georgie caught sight of a canteen van serving police and a rescue squad in what had once been one of those railed-in London parks with seats, and they found themselves sitting on a bench there drinking tea with sugar and milk in it that was like nectar, reflecting on air raids past and present.

'It's the endless din that gets me,' Patch said, 'our ack-ack guns going whang, whang, whang, on and on, drives me mad.'

'It's the flares,' Max said, 'you see a flare, you know something's coming, then the droning cough, as if the bombers are warning you, cough, cough, I'm coming, I'm coming . . .'

'Coming for you, yes!' Patch laughed.

Susanna glanced at him in surprise. He'd didn't often join in these general conversations, but he was making an effort tonight. A surge of affection helped her reach out and brush something off his shoulder. There was dust grimed into his best suit, a green mould-like stuff in his hair. He'd been through so much already! She must be kinder to him, stop bickering, let him go on dreaming of a future that might never come.

Georgiana passed him the plate that had been balanced on her knees. Her slinky party dress was filthy, all her skin and her beautiful blonde hair green. 'Try a bun,' she suggested, 'they're rock-hard same as the rock cakes but who's complaining? I'm dying for some chocolate actually. Anyone notice if they had a cocoa tin behind the counter in that van?' She leaned forward to peer across the grass to the van. 'I'll wait till the rescue men and police have finished. They need nourishment more than we do. Trouble is, soon as you think of chocolate, you have to have some.'

Patch groaned. 'You would remind me of chocolate, just when I was satisfied with rock cakes for once.'

'Susanna has cocoa,' Max began, when a cry came from the queue.

'Look out, something's coming down!'

But it was all right. Whatever it was, hadn't exploded. There'd be a few minutes before the bomb disposal squad arrived and they'd be shoo'ed off. Patch and Georgiana went for the cocoa.

Susanna watched them go. 'They are so nonchalant, aren't they?'

'They are different from us,' Max agreed. 'And I don't know what your mother would say if she knew her daughter was being carried about by goy blokes.'

'What?' She turned to him, astonished. 'Mr David? You mean he shouldn't have helped me down the stairs? That's really silly. He's a gentleman. It's what gentlemen do.'

'He's a goy.'

'Yes. I wasn't brought up to use such terms, though. Name-calling's where it starts. And when were you so proud to be Jewish? If you didn't look it, you'd pretend not to be.'

He shrugged. 'You go too far.'

'What, too far? Who else is there to be friendly with, tell me? Has anyone from the Jewish community sought you out? Anyone from the synagogue? I saw a rabbi for Madame Lola's funeral but he never suggested I go to the Jewish youth group, he never asked me how I was managing. It wasn't Anglo-Jews who took us in, was it?'

'Suzy, Max!' Patch ran across the grass. 'Quick, they've got one, they've got a bomber pilot, God knows where his bomber went, but he and his parachute were what we thought was a landmine. Come on, you can help the police ask him a few questions.'

'No, don't say anything, Patch, I can't . . .'

Patch was back at the van where a crowd was collecting. Voices rose, excited voices.

'Max. You'll have to.'

'I can't.'

'We must. It'll look so daft.'

'They won't understand.'

'No.' An extraordinary nausea sprang up in her throat. 'Will they lynch him?'

'This is England.'

He edged closer. She could feel the two of them sitting side by side amongst a litter of plates and cups, and how they would look to other people, faces gone as white as could be under their green-mould hair. And that pilot boy. What would he think, seeing them there, and seeing the smoky desolation of the enemy's city he had been ordered to help destroy night after night?

In the end, they had to step forward with the policeman and go up to the van where several police were grouped around their prisoner. One of them was making a big roll of his parachute.

The pilot himself wore a flying suit, all flaps and leather, but he'd lost his helmet so she could see his face quite clearly.

It was like Konrad's, the same hard stiff features, everything straight, the mouth a thin line. Nothing moved on it, as if he were made of wax, and he wasn't looking at her, he was looking at no one.

It occurred to her he was a very frightened boy who was going to be sick, as she was.

Respectfully, everyone stood back and somehow she got out her questions, stumbling, the words unfamiliar, foreign.

'He won't give me anything but his name and number,' she announced finally, sweat trickling down her spine. 'Max, you try.'

Max stepped forward. The tea ladies clattered their saucers and not far off to the south-east, another bomber dropped something.

'Max.' She'd thought he couldn't find the words either, she'd thought that his fiddling in his jacket pocket was to give himself time. But he was getting out his dagger, the one with Blood and

253

Honour engraved on it, she guessed that from the flash of a blade. She saw him lunge forward and heard someone scream.

'My God, the excitement of it,' Georgie said, as they sat back on their bench with the cocoa and watched the waxen figure led off in handcuffs. 'How did you know he'd have a pistol inside that suit?'

Max shrugged. 'Assumed he would.' His skin was ghost-white.

'Liked the way you flicked that pistol handle round and round,' Patch said. 'And the way you passed it so casually to the policeman. Didn't they admire you! I dunno, I think our police are as innocent as they were when the war started. Why haven't they been trained to capture a pilot and get his gun? I love 'em, I really do, but what if plane-loads of SS float down on us like that?'

'Max has always seen himself as a gangster.' Susanna felt a sudden fury emerge from her fatigue. She'd thought Max had been going to stab the boy. He had been. To show off! 'Now we've got to go to the police station tomorrow, we'll be all day making statements.' She heard herself shouting. 'All day. And it's not as if we found out anything, or as if there weren't masses of German speakers in London trained to interrogate properly.'

I wish I could die, she thought, I wish I could stay on this bench in all this din and smoky air and just weep and weep.

'Well, he's absolutely finished now, poor love.' Georgie put one of her long arms around Max's shoulders and rested her hand on Susanna's. 'You're both done in. Brandy's what you need, and a bath, and a sleep. What do you say we make a real effort and get on to Suzy's place?'

On her other side, Patch struggled to her feet again, draining the last of her cup. 'It wasn't really like the films back there for you, was it, Suze?'

'No. It was . . .' Susanna had to make an effort. 'It was . . .'

'Don't bother. It's private isn't it?'

'Yes.'

'D'you know what, Suzy?' Georgie disentangled herself and stood up.

'What?

'I often decide I can't stand another second of this war.'

'So do I.' Susanna felt her eyes fill with tears. She caught hold of Max's hand and helped him up.

*

254

It was dawn, a foggy smoky dawn. Charred paper drifted in the air. Every tree had lost its leaves and at its blackened base lay a scattering of dead sparrows. All along the river, the great buildings smouldered still. As David made his way through the rubble of the street, he saw the clearance squads were already working in a stunned silence, the only sound cranes swivelling into place. The last of the shelterers were dragging their belongings out of the mouth of the tube station, gazing about them at familiar landmarks, wordless. This dawn, there was so much more that was burned, shattered, gone to dust. London was done for, that's what they were thinking, and he was.

He was done for too, and nausea sat somewhere deep inside him. On the mountain of rubble that night, he'd come upon a woman's hand. It had a wedding ring on it, an engagement ring, and he'd found himself doing the stupidest thing – trying to clean it with his handkerchief and when he realised that's what he was doing, he wrapped it up in the handkerchief instead and laid it with the other body pieces on the sheet close to the baby already placed there, in case it should be hers. Then he got on with digging where he was told to dig, where cries had been heard.

Now he had one more task to do, and at some point, as soon as he could face it, he must get breakfast down, and he must sleep. Meanwhile, brandy had helped him on, and hope, and the memory of the feel of Susanna in his arms, her slender weight against him. The night had brought him that.

He was trying to hurry over the glass and the brick, but couldn't. His knee held him back, and a sense of horror, a fear that she hadn't survived, or Patch and Georgie, because the best were so often lost first.

Chapter 40

London, June 1941

'And it wasn't only the worst spite night of all, Sophie, but the last! Since Hitler decided to invade Russia instead of us, the poor Russians are suffering all those bombers, and we Londoners can't sleep because it's so quiet.'

Sophie stood in the late afternoon sunlight by the cutting table and slipped on the tacked-up dress Susanna was making for her. 'I wish I could have been through just a bit of an air raid though, to know what it was like. The sirens go sometimes at school and we have to line up two by two and troop down to the shelter in the grounds. We sing a lot of songs and then troop back to class.'

'God forbid I ever have to worry about you being crouched somewhere in the dark waiting for the bomb with your name on it. Me crouched in the dark waiting for mine has been enough.' Susanna knelt on the floor with her yardstick and fiddled with the waistline. 'This seems too high,' she said, 'you must have grown since Aunt Daphne took the measurements. I shall have to lower it. Hold still.'

She got to work with pins. 'That May Saturday was a mass attempt to burn down London, though. Hundreds of bombers came over dropping thousands of tons of explosive and incendiaries. There were two thousand fires, apparently, fourteen hundred deaths, invasion expected – again! I can't tell you how many invasion scares I've lived through, or how many hours I've spent expecting to die in some shelter. To think that night I was actually out in the thick of it when I mostly preferred to avoid putting a toe outside after blackout – and am still here!'

'Puh, puh, puh,' Sophie whispered, smiling down at her.

'We've gone back to the old ways already.'

'Yes! I've been counting our God forbids. Nanny's banned them when I'm there in the holidays.'

'Nanny would. And you can come here in the holidays if there's to be no more raids. Hold still.'

'Sometimes at school I find myself saying touch wood.'

'That's all right. Turn round a bit and . . . Yes, it's about a centimetre too high.' She sat back on her heels and considered the skirt length. 'I shan't do it too short, a bit longer's more sophisticated and I think you're going to shoot up the way I did and will suddenly feel silly with your knees showing.' She blinked up at her sister who had turned to gaze out of the window. 'They won't mind, you know. Mama and Papa.'

'No.'

'They'll expect it. And midnight feasts in the dorm.'

'Yes. I might be invited to one soon.'

'They'll expect you to be playing tennis and things. They'll be *so proud* of their English daughter.'

'Yes.'

'Have you spoken to the other Jewish girls there yet?' She edged herself round the hem with her pins and the yardstick.

'They're all much older. I've sort of made friends with a scholarship girl called Mary. She comes from such a poor family, she's an outcast too, and she doesn't seem to realise I'm anything but a poor girl from Germany who's got a rich foster-mother. The word Jewish to her is just like some sect, Methodist or something.'

'That must be nice.'

'Yes. We go about together more and more and when everyone has to find a partner or get into twos, we have each other. Aunt Daphne says I'm to invite her to stay at Downlands this summer when Mr Montgomery isn't there.'

'You must invite her here, Sophie. A poor girl won't turn her nose up at a kitchen that's also a bedroom.'

'Did you really sleep under Madame Lola's bed for shelter sometimes?'

'My bed, yes.' Susanna laughed.

'Your bed.' Sophie waved a hand around the room. 'And your salon. Madame Susanna, Court Dressmaker.'

257

'Just dressmaker, darling. There are no court occasions anymore. It's considered bad taste up here to bother about frivolous show in wartime. But when it's over, I'm going to have the plaque on the door downstairs changed to Estanna Modes. D'you remember, I wrote to ask you once which you preferred, Bestanna or Estanna, and you chose to have Mama's name in it? Keep still, please. I really want to get this hem right. I have a lot planned for your weekend here, we're going out and about a bit and I want you to have this dress to take back to Dorset. You've so little else to wear this summer.'

'Imagine Mama's face when she sees her name on a door and steps up here for the first time.'

'I do imagine it, Sophie, often, and I imagine her agony when she settles to the idea that it's true, I have been given this gift, but there's never been anyone to thank or be grateful to, poor Madame Lola being dead. How she'll bless her though!'

Susanna put in the last pin and sat back to admire her work and her sister in it. 'Yes,' she said, 'the deep pink is one of your colours, it brings out the pink of your cheeks and the blue of your eyes. I think the waistcoat effect of the bodice is nice too. I did a puff sleeve, they're all right at your age but not on big gawky women. Imagine Mama's face seeing you so grown and healthy! Sometimes I think she'll weep for joy that we've managed without her and sometimes . . .'

Her voice tailed off as she got to her feet. Sometimes, she thought, I am absolutely certain she'll weep for what she has missed and is lost to her for ever. The next dress would have to allow for Sophie's little breasts and she herself had had to broach the subject of periods. 'Take it off carefully,' she said, 'and lay it on the table. Max'll be here shortly. We're going to have the proper sabbath supper and then he'll want to go to a film. He adores them. He talks Hollywood, using words like "swell" and "guy", he has an American officer friend and he smokes. You'll be surprised at how different he is, though he's still Max, of course.'

On the kitchen table, Sophie spread out the Board of Trade instructions, the pieces of white cardboard Susanna had cut from trimming boxes and the coloured drawing pencils. 'I'll do the title in red, this RATIONING OF CLOTHING, CLOTH AND FOOTWEAR FROM

258

JUNE 1941, the number of coupons needed for each garment, and the rest in black.'

'Yes, but keep over to that end, the end by the stove's for our supper.' Susanna gave the candlesticks a last polish and placed them in the centre. 'I discovered Madame Lola had these hidden in her trunk and I think they're old and valuable, or at least a family heirloom, so I feel I'm looking after them for any family of hers that might arrive here after the war. I thought they wouldn't mind if I used them occasionally. And you know what I thought?'

'What?'

'Her first sabbath here, Mama will be lighting them, until we get our own again.'

'Why not my mother, she's the eldest?' Max called from the salon, where he was admiring himself in the mirror. 'She has these daft dreams, your sister. Maybe they'll come over together.' He strolled into the kitchen and sat at the table beside Sophie. 'Like my shirt?'

'That's his Ivor Novello look,' Susanna said. 'You're supposed to notice that fine-weave and loose cut with the narrow diagonal stripes and the tie with the stripes going in the other direction. His other look is what I call his black marketeer, which I hate. It's a best dark suit, Brylcreem and an Anthony Eden hat. I had to lend him fifty pounds to re-clothe himself after he was blitzed, but if he gets into the black market, I'll be furious.'

Sophie giggled. 'You'll be sent to the KZ if you're a black marketeer.'

'Don't be daft. You think I'd get caught?' Max grinned, leaned his elbows on the table and picked up the rationing instructions. 'Haven't you got this sorted out yet? All the Savile Row shops I deliver trousers to have proper printed lists up.'

'You should have worn the best suit, I told you it's a real sabbath supper.' Susanna stood by the stove in something of a panic, stirring the soup. 'Can't you smell it?'

'I can smell chicken noodle soup and I can see chicken noodle soup tins on the drainer. No matzo balls? Don't they come in tins?'

'I'm too busy to bother with travelling across half London to the kosher butcher and if you think I could have the thing bleeding in here all naked and dead! These are from Fortnum's.' She stuffed the tins into the rubbish bin. 'Don't expect gefilte fish either. I have got some trout poaching though and I suppose I'm going to fry these potatoes.'

'Not in margarine, I hope.' Max yawned.

'Margarine, and olive oil I got from Mrs Bertoni, it'll taste all right. I've saving the butter Flo sent with Sophie for our breakfasts.'

Sophie held up a card. 'I've done the word RATIONING in capitals, the three other titles smaller underneath.'

'And it's very nicely balanced. Now put WOMEN AND GIRLS in capitals on the left-hand side and copy under it that list there. Ordinary lettering, I should think.'

'For my new pink dress, I'd have had to give up five coupons. "Dress, or gown, or frock, woollen, Adults 11, child 8, dress, or gown, or frock, other material, five." '

'You would, if I hadn't already got the fabric. It's some left from what Madame Lola sensibly bought when war broke out. She bought crepe as well, neutral colours, some grey flannel, some nice brown fleck tweed and fur strips. Of course, I could buy in now whatever the wholesalers are prepared to let me have from present stock, but it's a risk as an investment in case I'm bombed out here. The accountant thinks I should buy in some of the classic fabrics. He wasn't very pleased I lent Max fifty pounds. "When will this young man be in a position to repay you, Miss Lehmann?"he said, personally hurt, I think, because Max has no collateral to offer me.'

Susanna watched the potatoes come to the boil and turned down the gas. 'I told him, with half-a-crown a week until he gets a better job. Is it three minutes or five you boil first for sauté'd?'

'And I've told you, use some of your capital, buy up whatever fabric you can for reselling later to less well-advised dressmakers. Or sell those candlesticks of La Lola's, or one of her furs. War can mean profit for someone, always has.'

'He thinks he's my partner,' Susanna said, deciding on two minutes and draining off the potato water.

'Heat the frying pan first,' Max said.

'You want to do it?'

'Why would I? Hurry up, I'm hungry.'

'It's not dusk yet.'

'It's near enough dusk. Which film are we going to see?'

'Sophie must choose, it's her weekend.' She sliced the warm

potatoes and gingerly slid the pieces into the oil mix. It didn't smell very appealing.

'A thriller, Sophie? *The Lady Vanishes* is on, or what about a George Formby? He's in something called *Spare A Copper*, having lots of comic adventures while discovering a nest of Nazi spies. I suppose we can imagine what that'll be like.'

'Yes, funny,' Sophie said, copying on.

Edging the potato slices around the pan, Susanna said, 'I thought we'd wander about London in the morning with Fritzi. There are such odd things to see these days, sheep-shearing in Hyde Park, and a pig farm, and it's got rows of Dig for Victory allotments. I often wonder if there are allotments in the zoo gardens in Berlin.' She removed the soup from the stove and tipped it into a tureen. 'Though I suppose none of our people will be allowed them, any more than they were before. They'll be allowed to starve though.'

'Why are you bothering with serving dishes?' Max said.

'This is a proper sabbath, that's why. Stop now, Sophie, and put the things away. Don't waken Fritzi. I'll give him his fish later. I do want this meal to be nice.'

'Nice,' Max said. 'Nice tinned soup.'

'You'd be a horrible husband.' Sophie laid everything on the foot of the bed, gazed fondly at the sleeping Pekinese and returned to her place. 'Elbows off.' She pushed at Max's.

Max put his hands behind his head, leaned back and smiled. He was in his most smug and impossible mood. 'I shall be a wonderful husband. I shall be so wonderful, your sister will never actually have to pick up a thimble. We shall have a big estate like Downlands, with a suite of rooms for you to stay in on your holidays from university, which I shall pay for. You can have a pony if you want. You want a tennis court, you'll have it, you'll have your portrait in the hall. You'll have your medical student friends to stay every weekend.'

Susanna manoeuvred the fish platter from the oven and in a flurry of activity put out the dishes of salad and rice. Finally she spread the potato in its dish rubbed off the burned edges and added it to the messy display.

Then she took her place and suddenly it was very quiet and still in the room. Outside the salon, the sun had dropped away.

'It's time,' Sophie announced.

261

'Light the candles.' Max.

'I'm going to.' Susanna stood up and laid the white silk scarf over her hair. One by one, she lit the candles and recited the words of the benediction. We are play-acting, she thought.

'Now you, Max.'

'What, me?'

'The father's part. I did ask you.'

'You weren't joking?'

'Max!'

He glanced up at her with his too-bright eyes. 'I can't, Suzy.'

'All right.' What did it matter? They were only playing at it.

'You should have made me practise. What exactly is that pink stuff representing the wine?'

'I got a tin of strawberries on points, strained off the juice and added water.'

'You've spoiled it, Max,' Sophie said.

'Yes.' Susanna sat down and lifted the cloth from the challah bread. 'I shan't bother with it any more. Help yourselves.'

'It was nearly right, Suzy.' Sophie's loving eyes smiled at her across the table. 'I liked what you did. Max spoiled it like he always spoils everything.'

'Oh, shut up,' Max said. 'Make me practise next time.'

Suddenly filled with irritation and resentment, Susanna cried, 'Just hurry up and get it over with. We have to do our Red Cross letter before we go out.'

A longing for other sabbaths welled up in her, for Opa and Buba, her parents, Max's parents, the aunts and uncles, all the ones who'd judged and criticised her and Max. She wanted the noise they'd be making. She wanted to be treated like a no-good together with Max, because being of no account was easier than carrying her present burdens.

'Don't expect any more sabbaths out of me. Your next one will be when the others get here.'

'Just do the blessing at the end, Suzy, please,' Sophie said. ' "May the Lord bless you and keep you," it's somehow comforting.'

'For you, darling, I will. Meanwhile, eat.'

Sophie picked up her spoon with a smile.

Max said, 'Congratulations, Fortnum and Mason. And may you dream on, Susanna Lehmann.'

262

Chapter 41

Berlin, September 1941

'You have sewn on the star very nicely, my darling,' Josef said, patting the yellow cloth shape on his jacket lapel. 'I shall wear it with pride.'

She could not speak. Eyes blurred with tears, she kissed his cheek, watched him disappear through the kitchen door and as always, listened for the sound of his boots on the staircase. This was her last sound of him until until he was safely home from the factory at night. Next, for her last sight of him, she hurried across the room to open the balcony doors. Today, of all days, she must have that glimpse.

She leaned out. He was taking his usual slow, measured steps in the newly assigned place, the gutter, his head held higher than usual, prouder. Her heart felt as though it would burst. She must make her own gesture, now, at once, and not stay inside as she had most shamefully planned to do until stars had been got used to.

Yes, I am ashamed of myself, she thought, dashing into the bedroom and drawing back Freddy's covers, for I am married to the dearest man in the world, the noblest, I have this dear boy here, and our girls. I have so much, still, when so many wives and mothers have had their precious ones snatched from the street. And I fear a few, furtive glances at my label, a few jeers, as if it were not in my blood to endure, as if there had not already been so much else!

She couldn't see if any of the hurrying workers in the street had noticed her yellow star because she couldn't take her eyes off the ground. Having set herself and Freddy in the space between the pavement and the tram lines, she found herself in difficulties. Behind them, the two Polish slave workers pulling a coal cart were trying to get out of the way of a tram. She was in their way, and the tram's, so coming upon a corner with a pile of bomb rubble around it, she pulled Freddy over the top before searching for the name of the street. Was it one they were permitted on? Suddenly, she couldn't remember any of the forbidden street names, but as they were mostly the great avenues and fashionable area roads, she was probably safe enough. 'We'll take this route to Aunt Lottie Merkel's,' she said.

'Those men had special armbands on their jackets,' Freddy said, jumping off the rubble with glee.

'Yes. It means they are special kinds of workers.'

'They are workers like horses?'

'Yes.'

'What do yours and Papa's stars say?'

'That we are a special kind of people called Jews. Papa has explained it to you and you can read the words for yourself.'

'Why can't I have one?'

'You will, when you are six years old. Quickly now, or we'll never get to Aunt Lottie's.'

'Why can't we go on the tram like we used to?'

'Because we are not permitted to any more.'

'Why can't we go the other way so I can see the green nets over the tops of the linden trees on the Linden? What are the nets called?'

'Camouflage nets, and they are there so that when the bomber planes fly over, the pilots think the Linden is a park and not an avenue with important government buildings in it. They don't want to waste their bombs on a park.'

'I should also like to see how the fir trees are fixed to hide the street lamps and I should like to know if the English bomber pilots flying over Berlin at night are the same men we shall meet when we go to England because I have questions to ask them about what Berlin looks like from the sky.'

'For now my son,' she said, pulling him past an ironmonger's she had once been permitted to frequent, 'for now, we are going to Aunt Lottie Merkel's because we have the Red Cross letter from the girls to show her. Max is mentioned in it, isn't he?' Not one person has glanced at us, she decided, glancing herself at the straggle of workers making for their trams. They are indifferent to us, and that is the best we can hope for.

'Aunt Lottie Merkel doesn't like living in that big house with lots of other families, does she?'

'Because she used to have a grand flat with a balcony over the zoo gardens. You went there often when you were a baby.'

'Why isn't she in the grand flat now?'

'Because our people are not allowed in grand flats.'

'Because of the war?'

'Yes. Perhaps after the war, she will go to England to live with Max, just as we are going to live with the girls. Hold your head up, my son, you are scuffing your feet.'

'Why must I? I like studying the cobbles. They have nice shapes and I might find something to play with.'

'You must hold up your head because you are with your Mama who's wearing a special yellow star because she's special and that means you're special too.' This is what I must offer us, she thought, because pride is free and I have only to think of Opa and Buba, God rest their souls, and I can take some more steps and some more with my yellow star and believe there will one day be an end to it.

By the time they reached the wretched district where Lottie Merkel and her sister-in-law had been driven, she'd drifted into a wonderful dream of Sophie at her English school, her proper English school. She was carrying a lacrosse stick and something called a satchel stuffed with school books and a severe head-mistress figure was breaking into a smile as she announced that the winner of the chemistry prize was 'our newest arrival, Sophie Lehmann . . .'

DOCTOR IN THE FAMILY, that's what the Red Cross letter said, the girls' way of telling them *so much*. But it's all right, my darlings, she thought, turning into Lottie's street, anything in the family will do, paupers, it doesn't matter, just try to go on being happy waiting for Papa, Freddy and me, because we are trying hard to go on living for you.

Lottie Merkel was of course still in bed and deep in depression in the lice and flea-ridden lodging-house room she was allowed to occupy. She had slept, she said, but had had nightmares again.

Esther lit the gas under the camping contraption Josef had found for her. Lottie wouldn't use the kitchen, and without her sister-in-law Leah living in the next room, she would have sunk further into her misery.

Somehow, though, in the oasis of her bed amongst the few possessions she'd managed to cling on to during her two forced moves, she retained a little of her old manner. She expected to be spoiled as her husband had spoiled her, and at her worst moments in that bed seemed to have something of Max's sulky, little boy's face.

'They moved another twenty in here yesterday,' she said, propping herself up against silk pillowcases. 'They want more flats for the French labourers they've kidnapped from France for the war armaments factories. That makes two hundred of us in a squalid house meant for sixty. The manager's giving up telling the SS he can't take any more, and what do they care? He says Leah and I will have to share this room if yet more are sent. Imagine that, Esther, she's never quiet. I wouldn't have a minute's peace for her cleaning and cooking and mending.'

'Now Lottie, you told me she'd made a lovely job of your nightdresses.' Esther placed a saucepan of water over the flame.

'I suppose I will have a tidy nightgown to be buried in, yes,' Lottie said. 'Pass me my shawl, please. Where's Freddy?'

Esther passed her the black and gold antique beauty from the foot of the bed. 'He's playing on the second floor with the boys he met on our last visit.

'Countless boys here there are, you should hear them shouting up and down the stairs, where the parents are . . .'

'Well, I have something in my bag about your boy, Lottie.' Esther took off her jacket and laid it where the shawl had been.

Lottie's gaze settled on it with evident horror.

'Leah has sewn on your star, Lottie?'

'You think anything can be sewn on fur?'

'Then you must have it sewn on your black suit jacket, or you won't be able to go out, and you'll have to make sure it shows.'

'You know I don't go out.' Lottie pulled the bedclothes around her breasts and stared fretfully into space.

'You ought to take your turn to queue at the market and not let Leah do everything. You're spoiled.' She poured the hot water over the camomile tea the chemist had let her have and took her friend's cup of it to what must be the bedside table, a poor thing covered in dirty oilcloth. 'But you don't know yet what I have for you.'

'What?'

'A letter from the dear Red Cross office.'

'Only you could love an office.'

Esther sat on the chair by the window and held up the piece of paper. 'The people who work in it are dear to me. You'll be having one from Max soon, I expect, Lottie. And how do I know that? Because our three are together. Or have been together.' She smiled. 'Imagine. I had trouble getting Josef to leave it aside last night and go to sleep. Shall I read it to you?'

'You're going to, Esther.' Lottie too tried to smile. 'I am pleased for you.'

'Sophie doctor in the family,' Esther read, 'Madame Susanna dressmaker Max Savile Row all three will have connections and together sabbath today longing for you all four.'

' . . . Josef and I think Sophie's school really must be one of those English private ones we used to read about, when we were girls, and Susanna must already be doing some paid dressmaking. I hope she isn't neglecting that design training, the darling girl has so much talent. Max, well, your Max, you think he wouldn't have found his way and got his start? Savile Row, Lottie, Josef says it's the very top name in tailoring.'

'You think I want to boast of a tailor for a son? You think I'm pleased, you think a proper son leaves his mother like he did?'

'He did it for you, Lottie, so he can offer you a good life when the war's over.'

'Yes,' said Lottie bitterly, 'but only you and Josef believe it ever will be over in the way you mean, they'll rule the world, like they say. You know they're snatching people off the streets now, children? If you think you're doing right by wearing that star, you haven't understood it's so the SS squads can pick you out more easily.'

'No,' Esther said quietly, 'I think it's part of their scheme of gradual humiliation of our people. I think they hope the Germans will spit on us as they pass, and I am sure that some will. They don't need these stars for picking out poor souls to go on the transports to the work camps. Frau Leona was taken yesterday,

267

and the Benjamins, our neighbours, if you remember – the milliner and that frail old couple.'

'I'm surprised you're not trembling in your shoes, Esther.' Lottie drew the shawl around her shoulders.

'I am trembling, Lottie, for everyone, but I am ashamed to say, not trembling for you, because I believe everyone herded into these lodging houses is to be left alone, and everyone necessary to their war effort as Josef is will be left alone also.'

'They've emptied that Jewish old people's home round the corner.'

'Yes. But listen, Lottie, this Allied bombing of Berlin, you think that's for nothing? You think they're are not on their way? All we have to do is *endure*.'

'You're better at endurance than I am, old friend.'

'Yes,' Esther replied, surprising herself. 'Perhaps because I have had to tread a harder path than you Lottie. But just think of our three together in England. However did Max find them, the darling boy? And together on sabbath. I wonder who gave the benedictions? There's no end to my wondering, I think, did some kind Jewish family invite them? Is Max with a Jewish family? I keep thinking and dreaming, Lottie, then I lose myself in nothingness.'

Lottie had begun to let go at last. There were big tears rolling down her cheeks. 'At least they are safe,' she said, 'my boy and your two.'

Yes, Esther thought, with a sudden fresh constriction of her heart, and soon I shall have to wrench myself away from my third and my last baby and send him out there into the great blank of my wondering. Could there exist a deeper anguish?

Chapter 42

Berlin, December 1941

'Why have we come to this railway station if we are not to go on a train?' Freddy asked.

'Because I have promised Aunt Lottie Merkel in my heart that I shall be here, somewhere, to see her leave for the work camp.'

'How can you promise in your heart?'

'Darling, don't talk so much, it is too cold, you will have a sore throat. Just remember, we are going to pretend to be walking somewhere and are lost and have to turn back and so on, right up until we notice the procession with Aunt Lottie and Aunt Leah in it is actually coming. Then we shall go home. If we do spot them in amongst the other hundreds of people in the procession, what are we to say, Freddy?'

Freddy looked up at her, his face pinched and grey with cold. He raised one of his mittened hands and tapped his mouth. 'I pretend I have not seen them,' he muttered between his lips.

She smiled, pulled his cap further down and wrapped her shawl tighter about her own head and shoulders, whilst keeping her star out of view.

They were about to cross the street towards the station when she heard the rumble of a truck, the bark of a dog, shouts. SS shouts, SS dogs, SS trucks. They were coming. A dark column appeared from the bend in the street, people, four abreast, and yet forming one shuffling line, families, children, yet somehow merged into a slow-moving unhuman shape, unprotesting, silent. No child's voice was raised, no baby's cries, only the SS noise echoed out into the cold winter morning, especially that very particular rumble of the many trucks carrying the sick.

She knew the trucks always carried the sick to the trains because this was the nineteenth or twentieth tranportation forcing Berliners away from Berlin to make way for slave labourers. Could there be a single Jewish lodging house or family left, except war-worker families like themselves?

She gazed and gazed at the mass, trying to decipher face and form. She'd have liked to run across and ask each one for their name; she could make a list, she could make the list into a long prayer.

She wanted Lottie to somehow feel her presence, to know she was witness to her departure, that one single soul who knew her loved her though she wasn't lovable, and would mourn her loss.

She wanted a thousand witnesses to be standing with her, for there to be one mourning soul for each suffering soul.

'Mama.' Whispering through his almost closed mouth, Freddy tugged at her skirt. 'I can see Aunt Lottie Merkel, I can see her suitcase and her special hat.'

Vision blurred from too much staring, Esther felt she too could make out the pale hide of Lottie's best suitcase, the Russian style of her Persian lamb hat.

Look this way, old friend, she thought, *feel me watching you leave, know I am here.*

Chapter 43

London, March 1942

'Max has been trying to be a nurse, Aunt Daphne, although of course, he's not exactly used to sickbeds.'

Propped up on pillows, weaker than she'd ever have thought possible, Susanna gazed at the glorious vision of Aunt Daphne standing by the kitchen table. She wore a silver fox fur hat, navy fisherman's jumper, navy slacks Susanna herself had made her, and a pair of boots that must have belonged to one of her sons. She looked prettier than ever and younger, and she was preparing an invalid's drink as if she were an ordinary housewife in an ordinary spotless kitchen instead of this grubby, neglected place which was half a bedroom.

'In between fetching and delivering errands for his new job as an improver in a Greek Street outwork tailor's, he dashes in to see me, and at night he's been sleeping in that Morrison shelter thing in the salon. Did you see it when you came in?'

'I did, darling, and it was a most sensible buy if it means no more trekking down to the shelters every night. Hitler may be concentrating on Russia at the moment, but he's still throwing a few bits and pieces our way, isn't he?'

'Yes, but isn't it the ugliest sight in the world? It's like some cage in a zoo. It's five feet high, you know, and seven feet long. You could keep a family of small monkeys in it. I didn't want to buy it, Max persuaded me, and I've wished I hadn't ever since the bombs eased off again. We hardly hear the sirens and I sometimes wonder whether it wasn't to have a reason to be able to sleep here. He does loathe that room of his in Wardour Street. I admit I couldn't have managed being ill without him but I do hate clients coming in for fittings with that thing in the salon, it seems so squalid. Madame Lola would never have allowed it.'

She glanced towards the open doorway where she could see Max finishing the hand-sewing on Mrs Windsor's order. He'd gone so far as to have adopted the proper tailor's position for it, left ankle over right knee. He was hand-sewing away as if he were born to it and she ought to be grateful. But the salon looked awful, the unmade bed inside its cage only one of its present horrors, fabric everywhere, the machines all crooked, the trimming boxes strewn about. I shall begin losing business, she thought, unless I force myself to be well again.

Aunt Daphne held up a startling lemon she'd produced from one of the bags she'd brought from Flo. 'Flo paid three shillings for that in Weymouth market for you,' she said. 'Having decided the sailors coming in from Gibraltar might be likely to bring in some illicit fruit, she went there specially. But three shillings, Suzy, eh?' She laughed, laid it on the table and cut into it with what was actually a carving knife. 'Pneumonia has to be treated with hot lemon drinks according to her, so here I am with this beauty and a bag of her sugar, and hot drink I'm going to make.'

Without knowing how to cut or squeeze it, Susanna realised, feeling herself smile in return. 'It's nice to hear someone laugh,' she said, 'no one in London does any more unless they've been drinking. It's been such a miserable winter, the worst for centuries, they say, and there are so many colds about and bad chests like mine. Somehow a kind of dreary boredom covers everything, then there are more cuts in the rations. It's going to be coal soon, apparently, and we're going to have to eat eels, according to the food ministry.'

Aunt Daphne laughed again, wiping her hands on a dirty teacloth and opening the sugar bag. 'Lord Woolton'll be giving his nice little radio talks on eels. Imagine. "Eels now, there's lots of eels this week." '

'It'll be a change from "Carrots, there's lots of carrots this week." I wonder if he'll be giving special talks for horse owners now that horses are to have ration books. "Hay now, there's lots of hay." '

'Yes, well, Flo'll be listening. She's determined to do the right thing always in case a food inspector turns up and demands to root through the larders. She'd die of shame if she were taken to court for hoarding, or worse, black marketeering, the poor love. She listens to that Lord Haw Haw propaganda chappie from Berlin on Sunday mornings with his horrible sinister voice. "Good morning, have you all come out of your holes?" "No," she shouts back at the wireless set, "no we haven't, you slimy toad." '

'I don't think Londoners even listen to him to give themselves a laugh any more. They can't be bothered about anything. Being bombed every night was somehow something to keep going for, and it was actually exciting, I suppose, to feel that every Nazi pilot was trying to make that night your last. My clients seem cross about everything at the moment, the worsening war news, the battles lost in the Far East, the fact only the Russians are fighting the Nazis. They're even fed up with Churchill, they say he's lost his touch. Of course they forget how terrified they were, how awful it was, the Blitz.

'D'you know what I did soon as rationing started, Suzy? After years of toying with a boiled egg, I suddenly couldn't stop eating. Flo doesn't know whether to laugh or cry.' Adding boiling water to the sugar and lemon juice, and with the aid of only one walking stick, Aunt Daphne came towards the bed with the glass on a saucer. There was only a slight stiffness in one arm and one leg now and just a tiny difference in her face. But what a joy to see her smile!

'You certainly don't look as if you've been hungry, Aunt Daphne,' Susanna said, pushing aside the collection of empty cups on the bedside table. 'Or as if you've been living in a hole, whatever Haw Haw means by that, like rats, I suppose, underground?'

'Well, you do look both those things, my darling.' She established herself on the other side of the bed by Fritzi. 'And I want to know first why you didn't send Max to fetch Patch and Georgie, they're only half a mile away.'

'I knew they'd gone off to their training camps now they've joined the FANYs.'

'They get leave. They'd have come. They're still in training, not in some vital war outpost just yet.'

'They will be. It's their French, isn't it, the French they learned in that French prison, Patch told me how the other prisoners used to give them lessons. I expect they'll be doing something

273

important soon to do with Occupied France. The FANY uniform's smart, isn't it, and it's issued with silk stockings, Georgie'll pleased and they'll both be pleased to be back in the thick of things, they must miss the excitement of their ambulance-driving days at the battle lines.'

'You are getting right off the point, Susanna, and the point is you have been very ill here on your own with only Max to dash in and out, though granted his staying the night must have helped. I suggest that when Patch comes back with the clean laundry she's gone to fetch, you let me help you have a bath, then the four of us sit down and see what is to be done. If you really won't allow Patch to take you back to Downlands with me while she has the petrol, you must promise us you'll never get so ill again without telling us, it isn't fair not to promise, we'll be forever worrying, and what if Max is called up to join the Pioneer Corps, what then?'

Yes, what then? Susanna thought. Everything was slipping away from her. She hadn't considered illness, hadn't taken it into account. Yet if she didn't keep up the work, she'd lose orders, she'd lose her income.

She put a hand on the comfort of Fritzi and closed her eyes.

' . . .in any case, darling, I think we must consider your moving from this place altogether when you're well. Two gas rings for heat in a room which is kitchen and bedroom is not exactly healthy.'

Susanna stifled another cough. 'I mustn't,' she said. 'You change your premises, you lose continuity, people get used to where you are, you're a familiar landmark, your door is, and one day they might just call in – and there's another order. I shall have four people to support with this business when the war's over, my parents, Freddy and Max's mother. He'll never be able to sponsor her himself. He's still an improver, doing the basic work on garments, and that's for an outworker for Savile Row. It's only because he does the errands, fetching and delivering cut-out pieces and the finished items to and from the Savile Row premises that he's been able to keep coming here to make me something to eat or see the doctor. He's even come so I shan't have to cancel a client appointment for a fitting – he's done the fitting, imagine, but I suppose he's learned enough.'

They both turned to stare through the doorway into the salon where Max still sat sewing. 'If his mother could see him there, she'd die of shame. It's so Jewish, you see, it's old Jewish ghetto life, working day and night in cramped quarters, fried onion smell getting into the cloth. He was brought up to be a dealer in precious things, silver and Flemish miniatures.'

'All mothers want the best for their children, Suzy, but these aren't normal times. She'll just thank the Lord her son's alive.' Aunt Daphne reached across the bed for the empty glass and got to her feet. 'I can imagine her and your parents dreaming up all sorts of horrors you might be going through. It's not knowing that's the worst, and now there are only the measly twenty-five words passing between you. I mean, take David. He let slip to Flo last month he was training for some secret mission in that new camp of his. He wasn't going to tell me, I suppose, so's I shouldn't worry, but I'd rather know.'

'Secret? What, Mr David?' Susanna asked. 'Whatever for?'

'Spying, of course, what else? Naturally I shall never find out unless he's lost on some spying mission in enemy territory and I get the telegram all mothers dread. I wish he'd bring a girl home before he goes off, so I can begin hoping for a grandchild. Unless you and Max?' She stood by the pillow with the glass in her hand and touched Susanna's hot arm with a cool hand. 'You are sure you want even to consider it? You know Max will never turn into a prince however much you kiss him?'

'I'm not sure. No. But he keeps pointing out I shan't be conscripted for war work if I'm a married woman with a husband at home. More and more girls over nineteen are being sent into the armaments factories, and if that happens to me, I shall lose what business I've managed to build up. It is mostly remodelling work and the slacks of my own design with the narrower leg. My clients seem to like them and they tell their friends. But this is wartime so I feel that if I can just make a living, that's all I can expect until it's over. And if it's enough of an income to serve as a sponsor, well, you understand, Aunt Daphne.'

She gazed up at Aunt Daphne's pretty, concerned face and leaned back on the pillows. She didn't want anything herself, didn't want to marry Max, didn't ever want to get up from this bed, not even for Aunt Daphne to help her bath and wash her hair.

'Marrying him is not what I foresaw for you, darling Suzy, but if it's for the best, if you're sure. It's just, heavens, you are very

275

young. You have known each other a long time, that's important, I suppose, you have been through the same problems. I wish I could do something as simple as telephone your Mama and your Papa for myself and have a long talk about about it.'

'If only!' Susanna managed a smile. 'My father will be against it and my mother perhaps not,' she said, surprising herself. Was this true? She couldn't gather her thoughts about home, or hardly ever could. They were just lost in an immense blank of uncertainties without a single fact to fix on, except that her parents were unlikely to be as warm and comfortable or well fed and cared for as she was this very minute.

'I can't afford to be ill without Max to keep the clients reassured, Aunt Daphne. You know his charm. And he's learned a lot.'

'It worries me he'll charm you into something you don't want to do. I can't deny being married gives one status. But the solicitor and your accountant, I feel they might refer every decision to Max automatically . . .'

'I've been considering that aspect, Aunt Daphne, and I don't think either of them will. The accountant keeps on about when Max is going to finish paying his debt to me, which won't be for years, and the solicitor tells me funny stories about his magistrate duties. Women really are kept down in court, he says, and he once saw a woman sent out for not wearing a hat – a defendant, a criminal I suppose, and she'd shown disrespect to the court by not wearing a hat!'

Aunt Daphne snorted, moving to the sink to make coffee, and producing biscuits from her bag to serve with it.

'And once,' Susanna went on, 'he almost decided to resign as a magistrate because some poor soul who'd been stealing wasn't actually spoken to at all. The chairman of the bench informed the husband he was sorry for him, having such a wife, and was only going to impose a small fine because of the shame she'd brought on him!'

'Oh, darling, sometimes I wish I hadn't wasted so much of my life lying in bed feeling helpless, letting myself be helpless. I could have struck out of my own after the children went to boarding school, I had money and the London house. If it weren't for Arthur, I'd let you have it rent-free for a year or two. The tenancy's coming up for renewal and it'd get you out of here into bigger premises. It has a proper heating boiler in the basement and plenty of big, airy rooms with electric light. You'd have enough rooms for a separate fitting salon! You could take on your own outworkers.' She sighed, turning on tap to fill the kettle. 'What a nice dream. But it wouldn't be a dream if Arthur hadn't taken everything away from me after my stroke, my bank account, my cheque book. He has power of attorney over me and gives me an allowance, damn him. If he has a heart attack at sixty like his father, I'll be free though, and then we'll just start getting everything we want. That house has a flat on the second floor and one on the third, masses of space for your parents and the little boy. I could have the very top one as my town flat, I get so bored in Dorset, I don't know why I stay there, I don't have to, it's not as if Arthur would care tuppence.' She put the biscuits on a plate and searched about for cups.

'They're all dirty. I'm sorry. Look, let me come and wash up.' Susanna didn't move, knowing she wouldn't be allowed to. 'Us all living there, Aunt Daphne, it'd be wonderful, so cosy and safe.'

'Safe! She's obsessed with being safe, with the coffee on the stove and the blackout up.' Max had appeared and was leaning on the door jamb. 'Any coffee yet, Aunt Daphne?'

'If you go and light the gas geyser in the bathroom. You can also collect those dirty cups and wash them and while Suzy's up strip the bed so that Patch can remake it with clean linen when she returns from the laundry.'

'OK.' Whistling, he strolled into the bathroom and shut the door behind him.

'OK! He has loads of American expressions from the films and this American officer friend he met at Patch's party last year. They go to clubs and drink and smoke, even now, when I've been so ill. He thinks I'm settled for the evening, off he goes. And I'm quite glad, Aunt Daphne, he's such a fidget. I'm sure he's too young for those Soho clubs.'

'He could pass for twenty-five.'

'Yes.' Susanna heard herself give another rattling sigh. 'That's part of the trouble. He thinks he can behave like a man, including staying out all hours having muttered conversations about petrol coupons and cigarettes and nylons.'

She closed her eyes again, suddenly wearier than ever. Talking was too much of an effort, thinking was, thinking about the future especially, and what would have happened if Max hadn't called in to see her one particularly feverish day. She could have died in this bed of Madame Lola's, in this salon, alone, as Madame Lola had done. Pneumonia kills. The doctor said so. And you're all alone, my dear? Yes. No family? No. Then, quickly, *None here*, because that one word had been so awful, and not true.

'. . . of course, if you and Max had a baby, then you certainly couldn't be called up for war work,' Aunt Daphne was saying.

Dear Mama, she thought, it seems I am to transform myself into a good Jewish mother. I shall have to start arguing with Max about the proper way to raise children, and being a shining light in a world which doesn't want another one of us, and circumcision and barmitzvahs for girls. And this without you and Buba to pass on the lore and side with me and shout at Max.

The baby would have no great-grandmother, no grandmother and a mother who couldn't remember a single thing about how it was supposed to be.

Even Mrs Merkel would be better than no one.

With this realisation, the tears that had been hovering for some time began to make their way down her face.

Chapter 44

Berlin, Late Summer 1942

Somewhere in these papers, I shall find the good, Esther decided, spreading them out on the kitchen table.

'May I go and play on the balcony, Mama?' Freddy had thrown off his jacket and stood waiting.

'If you keep on your cap against the sun.'

She sat down and considered the new issue of ration cards she had just collected. It seemed that in future, they were to be entitled to no more than two turnips each a week.

This must be one of their jokes, one of their ways of saying: We are going to starve you to death, it will be easier, and less wasteful than using up precious fuel transporting you to work-camps when it is needed for our tanks and our bombers.

Very well. But why this order that she report for work at the railway depot on Monday morning? If she had to report for work, she was needed for work, she was going to join the privileged group of Jewish people allowed to do war work in Berlin as long as they kept out of the way of Germans. No, not quite even that. She and Freddy were going to be allowed on trams and buses when travelling to and from the railway depot and the nursery, so long as they did not sit down.

She was so much needed for war work, her boy was going to be permitted to take up nursery space. A Jewish boy, in a nursery. Well, then, she must believe he would also be given soup at noon, that she would be given soup. She had seen other forced labourers being fed.

With the addition of Josef's wages and Frau Hahn's courage

and determination, perhaps then they would be able to continue surviving. Last week, half a pound of lentils was slipped into her bag in the market, yesterday a potato and a handful of haricot beans.

And yet, and yet. Freddy was going to be registered at a nursery. He officially existed, on their records.

This morning then, she was face to face with a simple fact: having indulged herself so wickedly in the anguish and joy of keeping him with her until the very last moment, that last moment might be gone.

Chapter 45

London, Late Summer 1942

He had sat too long in the little park at the end of the street. He had been too early and now he was too late.

His knee stiff, David got up from the bench and walked blindly along the pavement.

Then he heard them, his mother's cry, Patch's, and the crowd of them outside the place.

The boy looked very shiny in his best suit. He had a pink carnation in his buttonhole. They all had one.

They were going in, they were disappearing through the door. People were smiling to see the dressed-up, buttonholed collection. Everyone loved a wedding.

I cannot do it, he thought. He felt as if he were glued to the pavement. I cannot stand by her side as if I were her father as I am expected to do, as Patch and my mother have commanded me to do. I shall stand here instead and pretend I have been delayed. I am always expected to be late so they will not be disappointed. But I shall not have seen it happen. Susanna. Susanna married to that boy.

How would he pass the night?

In the end, knowing it would be almost over, he got himself up the steps and through the door, forced through because another wedding party was surging up behind him.

His were coming out.

All hope gone then? Yes. And he'd decided at one point he'd interrupt the ceremony to shout, Wait, there is an impediment . . .

He'd pictured himself doing it, his mother's horrified face, Susanna's, Susanna's lifting with joy.

He had watched too many films. Bloody *Jane Eyre*.

He saw the boy first. Max. He hated the name.

He couldn't see her.

'There he is, you absolute wretch, David, not even being in time for Suzy's wedding, call yourself a guardian.' Patch's voice, Patch flushed and happy, own fiancé on her arm.

'Sorry,' he muttered. Where was she?

'You missed it, darling, shame on you.' His mother, radiant. 'It was short, you know, but touching, and nice.' She caught hold of his hand. 'And see how lovely our Suzy looks. I so wish her parents could be here and oh, heavens, I hope we've done the right thing, not trying hard enough, you know, to make her wait. I can't say I like the boy, but well, there you are. They were brought up together, they know each other and that's more than most wedding couples.'

'Yes.'

'Here comes the bride.' Patch was singing, and his mother, Georgie and her French bloke, Patch's fiancé.

Susanna was wearing something with buttons down the front, cream-coloured, and one of her little hats and some yellow roses and a very pale set face which wasn't smiling. She looked frightened.

Everyone was singing, and laughing. He wanted to say something sour. Don't you know there's a war on, or, Don't you know this is a bad lot she's given herself to, a bad lot. Because he was.

She was smiling now, at him, a smile of a sort, her eyes bigger than ever.

He held out his hand to her. 'Congratulations,' he said. And something more foolish than usual. 'Got that over with then?'

He was holding her hand in his for probably the last time. There were strange blue shadows under her eyes, she was frightened at what she'd done, she was too young, but it was too late, she was lost to him, and he to her.

Sitting up in bed in the splendour of the hotel room, Susanna watched dark little trails of cloud drift across the moon. She had drawn back the curtains the maid had pulled and crept into the space the maid had laid ready in a glory of linen. She was a glory herself, in a cream silk gown with lace insets, a wedding gift from Aunt Daphne, and she had a new name, Mrs Max Merkel, soon to be Mrs Max Merchant because Max had decided an English one was better for business. Susanna Merchant. She tried it out on herself and turned to where Fritzi usually was, where he wasn't now, of course, he was being looked after by Patch. Max was going to be there, and she supposed he shortly would be. Tonight they were to have marital relations.

She wanted her mother so much a wave of longing seemed to take away her breath. It had actually come to pass, that she had gone through her own wedding without a mother's advice.

Aunt Daphne had tried. She'd said, Just don't always be available, darling, that's all, which was much less than her mother would have managed. She'd have had a long list of Jewish lore at her fingertips and not hesitated to recite it when Papa was out of earshot.

Shivering, silk and linen cold against her skin, she watched the moon grow bigger and whiter and sent across her message: Mama, I need you here, now, because today I was married to Max and I am sitting up in bed waiting to be a good wife to him in Claridges best suite, paid for by Aunt Daphne. Max has gone out to meet a chap in one of his clubs, very important it was that he should go, and I am the loneliest bride in the world.

She must have dozed. The moon had floated off to the corner of the window but the pretty white light of it still picked out the room, everything in it rich and solid and old. Mama, she thought, you'd adore Claridges.

She'd been dreaming of her mother sitting in the old bedroom feeding Freddy with her loose breasts and her own breasts had been hurting.

She turned her head towards the bathroom. Before, she'd been able to see the claw feet of the bath, the huge towels spread out. It was too dark in there now, no light, no Max, no Max in this room, only his suitcase where the porter had placed it and the maid laid out certain things for his use. You were well looked after in a good hotel and this was one. Earlier on, she'd been glad the maid had done that, because she herself wouldn't have done it well enough.

283

I shall never do anything well enough for Max, she thought, closing her eyes. Perhaps he had had an accident somewhere out in the blackout, or in one of those basement clubs where he met the good chaps, the handy chaps, the connections-for-our-future chaps.

She could feel her own skin in its silky covering, the soft linen on her legs. Aunt Daphne had been generous. If you have to have a honeymoon night, darling, she'd said, and I suppose you have, you'll have it in style, room service. Mind you have room service dinner, they'll lay it all up for you with lovely fancy manners.

Aunt Daphne had ordered champagne for seven, she'd said, which ought to be about right, then while the waiters are there, you order the dinner, that way you won't be too shy to telephone down.

She always foresaw problems of that kind, Aunt Daphne. They probably would have been too shy. They'd probably have expected a sharp reply, like No room service for Jews, or something.

The champagne was even now sitting in its ice bucket on a table in the sitting room next door.

Yes, Aunt Daphne foresaw most things about this wedding night but not that Max wouldn't be present.

She must have dozed again for the moon had quite disappeared. But Max had appeared. He was in the bathroom. The light was on in there, the door shut, water running. She could hear it, and Max whistling. He was happy. He'd been for his drink with the useful chap and now he was coming for her.

Her heart flew up to sit somewhere near her throat.

The bathroom door opened and Max was silhouetted against the light. He was wearing the silk pyjamas Aunt Daphne had given him, made down from a pair of her husband's. Suddenly, he lurched towards the bed and stood there contemplating the nest the maid had put ready.

Now, Susanna thought, I am to kiss Max to make him seem like a prince. He has a nice mouth. He has nice smooth skin. We are to kiss on the mouth for the first time, it begins there and moves on to other places. From tonight, neither of us will be lonely again or fear illness and dying alone. I shall not have to work in a war armaments factory, I shall be a wife.

Max didn't look at her. He said, 'I don't think we'd better bother with any of that stuff yet, d'you? Your mother wouldn't like it.'

She watched him turn himself slowly around so that he fell backwards against the bottom of the bed. His feet landed on the pillows beside her. He hadn't taken off his socks.

Nightdress folded, toilet things repacked with it into her suitcase, she gazed at her own reflection in the bathroom mirror: very white face, a hint of lipstick left, newly trimmed *pretty* hair done properly instead of being chopped off by herself, short at the back and over the ears but a mass of curls on the head which held the hat very nicely. The hat was successful too, the one Madame Lola had made for her wedding re-covered in brown linen with a brown silk rose from Berwick Street. And what a well-cut jacket, what unusual buttons! They'd taken her hours of evenings to make, each one torpedo-shaped and covered in the rough cream lace matching the cream linen of the Schiaparelli design she'd copied, a tight-fitting waisted affair no one else in London was wearing, certainly not other brides. The bride preceding her at the register office wore a full-skirted flowered dress under a contrasting coat tied at the waist, short-sleeved, a frightful mess of a hat with half a field of daisies on it, and of all horrors, black gloves above the elbow, black bag, black shoes, all the black on the lower half of the body therefore, the light at the top and nothing to bring the outfit together. She looked awful. She will be a married woman, a wife, this morning, and me, with my beautiful jacket, my plain brown skirt, my brown court shoes, my *chic*, what am I?

She unpinned the yellow roses from the lapel, ran some water in the basin and placed them in there for a drink of water. I have made a marriage of convenience, she thought, recognising in herself, not only hurt and resentment but something like relief.

Chapter 46

Berlin, March 1943

'You have finished your porridge, Freddy?'

'It has lumps.'

'The lumps are the best part.'

Esther stood beside him, stroking his thin neck and shoulders. Even his hair was thin and she could feel every one of his bones. How was she to go on feeding him? If ever he were to have more than a cold, his poor little body would have no resistance. 'You have been learning the poem for me?'

'No, it's too cold for lessons.'

'Never mind, we shall learn it together tonight when Papa is back and we have made the kitchen cosy for him. We have some wood left to burn and we shall collect more on our way home tonight.'

'From the bombed buildings?'

'Yes. Your Opa would say it is good out of bad, that we have fuel from the houses of the poor souls who've been bombed. Come on, now, leave the last lump. Let's get on your coat and cap. Today we shall hurry along laughing to my work and your nursery.'

'Why will we?' Freddy got to his feet and passed her his clothes from the back of the door.

'Because spring is coming.'

He frowned up at her, searching her face for clues to this silliness. He was a very old little boy.

'I'm a foolish Mama, aren't I?' She pulled the cap down on to his forehead and he levered his skinny arms into the jacket. The star was grubby. She must sponge it off tonight and tonight she must make up her mind to present Josef with the only secret she'd ever kept from him: the plans she and Frau Hahn had made to save their son. 'Soon it will be time for you to go on your holiday to the country,' she said. 'Papa will have such a lovely surprise when we tell him about it.'

'I don't want to go.' He brushed off her hand so he could button the jacket himself.

'There won't be any bombing there or any air-raid sirens every night to keep you awake like Berlin has now, and you won't have to wear your star which makes other children nasty to you and you'll live with some nice ladies until it's time for me and Papa to have our holiday with you.'

'Afterwards, we come back to Berlin?'

'Perhaps. But by then, we may be able to go to England to join the girls because the war will be over.'

'There'll be porridge with lumps in the country?' Tears threatening, infinitely sad, he looked up at her again.

'I can't promise there won't be and I know my big boy will swallow them straight down so I can be proud of him.'

'Will there be lumpy porridge in England?'

'In England, my darling, there will be boiled eggs and white bread and butter and jam made from oranges.'

He narrowed his eyes and frowned again.

'It's true. You'll see.' She set his cap at an angle. 'Go and fetch my coat and shawl from the bedroom please.'

Yes, she thought, I shall tell Josef that we can no longer pretend, the Jewish workers have been rounded up from three other Moabit factories, and yesterday, just as she arrived for her shift at the railway depot to start cleaning the trains, she'd seen the factory doors across the street open. Trucks drew up and a long line of workers appeared with their yellow stars, and soon the trucks drove off with them inside.

In fact, Josef, she must say, was going to say, you can no longer persuade me that the three of us will not have to follow the rest of our people out of Berlin to this east talked of so much, these Polish ghettos and the work camps into which such thousands have vanished, where Opa and Buba have vanished. And he will weep, because I have kept my plans from him, and then he will agree: Freddy must be given his chance.

*

287

As always, passing Josef's factory on the way to the tram stop, they slowed their step, because sometimes he had a task near a ground-floor window and there could be a glance between the three of them.

They were approaching the point where they could glance that way when a figure came out of the big delivery doors giving on to the street, a man, and he began to unload something, cartons or some such, and a carton fell by their feet. Instantly, she pulled at Freddy's hand for fear a supervisor might be watching, that the fault might be made into theirs, but the man dared speak. He didn't look at her, of course, yet she heard his whisper clear enough. 'Send the boy on a few steps, dear Frau Lehmann, and return as if you had dropped the coins for your tram.'

By the carton that had fallen, there were indeed some coins. Her own head down, she heard the man speak again. Josef must have sent him, she must trust him.

'Earlier this morning the trucks came, the Jewish workers had to line up, your Josef, dear lady, he was hit by a terrible pain, I saw him fall just there where I placed the coins.'

Esther leaned down and touched the ground where Josef had lain. 'Hospital?'

'Too late, I saw, he is gone, his heart, and be glad of it, dear lady, bless this day as I do. He was a noble man.'

'Yes. Thank you.' For a second longer, she let her fingers rest.

'Hide,' the man said. 'Your turn.'

'Yes. And may God bless you.' One by one, she slipped the coins into her pocket and walked on to the tree where Freddy waited.

'Darling boy,' she said, 'there is a message from Papa. He has been sent to Düsseldorf to work in the factory there for several weeks so I think the best thing will be for us to go home and make arrangements for your holiday to start today. Then I shall be able to do a double shift at the depot and earn more money for our journey to England. Didn't I tell you this was going to be a nice day? Well, so it has turned out. You are to have no nursery but instead a little walk round to the cellar store where Frau Hahn keeps her vegetables to sell in the market. We'll sit in there and have a nice word game until she comes.'

I feel strong, she thought, stronger than ever, because Josef will never go east, Josef is safe. He is in my heart now and for always and he will go on helping me to do what I must do. This evening they will come for me. I have not much time left

But I shall never have to say goodbye to my Josef. She felt as if she were filled with a warm glow. Josef. She had been loved twenty-two years by such a man.

'We are to wait here for Frau Hahn?' Freddy sat un an upturned box amidst a litter of more boxes, a sack of apples, two of potatoes and some turnip tops.

'Yes. She saw us pass by her stall in the market so she will be with us soon. I gave her a little signal and I already had the key to this cellar in my bag. Your Mama and Frau Hahn have been clever ladies.' Sitting on the box beside him, she began to unpick the lining of the string bag she had chosen to be the hiding place for the papers Frau Hahn's policeman son had stolen for her from the registry of deaths. It had been a hard choice, settling on that bag, but she had reasoned that it was one she could quickly discard if she had to without anyone blinking an eye.

'Shall we practise your new name while we are waiting?'

'I should like Papa to have heard it.'

'He will, one day. Now, what is your name, little boy?'

'Franz Kurt Buchert.'

'And your father's name?'

'Hans Kurt Buchert.'

'And where was he born?'

'Bremen, on the seventh of April, nineteen . . .'

Heart just beating, she thought, just beating. I am managing, Josef, watch me managing, listen to our boy becoming someone else. I am getting stronger and that is because I have you with me. I need not fear I shall fail in this final task of setting him free.

The birth certificate stowed safely in its rubber wrapping under a flagstone on the floor, she set her scissors to work on the star on Freddy's jacket.

'I am not to be a Jew any more?'

'Not while you're on holiday. Remember, I told you? And remember being a Jew has to do with sabbath suppers and special prayers and if anyone should ask about prayers or suppers, you

289

will say you only ever knew the prayers you learned at nursery school which were about the Fatherland. It is good you have been to the nursery, because you have also learned the songs about the Fatherland and you may have to sing them on holiday with the nice ladies. They will tell you to join in, and when to join in.'

Soon the second task was done. She'd brushed every thread of stitching from the lapel and it left no trace; she'd been careful to sew it on so lightly it had practically been hanging off, and now it was gone without trace too, cut into tiny pieces by Freddy and stamped into the soil around the sacks.

Opa, she thought, forgive me. Your grandson must pretend not to be a Jew, but he is going to live. As a Catholic! May the Lord forgive me, and you, my dear father, God rest your soul.

They were sitting trembling together on the box, he reciting his lessons, she reciting the prayer for the dead over and over to herself, when Frau Hahn hurried in and locked the door behind her.

'The time has come then.' A fierce little bird of a woman, an old Berliner, quick-mouthed, mocking, cynical, she wore the sacking apron, the headshawl, the man's cap of all the market women. And from her weathered face, her small grey eyes, shone goodness.

'So Franz Buchert, the bravest boy I ever knew, is going off on holiday without his Mama and Papa?'

Dumb, Freddy nodded.

Esther stood up. 'I shall go for his suitcase.'

'You think that sensible, Frau Lehmann?'

'All he needs is in it.' Esther took off her shawl and put it around her son's shoulders. 'I shall run home for it, bring it with my string bag to the market, shop with you and casually leave it under your stall near your feet. If I can, I shall tell you where my husband has gone, he has been sent to another factory, and . . .' She and the good Frau Hahn did not always need to make things clear to each other. She let her gaze rest on her several seconds and it seemed to her she was understood. 'You will remember to tell the nuns Freddy is big enough to wash and bathe himself?'

Frau Hahn gave a sharp laugh. 'I haven't told you what I have learned about Catholic nuns since our last meeting. Listen.' She put a work-rough hand on Esther's arm. 'They make the poor kids

290

wash under their nightshirts, yes, for fear the poor mites should think wicked things about their menkies! Did you ever?' Tears came to her eyes, from laughter, and they came to Esther's own.

Freddy stared at them both in astonishment.

Frau Hahn sat beside him, took off his cap, stroked his hair and produced an apple and a piece of bread from a pocket.

She saw Freddy hold one in each hand, glance up at his Mama, begin on the bread and say, 'I'm not going to be a Jew any more.'

Yes, my darling, Esther thought, but I have freed you so that one day you can be proud of what you are.

And now she must get ready. This evening, tomorrow, they would come for her. She was going to be put on one of those transport trains which held one thousand of their people exactly, and she was going to be taken in it to a work camp or ghetto in Poland, and there she was going to learn the worst of it.

Chapter 47

London Autumn 1943

'Well, how was the old girl?'

'Aunt Daphne's not an old girl.'

'OK. How was Aunt Daphne?' Whistling, Max was fixing some hanging contraption by the fitting cubicle.

'What's that?' Bags by her feet, Fritzi in her arms, Susanna felt the usual knot of resentment tie itself around her stomach. Coming home after a stay at Downlands made everything seem worse.

'It's a movable hanging rail for my stock.'

'I don't want you to bring your so-called stock in here, Max. I did tell you.'

'Where else can I put it? You want us to pay the next quarter's rent on the salon or not?'

'I shall be able to settle it as soon as my two clients have paid their accounts. I told you.'

'Yes.' He stopped whistling and glanced across at her. 'And I told you there's easier money to be had now clothes rationing has begun to bite. I buy up good quality stuff from people's attics, you remodel it, you sell it someone else, or else I just sell it on at a profit.'

'You think a second-hand clothes dealer is the big time, do you?'

'Bigger time than your bits of dressmaking, and besides paying our way, we'll have something to give us a start when the war's over and business begins to move.'

'I'd rather you had a steady wage as a finisher at the outworker tailors. At least we can be sure of it.'

292

'Oh, no, we can't. How long do you think they'll keep me on? Savile Row customers may be able to buy off-ration cloth, but the fact is they don't want to. For the rich, it's infra dig, it's unpatriotic not to keep to the rationing regulations. Well, for most people really, so, as I say, second-hand clothes remodelled or sold on are our best bet.' He paused again in his fiddling with steel tubes. 'This thing's second-hand,' he said. 'And d'you know what the rich don't mind being second-hand? Petrol coupons, that's what. Seems they're not like dirty money and it's not unpatriotic to be able to drive home to the country at weekends.'

'So you are dealing in petrol coupons too? The black market, in fact.' Wearily, she trailed past him to the kitchen.

'You've been sleeping in my bed,' she said at once, surveying the unmade mess of it and the squalor of the sink.

'Thought I might as well while you were at Downlands and didn't need it. Made a change from my Morrison shelter bed. It's cramped in there.'

She took off her jacket, set Fritzi in his chair, put water on to boil and turned to the task of remaking this room back into her own. She was crying, she realised, without surprise. She could smell his American cologne on her sheets, and worse, mothballs and cigarette smoke.

It was only on opening the wardrobe door in order to hang her jacket in it that she noticed something was missing. Several seconds passed before she realised exactly what – Madame Lola's furs, the full-length mink and the sable stole, two silver fox stoles, a genuine Persian astrakhan hat. 'What have you done with them?' she shouted, her tears of helplessness gone, anger in their place.

He strolled in, whistling 'You are my Sunshine'. 'Got the coffee on?'

'What have you done with Madame Lola's furs?'

'Our furs.' He joined her at the wardrobe door and squeezed her against him. 'Ours,' he repeated, 'and they gave me the start I needed. I had to buy in some stock, didn't I? You'd be surprised how much I got, over a hundred.'

'I was keeping them for her family.'

'If there is family and they do come here after the war, they'll understand. By then, we'll be able to repay them in cash anyway, or offer them something. But she did leave all her possessions to

293

you, so we have a perfectly moral right to them. I don't think she had any family. You never saw foreign stamps in her mail even when there was foreign mail.'

'You smell of mothballs already,' she said, pushing him away. 'And you've been smoking in here.'

'All right.' His eyes went dark and he shrugged. 'I'll make the coffee, shall I? There's some condensed milk, and I got you a tin of corned beef and a couple of tomatoes for your lunch, in case you didn't want to go shopping after your journey.'

'I don't want corned beef from your American friend. I do want Madame Lola's furs back, Max.'

'You must be more sensible about eating, the doctor told me. More meat, he said.' Eyes still dark, but hurt now, he could always look hurt if he chose, he stood by the stove waiting for the water to bubble. 'But if you don't want the corned beef, let me unpack your bag for you, then I'll heat up a tin of soup. There's fresh bread, I went out for that for you. We'll go for a nice meal somewhere grand tonight if you like, have one of those five-shilling meals to build you up. I only want to please you, and help you. I don't want you to have colds all the time.'

'I haven't one now.'

'The doctor told me your strength is gone and I was to see you worked less in this stuffy room in the evenings, the gas is bad for your chest and you strain your eyes.' He smiled his most boyish smile. 'But if you get pneumonia again, I'll be able to nurse you more easily as a self-employed dealer than as a wage-earner.'

'Just imagine your mother's horror when she gets here and finds you dealing in second-hand clothes when you were brought up to learn about lovely things, antiques. They're hardly the stuff of your mother's dreams, those rags.'

She saw him turn pale. He didn't answer. There was only the sound of the gas fizzing. He hated her to mention his mother.

After what seemed like a minute, he said, 'I sometimes forget I married a fool. How was Aunt Daphne?'

'How d' you expect?' Eyes full of tears again, she slammed the wardrobe door and sat at the kitchen table with Fritzi on her lap. She would let him at least make her some coffee. He'd suddenly find he had an appointment afterwards, he'd go out and she'd have her home back for the afternoon. If she were lucky, the entire evening and half the night too, even the whole night.

'Have those yokel policemen found the murder weapon yet?'
He poured the water into the jug.

'No.'

'Or God forbid, the actual murderer?'

'No.'

'Did they question you about your whereabouts on the night of
the murder?'

'Whatever for? I was here in London.'

'Thought they might question everyone who knew him.'

'Aunt Daphne's decided it was someone sent by his Irish
woman friend, the barmaid. He'd got tired of her apparently and
was having assignations with a girl from the next village.'

'Do the police think that?' He stood waiting for the coffee to
settle with his hands in his pockets.

'I don't know.' She reached for the bag on the floor and picked
out the tin of Flo's shortbread. 'Flo thinks they suspect a
disgruntled employee, he was always sacking people, the land
agent for one a few months ago and that's why he's been there
himself. I told you, didn't I? He's been shouting about the place
because the land agent was stealing something and the man who
saw to the fishing was poaching, and the farm tenant he'd given
notice to had nowhere else to live . . .'

'Long list of suspects.' With a burst of activity, he laid out
napkins and plates, whipped off three days' worth of dirty
crockery and poured two cups of coffee. 'So how's Aunt Daphne
managing to bear her grief?'

'Don't try and be funny.' She picked up a piece of shortbread
and dunked it.

'You mean someone's done her a good turn?' He helped
himself to two and crunched them standing up.

'Hardly. She feels guilty now. She'd prefer he'd died of a heart
attack.'

'Yes, much nicer, I see that, but you can't arrange everything to
order.' He swung to and fro on his heels as if considering the
profundity of this remark and with a sudden movement grabbed
the tin of corned beef from the dresser, took out the key to open it
and gave a cry of pain. 'I've cut my finger!'

'You do every time. You should let me open it. Not that I want
corned beef.'

'I thought you might if I made you a nice sandwich.' His skin

295

white, he stood looking helpless, blood soaking into his handkerchief.

'Put your finger under the tap, don't spoil the handkerchief.'

'You know I can't stand blood.' His eyes closed, he turned on
the tap and let it run.

'You are a baby.'

'Get me some plaster, Suzy, please.'

'We haven't any.' She dunked another shortbread and
resolutely sat in her place.

Groaning, he flopped down opposite her and put his head in his
hands, the finger sticking out, the stained cloth back on it.

'What's the matter now?'

'Tired,' he said. 'I was up late finishing that jacket of Mrs
Deacon's for you, then I realised I wouldn't be able to sleep, I'd
gone past it, so I went to the club.'

'You mean you were up all night drinking in that basement
place with your American officer friends and those girls?'

'Couldn't get home. There was a raid. Yank military police
arrived to search the club for deserters, but they were spotted on
the top step so the barmaid locked the door and didn't answer
when they pounded on it. They waited outside until dawn so we
waited inside till dawn was past.'

'You mean your American friend is a deserter from the
American army?'

'How should I know? Look, Suzy, I'm going to lie down for a
while in my Morrison. Will you wake me around five? We'll go
for a nice early supper, you can get to bed early with a nice book
and I'll do the same, honestly, we'll be a cosy married couple like
you want.'

'You were not meant for cosiness, Max, or marriage for that
matter.'

'Did Aunt Daphne mention the London house she owns?' He
was standing by the Morrison, taking off his jacket and laying it
on the mess of boxes on its top surface. He was also ignoring this
last statement of hers, because that was what he always did when
she bothered to begin on the truth. 'Yes,' she said.

'And?'

'She's coming to discuss it with me next week. Mr David will
probably come too.'

'Good. This'll be the start for us, Suzy, you'll see. There are so many rooms in that house. I can have two or three for my dealing, we won't get in each other's way. I won't irritate you any more. It's going to be wonderful, you'll see. We've got a bit of capital ready, selling those furs came just right.'

He was using his gentlest voice and flashing her glances and smiles. 'I did try to bring over some of Pa's money, didn't I, so we could have a proper start. Our bad luck's piled up though, hasn't it? Years of bad luck we've had, through no fault of our own, I mean I even lost the sapphire in the end, but you'll see, if Aunt Daphne lets us have that house in Mayfair, it means our luck's changing, we're due for a patch of good. I mean, poor old Montgomery's murder was the bad, obviously, but it's freed Aunt Daphne to do what she likes with her own house. Mayfair, Suzy, think!'

Susanna sat on at the table. She was thinking. She was thinking how nice it would have been to have come home from Downlands to her very own rooms, with just her and Fritzi in them, and their routine, her work, his walks, and silence, and space. She was not made for marriage either, and she wished she had not let herself need him and consented to it, that she had not let him bully her into it. How many many years now must she endure this dread of his schemes, his interference, this skin-itching longing that he should be gone, that she could get up from this chair and tip his things into the street, his nasty frowsty bedclothes, his mess, his awful low-class second-hand clothes?

With a surge of anger, she dashed into the salon and stood with her arms crossed, staring at them. 'I want you to buy the furs back, Max,' she shouted, 'I want you get rid of all this stuff, now, at once, sell it back to whoever you bought it from, and if you can't by proving to me where the furs went, then I want to see the exact sum you got, in my bank account, the exact sum. I mean, over a hundred, is it a hundred and five, a hundred and ninety, there's a difference. And please don't pretend you're keeping it as cash to avoid my having to pay income tax. What you really mean is you're keeping it for yourself.'

'No I'm not, Suzy.' His gentlest voice. He'd got into the Morrison and was lying there with his hands behind his head. He looked about twelve again. It was his greatest gift to be able to, and he used the gift more and more often. It didn't touch her. It had never touched her.

'You will have to prove it to me.' Exhausted, she nonetheless kicked a foot into the base of the rail. 'And this is just in my way, d'you hear me, it is just too near the fitting cubicle, my clients won't like it, and I don't like it and it will have to go.'

'Suzy. You remember you said you could remodel old blouses and dresses for your clients if only you had some material to make inserts and trim?'

'I'm not using that old stuff. I was just wishing the rationing wasn't so strict, that's all. Don't try and make me believe you've been thinking of me, because you haven't.'

'Suzy, look at the end of the rail. Something in a sort of cream colour, I can't describe it, you're best at that. Go on, have a look.'

'I shan't bother, because I don't want it.' Heart thumping from wasted emotion, she shot back into the kitchen and closed the door behind her. She had bothered. It was something cream-coloured. It was a Vionnet dress from the twenties, an exquisite thing made up of petal shapes fitted into each other, each petal the finest silk muslin delicately embroidered and edged, each petal usable.

The very worst of Max was sometimes being right.

'I still want Madame Lola's furs back,' she shouted, picking up Fritzi and bursting into tears.

Chapter 48

Autumn in Auschwitz-Birkenau, Poland

'Out! Out!'

The room elders' door at the end of the block flew open and they strode along the aisles banging their sticks on the layers of shelving where hundreds of women were packed together under pieces of blanket.

'Out! Out!'

It was, as always, four a.m., but Esther was awake. The chill of Hella's body on her right side had woken her, and she was carrying out the morning check on her possessions in case any should have been stolen whilst she slept, or nibbled at by rats. They were all there: in her left hand, the half-crust of bread from supper, on their string around her waist, the tin bowl and spoon, in the hem of her dress, just past the tear, Buba's talisman, kept in place by a ball of dried grass. Around her neck was the kerchief that had prevented her scalp from burning that summer and on her feet the shoes that had cost her two half-crusts and a piece of soup turnip.

She eased her hurting body into a sitting position and felt along her limbs for swellings around her mosquito bites. None. Lucky so far. Next, she allowed herself to rub the area of her stomach and chest where the agony of hunger seemed always to be but wasn't. It was all over, inside and out, it was a presence. 'Hella's gone,' she whispered to Sonja as her friend eased herself up on the left side of her.

'I'm not surprised.'

Quiet as they could, they whispered the prayer for the dead and levered themselves on to the floor over the heads of the occupants of the lower shelf who were attending to one of their own deceased.

On the top shelf, women were waiting to be able to deal with theirs.

'Someone has died in here?' Ruth, an arrival on the previous day's transport, who had twitched and moaned all night on the other side of Sonja, had given her usual new arrival's whimper of shock and disbelief on opening her eyes, and was now staring about her with horror, both hands clutched to the nakedness of her scalp.

'There is always someone dying,' Esther whispered, taking hold of one of Hella's swollen blue legs and one of her stick-like arms. Work had killed her, and having no proper shoes so that her feet had been cut, and the cuts infected.

'Who is that woman shouting?' Ruth put her slender young undamaged, unworked legs over the edge of the planks.

'A room elder. They're like us but chosen to keep us in order and deal out our bread. Do not speak to them unless they speak to you and do not dare ask them anything. They will beat you. That is their job.'

She and Sonja managed to get Hella's body far enough out to pull it the rest of the way down. Though she was a skeleton, it had taken their strength and they paused to rest as a room elder strode past on her second round, thumping the shelves so hard they rattled.

Esther glanced up at Ruth who was staring down at her, expecting to be told there'd been a terrible mistake, she should not be here, she should be allowed back home. 'Follow the others to the latrines,' she said, 'you will not get another chance.'

All big blue eyes and skull with a sweet little triangle of freckled face like Sophie's, Ruth slipped on her clogs and jumped down.

'Come on.' Sonja picked up her share of Hella's body, and the two friends, chests wheezing, got her through the doorway and laid her outside against the block wall to be counted.

On the camp road running the length of the compound, other dead were being dragged from other block doorways and someone had been assigned the task of removing the suicide bodies from the electric perimeter fence. Most nights, several prisoners waited for the searchlights to pass by and made their bid for oblivion in one dash.

Checking Sonja's face and arms for signs of infected bites or cuts under the light from the door, Esther said, 'Let me see that boil.'

Gingerly, Sonja bent her head and she lifted the collar at the back of her dress. 'Is it drying?'

'I think so, it's smaller, but we must try and get some more ointment organised.'

'Esther, it costs!'

'Yes, but who knows I might be passing the kitchens next Sunday and find a potato peeling falls at my feet again.'

'Don't risk it yet. The boil's going.' Sonja squatted beside Hella's body and laid her arms across her chest.

Tonight, she'd sit *shiva* for her, as she had for all the others, and she was, Esther reflected, a privilege to have as a friend. They had been together since their arrival, their silence seeming to draw them together in the midst of so much agitated confusion. Each had been is mourning for a beloved one. Sonja's boy of three had died in the transport train.

'We'd better try and organise some string for the little Ruth,' she said. 'She'll lose her bowl and spoon.'

'Yes.' Sonja got to her feet and considered the matter, her strong face and dark eyes, her arched black eyebrows not needing a frame of hair to be beautiful. 'We'll wait a while. She may not last the week.'

'All right.'

Around them a drift of east wind stirred the dusty soil. The orchestra members were taking their chairs over to the front gates, and the sky had a hint of light. Esther looked up at it. So far, each morning, she had managed that.

'This is roll call?' The wind had increased, with a feel of winter. Ruth tried to draw her sacking tighter around her neck, a waste of energy.

'It is and it lasts at least two hours, sometimes all day. Once the guards get here, put your hands at your sides, do not move or speak, do not yawn or flinch whatever you hear, or see.'

Along the camp road around them, hundreds of other women were stumbling into their five-abreast lines to be counted, the sick too, supported by their friends. To be counted, they also must stand upright and not moan or shiver.

'I am so hungry. What was that liquid splashed into our bowls at the barrack door just now?' Glancing about her with horror at the looming skeletal figures, Ruth couldn't stop her teeth chattering.

'Herb tea maybe, acorn coffee perhaps, perhaps coloured water,' Sonja whispered, 'but you will learn to love it, and if you think you are hungry now, you are not, because a few days ago you were at home, eating three meals I expect however small. When you have been here a little longer, hunger will be in you like a pain, but never ask for more of anything. Never, never ask for more in the fields at noon when something resembling soup will be splashed into your bowl. The soup will help you survive the afternoon's work though it is mostly water.'

'What work must we do?'

'We help build more barracks like the ones you see stretched along this road. We call them blocks and there are many of them. The compound covers miles, it has hospitals, hundreds of SS live here, doctors, nurses. There are workshops, laundries, sewing rooms.'

'Oh, Esther,' sighed Sonja. 'If we could get an inside job for the winter!'

'What are those guards?' Half-craning her head, half-crouching into herself, Ruth had already learned to whisper without moving her lips. Her skin had turned blue; only her scalp was freshly red, from its shaving.

'Kapos. They are prisoners like us, but criminals. They serve their sentence by supervising our work details though they do not work themselves as they are not Jewish. The coloured triangle over the number on their uniform means certain things, red for communist, black for prostitute, green for a murderer. Green are the worst. Our present Kapo, Greta, is one. If you're assigned to her work detail with us, do exactly what she orders you to do.'

'Sssh,' Sonja whispered, and she and Esther shuffled themselves into an exact, five-abreast line with two others from their block, Ruth between them in the middle.

Where there had been quiet before, with only the sound of feet and the room elders banging about, now there was silence. The SS guards had strolled in with their dogs, and several female SS.

'If one of those women speaks to you,' Esther muttered quickly, address her as Frau Wardress.'

'Ooh,' whimpered Ruth, 'I shan't be able to remember . . .'

'Sssh.'

Thousands of women waited in their lines. The east wind whistled through their dresses and lingered on their sorest places, the nipples where the sacking had rubbed, their thighs where the menstrual blood had dripped unchecked.

On it went then, in and out of the barbed wire, seeming to pause by the front gates in order to tear at the sheet music of the orchestra who sat waiting on their chairs, and swirling over the watchtowers before speeding off to shriek around the chimneys at the camp perimeter and on to the plains of Poland.

'Get in line, you shit Jews!'

Up and down the column the SS guards strode, hitting out with sticks and whips. 'Keep in line!' the female SS repeated, strolling behind with the dogs. Elbows were their favourite for counting aids, and shins.

Somewhere behind Esther, a thud sounded louder than the others, and a scream, a laugh, the click of a gun, followed by the collective gasp, the wait.

The shot rang out – into the sky! He was playing games.

No one had long to wait for the second. The one who had dared blink, who had dared shiver, was gone. Esther pictured the dribble of blood that was now seeping into the dust to join the lake of it beneath Auschwitz soil.

But it was an easy roll call for, two hours later, the orchestra was ordered to strike up and thousands of women trooped out of the gates and into the fields.

Keeping her head well down, Esther threw a shovelful of earth over the side of the ditch and saw that Kapo Greta was several ditches down the field beating poor Lenka on the head. 'You call that fast enough, shit Jew!'

The wind seemed to snatch her shout and fling it with the others up the slopes where hundreds of women dug and sifted earth for their companions to load into the trucks they had to push towards the area where the men laboured.

303

'Rest a second, Ruth,' she whispered. 'Greta's occupied.'

Whimpering still, dirt spattered all over her, Ruth leaned the shovel against her waist and held out two swollen, blistered hands.

'Those will burst and tomorrow you will work with bleeding skin. Then your skin will harden, as ours has, and your heart will harden too and you will survive.' Esther wanted to smile at her but there was never any smiling in Auschwitz-Birkenau.

'No talking, and no slacking, you shit Jews!'

Ruth ducked her head, grabbed the handle of her shovel and slammed it into the side of the ditch at the very same second Greta's boots appeared. She was learning.

'Get that truck moving!'

Esther threw up another shovelful and turned back to Ruth. 'When we start pushing up the trucks, never look at any of the men. Yesterday, Greta beat a girl to death because she got too close to the fence.'

'They are slaves too, aren't they, and we shall never get out, shall we?' Ruth's voice rose. She scraped up some earth Esther had dropped and threw that over.

Esther knocked out some more for her. 'God forbid you think that, or you won't. You must tell yourself you will endure what you have to and there will be an end to it because the war will be lost. Every night, you must wash yourself all over, using your soup bowl and the cold tap. You will pretend it is hot water and you have soap. You must keep your skin clean because scratches and insect bites get infected here. You must pretend your appearance matters because it does, for your self-respect. You will be proud of your pretty bald head and welcome every third Sunday when it is reshaved because that is also clean-dress and delousing day. You must save half your supper crust of bread for your breakfast, hold it in your hand as you sleep and you must stay dumb and invisible as Sonja and I do. You must keep lice from your body by picking them off and not minding and there is no need to mind the rats. They don't beat you or shoot you. You must find someone you love from home, your mother, your father, your Buba, and even if they are dead or you don't know where they are, you will carry on a conversation with them in your head. You will tell them you are going to survive, for their sakes, or because they would want you to.

304

Each day you will get through somehow and at night you will start building your strength for the next.'

'You see, I told you there would be an end to the day,' Esther whispered to Ruth from the corner of her mouth as they marched in their five-abreast column down the fields towards the barracks.

'I shan't be able to stand another day and I cannot walk in these clog things.' They were caked with earth and her young legs could barely carry her.

'Is that nice Polish girl still working in Canada?' Esther said. 'Only I was thinking, about the ointment for your boils, Sonja.'

'Died last week, dysentery.'

Giving a cry of distress as she almost fell, Ruth whispered, 'Canada?' She took in a great sighing breath and stared ahead of her at the trail of skeletons in their blue and grey sacking and the desolation of the barracks stretching to the horizon. The beams of the searchlights arched and faded, dipping over the barbed wire, making ghostly shadows.

'Canada?' she repeated.

'Stores block,' Esther said. 'For the clothes and shoes stripped from you when you arrived, and all you had in the suitcase you had to leave on Auschwitz station. D'you remember being so careful to choose what you should bring? Well, it was all taken to Canada, as ours was, to be sorted and folded for delivery to the women of Germany.'

'You shit Jew.' Greta appeared alongside them and pointed at Sonja. 'Go back and help.'

Esther watched Greta walk on. 'If you are prepared to forgo two crusts and any pieces of potato or turnip you find in your soup, Sonja and I may be able to organise a pair of shoes for you from Canada, just as we had to do for ourselves. We shall have to find another contact there somehow.'

'Why does Sonja have to go back and help?' Ruth was too exhausted to make the mistake of following Sonja's departure.

'Someone's been beaten to death, I expect,' Esther said. 'Greta often kills several a day, as I expect I told you, and Sonja has to help carry them back for roll call. She looks so strong still.'

But Sonja wasn't strong, or only her will was, and how much longer could it drive her on? How would she herself be able to go on, without her, she thought, desperate suddenly to glance back at her friend struggling with the broken body.

'Why does Greta want to kill several a day?'

'There's never any point in asking that here, Ruth, everything at Auschwitz just is.'

'The band's playing again?' Ruth was very nearly at the end of her strength. A faint tinny sound had reached them, and a drift of smoke.

'They play us in and out of the gates. Be careful to keep in time to the music, some Kapos are very particular and they use whips or sticks.'

'I will be beaten because I don't keep in time to the music?'

'Of course,' Esther said. 'And never look at any of them, did I tell you that?'

Roll call that night seemed to pass more quickly. The SS had seemed not to be looking for trouble. But when it was done, they were not dismissed. There was a hold-up. An almost tangible pall of anxiety settled on the women.

'A new transport's coming in?' someone suggested. 'The chimneys are lit.'

And along the camp road, out of the gloom of the night, there was indeed a column making its way towards them, and from the head of their column right down to its distant tip the same gasp was repeated over and over and with it the same words, 'It's children, it's all children.'

The hundreds of children were five-abreast, as they were. Their marching feet made no sound. No one shouted because they were being good. The bigger ones held the little ones by the hand. The little ones had been permitted to keep their toys. They'd pressed them up close into the warm place in their neck, where coat collar met knitted hat. Big round eyes glanced at this other column with madwomen in it, staring at them, madwomen, sobbing.

'They've emptied an orphanage.' Someone said this out loud.

'Yes.' Someone, a guard, a female SS guard, replied. And she added, 'Where is your God now?'

Esther heard this because she was on the outside of her row. Impatient, she waited until the creature had passed on and turned

306

her head back to the other column, *where Freddy was not*, where she glanced down and tried to smile her first Auschwitz smile in case any of the little ones should look her way and see a madwoman smiling a sweet smile like their Mama's.

They were going to the gas, of course. That was why the chimneys were lit.

Tonight the smell of smoke would keep every woman awake.

Chapter 49

Hertford Street, Mayfair, Autumn 1943

'You're trying to copy the Downlands kitchen,' Max said, 'and in this dump of a place, it won't work.'

He was lounging by the stove in one of the fireside chairs she'd discovered in an attic room and had re-covered in the blue and white mattress ticking which didn't need coupons.

Furious, Susanna went on laying out tea for four with the striped blue and white cups and saucers. 'I spotted this china on a stall in Soho market,' she said, 'and bought it because I like it. It's not a full set and I was lucky to get it, and those pink dishes on the dresser.'

But she was trying to recreate the Downlands kitchen, for her parents to come to, because she'd once told them so much about it in her letters and had longed for them to know it. 'This isn't a dump of a place,' she muttered, 'it's a lovely old town house which has had war damage and over the years too many tenants. It has a very odd mix of furnishings, hardly any kitchen utensils, it's seen better days and it'll see better days again. Aunt Daphne has not only let me have it rent-free for five years, she'll pay for the repairs as soon as any wood is available, and a carpenter.' She laid a clean teacloth over the macaroons and éclairs she'd carried across from Sherry's teashop. 'Did you fill the coal scuttle and is the boiler banked up? I did ask you.'

'Why don't you have some ideas of your own? We could get Art Deco stuff in here, or really classy bone china. I'll start looking out for things on my buying trips, shall I? It's time we started to get a home together.' He took a pair of scissors from a pocket and began to clean his fingernails.

'I want a cosy kitchen. I don't mind odd bits and pieces. I like them. And please don't do that here, it's not as if we don't have a bathroom, we have two.'

'Yes, we have, and I could have one and you the other. We needn't even meet.'

'Max, I am not having second-clothes dealing in this house and since my agreement is with Aunt Daphne I have already told her I hope to let those two spare first-floor rooms to a milliner after the war. A dressmaker and a milliner on the same premises bring each other business. They go together. You keep talking of class, Max, well, class is what I want here, I want to make a fresh start as a dressmaking business with class. I shan't have another chance at a Mayfair address. This is my chance. Aunt Daphne is offering it.' She found she was standing over him with her hands on her hips and was ashamed of herself. Had this become a wifely habit?

She glanced at her reflection in the glass over the mantelpiece. She was frowning. She looked ugly.

'You've done very well so far out of my second-hand clothes business. If it wasn't for me bringing home that twenties Vionnet gown, you'd never have been so successful remodelling blouses with the insets.'

'I admit that. Surely I don't need to go on thanking my own husband?' She set the kettle over the stove for it to simmer and spooned some coffee from its tin into the coffee-pot. 'But I shan't always have to depend on remodelling. Soon the war will be over. I have to think of the future and even if most of my orders here are still for remodelled blouses and my slacks, I expect to get proper garment orders from ladies using their coupons once my reputation spreads.'

'You think I couldn't get you orders? You think I couldn't get connections around here, I soon would. I already have, as a matter of fact, I do some of my buying from grand Mayfair ladies. I could bring you all sorts of clients, but I shan't unless you give me those two big back rooms on the ground floor, if not the first-floor ones. You won't use them. I can bring my stock in the back way through this kitchen, no one'll see me. And I won't expect to have a notice up, no one'll know you have a second-hand clothes dealer for a husband. I need more space. Anyway, I'll charm 'em, they'll love me. Your clients'd rather have me to fit them than you.'

'They won't rather, Max, because you are going to stay at the salon.' She took her brown jacket from the back of the chair where Fritzi slept and shrugged it on. 'You can have the bedroom to yourself, the whole of the salon space for your stock, you can have a boy to run your errands, you'll soon expand from there. I'll send the charlady who's worked in this house for twenty years to clean for you twice a week. I've asked her already. She'll change your bedlinen and towels, see to the laundry. You'll be able to have your friends in whenever you like and smoke as much as you like. She'll wash the ashtrays.'

'Trying to be a wife now, are you?'

'Yes. I always have.'

'And I've tried to be a husband.' He swung the scissors from a finger, round and round, and threw her one of his darkest glances.

'By the way,' she said, buttoning her jacket and brushing off imaginary fluff. 'Please don't forget when they get here to offer Mr David your sympathy for the death of his father. You haven't seen him since Mr Montgomery was murdered. He's also lost his younger brother, Henry, in the desert campaign. I think I did persuade you to send Aunt Daphne a note of sympathy for both those deaths at the time. I don't suppose either of them are going to be exactly cheerful this afternoon so don't make any jokes, or any of those remarks of yours which are meant to be jokes.'

He'd folded his arms and was staring into the glow of the stove.

'Max, please, are you listening? If Patch should be with them, or when you next see Patch, remember to offer her sympathy too, not only for her father and her brother; her husband died in Libya this summer, I did tell you. She's been really sweet to you in the past, they all have.'

'Very sweet, they all have, yes.' He stood up suddenly, hitching at his trousers. 'Don't worry, I'll put on a show for you, I always do. I'll be as goy as can be, but they still won't like me, they look down on me, they think of me as a Jew but they're too English gentry to be anything but perfectly mannered, extra-perfectly mannered, to my face.'

'Don't be silly, they don't think like that.'

'Not about you or Sophie. A pretty girl passes all sorts of boundaries, anywhere, but a ugly bloke like me, that's different. Bet they didn't want you to marry me.' His eyes had taken on their most glittery, black appearance.

She stared into them, weakening. 'Why can't you show your

nicest side to the world, and to me, Max? As your father would have wanted.'

'My father wanted me to marry you. He was the only one who did in our entire clan.'

'I know. Your mother certainly didn't want it. Or my father.'

'No. He's going to be cross with me, when he gets here, is that what you're going to say next? He's going to have a fatherly word with me for not making his precious daughter happy?'

'He decided your constant teasing went too far, wasn't ever funny and never made me or anyone else feel better about themselves. My father believed the very best of people, always, and he brought out the best in them, but he won't be having a fatherly word when he gets here because he'll know we did the best we could to help each other, and he'll be too busy being full of the greatest imaginable joy seeing me and Sophie again. And you, Max.'

'Oh yes? Suzy, you're a fool, he's not coming to England, your father, or your mother, or mine, they'll never set foot on those front steps you keep sweeping, they're in Nazi work camps or in the ghettos, I've told you.'

Stumbling, she began to run up the stairs. She couldn't hear him, didn't want to, wouldn't.

'You know it, don't you, you just can't face it.'

'No, I don't know it,' she shouted, pausing at the top to turn around and send her voice echoing back at him. 'And nor do you because even if thousands and thousands of our people have been sent to work camps, thousands and thousands haven't, and my parents and Freddy are three of them because Papa's skills are needed in the war factories. It's a pity your mother only ever managed to parade about in furs and jewellery having coffee and cakes every afternoon, even the Nazis won't have any use for your mother.'

She stopped, horrified at herself. 'I'm sorry, I didn't mean it. Max.' She peered down through the gloom of the stairwell. He was standing there looking up at her, his face all white and black.

'I'm sorry.'

'You did mean it,' he said. 'And you often say things to hurt me, but it's all right, I understand. Isn't that the doorbell? You'd better answer it while I put some more coke on the stove. You wanted it to seem nice and cosy like Downlands, didn't you, well

311

it is, and I'll stay a while and be charming, I can do that, can't I? Then I'll get back to Soho where you want me to be.'

Clattering across the polished wood floor of the hallway where the walnut table she'd bought, the vase of roses, the painting she'd cleaned, were all suddenly *dust*, she opened the door. Aunt Daphne stood there, flushed and pretty, her face framed in dark sable, and Mr David with his gravest, deepest gaze which she had always thought could see right into her heart, because that's where she felt it.

Chapter 50

Winter at Auschwitz-Birkenau, Selection Day

The worst of it was, today of all days was selection day. There'd be no work, but no soup either, and maybe ten hours of standing naked, waiting their turn.

In the middle of their row, Esther and Ruth struggled to hold up Sonja, each gripping an elbow as she shivered and swayed. The fever showed far too bright in the beacon of red on her cheeks, the glaze in her eyes, her wheezing, each one a signal for the gas.

'I can't, Esther, I can't any more. Let me go.' Sonja managed these few words.

'You think I organised the powder for you for nothing?' Esther muttered. 'It cost me my mother's talisman and how long did I carry that under my tongue before I found a hiding place for it? You take the last dose tonight, in the morning, the fever'll be gone. Ruth's got the water saved, you'll swallow it, you'll sleep.'

Brave little Ruth stood shivering from cold. There'd been frost on the road that dawn, a sprinkling of snow, but it was already churned to grey Auschwitz mud by thousands of feet. 'You think I got that water for nothing, Sonja, good, clean water?'

A faint whisper travelled down the rows. 'It's Taube.'

Through the gloom, the shape of Taube's heavy body could be seen stamping his boots. He was cold too. He was slapping his arms in their black finery as he advanced down the rows.

Thousands of women held what breath they had. Sonja whispered again, 'I can't, Esther.'

'You can.'

Taube was in jovial mood. 'Well, you shit Jews. We'll have some gymnastics to begin the morning, shall we?'

Instantly, the women fell to their hands in the mud.

'Up, down,' he shouted, 'up, down,' laughing and hitting out as he strolled, his drooling, expectant dog beside him. 'Up, down!'

Somehow, most of the women raised themselves, and fell, and raised themselves again.

'Esther, I can't.'

Esther could see Taube and the other guards getting closer and closer. They were so close, she could see the spattering of mud on their shiny black boots, the dogs' paws, their dribble, their steaming mouths. *Go past, she begged, go past, go past Sonja*. If she could will them, if she could will them, just this once! She edged her hand under Sonja's shaking, burning wrist. 'Try. Try, Sonja.'

Sonja laid a blue and red cheek in the mud with a noisy, rattling sigh.

'Up, down!'

'Up, Sonja, up, please, now, now, up.' Frantic, she tried to shield the bony head with its fluff of dark hair among the boils as the last spark of strength left it.

But Taube stopped. 'Ah.' His voice. He was reaching over Ruth's struggling body and poking Sonja's with his stick.

Crack.

A sharp noise, and yet not. It was like no other, the splitting of a skull.

'Better make sure though, eh?' The black boot appeared and stepped on Sonja's blue and red cheek.

Esther felt the blood dribble over her hand and was glad of this last touch of her friend's warmth. *Rest in peace, dear friend*.

Hours passed. Most of the day was gone and the survivors went on shuffling forward round the skull-smashed dead and those who'd died with a dog at their throat, or more simply, from exhaustion or cold. One by one, they reached the judgement table and held up their naked boil-covered heads, willing their skeleton bodies to suggest sturdiness and strength.

Side by side, getting closer, Esther and Ruth awaited their turn. The chimneys had been lit and the smoke was drifting over the camp road. Not far enough off, to the left of them, the girls and women selected for the gas huddled in the open trucks that would take them to it.

'Esther, I shan't be able to jump this time.' Ruth reached out an almost frozen arm to touch Esther's.

'You will, Ruth,' Esther whispered. 'Think about your darling old Buba who's waiting for you somewhere this very minute, you'll live with her when the war is lost. You want her to have no one to go on for?'

'I can't go on.'

'No talking, shit Jews!'

Somewhere, a whip hit out and somewhere someone screamed. The lines shuffled on, towards the table, and the ditch.

And me, Esther thought, without Sonja, can I go on, when I am nearly forty, when at forty, I shall go to the gas, and now, today, when I cannot do it any more, I cannot hold up my head and my shoulders and tell them I can go on working for them, go on digging their ditches, witnessing their killing and my friends I cannot save breathing their last breath, though I have given up all I had, my Mama's talisman . . .

It was her turn. She stepped forward, holding up her head and her shoulders, watching the black cap visors behind the table, the papers, a flash of glasses, Taube's hand deciding her fate. *I shall defy him one last time*, she thought, and saw his hand point right.

No run-up was permitted. Walking the few steps to the test-ditch, she gazed at its terrible few feet of width. *Josef, help me one last time*.

'Jump!'

She jumped. And somehow, landed on the other side.

Half-blind with exhaustion, hunger and thirst, she milled about with the others judged still fit to work in the place allocated them between two blocks. They did not have to stay in lines. Restless, watching and not watching, they waited for the rest to be pointed left or right.

Now it was Ruth's turn. She seemed no more than eleven or twelve, a little girl with her head up, trembling so hard they could see it.

Esther breathed across her message: Ruth, Ruth, gather your strength, it is in you somewhere, find it, find it.

Ruth got as far as the ditch and stared into its depths.

'Jump!'

She didn't even try, she just seemed to fall in. Oh, Josef, Esther thought, can you see? This is what we have saved our girls from. Stock-still so that Ruth could pick her out when she could, she watched the tiny blue body being dragged from the ditch and ordered into the trucks.

And there she sat, with her still-pretty face turned Esther's way, hands clutching the sides, as the ones who had died that morning were thrown in behind her. This meant it was nearly the end. May it be very quick, darling girl, Esther thought, may I never forget you.

In fact a few lines remained, but the SS had begun to yawn and stamp their feet. A Polish winter night's glacier-chill was edging along the road. The gloved hand kept pointing left, the trucks began to rev their engines and rattle off towards the gas chambers.

Straining for a final glimpse of Ruth's face, Esther watched it disappear. Only one truck remained, with a solitary figure sitting in it, Tomcia, a small Polish girl whose arm Taube had absent-mindedly broken that morning, rendering her useless for work. Tomcia was waving, the still-good arm raised. Tomcia was smiling. Dimly, Esther and the others could see that. In unison, they willed across their own smile, their own wave. *Rest in peace, Tomcia.* You'll soon be free.

Night had fallen. Red flames licked out around the top of both chimneys and the thick black smoke smelling of flesh crept under the block-room doors. Though there was plenty of space to enjoy on the planks now – and would be until the arrival of the next transport – the survivors huddled together, exhausted and sleepless.

Close up against a woman she hardly knew, Esther wrapped her arms around herself, thinking of Sonja and Ruth, their long struggle, the last moments, her own to come without them to bear witness, to bless her, to know her.

There was an audible collective cry when the door flew open, quickly silenced when Frau Wardress Muller strode in with her dog and made her way to the room elders' quarters.

316

They waited. Who?

The shout came. A number. Her number, the one tattooed on her forearm, that she never glanced at and could never forget.

She tumbled off the plank. There had been a mistake. She was to go to the gas. And she was glad of it. She was ready. She wanted to join Sonja, Ruth, Tomcia, so many many friends, she wanted to be free. She wanted to be with Josef.

She looked into the small brown eyes and heavy, ungracious features of Frau Wardress Muller, about to utter the very words, I am ready, as if, thus, she could remove something from them with this readiness.

Muller said, 'You can sew, right?'

'Yes, Frau Wardress Muller.'

'Proper tailoring, right?'

'Yes, Frau Wardress.'

'You better prove it good. Report to Canada tomorrow after roll call. I want stuff remodelled, proper tailoring.'

She was gone. The door slammed behind her, the room elder returned to her quarters and the little flutter of agitation settled.

An inside job. Esther climbed back on to her planks. She'd maybe survive the winter.

'An inside job, you'll live, Esther,' Magda whispered, and Rebecca.

'Yes.' In a moment, an hour or two, a day, she'd find something within her to help her feel glad.

Chapter 51

Sherry's Teashop, Mayfair, July 1944

'Only I couldn't bear it if I lost either salon to one of these new flying bombs,' Susanna said, 'but especially the Hertford Street one. My mother will so love it here, you see, with Shepherd Market just round the corner for her daily shopping. There's everything there for her, fish, groceries, haberdashery, bread baked three times a day. She used to love fresh white bread and she'll love this little teashop with the samovar in it and its refugee owners and customers. She'll feel at home, the dressmakers around take their tea at these very tables, the mannequins pop in. My father'll prefer Soho, I think, and I intend to send him off in the mornings to look for the exact kind of buttons and trimmings we need, because he'll so love getting to know people. He'll soon rout out a favourite café to sit in reading his newspapers and discussing the world. I expect he'll find himself other work that way, and he'll deal with the boiler, thank goodness, and probably take Freddy to school. He'll have kept up Freddy's English, I know that, with a view to his fitting in straight away and his future education. What I couldn't bear would be for him to feel a burden on me, he's such a proud man.'

Oh, my darling, David thought, leaning across the table, watching the lips he'd never kiss. Her eyes were green today, for she wore a green dress and a little green thing of a hat perched on her forehead. She seemed older, grown-up, beautifully grown-up, though with a slender girl-like quality about her still. He had come to say goodbye.

'Your parents would rather have a whole, live daughter to greet them than any number of buildings,' he said, 'so please make sure you protect yourself for this new horror the Nazis have managed to create.'

She turned her head towards the window and he could see that strong profile of hers, courage written in it, and determination. He drank in its lines, the shadows, and the poignant, tender skin under her ear and neck where the collar of her dress lay. I can gaze at the blue veins on the inside of her elbow, he thought, and the swell of her breasts, and I can wonder over and over what that boy husband has taught her about love because I have come to say goodbye to her and may never see her again.

'Shall we take Fritzi for one of our walks? Aunt Daphne will be ages yet at the hairdresser's and there's no sign of Max arriving to join us as he threatened to do.'

She had turned back to him and something in him seemed to loosen as if this suggested intimacy, this 'our', cutting out the others, gave him the right to begin edging towards some future where they might be together, or where, at least, her married unhappiness might be talked about between them, and hasty war marriages and the number of war divorces, and she could have things to think about while he was away, and he things to return to. And his awkward leg wouldn't matter, or the scar on his face, or his non-Jewishness, because the depth of his love would make up for them.

'Oh, listen, can you hear it?' Her face had lost its brightness. She was frightened, and he thought, now, and he stood up as if to hold out his arms to her, as any man would with a bomb about to fall. The teashop chatter had stopped, spoons and cups were as if suspended, the cashier's face had taken on a mask, as Susanna's had, a mask of careful listening, and fear.

He was stricken with fresh pity. She had endured so much! Yet it came to him in that eerie waiting moment that he'd be glad if the rumbling sound of its engine coming closer actually cut out and the robot thing fell now on this little place, so he and she could be together in death.

The rumbling did stop. He held his breath and gazed at the mask of her face, lovelier than ever in its stillness. The engine had cut out and the silence was tangible as this awful thought came to him and then another, that he'd rather she die now, with him, in

319

his arms, than ever learn the war had gone on too long and she and Sophie were the only ones of their family left.

The thud of its landing came next, just far enough off. Window panes rattled, the floor shook, hands and cups moved to their positions, the chatter restarted and Susanna's face broke up into laughter, at him. He was the sole occupant to have got to his feet.

'You're obviously not used to the new robots,' she said, unwrapping the dog from the folds of her skirt. 'We Londoners simply wait and see if it's got our name on it, and continue with what we were doing when it's clear it hadn't.'

She had laughed at him, and that seemed an intimacy too. He liked it. He said, 'I'd rather you didn't wait about being London-blasé, and ran for the nearest shelter instead.'

She shrugged. 'It's best not in some ways. There isn't much time with these. But nobody goes to the window any more to see if they're aimed in their direction. They have the most tremendous blast and you can be just drawn up in it and killed if it's close enough.'

'Never go to the window, please, Susanna,' he said sharply. 'You do realise that you Londoners are more in the front line than some of the troops on the battle front? I do wish you stayed a safe Dorset yokel, you know.'

She ignored this remark. 'If you do see them, they're the shape of little planes. Their starting now does seem especially terrible, doesn't it, when the Allies are finally managing to get into France and begin the liberation of Europe. I don't understand how the Nazis are able to manufacture new weapons. Surely they need to concentrate on driving the Allies back, or trying to.'

'They can do both, I'm afraid, they have the materials, the skills, the millions of slave labourers kidnapped from Poland and Russia and the other countries they've occupied. These new doodlebug planes will have been built by slave labourers, prob-ably in underground factories our bombing can't touch.'

'Well, shall we go for our walk so I can show you what one of them did to my favourite trees, the ones we used to sit under, if you remember. It's wonderful having Green Park just across the road. Fritzi gets more walks than he ever dreamed of.'

Again, a hint of intimacy, and better than nothing to carry away with me, he thought, collecting the cakes into his handkerchief. 'For Fritzi,' he said, knowing she'd later wash and iron the handkerchief for his return. It will be my talisman, he thought, near her, next to her possessions, reminding her of me.

'Chairs still tuppence?'

'Yes, but look, no more barrage balloons and no barrage balloon base. They've all gone to the Kent coast to stop the doodlebugs getting any further. The searchlight girls' huts are empty too. We miss them. On sunny days, off-duty, they used to sit knitting and gossiping in the little garden the men made, when the men were on searchlights. They've gone to the Second Front in Normandy now, I suppose, like most of the Americans, the Free French, the Polish airmen. It feels quite empty around here.'

She ran away from him, down the slope, where she paused by the firemen's reservoir and called to him. 'Come and see this.'

She was knee-deep in fresh green leaves. 'Blast swept every one off its tree. Isn't it amazing, a carpet of green leaves?'

'It is.'

'And the newspapers said a flying bomb had fallen on waste-land somewhere in southern England! I'm glad Hitler and Goebbels and the rest of them don't know exactly what they're doing to the heart of London. Goebbels would gloat so on the radio. I'd hate to think of my parents hearing the worst war news and longing to be able to struggle over frontiers to help me and Sophie, and being desperate, and fearing they'd done the wrong thing, letting us go.'

The man was just putting the chairs out after the rain. It had rained all summer but for the moment, the clouds were rolling off. He fumbled for fourpence and she ran up to sit down, settling the the little white Pekinese at her feet.

'At home,' she said, looking up at the patch of blue in the sky, 'in Berlin, I used to do comic drawings, I can't think why I started doing them, but I did. I made Goebbels into a jackal in a cage at the zoo, Hitler was a hamster with mad marble eyes. They used to make Sophie laugh, we'd been laughing about them that night when the stormtroopers smashed the Jewish homes and shops and my parents decided Sophie and I should join the children being helped out of Germany.'

The pity of it, he thought, listening to her sweet, low voice talking about things that should never have been, could never have been imagined, drinking in the sound of her, the colour of her skin, the way her hair curled at her temples. She had the loveliest blue veins there . . . He must begin, he must find some natural approach.

'. . . of course, if as you say, there will be an end to this war, the Allies will finally somehow win through even though the Nazis are still building new weapons and Churchill's warned us there may be another one to come at us, what will actually happen to Goebbels and Hitler and the others when they have to surrender?'

'They will be tried for war crimes.'

'They haven't enough eyes to give though, have they? If it's an eye for an eye?'

The chair keeper put out a few more seats. Fritzi set off again to the slope and David gazed down at the camouflage netting on the pond. Insects danced over it, mosquitoes. 'I have something to tell you,' he said, with a thump of his heart. He would begin with giving up something of himself, that he'd revealed to no one. 'I shall be one of the men sent out to investigate war crimes, Susanna.'

She didn't seem to respond, she was watching the dog, so he went on. 'My new unit will be following behind the Allied attack. Once we get into Germany, our task will be to arrest members of the Nazi party and the entire army of SS. Eventually, they will be tried in the courts of law. Anyone who's ever been part of the machinery persecuting you and your family, or any of your people, any dissident, resister or innocent, will be brought to account.'

Still she said nothing and he dared not look at her. He felt she was as horrified by his admission as if he were a member of the Nazi party himself. But he had to finish. 'For some time, since it was clear after Dunkirk that I couldn't fight in the front line, I've been getting ready. Of course, I had a particular reason for choosing to join this particular unit.'

He couldn't look at her now. He'd held it all in far too long, waiting to tell her. 'Just before war broke out, I learned my father was not Arthur Montgomery, but another man my mother had had a love affair with. I'm glad she had that, in spite . . .'

Finally, he did glance at her face and saw there, what? Sorrow for him, pity? He rushed on. 'My father was actually German, Susanna, and when my mother told me just before war broke out, I found I minded very much indeed. I felt I wasn't the same

322

person, I belonged nowhere, I had no right to the inheritance of Downlands or the life I led there. It's often struck me we had this sense of displacement in common, you know, but the worst of it is, I feel I may have something dark lurking in me, some genetic link to the savagery of the Nazis. I'm no longer the same unthinking sort of a bloke with my life mapped out and I shan't be able to rest until I find out what this real father of mine is, and the half-brothers I might have are. I lay on that beach at Dunkirk and wondered if any of the gunners in the fighters over my head who were aiming for me and the other thousands of helpless men were of the same blood as me. Do you understand? I should like you to, especially you, Susanna.'

Frantic, because she didn't seem to understand and had not uttered a single word to help him on, he got his stiff leg to move and stood up.

She stood up too, reached out and put her hand in his. He gripped it, tight, relief flooding him, and joy. He wanted to laugh. He said, 'This is the first time you have given me your hand.'

'Yes.' She'd gone very pale and her eyes had filled with tears.

'It feels right.'

'Yes.'

'Coo-eee!' His mother's voice. His mother must be standing on the path, and the boy.

'We are being collected by my mother and Max.' He gripped harder.

'Yes. What a pity.'

Three words. They were so many. They were enough. He said, 'I am leaving this afternoon for Europe and I shall be I don't know where. I shan't be able to write to you, but if you need me, will you write to this new Army number of mine?' With his other hand, he took the slip of paper from his pocket where he'd had it ready.

With her other hand, she accepted it. 'Thank you.'

'Aunt Daphne wants her tea.' Max's voice, harsh, echoing.

'I shall add you to my list of worries,' she said, not moving.

'May I be first on it? I'm going right into the thick of things, you know.'

'You've often been first on it.' Then, at last, a smile, faint. And so shy, heart-rending.

'Give me an example of when, to prove it.'

'Dunkirk. I used to go to the stations, to see if you were amongst the troops being brought home. I was terrified you'd been left behind on the beach and would be thrown into one of their prison camps, or worse. I couldn't sleep.'

'Ah,' he said, ready to shout for joy, turning instead to grin like an idiot at his mother and the boy-husband who were making their way across the grass.

He didn't mind their arrival. He had all he could expect for the moment.

Exhausted, Susanna stood at the bottom of the Hartford Street house steps holding Aunt Daphne's stick whilst David helped her into the taxi. He was going to see his mother off to Dorset, then take his own train to his unit.

He was going to Germany. This extraordinary fact alone she could barely take in. And his father wasn't Mr Montgomery. But he wouldn't be Nazi. A father of his, if German, would have been a resister, therefore dead long since.

In a minute or two, he'd be gone again. Desperate, she kept her eyes fixed on him. He was trying not to limp, in case she should mind he was wounded. He didn't know how vulnerable it made him seem, or how she yearned to comfort him for it and touch the scar on his cheek. He always had tried to hide that too, as if it did anything but add to the interest of his face, the bony shape of it, the frown that was never angry, only concerned, for her.

'Goodbye, Max.' He was smiling nicely at Max.

Now her. His gravest smile, the one she couldn't endure. A stab of anguish took away her breath. 'Goodbye, Susanna.' His hand, holding hers again, seconds flying past.

'Goodbye.' She and Max waving, the two faces, Aunt Daphne's pretty, smiling one – she'd had an affair! Mr David's from the rear window, not smiling now, telling her things.

When had she begun to love him? Years ago; perhaps that first day in the kitchen at Downlands, because ever since his merest glance had gone straight to her heart. Her heart hurt now.

'Thank goodness they're gone,' Max said, running up the steps.

She wanted the taxi to stop, the door to open and Mr David to come limping along the pavement towards her, his arms held out, because her whole body yearned to feel them.

Chapter 52

Canada Block, Auschwitz-Birkenau, September 1944

'You wait your turn,' hissed Bertha, a sharp-eyed little woman working at the central table where clothes had to be folded and tied into bundles for removal to Germany. Her fingers worked fast in and out of pockets, up and down linings and hems.

'Wardress Muller sent me,' Esther said. 'I have to find the right sort of coat for her.' She glanced away as Bertha slipped something she'd found into the waist of her own dress.

'You wait your turn,' Bertha repeated, laying out a grey flannel jacket and folding it.

'No talking!' The SS guard on duty strode round the table hitting out with his stick. 'Get on with it.'

'Frau Wardress Muller sent me.' Esther flinched as the stick caught her on the shoulders.

'Hurry up with whatever it is. You help her.' He prodded the stick into Bertha's back.

'What sort of coat does Frau Wardress Muller require?' Bertha asked, not looking at her, inspecting the skirt belonging to the jacket she'd just robbed of some secret, a talisman hidden there by its owner, a little square of chocolate, a sweet to soothe a child, hidden there not long before when the owner was preparing for the transport train, unable to imagine what awaited her.

'Frau Wardress Muller would like a cashmere coat for the coming winter,' Esther said. Always, in this place, she felt her dry, cracked skin prickle with some other, deeper dread, a horror without name. 'I must also collect a fur as she would like her coat to have a good, warm lining.'

325

'Look over there.' Bertha pointed to a heap of coats on a table at the far end of the room. 'You think transports are arriving with winter coats when it's still summer? You think the suitcases are filled with winter coats this time of year? The pile over there's still the backlog from the Hungarian intake, you can search, you won't find cashmere. There may be a few furs.'

Esther made her way around the other women working at the sorting table and paused in front of the mountain of coats. All fabrics were represented, linen, fine wool, heavy wool tweed, and all colours, natural, beige, navy, brown, black, grey, and yes, some of the Hungarian women had thought to come prepared for the winter. They hadn't known they'd go straight to the gas and every stitch of their clothing would be picked over and folded in Canada in order to one day grace the body of a German woman.

With her own expert fingers, she turned the garments, feeling as she did, just as Bertha did, and everyone on Canada work detail, all along the hems, the pockets, the linings. On her last trip, she'd discovered three Hungarian cigarettes in a packet and had been able to barter them for three whole cooked potatoes and three slices of sausage. The Polish prisoners who worked in the kitchens gave real food for cigarettes and she and her five companions in the sewing room had feasted.

Holding up a box-shaped three-quarter brown wool which would be full-length on Muller, she considered a fine grey worsted and discarded both. However well remodelled, Muller would appear as she was in them, a short, stout farmer's daughter with heavy jaw and very little intellect whom no dressmaking skill could transform into a chic, elegant woman like the commandant's wife.

Yet she suffered envy, Esther thought, ready for the weakness of tears as she always was in this place. Muller is a human being, she suffers envy and jealousy of another woman's beauty, and that is normal, yes, but which part of her can live and work at Auschwitz-Birkenau? That was the puzzle.

Just at the point she felt she couldn't breathe, she came upon a jewel of a coat in fine black cashmere. So austere was its design, it must have belonged to a lady of refinement. For Muller, she would add things, a big shawl collar, bigger leather buttons in extended buttonholes, some braiding. Muller liked more.

*

Outside the block in the autumn sunshine, she rehearsed her explanation to Muller that a complete fur lining would make the coat too heavy and that in any case, a half-lining was smart. This would be safer than having to admit Canada was without full-length furs until the next transport, for the fact would be her fault.

The cashmere under one arm, a sable cape under the other, she let the sun's warmth soak into her and walked as fast as she could. She must at all costs avoid looking around her. Last trip, she'd been careless, she'd glanced up from a window in Canada. And next to Canada block were the chimneys.

Every day, she thought, every day, the workers in Canada block could watch from the windows as the SS man climbed the chimney ladders to pour in the liquid gas. It had to go through a a little opening with a shutter. He had to close it quickly.

There was more than one reason why Canada detail shrivelled the heart.

'Out! Out!'

Barely established in her chair beside Paula in the sewing room, Esther saw the same horrified stare on her face as must be on her own. What time was it? What was it for? They stood up.

They did not speak. They had not become careless.

'March! Keep in step!'

March? At this time of day? When you worked in the sewing room?

On the camp road, the entire population was marching. Fear spread in whispers. Were they all to be gassed because the war was lost? Were the rumours the Polish prisoners passed on from their secret radio therefore true, the Allies were coming, the Russians, the SS were going to have to fight the Russians and could no longer guard?

Were the chimneys lit? Yes. They were going to the gas. They were going to die just as the war was lost. Only the other day, a bomb had fallen on Auschwitz. Auschwitz did actually therefore exist, they hadn't been living out nightmares, a bomb had fallen on it, on the SS quarters, ambulances had driven up, there'd been SS deaths and billows of smoke, good smoke.

*

327

It was for an execution. The band was playing especially and just beyond the gates, a platform had been set up with gallows on it. Their own woman commandant and other SS stood there. Taube was there!

The band ceased playing as thousands of women shuffled into their lines and the news spread in more whispers. It's Mala. Not Mala? Mala, their dream figure, yes, beautiful Mala, nonchalant Mala, the charmer who knew so many languages she'd been given the task of runner in the camp. There'd never be another runner. Mala had escaped.

Mala had been recaptured.

It was a calm, smiling Mala they brought out. She was holding her bloodied hands in front of her. They'd beaten her, but they couldn't make her carry the placard for them to read, as other escapees had had to do. HURRAH, I'M BACK, would be written on it, but none of them would have looked at it, and anyway, Mala wasn't carrying it.

They looked at Mala though. She was more beautiful than ever. Her hair had grown while she'd been in the world. Hair! A deep sigh seemed to sweep towards Mala from thousands of hearts.

And she was busy. She was taking something out, a razor blade, she was slashing her wrists, she was going to die by her own hand.

Taube himself went for her. 'You shit Jew whore, I will kill you, you will die by the rope!'

Mala was ready for him. She struck him in the face with her bloody fist, there was good Jewish blood on him, on Taube! 'Murderers!' she cried, the cry echoing out across their rows. 'Murderers, you will pay for what you've done, the end is near!'

Taube bellowed,

'She will die in the flames,' and SS clubbed her to the ground.

It was as if each one of them felt the blows and flinched as her body was thrown into the wheelbarrow. An arm trailing over the edge appeared to make one final gesture, for them, as she was raced away, and every single eye strained for a last glimpse of it vanishing through the camp gates.

Mala's body was going to the ovens and an almost audible sigh rose up, Die now, Mala, die quickly, die free.

328

Chapter 53

Transportation from Auschwitz-Birkenau, November 1944

The most recent events had, in their extraordinary way, been amongst the most terrifying.

First, they had been permitted to cease all work, enter Canada block and choose clothes for themselves.

Second, they were taking this, the second cattle truck journey of their lives, *away from Auschwitz*.

And dressed like normal women.

So far, inside the jumpers, skirts, hats, coats, thick stockings, real shoes, their un-normal, starved and shivering bodies had remained unfed for two days and nights.

Esther, huddled against three friends from the sewing room, was squatting amongst the others on the floor of the truck. They'd been singing. There'd been rounds, and solos, a little concert by a girl who knew entire sections of Beethoven she could la-la and hum, but now the cold had reached so far into them, their voices failed.

Whispering kept them going, and rubbing each others' limbs in turn, and the speculation.

Back to back with Olga, Esther tried to rub some life into Paula's right arm. 'Why didn't we think of taking gloves?'

'Because we didn't know we were going on a journey, and it was so quick.'

'They were always quick.'

'Quick, quick, out, out,' murmured Paula.

'Out, out, you SS creatures, the Russians are coming, the Russian tanks are rolling across the Polish plains, and my word, *how* they will avenge themselves for their own dead.'

'How many Russians killed by the German army, Olga?'

'Millions.'

'Perhaps that is why they have blown up the chimneys and the ovens, so as not to be flung in themselves.'

'The Russians are devils,' Olga said, 'that is well known, they will demand revenge for their own, an eye for an eye, but they are not creatures.'

There was never a suitable word, Esther thought, resting a moment. Somewhere inside her shivering shell of a body was a desire to be angry, that she would not be witness to the terror of the SS. Would they tremble before their Russian conquerors, beg for mercy, throw themselves on their own electric fences? 'We shall not see the Russian revenge,' she said, 'but we have seen the chimneys dismantled and the ovens blown up.'

'Yes!' A croaking cry of delight.

'They don't want the world to know what they have done.'

'Even the SS realise they have done terrible things.'

'Before, they assumed they were going to rule the world, so it didn't matter, they were going to build gas chambers over the whole globe.' After a burst of excitement, Paula's voice faded.

'But the Russians are coming, oh, glorious Russian devils, my ancestors' countrymen, I shall kiss every one.' Olga croaked to a stop too.

'If you live, Olga, if you live long enough,' someone said.

'Maybe we are going home, they are taking us to Berlin stations in order to have us ferried to our homes from there, they are sorry for what they have done to us.'

This was almost funny. They wanted to laugh.

Paula whispered, 'Home? There is no one left.'

'Is Berlin left, hasn't it been bombed? The Polish prisoners heard it had been on their secret radio and from the SS radios when they delivered the meals. Berlin, and the other big cities, the British are bombing them, the Americans.'

Home, Esther thought, a home without Josef in it, without the girls in that cold-water flat where someone else has been sleeping in our beds, our linen, ferreting in our cupboards, tipping our photographs, our letters into our stove. The same someone would have found the last lump of porridge she'd allowed Freddy to leave.

She had never considered the future, only survival.

She tried to conjure up the feeling of Josef being with her, being safe in her heart, helping her. Such a man! She had lost him somewhere, a long time ago, she hadn't been able to keep hold.

The truck rattled on and moaning, wheezing, huddled tight up against Paula, Esther went on trying not to let herself die. Josef, she thought, come back, help me take the next breath of this foul and icy air with the death gasps of my friends in it, and their emptied bodies, for it seems that if they cannot kill us in this new way, we may be going home, and I am trying to remember how much our children need their Mama.

Another two days and nights later, without food or water, they'd arrived at some station and the cattle truck doors were finally opened.

Esther knew she lived still for she blinked at the sudden light, but Rachel had lost the fight, and Magda, and dozens more in their truck alone. Olga would never kiss a Russian conqueror. She lay stiff and staring in filthy straw at their feet because they hadn't had the strength to roll her decently against the side farthest from the spill of excrement.

'Throw out your dead!'

It wasn't over.

Of Esther's friends, Paula was with her when they finally straggled through the gates of the camp. Another camp existed beside theirs! Its name was Bergen-Belsen and over its archway entrance were the familiar words in iron lettering: WORK MAKES YOU FREE. Beyond that was the familiar wasteland of roads and blocks like theirs, containing thousands and thousands of walking skeletons like them.

Chapter 54

Hertford Street, London, Late December 1944

'So this done-up blonde of a Piccadilly commando says to Max, "Want to come home with me love?" And he was *furious*.'

Giggling, Patch dumped the chicken on the kitchen sink draining board and peeled off the newspaper wrapping. 'God, I'll be glad when we're allowed greaseproof again, this is disgusting.'

'What, one of those ladies of the street who are all jammed around the Circus every night?' Gingerly, Susanna approached the bird and inspected it. 'I've had the oven on for ages in case we decided we had to roast it tonight. I mean, we could, then we could make it into the soup for sabbath tomorrow.'

'That's not how you make soup,' Max said. 'And I wasn't furious. Don't start about the blood either. You should have ordered it from the kosher butcher like I suggested.'

'I'm going to try and drain the blood off for you.' Patch threw her jacket on a chair and followed it with the knitted pompom hat which made her seem like nothing so much as a blue-eyed, red-cheeked snowman. 'You should have seen them, though, Suze, tart after tart looming up in the fog and all these blokes shining their torches to get a proper look. Talk about a cattle market.'

'Don't bother about draining the blood, Patch.' Susanna lit the gas under the kettle. 'It's not as if we don't eat in ordinary restaurants every day of our lives. We haven't had a kosher chicken since Max's foster family died in the Blitz.'

'I'm the only one who knows how to do it, and I shall do it.' Max muttered, throwing his jacket and cap on top of Patch's. 'You lot keep out of it.'

Susanna could see he was still furious. His eyes had the glittering black look of his worst moods. 'Why go to all that trouble?' she said, to worsen it. 'Can't we have our special meal to celebrate Christmas, New Year and sabbath together in a nice restaurant? It's not as if we're all here. Aunt Daphne can't get through the fog in Dorset, never mind the London fog, it won't be the same without her and it's not as if we're feeling exactly like celebrating.'

'Too many deaths,' Patch sighed, plumping herself down at the big table in the centre of the kitchen where Sophie was engaged in sewing up a hole in her gloves.

'And the war not going as well as it was,' Sophie added.

'Yep.' Patch twisted one of her curls around a finger. 'Bet those Piccadilly commandos are feeling the pinch with most of the Americans gone to fight for Europe. I dunno, it seems worse somehow, to have got so far and here we are with a chance of being pushed back into Belgium and the Nazis actually winning.'

'What'll those Piccadilly and Mayfair girls do for nylons?' Susanna watched the coffee settle in its jug and took it to the table where Patch had set out the biscuits from Flo.

'What'll they do for cigarettes and booze, never mind the readies?' Patch offered the biscuit to Sophie. 'Close your ears, kid, this conversation's not suitable for fourteen-year olds.'

'I know about street girls!' Sophie broke off her thread with her teeth and snatched some shortbread.

Susanna watched with pleasure as the blush spread on Sophie's cheeks, making her prettier than ever. The freckles were nearly gone now, and the frantic look in her eyes that meant tears were coming, and a bout of thumb-sucking, a refusal to eat. The school had calmed her, she had a routine there and she was top of the form in chemistry and physics. 'Emile gave her a lovely cut this morning, don't you think, Patch? He agrees the fringed bob is her style.'

Patch nodded. 'She's going to be a beauty, Suze. And she's as tall as you already.'

Blushing deeper, Sophie considered the darn in her gloves. 'Max could set up a pavement stall in the Circus selling those girls black market cigarettes and drink.'

Max threw a teacloth at her head. 'Did you get the onions on the way back from the hairdresser?'

'We did,' Susanna said, pouring hot milk in her sister's coffee. 'Four, imagine, the most I've ever bought, and don't say it isn't enough for chicken soup, it is. Sophie has chopped two for you and they are under a plate in the pantry. Have you washed your hands after touching that dead thing? Don't put your finger in the pudding I'm keeping cool in there even if you have.' ·

'Oh, shut up.'

'He'll go out on his own if he's in a mood, won't he,' Sophie whispered. 'Shall we just have toast and cocoa in here for supper if he does? It's so cosy, with the stove lit. It reminds me of Downlands kitchen.'

'It's meant to, darling. Have your noticed the new plates on the dresser? I've been picking up those in the markets since you were here in the summer. They're not all blue, but I think the pink ones are pretty. The last tenants left a few saucepans behind and I've cleaned them all. When Max can be bothered, I want him to put up some hooks on the shelves by the stove so's I can hang them up. I know it won't be quite the same as our description of Downlands kitchen in the letters home, but when Mama and Papa get here and see this, they won't be disappointed, will they?'

'They'll be speechless with surprise.'

'Yes.'

They gave each other one of their private looks across the table. These were rarer now, but Susanna thought they expressed more than words, and in any case, there were things that were better left unsaid.

'Might as well stay here,' Patch said, yawning. 'I dunno whether I can be bothered to have another eat-drink-and-be-merry night for tomorrow we die. I just feel it'll be easier to let the V2s finish us off. They're a bomb too many. I mean, here we are, France is liberated, Paris has been liberated so long, the collaborator trials are going on – and I should know because I've been living there for months – I come home to see my poor Ma and you lot for Christmas and New Year and I find dear old London's having some frightful new weapon thrown at it from bases in Holland and they are hurtling down on the city faster than the speed of light.'

'Where's the rice?' Max shouted from the pantry doorway.

'Where it always is,' Susanna replied. 'And if you're going to cook it tonight when we're supposed to be going out, don't forget to put plenty of water in the pan, because we shall forget to turn the gas off under it. I don't want to lose another one, there may never be any aluminium for new ones ever again.'

'No,' Patch said, 'there won't be, because there's never actually going to be an end to this war. The whole of Europe will be a battleground forever. I mean, the Russians are rushing in from the east to extract a terrible revenge for their millions of dead and their further millions living like rats in the sewers, for their churches that were crammed with women and children and set alight, the French are starving and freezing to death even now, the Belgians are not much better and the Dutch are dropping dead in the street, they've been starved so long by the Nazis, and still the Nazis have plundered so much and kidnapped so many slaves to work for them, they can fight on.'

'My headmistress called the Allies trying to break through at Arnhem the world holding its breath,' Sophie said. 'If they do break through, and Germany is occupied . . .'

'If they break through in Holland, it'll be something, the V2 rockets are being launched from there. Sophie and I saw the damage one did in Oxford Street the other day, a school was hit, and Selfridges, their Christmas decorations were all over the road, and there were lots of deaths.'

'There would be lots of deaths,' Max shouted from the area of the sink. 'The things can drive entire houses into the ground as if they had never existed, only a huge crater's left. And what about the one that just disappeared into the Thames?'

'They're so silent, Patch, they're absolutely terrifying, there's no chance of you seeing them so you can run, and no chance of their not killing you if you're in the way.' Please God, she thought if I am to be targeted one last time, let it not be this house that disappears into a crater, because this house must be standing, Estanna Modes on a plaque outside, when my mother, my father, come up the steps and there it is.

'We won't be in the way,' Max said, 'we've had our share.'

'Puh, puh, puh,' whispered Sophie.

'Puh, puh, puh.' Susanna reached for Buba's little gold talisman which she'd taken to wearing around her neck on a ribbon.

'Touch wood.' Patch tapped her knuckles on the table and dunked another biscuit. 'The awful thing is, I can still eat. I've lost my husband in this war, one of my brothers, my father, and probably my best mate, Georgie, yet my appetite's the same.'

Or she tried to pretend it was. Susanna glanced at the shadows in Patch's face, its thinner, drawn look. When she wasn't making an effort, sadness lay on it and a deep weariness as if in fact she couldn't bear any more. 'Have you news of Georgie yet? You did say you might when you started that new job of driving for the American general in Paris.'

'Some news.' Patch pushed aside her coffee cup and leaned her elbows on the table. 'First thing I did over there of course was find that old friend of ours, Misha, English father, French mother, I think I told you about her. She was caught up in the French retreat in 1940, we picked her up in our ambulance and she was imprisoned with us in the Cherche-Midi. She was accused of a hostile act against the Germans actually, but that's another story. She was sentenced to death for it anyway, but was somehow got out by her mother's lover and taken down to her grandparents in the south, where she became involved in the French resistance.'

'And met Georgie?' Susanna gasped.

'For about three minutes, in a café, then Georgie got up from her chair and disappeared into thin air. She must have seen the Gestapo outside in the street and left so's Misha shouldn't be implicated. 'Course, Misha went mad wondering what had happened to her, I mean, there she was, sitting in front of her, Georgie in all her bloom, dressed up like a classy sort of French housewife, in the French resistance no less, she is gone in a flash and Misha has years of wondering what happened to her?'

'Did the Gestapo get her?'

'Yes. Misha meanwhile had this gorgeous French bloke who was naturally also in the resistance. They were married a couple of months back. He'd been making enquiries about darling Georgie and it seems it's possible the British resistance women captured by the Nazis in France have vanished without trace. They may have been sent to German camps but their names haven't been found on any lists and the Nazis made lists for everything they did, even their murders and their deportations.'

'But there is hope, surely?' Susanna said.

'We've always lived with hope!' This exclamation burst from Sophie and her eyes filled with tears.

Yes, Susanna thought.

Soon the three of them were tearful, each with their separate images of Georgie's possible suffering in a KZ.

They could smell rice cooking. More coffee had been made and the evening was edging forward.

Sophie said, 'Who's going to do the dumplings, Max? If we are having chicken soup, I want matzo dumplings. I want fried skin as well.' She'd recovered enough to be gazing at the reflection of herself in the mirror on the dresser.

Patch had returned to the subject of Paris. 'Misha's been trying to set up a little dressmaking business to give her mother something to do, otherwise she's afraid she'll go bonkers. She had a German lover at one point and the street mobs got her and the other women who'd had Nazi lovers, and on Liberation Day they paraded them through the streets, having shaved off their hair. It wasn't very nice, and a bit pointless I think. They were only the small-time ones. The others were able to get out before the Americans rolled in. The worst sort were the black-marketeer women, not just the wives waltzing about in their furs bought with death-money, but Parisian women who actually dealt in property the Nazis had stolen from its owners, mostly Jewish of course. They deserve to be strung up. They were the ones who kept Paris couture going. And as for that Chanel, it's rumoured she tried to have her Jewish partners in the Chanel No. 5 scent business deported.'

'Did Paris couture really continue throughout the Nazi occupation?' Max strolled across to the table, wiping his hands on a teacloth.

'It did,' Patch answered. 'Hitler himself, no less, wanted it moved to Berlin, the hundreds of skilled seamstresses, the designers, the lot, but one of them, Lelong it was, went to Berlin to plead it should be allowed to serve the Germans from its Paris base. I imagine he feels he saved the couture workers but there's something nasty about it, all the same. I mean, any sort of woman parading in the finest of fabrics when the rest of Europe paraded in rags and make-do-and-mend. They're a slur on our sex.'

'Seen any of this finery on display since you've been in Paris, Patch?' Max sat down.

'I suppose I have, though I expect most of it's been hidden until the worst is over. Some women must be pretty busy buying

337

themselves out of any whisper of collaboration. I can tell you some very strange fashions have been developing over there and all the girls are looking absolutely hideous.'

'What way hideous?'

'I sent Suzy a picture from a magazine to show her.'

Susanna got up, found the cutting under the mantelpiece and put it in front of him. 'I was going to show you. Look, the hair's about a foot high with the silliest little hat on top, and the shoes! Thick ugly wedges. And sheets of material in the skirts when all this time we've only been allowed the skimpiest of garments imaginable.'

'Yes,' he said, frowning over it. 'But if sheets of material are being worn, that means sheets of material are able to be bought. You say the French are starving, Patch? And freezing?'

'They are.' Patch yawned.

'So they'll sell what they have?'

Patch shrugged. 'They might if they had anything to buy but they haven't. I've heard some workers use their wages by dealing in cigarettes. They stand around the railway stations bartering with any travellers coming in from the outside world. If a bloke can get some cigarettes, he has a chance of bartering them for food for his family.'

'Yes. I think I might go over there and see if I can't help. I can get you some fabrics to start you off properly, Suzy.'

'In Paris?' Susanna heard herself give out a nasty sound like a snort. 'How? You know only officials are allowed over, and military staff like Patch. You couldn't even buy a train ticket for Paris.'

'I have contacts.'

'Not that sort, don't be silly.'

'This is one of the first end-of-the-war openings, it seems to me.' His eyes had lost their glittery look and had taken on the blank, stubborn glaze. 'You have cloth, your clientele'll grow like magic.'

Patch whispered, 'He won't get over there, Suzy, don't worry.'

'I certainly will.' He stood up and grabbed the saucepan of rice. 'I'll leave this to absorb the water,' he said. 'And I've dealt with the chicken, more or less. Just don't bother with it. I've got the skin off, Sophie, so you can fry it yourself and make it nice and crispy. You could have it spread on that bread Patch and I brought in with us, it's fresh. In fact, why don't you girls make yourselves a nice girls' supper with cocoa? I want to go out, if you don't mind, I've just remembered I'm supposed to meet a chap at that place in Frith Street.'

He swung his jacket across his shoulders and glanced at himself in the mirror. 'I'll have a shave and brush-up at Emile's on the way. Don't wait up, will you? Get on with planning our new lives for next year though. Next year's going to be the best of all, you'll see. It's going to be the start of Maxanna Modes.'

'Estanna Modes,' the three of them yelled but Max was gone.

Chapter 55

Bergen-Belsen, April 1945

Had other Aprils been as hot as this? Esther could not remember. Marooned on a patch of dusty earth as yet unsullied, she squatted, feeling the sun. She wanted to go across to the tap to ease her split and swollen tongue. For seven days there had been no cup of water, no soup, no bread. Roll calls were long gone, and most of the SS. The rest were waiting, and the inmates were waiting. A near-silence reigned over the wooden huts and the filthy ground and the mountains of the dead. And the tap was so far away. More, it was maybe a mirage of a tap, it was maybe one of their jokes.

In front of her, a skeleton was dragging herself along by her hands, searching for something she would not find because even the worms had been eaten. A centimetre at a time, she moved though and the lice on her moved, busy black threads where her eyebrows had been.

Next, the boots of an SS guard appeared, and a dog's four paws, and a drooling tongue. It was thirsty, as she was. Go and find your dog water, Esther thought, in her blur of thoughts, and may it return here and splash some drops on me.

The crawling skeleton meanwhile managed a few last rattling breaths and lay down beside some others. The guard's boots paused, and the dog's feet paused.

She forced her eyes upwards and saw the guard gaze about her, recognise they were not all dead and open her mouth, a red, blazing mouth, a blood-red mouth, a mouth which that very morning must have felt water in it, tea, coffee, soup.

'We'll soon be liberated,' it said.

She searched for some feeling within her to respond to this remark. The woman was frightened. Yes. That is good out of bad. She had found something to think. I have to be glad the woman is frightened, she decided, for the sake of the others, the names she could list, the ones she had seen suffer their deaths, whom she had briefly loved in their suffering, and then the thousands and thousands of nameless ones whose flesh made smoke she had breathed. Thousands and thousands. And she had another thought: the Allies are coming. It is over. All this.

It was as if she had waved a hand to take it in, the entire wasteland with its huts stacked with the living dead on layers of planks, its hundreds moaning that very second in their last typhoid-agony, its thousands buried in pits, its ooze of excrement and vomit, its mountains of decaying flesh, all this holding so many different ways to die, it is going to end.

If she listened intently, she thought she could hear the guns. Josef, she muttered, here I am. Help me live to see the tanks pass by on the road outside. Help me crawl to where the tap is. We are permitted to use it. But we cannot get there.

She'd been dreaming of Josef. She could hear his voice calling, Esther, Esther.

But it was Paula. Paula had crawled from where she'd been lying over towards the gates, where there was supposed to be a *tap*, where she'd had to rest. 'Esther. Listen.'

She opened her eyes and through a dancing mist saw Paula's face. There was something different in it. Paula was trying to laugh.

'They are sending us a message, Esther.'

'Who?'

'Soldiers.'

Soldiers. She tried to find the words for a question. 'What kind?'

'The right kind. British. Esther. Listen.' Paula dragged her bones to sit beside her, edging her knees up one by one so that she could support her arms and thus her head.

'They are speaking to us. To us.'

Esther felt herself begin to tremble. There was someone speaking, someone shouting. There was too much noise. But such a voice, such a beautiful voice.

341

'YOU ARE LIBERATED, YOU ARE ALL FREE. BRITISH TROOPS ARE AT THE CAMP GATES, YOU ARE FREE. STAY CALM. YOU ARE FREE.'

'We must stay calm, Esther.' Paula's bones shook.

'Yes.' Her eyes hurt. She tried to peer across the mounds of the dead towards the gates. Something was moving there, a big dark shape. A tank.

Chapter 56

London, April 1945

This is the new night-sky, Susanna thought, gazing up at the flashing lights of the bombers going over to Germany. The new night noise was the throb of their engines. And unless Hitler had some other weapon he planned to launch from yet more underground factories hidden in forests, the present dim-out would soon be transformed into the old-time glare of full headlamps, lit-up shop windows and WRIGLEYS CHEWING GUM in red neon tubes at Piccadilly Circus.

'Evening, Mrs Merkel,' the newsagent called from his doorway. 'I see hubby's just back from his trip.'

'Yes.' She rubbed the sleeve of her jacket across the lettering MADAME LOLA COURT DRESSMAKER and hurriedly turned her key in the lock.

'Seemed worn out, he did, like as if he was hoping to find his slippers warming and his supper on the table.'

'My husband really prefers to eat out, Mr Harvey.'

'Staying the night, are you?'

Pretending not to hear this last remark, she closed the door behind her and stood listening. No sound. I hope there's at least coffee up there, she thought, and the bread, milk and margarine I asked the charlady to bring this morning. I hope she has also cleaned the place and there are fresh sheets on the bed. I hope the wretched Hank is not with Max.

'You took your time getting here.'

He was slumped in the armchair beside the salon hearth.

343

'Why are you sitting in the dark?'

'Couldn't be bothered with the blackout.'

'It's dim-out now.' Releasing Fritzi, she switched on the light and went into the kitchen to put on the bedside lamp there, relieved to find Mrs Smith had temporarily cleared the place of its squalor.

'I keep forgetting no blackout.'

'You want coffee?'

He'd got himself out of the armchair and was standing in the doorway.

'Where's your luggage?'

'Lost it.'

'Lost it?' His face had its most glittery, wild look. He was unwashed, his skin shiny, his suit rumpled. Something had certainly happened. 'Is that why you telephoned me to come?'

'Hardly.'

'Why then?'

'I can't call my wife to come and be a wife to me now and then?'

'You never have before. You usually have your American friend with you and don't need me.' She poured water into the saucepan and lit the gas under it. 'Where is Hank?'

'How should I know?'

'I assumed he went to Paris with you.'

'He didn't. He just gave me the name of his contact over there.'

'All right. Would you like me to run a nice hot bath?'

He didn't answer, but she folded back his bedclothes, took a pair of his pyjamas from the drawer and went into the bathroom.

He was still in the doorway when she returned feeling obliged to say something further to please him. 'Anything worth my looking at on your rails? I'll never forget that first Vionnet dress you found me. Appliquéd muslin it was, if you remember, and it started me off remodelling blouses with insets, didn't it? Such workmanship in a Vionnet though, I don't suppose it'll ever come back . . .'

'Have you run my bath?'

She could hear him swishing water about. 'I'll get you a toothbrush and flannel tomorrow,' she called. 'You'll have to find yourself some new tortoiseshell brushes. Or maybe the suitcase will turn up.' Whatever had happened to Max in Paris, she realised, it hadn't been a successful visit. 'If you are planning another salon here for your mother when she arrives, you'd better start looking out for a second sewing machine. I imagine that Sam will be able to do machining at some point.'

There was no answer, but she went on talking, as if compelled. She was waiting for bad news. She knew bad news was lurking in the very air of this flat and shortly it was going to hit her in the stomach.

He seemed better sitting at the table in his pyjamas, his coffee in front of him.

'You've had supper?'

'How could I have had supper?'

'On the train.'

'You think there's a buffet service, with a war on? Don't be daft.'

'On the way from the station.'

'I haven't had any supper, and I don't want any.'

'All right.'

'I'd like toast.'

'Good. I did ask Mrs Smith to bring in some essentials this morning.' She stood up and busied herself slicing and toasting, knowing his eyes were on her.

'Like old times, Suzy.'

'Yes.'

Greedily, he dunked toast fingers.

'You will stay the night?' He was feeling lonely. The bad news wouldn't be long coming.

'I can't. I've an order to finish.'

'Please.'

'All right. But I'll have to leave early.'

'You can have some of my pyjamas. Look, I think I'll get into bed for a while, I'll feel better if I can have a sleep.' He leapt up and opened a drawer, passing her the cream silk pair Aunt Daphne had given him for their honeymoon. 'Let's have a talk in bed. I am tired, you know. It'll be like old times. I have lots to tell you, wait till you hear about Paris fashions, hideous they are, like Patch said.'

*

It wasn't like old times, Susanna decided, it was very strange. Fritzi tucked inside her left elbow felt familiar, but the room itself, with a view of kitchen sink and kitchen mess, she'd almost forgotten. She'd become used to a proper bedroom with a decorative washstand in it and a picture of Westminster Bridge.

'You didn't actually do any dealing?' she said. They might as well get out the bad news, that he'd been gambling or something, or robbed. She'd be nice about it, it was only money; money didn't matter, only people did, and soon her father was going to be here to remind her of the preciousness of life for himself.

'No. Hank's contact wasn't the right sort. I'll have a thing or two to say when I see him.'

'But your next trip might be more profitable?'

'Yes. Next trip.'

'And you didn't like Paris as much as you felt you would?'

'No. It's a miserable place with a sort of furtive atmosphere as if there were Nazis round the corner.'

'Even in the spring? The song? Paris in . . .'

'I didn't notice it was spring.'

'What was your hotel like?'

'Didn't stay in one, did I, I told you. I stayed with Hank's contact. It was cheaper and he invited me to stay.'

'What was he a dealer in, this contact, if it wasn't clothes?'

Max didn't answer. He'd shut his eyes again and a little snore like Fritzi's was coming from him.

She too closed her eyes. Tomorrow, she must waken early and catch a cab back to Hertford Street to finish Mrs Whittaker's jacket. She'd cut it in the same design as her own wedding jacket, almost a copy of a Schiaparelli one. I shall concentrate on getting some nice linen this summer, she thought, if there is going to be any cloth released at all at the end of the war. I shall then swear never to make another nasty short boxy skirt.

'Suzy, he was a dealer, Hank's contact.'

'Was he?'

'But not in clothes.'

'Yes. You said.'

'He lived in a wonderful flat in the poshest district near the Bois de Boulogne.'

346

'But it was cold? There's still no coal in Paris or hardly anything to eat?'

'No.'

'So you didn't feast?'

'I could have, but I wouldn't have gone in one of those places, would I?'

'They'd have been collaborators' places.'

He fell silent again and she glanced at the clock. She'd almost like more toast and some cocoa but she must wait until he was properly asleep. He needed sleep rather than food. He had a battered sort of appearance, as if he'd been through too much. Poor Max, she thought, after all his boasting, Paris was perhaps real big-time. Well, he must settle for what he had, which was unfortunately what she herself had. Frau Merkel might one day be sleeping in this very bed, *of mine*, she reminded herself, but I shall be beautifully gracious about the matter, for my Papa and my Mama will be with me and I shan't care what Frau Merkel has then or what a superior face she puts on, with her wicked-stepmother eyes inspecting this ghetto kitchen-bedroom and the rows of second-hand clothes in its only other room and an errand boy called Sam employed by her son, the dealer, the black marketeer.

'Suzy?'

'Yes.'

'You awake?'

'Yes.'

'Hank's contact, d'you know what he was?'

'No.'

'He was a profiteer.'

'I guessed he was some sort of a one.' And somehow, she thought, he has got money out of you, which will never be returned, but I am not going to mind.

'Not my sort, Suzy, I mean, a few black market coupons is all I dealt in.'

'Well, hundreds, not a few. It doesn't matter now though, the war's nearly over and you're going to be legitimate.'

'Yes.' He laughed. 'I can be legitimate.' He sat up and put his hands behind his head. 'Everything's going to be all right, isn't it?'

347

'Yes.'

'I've made a lot of money, you know, so you can make your start in the couture once fabrics come off ration.'

'As you keep on telling me.'

'It's true, wait until you find out how much.'

'When can I?'

'Soon.'

'You'll be able to take on several girls because they're coming out of the war factories. Begging for work they'll be, so don't go taking on the less skilled ones, you're going to be big, you've got the right address, Mayfair, you have to start class and stay class and that's what I've been making money for.'

'We'll wait until the war's actually over first.' And also, she thought, until you get around to admitting how much of it you lost in Paris.

'Part of it's in gold.'

'What is?'

'The money I've made for you.'

'Heavens. How will I exchange it for usable money?'

'See that accountant. Make sure he doesn't declare all of it and gets you out of as much tax as he can.' He yawned. 'I'm tired, you know.'

'Go back to sleep. Shall I switch off the lamp?'

'No.'

She was just ready to sleep herself when he startled her awake.

'That contact of Hank's, guess what he had in the flat.'

'What?'

'A prayer shawl.'

'He was Jewish?'

'Of course he wasn't Jewish.' With a bound, he was suddenly out of the bed. 'Of course he wasn't,' he yelled from the bathroom.

The last thing she heard was him passing water.

When she woke again, Max was sitting at the kitchen table with a big black box in front of him.

'It's all here, Suzy,' he said.

'What is?' She sat up, eyes pricking.

'The gold, the various bank accounts, all the papers you'll need after the war.'

'Good.'

'Listen.' He picked it up and carried it to the wardrobe. 'I'm going to put it at the bottom where you used to keep Madame Lola's furs.'

'All right. There's no need to show me now, is there?'

'Yes. And I'm sorry I sold the old lady's stuff without your saying I could. I just felt I had to make our start and that was the only way left to do it. The sapphire was gone, everything. I was right, as it's turned out. You'll be surprised when you see how much there is in there.' He wiped his hands on his pyjama trousers.

'D'you you want some cocoa? It might help you sleep.' She was almost amused by this performance. She really ought to relieve him of his anxiety and admit she'd realised what it was all for.

'I'll sleep in a minute. I just thought I'd show you.'

'You have now, and you're overtired. I'm going to get cocoa and aspirins.'

'You'll take care of me? That's nice.' He returned to the bed while she busied herself again at the stove, more wifely than she had been for a very long time.

'There,' she said, tucking the tray near him on the coverlet. 'I haven't often taken care of you, have I?'

'I haven't been much of a husband to take care of. I've been a pretty bad husband in fact.'

She sat on the bed and felt his forehead. 'I think you've caught a cold, you're getting more feverish by the minute. I just hope this Paris trip hasn't given you more than a cold. You'd better rest tomorrow, I'll come over in the evening.'

'That'll be nice. I do feel ill.' He gazed into space. 'Suzy, I'm sorry I couldn't manage, you know, love.'

'It doesn't matter, we weren't ready for it. We were too young. We married to be company and protection for each other, didn't we? And we have been too.'

'Your mother wouldn't have liked it. The wedding didn't seem right either, did it, with them not being there.' He swallowed two aspirins and the cocoa and went on staring at nothing. 'You're fonder of that dog than you are of me.'

'I'm fond of you both.' Yet her tenderness was for Fritzi.

349

Perhaps she had none left for Max, even when he needed it. This recognition was followed by another, more unwelcome: Max has always needed it, and I have failed him quite as much as he has failed me.

'It should have been different, Suzy.'

'It will be, after the war. I mean, think what we've been through, loathed and unwanted in our own country, enemy refugees here, threatened by death from bombs practically every day for years, without parents or family except the Montgomerys for me, and the Lipinskis for you. And they died, horribly. It's a wonder we're still here ourselves. But we'll be a proper family again, soon, when ours get here, and we'll have to do as we're told, never mind how well we've been managing on our own. I can almost hear all that old emotional blackmail they'll use to get us around the table for the festive meals and we'll never again want to miss any of the rituals, will we, we'll be only too glad to sit through the droning on. You'll ask my mother to sing some nice Yiddisher songs for you, and you'll cry, I expect.'

'Suzy.' He sat up, carefully moved the tray to Fritzi's side and got himself out of the bed. 'They are never going to get here, why don't you admit it?' Dashing across to the kitchen chair where he'd hung his jacket, he frantically searched its pockets and dashed back to lay a newspaper cutting on her knees. 'Those KZs where you've consoled yourself by picturing them busily working away for the dear Nazis, they were that, Suzy, that, and they will never come, never, Suzy, because they are dead.'

She didn't look at the photograph, not needing to, not wanting to, only letting it into the edge of her vision. 'That's been printed in the English newspapers,' she said. 'But your mother couldn't have been in a camp like that because she wouldn't have been able to do any work, not like those poor souls were obviously expected to do, and as for my father, his skills were vital at the AEG factory in Berlin, so that's where he would have remained, and my mother and Freddy with him. I do realise that if he was no longer wanted, he and Mama and Freddy might have been sent to one of the ghettos to toil in some factory, making uniforms I expect, and being just about fed, but surviving. They needed slaves, the Nazis, they must have looked after them, they'd have had to. Your mother might have been chosen for a uniform factory, she's a fine seamstress actually. What we must remember is that the Nazis had to have millions of workers in order to conquer the world, and in those millions, somewhere amongst them, working even now I expect, because the Nazis haven't given in, somewhere, Max, are our parents. And won't they have to be cosseted, after what they've been through. Your mother'll spend weeks in that bed, recovering, you'll have to use the Morrison.' She was shivering and suddenly spent, they both were. 'Get under the covers,' she said.

'You think I can sleep? You tell me how. I see that in the Paris paper, those mountains of skeleton bodies, you think I want to sleep, my Ma's in there, Suzy, and yours!' He grabbed her arm and shook it hard.

'They aren't, Max!' She was shouting. 'For once, I am not fearing the worst. If thousands and thousands have died in those camps, thousands more survived, not even Nazis would deliberately kill the slaves they wanted for their war, it wouldn't make sense, and now they've lost it, thank God, our parents will be free, Max, to come here, to us.'

In the end, they had to sit at the table for more cocoa with the gas rings lit. It had turned chilly.

'It was the prayer shawl,' Max began, before she'd taken a first sip. 'Hank's contact, he was using a prayer shawl on the back of a chair, as a chair protector thing, and I asked him, I said, "Are you Jewish?" "Do I look Jewish?" he says. He was blond, you know, like Hank, he had a face like Hank's, face like the Hitler Youth we went to school with. "There isn't a single Jewish look, is there?" I say. "Well, you have it," he says, "and I like it, I had lots of nice Jewish boys before they were deported, one of them lived here, his father was an antique dealer, that's why there are some good pieces, and when it was empty, I moved in."

'Suzy, he stole that flat, I assumed it was his, but no, he'd stolen it, he walked into it after the Paris Jews were rounded up and deported to the KZs. I knew then I must do something, you see.'

'Yes,' she said, eagerly. 'You robbed him, you took something back, I understand, but it wasn't wrong, it was making a gesture towards righting a wrong.' She felt herself smile. 'I decided he'd robbed you, or you'd been gambling, and you were too frightened to tell me.' Then she thought, now I understand, about our wedding night, and it doesn't matter any more, it hasn't mattered

351

since the day I realised that David loved me. As always, this reminder made tears come to her eyes, from some mix of joy and fear.

'It's all right, Max, listen, are the police after you? The French police? They won't arrive on our doorstep, don't worry, there's still a war on, why should they fuss about something stolen from a flat that was stolen? There's worse things going on in Paris, weren't half the French police Nazi collaborators, they'll be too busy pretending they weren't . . .'

He wasn't listening but he'd caught her gaze in a terrible, suddenly terrible stare. 'I got out my dagger, you know, the one I took off the Hitler Youth gang at home, Blood and Honour's written on it, their little motto, and I went for him with it and I slit his throat and I watched the blood spill out all over the Aubusson carpet he'd stolen from a dealer like my Pa, and I said, out loud, I said, "There you are, Pa, that's for you." Because they beat my Pa to death with shovels in the Sachsenhausen KZ that night in November '38. Your father would have gone the same way if he'd been rich, he was lucky, he didn't have anything worth stealing but they had this big welcome ready for the rich Jews, double line-up reception at the gates they had, double SS line-up, with shovels, and they beat them till their eyes fell out, a policeman outside saw it, he came to tell me, I didn't tell Ma, though, and d'you know what, I wish I could have beaten that Paris bloke with a shovel, slitting a throat's too quick. Did you know that, Suzy? It's too quick.'

She found she was shaking her head to indicate a silent no, as ice crept from somewhere in her stomach, made its way into her chest, her arms, her throat, and began to freeze her skin.

'I knew it before, of course. I should have gone to look for a shovel. I told you I used the dagger already? First time, I killed the guard dog on the Dutch border when I was trying to get across, it was him or me, then the second time, it was Pa Montgomery, I thought, everyone hates him, I'll be doing them a good turn. Aunt Daphne's done well out of it, hasn't she, and that David you're so fond of, and you, Suzy, Mayfair, that's where you started, and that's saying a lot.'

He began to drum his fingers on the table, the cocoa in the cups was trembling. She dragged her eyes away from his stare. It was her fault, she wanted too much and now it was dust, as she knew

352

it would be, it was dreams gone to dust, Mr Montgomery dead because of her and Max, murdered because of them, and now she must help him, hide him somewhere safe, look after him, because she always knew she'd have to, and she'd made a bad job of it so far.

She said, through her mask of ice, 'It's certainly saying a lot,' and then, 'Have you still got the dagger, Max?'

'I felt I wouldn't need it any more, so I left it stuck in him and I wrote a message on the bathroom mirror, FOR SACHSENHAUSEN. I used his lipstick. Did I tell you the creature wore lipstick?' He yawned. 'I'd like a sleep now. Will you sleep beside me one last time?'

'Yes.' She stood up and reached for his hand. It was burning hot, all his skin was, and his eyes seemed as if they were coals about to burst into flame. 'I'll tuck you up, like you used to me, when I had pneumonia, d'you remember? You were a good nurse.'

'I was good at lots of things, wasn't I?' Suddenly earnest, getting to his feet, he said, 'I was a good dealer, a good picker-out of gowns you could use, wasn't I?'

'I couldn't have made such a solid start without you, not once rationing began, because you gave me the idea for blouse inserts, didn't you? Come on. Sleep now, then more talk, and deciding what we must do in the morning.'

'That's nice, that "we", Suzy. I wish I'd been a good husband, you know.' He allowed her to lead him to the bed.

'You were. You gave me my start, and I felt safer knowing I wouldn't die alone in this very room. I was afraid of many things, but got better at bearing them once I was Mrs Max Merkel and knew I'd always have you.'

'You knew I'd never let you down.' He slipped between the sheets and leaned back on the pillows she plumped for him. 'Mrs Max Merkel. It sounds nice, doesn't it? Maybe we won't change our name to Merchant after all, or perhaps we will, it'd avoid confusion between you when my mother gets here.' He yawned again. 'We'll talk about it in the morning.'

'We will.' Making her way to her side of the bed, she edged Fritzi along and plumped up her own pillows. Your body could go on doing things of itself, she knew that. 'We'll have a proper sleep,' she said, 'and in the morning we'll have a real breakfast.

I'll run out to Antonio's for fresh bread. He might let me have a pat of butter if I'm nice to him. Then we'll talk about what to do.'

What to do about calling the police, she thought, and admitting to Aunt Daphne who had killed her husband, what to do about Max having to manage without her once the police came to take him away. Because how could she hide him? And where?

Something awful closing her throat, she gazed at his face against the linen. It was really such a pleasing face in its perfect symmetry of brow and hairline, its dark dark eyes and smooth matt skin. And it was soon to be no more, Max was to be no more, he was to cease to exist, he wouldn't be able to help her endure what must now be endured, the terror of waiting to come, and the going-on afterwards, his mother and her parents arriving to a trial for murder and a hanging. There'd be a great space beside her where he'd always been since they were nine or ten.

'Get in,' he said. 'I want to feel you near me.'

Switching off the lamp, she settled herself with one arm around his shoulders, the other around Fritzi. 'It feels cosy,' she said, hugging him close to something rigid which was her, trying to comfort too late.

He laid his cheek against her neck. 'I did love you, Suzy.'

'I know. And I loved you, even if we did argue about every single thing.'

'Married people do, don't they? We got that right.'

'We did.'

'Tell your parents I tried to look after you, won't you?'

'I will. Sleep now.' She drew him closer, feeling the thud of his pulse, hearing his heart. Her own heart raced. She would never sleep again. Images of death would pursue her for the rest of her life as they did now, Mr Merkel's head being beaten, one of his eyes was stuck to his cheek and begged and accused her both at once. Mr Montgomery's ugly face kept accusing her too, but it didn't stay long, for Paris was butting in, and blood mixed with lipstick.

She must have slept though, for she woke with a terrifying start, registering the fact she was in the salon bed, registering also the cold pillow next to her and remembering the night, letting the horror of it spring back into her throat.

She sat up. 'Max!'

No answer.

Throwing off the covers, she wakened Fritzi and padded with him to the bathroom.

The door was shut, and on it, scribbled in tailors' chalk, was the message, DON'T COME IN, CALL THE POLICE.

And somehow she knew, almost before she glanced down, what Fritzi was so excitedly sniffing at. It was blood. A sticky puddle of it had seeped out on to the lino.

Chapter 57

Victory-in-Europe Day, May 1945

'Yes, Aunt Daphne, honestly, I am all right. I do miss you, but you did have to get home for Will. A mother can hardly allow a war-wounded son to be sent back in a wheelchair without a proper welcome. And I've been out with Fritzi this afternoon, we did our Green Park walk like we used to, then I got us both through the crowds in the Mall and had a glimpse of the King and Queen and the princesses on the Buckingham Palace balcony with Mr Churchill. I heard he was going to be making his speech in Whitehall later and I went off again to hear it at about five o'clock.'

Telephone receiver to her ear, Susanna stood in the hall of the Hertford Street house, gazing through the open doorway to the Union Jacks fluttering from the windows opposite.

'Well, yes, it was rather daft, but they were very nice crowds, not, you know, wild, or drunk, and I decided I must make the effort. I mean, I've been through this entire war and practically heard at least the whine or felt the tremor from every single bomb that ever fell on central London.'

Absently, in a familiar gesture, she used the skirt of her dress to rub over the new brass plaque with ESTANNA MODES on it. She'd had to bribe the Soho craftsman to find the brass and get it done in time.

'And I did see Mr Churchill, it was worth it, and I'm exhausted now, so I might sleep. His car had to crawl there apparently, people wanted to touch it, which must have been wonderful for him, and a change from before the war when he was sneered at for being a warmonger and frightening everyone. He knew the Nazis intended to conquer the world by savagery and no one wanted to believe him. I loved hearing him use those glorious hissing words like *Nazi pestilence*, and calling Hitler a monster of wickedness and a bloodthirsty guttersnipe. He really seemed to understand how it was for our people and those other millions suffering Nazi horrors. Anyway, the crowds were dancing and singing and shouting for him, "Winnie, Winnie, we want you," until someone spotted him on a balcony and there was suddenly absolute silence. I just heard "Dear friends, this is your victory," before I started crying again.'

Wiping away fresh tears with her skirt, she listened to Aunt Daphne trying to comfort her.

'Yes, but I realised Max should have been there. He deserved to see the end of it all, he was only nine when the Nazis started at us. I wish I hadn't been so hard on him, Aunt Daphne, why was I? I wish I'd known about his, you know, his problem. I would have understood better then, wouldn't I? About, you know, the honeymoon and so on, it really didn't matter. I was relieved actually, it didn't seem right between us, that sort of thing, but of course, I had to feel resentful, and rejected, why couldn't I just have talked to him about it, we could have gone on as we always had, bickering, yet being together. We were more like brother and sister, I suppose, but he must have been so ashamed of himself, I feel he must have been, it must have made him feel furtive or something, he did so admire class and style and he yearned to belong. How he would have managed after the war, I can't guess. I can see myself behaving just as badly towards him though, if none of this had happened. I used to feel angry enough to hurt him, I wanted to hurt him and I don't think he was ever angry with me, or wanted to hurt me, except through that teasing of his, which was just him being clever. And being unhappy, I suppose. He was always unhappy, but if I'd loved him!'

Struggling against more tears that would keep coming and coming, she leaned against the door jamb. 'What? Yes, I will stop crying, I promise, and I'll get myself something to eat when I prepare Fritzi's. I don't know what I'd do without this dog, probably lie in bed brooding all day. I'll telephone tomorrow to report I have got up and let you know if the police or the solicitors want any more information. Have you told Will it was my Max who murdered his father? Well, yes, he did loathe him, but murder, Aunt Daphne! Millions of murders in this war? Yes. And he was a war casualty, Max, if you trace if back to his poor father and that awful death, never mind Max's walking across most of Germany and getting himself over the Dutch border in 1939. On his own, he was always on his own, when did I ever make . . . No, he wasn't ordinary, was he? But goodnight, darling, sleep well, I won't keep going on.'

A fresh sob rising in her throat, she replaced the receiver, picked up her little Pekinese from the doorstep and stood listening to the strange crowd noise drifting over from Piccadilly. The victory celebrations were building up, and across the street two houses had every light on, blatant lights and bare windows.

Reaching behind her, she switched on her hallway light and went on sobbing, not caring if the neighbours saw her. No one had called in with the offer of sympathy for Max's death, but then she wasn't a decent war-widow. She was a suicide-widow, a different matter, and moreover the widow of one of those Jewish refugees – who to show his gratitude had stabbed a member of the English gentry!

Yes, yes, she thought, and just let me tell you, oh God, let me tell you English citizens out there, what it was like for me and Max, in Berlin. Ugly old Berlin he used to call it, and if it had only been ugly! Imagine the Nazi invasion they planned actually happening and this London street being forbidden you with notices saying DOGS AND ENGLISH KEEP OUT, and your parks having them up and your cinemas, and your parks and cinemas filled with Nazis, their wives and their children – who'd have been taught to despise you and spit at you. Imagine not being permitted to work or receive your pensions, thus starving to death very slowly, and if you are proud and noble like my Papa having your spirit broken, and if you are rich like Max's father having your head made into pulp with a shovel, and if you are Max, knowing it and bearing the weight of it in your heart, somehow, until your heart can't stand it.

I wish, she thought, sobs rising in great choking waves, I wish I'd never heaped more hurts on Max. He'd be with me today then, and I wouldn't be pierced with this guilt and this cold horror that every echoing step I take in my polished hallway and up my polished stairs is a guilty one. She'd banished her own husband, in fact, whilst she went on creating foolish dreams that to anyone

358

else but her were more and more obviously based on a denial of the truth. She'd spent years denying the truth, years living on the surface, never giving rumours so much as a glance, never daring to.

And it had been for nothing, for this day-and-night weeping in a vast, empty shell of a house her parents and Freddy would never come to, or Max's mother, because they couldn't, because they were in those piles of bodies.

She was down in the kitchen, almost asleep with her elbows on the table, when the doorbell rang. It took her so long to decide to answer it she expected the caller to be gone, but he wasn't.

'Telegram, Mrs Merkel.' The telegraph boy was trying not to smile at her, in case he was passing over grief, but victory excitement made his eyes sparkle. 'Hope it's good news, especially today, like.'

'I hope so. Thank you.' She reached for a threepenny bit in the hallstand and handed it to him.

'Ta, missus.' The boy winked. 'It'll help me celebrate. There's dancing in the parks later, and bonfires, you should see the people getting ready to burn old Hitler, he'll burn thousands of times tonight, wish he could feel it, that old devil.'

'Yes.' She watched him throw his leg over the bar of his bicycle and pedal off whistling 'Land of Hope and Glory'. She was postponing the moment. Who was the telegram about? Aunt Daphne of course. She had been asleep, and not heard the telephone ring again, and it had been Bert telephoning, or Flo; they'd sent this telegram instead because Aunt Daphne had had another stroke, from worry over her and Max.

She tore open the envelope and in a blur read the words, MOTHER TRACED IN CAMPS, RECOVERING WELL, REGRET FATHER DIED HEART ATTACK TWO YEARS AGO AT HOME, REGRET MRS MERKEL DIED AUSCHWITZ, AM TRYING TO TRACE FREDDY. LOVE DAVID.

Outside the kitchen window, the sky had a rosy glow. The lights were on in London town, at last, like the song.

Elbows on the kitchen table again, Fritzi in her lap, she stared into space. In a moment, she was going to settle into one of the blue and white chairs with cocoa or something.

Her father was never going to sit in it now. He'd never walk up the steps she'd been sweeping, never choose his café in Soho, never hear her war horrors, or tell her his. He'd never know the war had ended.

He'd never been one of the bodies either.

You see, Papa, I have found the good? If she closed her eyes, she could almost conjure up his face, the smiling, tender look of it. And Mama has known the end, she will be here, and she will walk up my steps and will see her name set in brass. I own a salon, Papa, and I am only twenty-three and because of you I am not one of the bodies, and our little Sophie isn't. You should see her now! And Max isn't either, he had a cleaner death than that. So that is good too. And listen. There is more good. Mrs Merkel has not lived to know what all his hurt has led to, or that he killed himself to spare me the agonies of a court case. But Mama will listen to every detail of what I have been through, and she will comfort me. I am to have a mother again, and it will be wonderful. I have been lonely beyond bearing, trying to be a mother to Sophie and she will lift this burden from me and be proud of how well I've done.

Having suddenly decided to run upstairs to her bedroom for the photographs of her parents, she placed them on the table in front of her and reread the telegram for the hundredth time. And the LOVE, DAVID. Love!

Yet he sent news like that through the air, to be tapped on to a piece of paper and brought by a boy on a bicycle.

He should have brought it himself.

If he cared enough, he'd be there now. He'd be across the table, his gaze as always going straight to her heart, going right into it and letting out some of the pain.

Chapter 58

An Interrogation Room near Bergen-Belsen, Germany, May 1945

David thought, While I was mucking out horses, that man was being trained in torture techniques.

'You chose to join the SS, did you? There was no coercion?'

'It was an honour, of course.' Ramrod stiff, he sat in his SS uniform, the badges removed from it, the marks of rank he was almost certainly still proud of.

'An honour to murder? How many have you killed with your boot, your whip, an axe, a pistol? Your rank tells me many. Wasn't it so, that promotion meant special qualities in brutality were required? How many women did you rape before you despatched them?'

'We do not rape sub-human trash.'

'Only human trash?'

'We leave rape to the Russians. The barbarians.' His face had a peculiar, stiff, blank appearance, monochrome almost, skin, eyes, yellowish-white, hair too.

'The Russians can in any case do as they wish, they are the conquerors now, and they have twenty million deaths to avenge. I am very surprised you dare call them barbarians.'

'I wasn't at the Russian front.'

'No. You had an easier time. Concentration camp life was pleasant for you and your colleagues, I believe. On the other side of the barbed wire, you lived in splendour from the fat of the conquered lands. Perhaps you regret those years?'

'I regret that Germany has lost the war.'

David stood up and wandered outside into the glare of the sunshine. 'Take him back to his cell,' he told the guard, making his way around the barracks to wander amongst the trees there. They were in full leaf, bright green in the June sun – and this, so close to the burned-down compound of Bergen-Belsen, seemed like a miracle, or an unnatural disgrace, he could never decide which.

Well, he thought, taking a deep breath of fresh air, I have at least rid myself of self-pity.

Now that he was here in Nazi Germany and knew exactly how it had been, he could tell himself with absolute certainty that he would never have put himself forward for special training in brutality, or stood watching while a doctor demonstrated how to avoid being spattered with blood when murdering by a shot to the skull. There was a particular point, apparently, at the back, and the condemned Jews had to lie face down on the ground in batches of ten.

It's most extraordinary, he decided, blinking up into the sunshine, I have here learned what darkness is, I have been face to face with it. And I have been released. I do know what I am. I am not that darkness, I have none of it inside me, and what is more, I don't give a damn that the SS horror in the room I have just left is possibly my half-brother, or that his father was possibly mine, because the man died in 1915 and I can never know whether or not he would have chosen savagery. I can decide he would not have done so. I can decide what I damn well like. I can decide to dismiss the whole moral issue of my right or non-right to Downlands, or, preferably, probably, discuss it openly with Will. Perhaps he'd like the Scottish place for his own, since he always preferred it, we'll sell the Irish one, and I'll keep Downlands. We shall both need a house for a wife and family.

In fact, to celebrate his *release*, he was going to get into the truck and drive over to see Esther Lehmann again. Susanna's mother shone to him like a light after the desolation of the Germany he had travelled through and the black truth of Nazi rule.

And he had found her, for Susanna. Every time he reminded himself of the moment he first saw her name on a list, an indecent, stubborn sense of joy began somewhere under his ribs and spread upwards into his throat until he wanted to laugh. In Bergen-Belsen, he wanted to laugh!

*

362

'Such a letter you brought me yesterday, Major Montgomery,' Esther said.

'I did?' Delighted, he watched the tentative smile on her face, the glow in eyes which today, suddenly, seemed to be set in flesh.

'From Susanna, and she promises me one from Sophie very soon.'

'And I'll bring it over to you myself. I hope it will be soon, but you remember there is only the British Army mail?' He settled himself next to her on the bench outside the barrack hut where she lived and which was far too much like the blocks she'd once suffered in, now, thank God, gone for ever. 'Anyway,' he said, 'it won't be all that long before the paperwork's been dealt with and you'll be travelling to England to see them for yourself.'

'Yes. And I shall see your dear mother to thank her for myself, for caring for my girls.' Her fingers, holding Susanna's letter, were blue with veins and had the strange Belsen and Auschwitz skin of an unnameable colour. He could make out every one of the bones of her hands, and just, the figure 4 of the tattooed number on her left wrist, which, pitiably, she kept trying to cover with her sleeve.

'She'll be the one to thank you for the pleasure and interest they have given her, Frau Lehmann.'

'They were good children.'

'I'm sure.' Her breath came in faint gasps. She couldn't yet talk much, and inside the mismatch of clothes given her from the collection the Army had made from each German family, her body was as near skeletal as it was possible to be. Skeletons in such clothes were all around the compound, walking, sitting, dream-like yet agitated and restless. Often, he'd spotted someone holding a piece of food. He'd once seen a crust in Esther's pocket, and the worst of it was, she would repeatedly feel for it.

'May I hear Susanna's news?' he asked. 'I have none from home, we're only bothering to send through anything vital, communications are almost impossible, and transport. Hitler promised in his writings that if Germany couldn't conquer the world, he'd destroy it, and as far as most of Europe goes, he's pretty well succeeded. Germany itself is a devastated country, Frau Lehmann, its cities bombed over and over by the Allies to force a surrender on the Nazis. Millions of Germans were well fed and clothed with the Nazis' spoils throughout the war, but many are now homeless, without food or fuel, and only the British Army, the Americans, the Russians are in a position to supply these things.'

'And I must wait for news of my boy, yes, I understand.'

'I'm afraid so, but as I've told you, I had Freddy's real and his false name put on the search lists, Frau Hahn's also, your addresses and the area of the convent where she took him. I'm going into Berlin myself this afternoon and might find out something.'

'We here have been wondering if the linden trees still stand on the Linden. There's an old Berliner song about those trees, claiming the city will fall if the trees do.'

'Let's say I doubt they'll be giving out a single bud this spring. Russian tanks roll down the Linden at the moment, and their cannon. They took Berlin from the east with tremendous artillery bombardment and any Berliner left will be living some kind of medieval existence, in cellars, and in a state of terror. They will expect no mercy from the Russian soldiers and will get none. But I pity them. They've been trapped for many months, forbidden to leave though the city was being blown to rubble. Hitler apparently ordered anyone trying to get away to be shot, he wanted Berliners to die for not fighting hard enough.'

She seemed to sink back into herself at this news, retreating from him, as she had done before. He waited, gazing about him at the other survivors in their own Belsen separateness. From that, and from those words which said too much, 'the gas', the woman beside him had saved Susanna, and Sophie, and her boy.

'Perhaps,' he said, to go on, because if you began to think in this place, you wouldn't be able to utter a single worthwhile statement, 'perhaps, who knows, your apartment still stands. I should like some of your family things to be returned to you, photographs, photographs hold memories, don't they, they are better than nothing. Meanwhile, though, Susanna?'

'Oh, Susanna's news!' Trembling, she began to extract the letter from its envelope. 'You did not inform me my girl was a married woman, Major.'

'No. I decided it was better she let it all out to you herself, gradually. She's had an eventful six years.' He had avoided the subject deliberately, having reached the stage of almost denying it to himself, or rather, the stage of leaping forward to the divorce

364

and Max moving on with his own concerns and not causing any problems – almost, dear God, of thinking of Esther as his mother-in-law-to-be.

'So that is why you couldn't reveal to me that Susanna is a widow?'

'A widow?' He felt his mouth had dropped open. He was stunned. He must go to her, at once, he'd have the right now, and she'd need support, because with her tender heart she was going to be stricken with grief. They had so much past in common, she and the boy.

'I have to be glad, I think,' Esther was saying, 'that Max's mother has not lived to learn her only son killed himself, just as I am glad poor Lottie went straight to the gas and did not have to endure Auschwitz for long.'

'Max committed suicide?' The worst, he thought, and then, crass as could be – he'll be forever a shadow between us, because she will blame herself, suicides always leave blame behind. Yet she hadn't sent for him. She hadn't understood.

'It seems so. She tells me not to worry, everyone has been very kind to her, the police . . .'

'Yes, of course, there'll be police,' he muttered, 'questions.' Hadn't she been keeping those last moments together close to her heart, as he had? If so, where was his telegram, PLEASE COME AT ONCE, I NEED YOU, SUSANNA? 'My mother will no doubt have been with her, my sister, she'll be all right.'

All right without me, he thought, a ridiculous, inappropriate fury making him get to his feet. She could have made it simple. The telegram. His going to her, nothing much declared, from delicacy, yet there, waiting for a decent interval to pass, a growing certainty, and not far off, the rest of the their lives together. He touched Esther's shoulder. 'I'll call again the day after tomorrow,' he said, setting off under the trees.

He hadn't even asked why the poor devil had done it, he realised, climbing into his truck. Perhaps picturing your mother crammed into a huge chamber designed and built for the murdering of hundreds of people by gas was reason enough. Lottie Merkel would have taken between fifteen and forty-five minutes to die, depending on the strength of the gas, and on her own strength; the stronger ones crushed the weaker to the ground, fighting for another agonising breath. The children, stuffed in last

365

to fill in the spaces must, please God, have died the quickest. But what malignant mind had decided on the babies' particular way to die? There must be a species of mankind quite different from the ordinary run of good and bad, and all the while hidden until some horror like Nazism lets them out.

The nausea he'd carried with him since the day he'd entered his first death camp swung into his throat with one of his blackest moods.

Having watched him drive off, young Naomi staggered across towards Esther from the kitchen block with their tea on a tray. 'Isn't the Major handsome with that scar on his face and his limp, Esther? War-wounds! They are somehow romantic, aren't they? Is he married?' She placed the tray at their feet. There were two cups of sweet Army tea on it and a plateful of bread and butter cut into squares.

'I don't think so. I have not asked him. But there is much he has not told me yet.'

Naomi indicated the bread and butter. 'You are going to eat yours straight off?' She sat down beside Esther and swung her feet in their too-big sandals.

'I might.'

'I am.' She leaned down and passed Esther a piece. 'If he'd just take me for a stroll under the trees or something, he might fall in love with me and send me to England to be his wife, so I am no longer a displaced person no country wants.'

'You are young,' Esther said, accepting the square. The smell of rich food was sometimes almost too much to allow her to eat. 'The world is out there for you to explore one of these days.'

'I feel I want to stay here being looked after by the British Army for ever, yet I also want great crowds of people to be ready to welcome me. Oh, they will say, poor child, how brave you have been, how you have suffered, what a special strength you must have, come, there is a place with us for such a girl as you.' She sighed. 'How did we survive, Esther? Why you and me and not some of the others?'

'I often wonder,' Esther said. And I wonder, she thought, how I am to become a mother again, so that my children do not find themselves orphans, for I may not have the strength, I do not have it, and they will not be as they were when I sent them away, they will be strangers. Even my boy will be a stranger, and my Susanna has been married, and widowed, without me.

There was a well in her somewhere ready to send up many tears, but she didn't know how to cry either.

'Your butter is melting, Esther, start.' Naomi reached down for another piece of bread and took a tender, loving bite of it.

Sometimes, Esther thought, good food in my mouth feels wrong, and these clean clothes on my body also, though sometimes they are a joy beyond expressing. Sometimes being alive is dizzyingly vivid, every second of it giving up treasures of reflection and a whole day not enough to watch the patterns of sunlight on the bark of a tree.

But mostly, being alive was this yearning pain in her chest, and this sense of betrayal, because she should have died, with the others.

Chapter 59

Berlin

They left the truck in charge of the driver, although he wasn't too pleased to be abandoned in a wasteland of rubble, where barely another soul moved, but where watching eyes could be felt, and somehow feared. David glanced back to see him light a cigarette and get out his pistol, for the show of it.

'Only ever see women and kids around, sir,' Sergeant Bevan said, 'and really old men.' He was whispering, as if they could be heard, or understood. 'Them last days when they was trying to save Berlin from the Russians, the SS dragged out any blokes under seventy or so and made 'em join that home guard of theirs, they even took the sick from the hospital beds and gave 'em nothing to tackle the Russkies with. Don't suppose many of 'em has ever made it back home. But the women look like men, and they're digging in this mess, sir, trying to make order out of it and build shelter for their kids. There's some clearing a space for themselves to set up a market again, though God knows what they'll be selling, or bartering, I suppose it'll be.'

David coughed on the dust as they stumbled along what had been a main street. The evening air seemed to be filled with a smoke and a kind of ominous gloom. But if you didn't know how the Berliners had suffered, the landscape itself, the terrible acres of devastation, had a kind of beauty, as London's had. There were half-walls standing, parts of church spires, the familiar piles of bombed-out buildings and the debris of war, burned vehicles, jagged shapes of shot-down aircraft, with amongst it the pitiful evidence of flight and death, a shoe, a scrap of clothing.

'And the women live in groups with their young like, I dunno, is it lionesses in Africa, sir?' The sergeant paused on a corner by a heap of mess thirty feet high. 'Anyway, this is the street you asked me to find, sir, there's a bit of the road name stuck up still, and it had a bakery because I spotted a bakery sign on my first trip, and see, there was definitely a series of those typical Berlin flats built round central courtyards, you can tell by the way the concrete's fallen. There's the pillars of an archway left as well, and look, there's even the number you gave me. It's been scribbled with charcoal on a piece of wood over a list of names, the present inhabitants I suppose. What's more, a pathway's been made through that arch, and I've seen airway piping sticking out of the rubble, which indicates to me women and children in the cellars, sir.' He waved an arm to take in his find and stood back, as if to admire it.

'You've done well, Sergeant.' David gazed from the blackened pillars of the arch, where Susanna and Sophie had run in and out, and on up at the jumble of concrete which had once formed the rooms they lived in. He could see here and there some ends of wrought iron – balcony iron, perhaps the very railing Susanna had leaned over after that November '38 night to pick out her father's Shakespeare and her own English school story amongst the splinters of glass. And Josef Lehmann must have walked past this spot with his head held high, the first morning of the yellow stars. 'It certainly fits in with all that Frau Lehmann and her daughters have told me.'

''Course, I'm not saying the Frau Hahn on that list is your one for sure, sir, but she is the right age, sixty odd you said, and luckily she's registered for medical treatment with us, giving this address as her former and her current one. That's how I found her and why I thought it was worth you coming yourself, sir.'

'And you did right, Sergeant. Know what medical treatment she had?' He gazed down what had been Susanna's street, where she'd dreaded going into the bakery shop and meeting some Hitler Youth thug, Konrad, his name was. He remembered it, and if he was right, he'd been her first near-taste of young love.

'Well, sir.' Sergeant Bevan was hesitating. 'You know, the women, sir, antiseptic, I suppose, and I dunno, cotton wool maybe? Or stitches?' He was embarrassed.

'You mean she was raped?'

369

'As far as we can gather, most Berlin females have suffered multiple rapes, sir.'

'Even at sixty? Dear God.'

'And older, sir. Them Russians, they're savages if they're let loose, and they were let loose, revenge you see, revenge for their own women the Nazis took and their own men, millions dead and millions prisoners-of-war. Those troops have travelled across most of Russia to get here and they've learned what's been done to their own people by the Krauts, they must have come upon some awful things, and I mean, they were the ones to find Auschwitz, weren't they, but I don't know as I could bring myself to take revenge on the women, even if some 'em were the worst of all in them camps, or especially because they were, really . . .'

'Yes,' David said, the nausea shooting right back up into his throat.

'Anyway, sir, come on.' Sergeant Bevan set off past the pillars and along the pathway between the heaps of broken concrete, choosing a collection of slabs to serve as a bench. 'We'll sit here nice and easy like and sooner or later we'll be aware of something that suggests we're being spied on from the cellars. The women'll be down there, see the pipes for the air? Laundry cellars they'll be and that's something we could copy from the Krauts to my mind, blocks of flats with their own laundry area and drying rooms in the attics.' He waited for David to settle himself before taking his place beside him and offering him a cigarette. 'We'll show 'em we're prepared to offer a few of these. Like as not some kid's head'll appear shortly, and fags is the best currency, and coffee, and I bet them women wouldn't mind the packet of dried milk I got with me.'

With a sense of unreality, David smoked, thinking of the extraordinary nature of his presence in the courtyard Susanna had known, and Sophie, Esther, where Olympic music had blared out in August 1936 and where never once had they been greeted pleasantly by any neighbour other than Jewish tenants and Frau Hahn. But now, they have Mayfair, he thought, and Downlands, and dignity, thank God.

He jumped when the sergeant suddenly shouted, 'Frau Hahn, please!'

'She's here?'

370

'No, some kid's head I just seen down there, it's gone now. Maybe the lady will be next.'

More minutes passed until the sound of scrabbling broke the silence. A small figure emerged from somewhere near the archway and began to make its way towards them. You could only tell it was a woman from the stick-like legs under a sacking apron. Otherwise she seemed to be dressed in men's garments, a cap, a soldier's jacket and boots she'd probably taken from the dead. There was a frill of sacking around her ankles for the boots were too big, as the cap was, but from under the cap two quite sharp eyes appeared in dark, wrinkled skin. This poor soul has been raped, David thought, getting to his feet with a lump in his throat, because Flo had come to his mind, and his mother. 'Frau Hahn?' He held out his hand, and Sergeant Bevan held out a cigarette.

It was the cigarette she chose to take, ignoring the lit match and stowing it away in some inside pouch of her clothing before inspecting him from his boots up.

'I am come from Frau Lehmann,' he said.

She looked back at him for a long moment, expressionless. 'She lives?' she said finally.

'She is getting well in Bergen-Belsen.'

At this she dropped her gaze and sat down on a heap of rubble, nodding and nodding, as if to say, Yes, of course, and then sniffing, because tears had begun to roll down her cheeks. 'Is good,' she said.

'Yes.' He sat down too and accepted another cigarette for himself.

'You want to take the boy from me?'

'You mean he's actually with you?' He felt himself smile. 'That's wonderful, and far more than we expected, we were just hoping today for the address of the convent so the sergeant and his men could try and find it. Just to find you, Frau Hahn, has seemed like a miracle . . .'

'Didn't leave him at the convent because they refused to have him when we arrived on their doorstep. Those good Catholic ladies decided it was too risky.'

'Freddy's been with you all this time?'

'He has. We lived in my storeroom. We survived every one of your bombs.' This, with its hint of irony, made him smile again.

'You have your own son with you too, I hope? Frau Lehmann

has told me how many risks he was prepared to take to get those papers for the boy, and she's anxious to thank him.'

'He was a son to be proud of and he wasn't no Nazi either. But I haven't got him, how many of our lads d'you think came back from the Russian front? If he was lucky, he froze to death, my son, so the boy you call Freddy is all I have now. You'd better take him quick.'

In the end, they reached an agreement. Frau Hahn was to tell Freddy his mother was alive but very ill, and that meanwhile he'd live with Frau Hahn so he could accustom himself to the idea of leaving her and going to England. Meanwhile, Sergeant Bevan would arrange for them both to receive extra rations. One day soon, his mother would visit and they could go on from there, without haste, for their own and the boy's sake.

He didn't want to stay any longer, he felt cold, and tired to death. It wasn't until they'd given Frau Hahn what they'd brought and they'd reached the street that he realised he hadn't seen Freddy. But Bevan had seen him. 'Look back a minute, sir.'

A shrunken little boy stood close up to Frau Hahn, watching them go. He was dressed in sacking oddments, with huge boots stuffed with something on his feet and a tiny white face with dark holes for eyes. Around them appeared more figures, women, women holding rags in their arms that were probably babies, or pretend babies, because they were asking for food, begging, for Army milk, Army bread, bully beef, anything.

Yes, he thought, your babies are starving. That's what you're telling me. Has anyone ever told you what happened to the Jewish babies in the camps? Well, if you dare admit to yourself there were places for murdering hundreds of thousands of people, ask yourself how the babies were killed in some of them. Very special minds worked it out, your brothers perhaps, your father, your sisters, God forbid. There was the boiling human fat streaming from the ovens cremating those gassed bodies, you see, and the babies were thrown in it. Clever, eh? Such a saving of time and trouble.

'Let's hurry, Sergeant,' he said, 'I want to breathe clean air.'

'So do I, sir, but we found him, my word, we found him straight off.'

'We did, Sergeant, thanks to your diligence.' And whatever

else in all this he thought, I shall have two Lehmanns to take home for Sophie and Susanna. And that's not a bad tally. Most of the refugees sent to England on those special trains would shortly find they hadn't a single relative left and the only trace of them would be names on a list.

Chapter 60

Hertford Street, London

David stood on the doorstep. He said, 'You know who told me about Max?'

Susanna shook her head.

'Your mother. And she couldn't come to you.'

'Neither could you. You were in Germany doing far more important things.'

'I could have got a few days' compassionate leave. That is what I have now. I asked for it. I said, a member of my family has suffered the loss of her husband in very harrowing circumstances, sir, and my CO said, then get the next flight going out, Major.'

'Aunt Daphne's been wonderful.'

'My mother's had enough disasters to cope with.'

'Yes. I didn't want to worry her with this one, but Patch told her and she came straight away although Will was due home, and the police were very nice.'

'The police were very nice! Susanna, look at me.'

She wouldn't. Her eyes were fixed somewhere near his boots, her face was ghostly pale, there were shadows it shouldn't have. Yet she seemed about sixteen in her little blouse and slacks, and so fragile, pitiful to him, and lovely.

'Aren't you going to let me in?'

'Sorry.'

He stepped inside, closed the door behind him and followed her along the hallway. 'I should like some coffee, please. I have been on a very long flight in a very slow bomber. Coffee wasn't served on it, but I feel it must be time for coffee.'

As quiet as a ghost, she'd slipped down the stairs with the dog in her arms and was moving about the kitchen.

'You've made this cosy,' he said, taking off his jacket and cap and throwing them on the end of the table as if he were at home – and where he noticed the telegram lay, the one that told her he'd found Freddy. He wasn't to have any thanks for that either. 'And you managed to pick up a rocking chair like Flo's?'

'Second-hand of course. I've re-covered it in the same mattress material as the other two. It was for my father. I had this dream of the three of us sitting here on winter evenings, around the boiler, when Freddy and Sophie were in bed. If you open the front of it, you can see the glow of the fire and that makes it a bit like the stoves we had in Germany.'

His fury was whipped away. He'd been furious, with her! 'Susanna, I should just like to know how the position with the police has been left, in case I can help, even at this stage, there are ways . . .'

'Of hushing things up, yes.' She was filling the kettle but turned around suddenly and looked up at him for the first time, her eyes huge and veiled, agonising. 'The solicitor's been doing his best.'

'My mother told me that in a very crackling telephone conversation last night.' He could hardly stand still. There was such hurt in her. 'Susanna, did you find him?'

'Yes.' She put the kettle on the stove. 'We were at Madame Lola's together that night, he called me to go to him, he told me what he'd done, in Paris, and to Mr Montgomery, and we went to bed. When I woke up, I found a note on the bathroom door telling me not to go in. He'd cut his wrists with a kitchen knife. He was lying in the bathtub, so the blood could drain away. One of his arms had fallen out. I always thought I'd have to watch over him, but I didn't do it well enough, did I?'

'Oh, my poor girl.' Stupidly, he stood there, watching her busy with the coffee.

'But it's all right.' She picked up a coffee-pot and another of her gazes pierced his heart. 'I am beginning to recover, if one ever can. I realise it was for the best. He suffered inside, Max, and he couldn't share his misery, he couldn't speak of it, especially not to me, because he had to look after me, he had to give me my start. Really, he couldn't manage to go on living, and I am glad for him, that he's at peace now.'

375

'And you, Susanna? Why didn't you write to me at that special address I gave you? Haven't I always given you an address? There's not been a single moment in this war when you haven't been able to write to me. Only you and my mother ever had it. I used to think, if Susanna ever needs me, she'll send for me.'

'Yes! But as soon as you arrive, you have to leave. I expect even now the plane's revving up on the airfield and you have to catch it.' She was angry with him, and suddenly, he couldn't breathe. Stifling, he said, 'If you will tell me you need me to stay, I will let the plane go without me. I've been waiting a long time, six years, Susanna, for you to reach out to me.'

Susanna, searching blindly for matches, heard her own voice raised very loud, and somehow full of tears, there were tears in her mouth. 'And I've been waiting for you to come here to me and you didn't, you sent me news of my father's death on a piece of paper, don't you think I've had enough deaths to bear without you?' Horrified, frantic, she tried to wipe her face with her fingers, sniffing, and weeping, ugly.

'Susanna. Susanna.' Her name, and his special way of saying it, he was saying it over and over, wiping her face for her, holding her hands, wrapping his arms around her.

'At last you've come,' she sobbed, giving herself up to the feel of him, and to something wonderful beginning deep down and spreading up to her throat, joy, relief.

He said, roughly, 'At last you are where you are meant to be, Susanna Lehmann, isn't that so? Isn't it?'

With a final racking sob, she said, 'Yes,' and he, almost laughing, said, 'It will have to be where you stay.'

Epilogue

Hertford Street, London, June 1946

Choking back a cry, Esther emerged from the weight of her dreams.

'Mama.' Freddy's voice, from the bed beside hers.

'Yes, darling.' With her old woman's wheezing, she eased herself further up against the pillows. She'd fallen too far down into the awful softness of the mattress, she'd been drowning in it.

'I am writing to my other mother.'

'Good boy.' Slowly, she turned her head to take in the sight of her son sitting up in the comfort that delighted him. Fair hair curling off his forehead as Josef's had, very pale still, and thin, tiny for his age of a full ten years, he had the same air of an old man that he'd had before, and the same concentration. She remembered much of her last months with him, their anguish, but often different memories got in the way.

'I've done one page describing our bedroom, the new pencils and the notepad my sisters have given me, and the bag of caramels from their ration. I shall draw my new jacket and trousers at the end of my letter to show her how I shall look as an English schoolboy.'

'Frau Hahn will be happy you have such clothes. Tell her we are very sorry she cannot come to visit us in England yet but Major Montgomery will bring her to us as soon as it is allowed for German people to leave the country. It's taken a whole year for our papers to go through.'

Today, she thought, I am to force myself out into the noise and rush of the streets, in order to be a proper mother, to see my

377

daughter married, even if I am superfluous to her. I shall pretend, because my girls need me to pretend, and then I must somehow live on for their sakes, although there is something inside me shouting, Listen, listen, and they won't listen. Anything else I want they will give, food for ten mothers, chocolate, they will dress me head to toe, they will give me love, so much love, too much, and flowers, there are flowers in a dear little blue pot by me now, smelling of rotting things.

Freddy said, 'Perhaps my other mother is too busy to come and see us, perhaps she won't until her work with the rubble ladies is done and Berlin is rebuilt stone by stone. I'm telling her I'm going to have my hair cut this morning in the bathroom because I'm too frightened of London to go into a shop.'

'It's your Mama who's frightened, not her brave boy. Susanna is pretending it's you because she cannot admit it's her big grown mother.'

And somehow, I must manage, she thought, for even if I explained, they'd remind me Emile, the hairdresser, is not an Auschwitz barber. God forbid, Mama, they'll cry. But their Emile will bring it back to me, that first night in Auschwitz, it will be *as if* he is one those poor barbers we arrivals decided were lunatics. They were not lunatics, they were inmates, like us, and somewhere, in some part of me that does not show, I shall hear the others wailing and sobbing, I shall be naked again and blue and red with cold and shame, and Emile saying nice soothing things to me won't matter because from his mouth I shall hear, Quick, quick, we don't want to hurt you, Next, next, we don't want to hurt you, but those Auschwitz barbers did hurt, they couldn't help hurting, and swathes of hair all colours piled up, black, red, blond, and the pubic hair danced across the floor in puffs as the SS boots stamped and the whips cracked, Quick, quick, and they tried not to hurt, tried not to touch the most intimate parts of women like their mothers, like their sisters, good Jewish boys they were, weeping, every one destined for the gas.

'My other mother used to cut my hair. She'd borrow scissors from Frau Fest, she had scissors, we used to share things, my other mother had a cooking pot.'

'In the Berlin cellars?'

'Yes, and when the bombs fell we'd curse the English and the

378

Americans and when the shells came from the artillery, we'd curse the Russkies.'

'You remember going into the shelter under the stairs at home with Frau Leona and Papa and me?'

'No. Sometimes there were flames bursting into the cellars all along the apartment buildings because the ladies had knocked holes in the walls so we could keep running to escape whatever there was that was worst. Mostly in the end it was the flames that were worst, we didn't want to get burned to cinders.' He put down his pencil and pulled a caramel from its bag under the bedclothes. 'I saw a lot of cinder bodies in the streets in the gaps between bombing, they looked like burned wood, and the trees had parts of burned bodies hanging from them.' Pausing long enough to unwrap the sweet and sniff it, he went on. 'The zoo was bombed and in the zoo gardens there were animal bodies burned to cinders, but I didn't see them, I wish I had. There was a whole elephant there which couldn't have been burned to cinders because lots of men arrived to cut it into pieces for people to eat. They went right inside it, apparently, and nothing was wasted. It took days. Frau Fest was afraid the crocodiles hadn't died and they might crawl through the drains to get us.'

Cheek bulging, he resumed his task and Esther thought, Yes, my darling and you may tell me that story many times, as you have already, and I promise I shall never stop you and I shall always listen, because that is very nearly all I have to offer you for the moment.

'Tell Frau Hahn Suzy has made me a suit too, a good black it is, say, she'll understand, and a beautiful white organza blouse for the wedding, with a black silk rose set in veiling for a hat. Remind her the dear girl is going to send her a warm suit for the Berlin winter and a coat if she can get enough material, because she's grateful to Frau Hahn for caring for her brother.'

'I think I shall send her some of my treasures.'

Esther turned her head towards her own treasures the girls had laid out on the bedside table, American marzipan in a pretty box, a tin of biscuits made by the cook at the country house, a fine silver chain necklace and a locket containing a tiny photograph of the two of them. There was also a box of letters they'd written to each other during their war so that she could learn about it, and the craftsman's design for the plaque of Estanna Modes.

379

I long to be grateful, she thought. I am grateful. And I am proud. Only feeling seems to sit somewhere on the surface of me, it is not deep down. Deep down is maybe full, or is it empty?

I am struggling to understand myself, she thought, with a flush of horror. I think I have lived too many days in other places for their sakes, and the fight was too much for me, I have grown too old. Josef, if he'd lived in those places, he'd have sloughed them off, he'd have walked up the steps laughing with joy, true joy, and he'd have gazed down Hertford Street. Look, he'd have said, look at this fine city street, this is going to be my street, I am going to be happy here. And he would have been happy.

Sometimes, she was lucky enough to have a sense of him back, a glimpse of the way he was, his loving presence, and once, she'd woken with the weight of his right arm across her right side the way it used to be, a mirage of an arm it was, but it felt as if he'd found her.

'My sisters are down in the front hall with your coffee and my cocoa, Mama,' Freddy observed without lifting his hand from the page. 'I can hear Fritzi's paws on the wooden floor.'

'You have good hearing, my son.'

'I used to listen for my other mother because she's hard of hearing. I'd especially listen for the Russkies coming, she was very afraid the Russkies would find her and the other women, but they never hurt children, so I'd creep as near the street as I dared, listening for the Russian soldiers and sniffing for their tobacco smoke. She used to call me her little man.'

'Which is what I used to call you, Freddy,' Esther said sharply, surprising herself. Was she to begin to feel, to suffer afresh for what had been taken from her? She must be careful. If she was to come quite out of those other places into this wide-awake real world, she might run about weeping as she did in her dreams.

'My sisters and Fritzi have reached the first-floor landing.' Throwing down his pad and grinning with delight, Freddy swung his legs over the side of the bed.

'Mama! Freddy!' They heard Sophie's voice, girlish, giggling.

'Be careful.' Susanna's then, a grown woman's voice, low and steady, delightful.

'I am being careful.'

'You'll knock the vase over.'

The door burst open, her two big giants of girls strode in with a

380

tray and more flowers, and the little dog flew across the room to be swept into Freddy's arms.

'Don't let Mama see Fritzi licking your face,' Sophie cried, thudding the tray on to a chair. 'You'll be stripped naked and have to sit in the bath to be scrubbed free of dog germs.'

Esther felt herself smile, they expected her to smile. This was already an established house joke. 'Scrubbed by his Mama,' she said. They hadn't understood about the germs where she'd been.

'Good morning, Mama.' Pounding across the floor, Susanna kissed her tenderly and as tenderly plumped the pillows behind her. Such a golden giant she was! She smelled of soap and glowed with colour, ivory skin, blacker than black curls, dress a blazing yellow, and she was noisy, so noisy, she took up so much space, they all did here. Gently though, she placed the tray on her mother's knees and lifted the roses for her to smell.

'Lovely, my darling, and toast today, English toast like your Papa used to try and make us, d'you remember?'

'I do, Mama, but what d'you think Papa would say to my nails, look, red as red, aren't they? Sophie painted them for my wedding day.'

'Your Papa found everything about you beautiful.' She had already seen the nails. She watched her own ugly fingers reach for the toast. 'The last time I saw red nails was at the camp just after the Allies liberated us. They lined up the SS guards, female ones and all, and made them lift the bodies into trucks to be driven to the pits for burial. I remember the red nails on the flesh of my friends, they had lipstick too, those guards, right to the end.'

'Yes, Mama. You told us.' Susanna eased herself on to the bed beside her and put a loving arm around her shoulders. 'We've been talking about Papa downstairs this morning, discussing the future, you know, because straight after David and I come back, decisions are going to have to be made about Sophie's school.'

'Yes. Oh, Mama, what do'you think?' Sophie left Freddy and the dog and thudded on to the other side of the bed. Esther felt herself shrink back into the awful comfort of her pillows and her grey and yellow old woman's skin.

'I mean, now Suzy's marrying into money, Mama, we're safe, aren't we, nothing can happen, David will never let down me or Freddy or you, much less Suzy, and I mean, I'll still have Matric. as a safeguard, and it's not as if I'm aiming for the concert hall, just orchestra level, and I think Papa would love me to do something with my music, he never really wanted me to be a doctor, did he?'

'Papa would want you to be happy, child.' She almost put her hands to her ears. How they shouted!

'He would, wouldn't he? Yes!' Sophie sprang to her feet and threw herself on to her brother's bed where a lot of whispering and giggling began.

Susanna said, 'Mama, what d'you think? She's more or less turned against the sciences, but I think she'd have kept them up, for your sake, if you hadn't been able to come to us yet. It was really a vow she'd made you, and she's done well at them, she's cleverer than me. Your being able to get here this summer before the September term has released her, in a strange way, and of course, she has Papa's talent for music, her teacher at school says there's no doubt it's worth her trying to get into the Royal College. Will you give it a good think, please while I'm away?'

'Of course, my darling,' Esther said, tears welling up from somewhere, real tears. And I try and load my girls with my darkness, she thought, as if they have not done enough. 'But I think yes for Sophie.' The good Jewish mother, yearning for good sons-in-law, had been her. And there was nothing left of that woman.

'And yes for David?'

Esther nodded. 'Yes for David. He is maybe good enough for my Susanna.'

'Is he such a man? Like Papa?

'He's such a man, like Papa.'

Susanna sighed. 'Yes! And now, after your coffee, you'd better be thinking about baths for you and Freddy, then breakfast, then Emile will be here. After that, we can have fun getting ourselves dressed for my wedding day.'

With a kiss on her cheek, she leapt up and pounded to the doorway where Sophie joined her with the dog.

Exhausted, she and Freddy lay back, as the sound of the girls' steps receded.

'My sisters are very tall, Mama,' Freddy said, 'but I have grown to love them. We are lucky to have them, aren't we?'

'We are, my darling.'

'I'm tired now.'

'So am I.'

'But we must get ready.'

'Five more minutes.'

'Can I come into your bed?'

Esther drew back her covers and held out one of her unmotherly arms. Soon he was nestling tight beside her, a little boy you'd think eight or so in body, with an old mind and too much to forget.

It's as if we are on a raft together, she thought, on a sea invisible to people in this real world of London, England. What an easy, clean war they'd suffered!

'We're going to be happy today,' she said. 'For Susanna.'

'How d'you think she is this morning?' Susanna took the breakfast cutlery from its drawer and began to lay the table.

'The same,' Sophie said, stirring the porridge at the stove. 'Not really here with us.'

'It's going to take time, I suppose. David keeps saying all the survivors have her hollow-eyed, frantic look and her sort of distance.'

'Yes, he told me not to worry too much. Are you sure they'll want this porridge?'

'I decided to make it in case they're disappointed, but I could tell it was going to be hot today.' She wiped the stickiness from the golden syrup tin and put it on a plate. 'Freddy can't get enough syrup, he has everything soaked in it. I hope it makes him grow to a normal size or he'll be teased at school, which won't help. Being Jewish and having a German accent'll be enough.'

'I just feel she doesn't care about anything.' Sophie held the wooden spoon in the air and turned to gaze at her. 'And certainly not my education or my future.'

'And yet she must,' Susanna said, again. They'd had this conversation before. 'When she gets back her physical strength, she'll be our old Mama.'

'You think so?'

'I'll be expecting some improvement when I'm home from my holiday.'

'Your honeymoon,' Sophie said.

'My honeymoon,' Susanna repeated, a blush spreading up from her toes. David beside me, she thought, David and me, David's hands, his mouth.

'I shall go right away for mine, I shan't have it at Downlands.'
Sophie dropped the spoon into the saucepan and folded her arms.

'Why ever not?'

'Well, everyone around'll be watching the next morning.'

'Of course they won't.' Susanna laughed and with a flourish
placed the pot of freesias in the centre of the table. And anyway, I
shan't mind, she thought, because David and I will be together, at
last.

'I'll creep away for my wedding and my honeymoon, they'll
both be secret.' Sophie strolled to the back door and opened it to
the summer air.

'From your husband as well?'

'I'll go somewhere with only strangers present, so no one will
realise we've been to bed for the first time.'

Susanna picked four nice big Downlands eggs from their basket
and reached for the timer on the mantelpiece. 'In some country
places, the villagers celebrate outside the window all night, then
crowd into the bedroom with jokes, I think that's in rustic France
so you'd better not choose France for this secret honeymoon of
yours. Apart from that, what a subject to be talking about today of
all days.'

'Here comes Mrs Smith to join in.' Sophie edged the door
wider for the charlady to scurry past, a toothless grin on her face.
'My, my, ain't you two had breakfast yet? And where's your
mother and the little lad? You got this boiler going for their baths,
I hope?'

Susanna gazed dreamily at the small figure coaxing more heat
from the fire than she herself ever could. She had on a clean,
flowered apron, and what seemed to be her Sunday hat, a pink
straw with daisies. 'Where was your honeymoon, Mrs Smith?'

'Oh, Lord, me and Albert didn't have one, didn't wait for one,
neither, if you sees what I mean, and if I'm not mistaken that
telephone's ringing.'

Sophie rushed up to the hallway to answer it while Susanna
began to read out her list of the extra duties Mrs Smith would have
during her absence.

'It was Aunt Daphne,' Sophie announced, dashing back down
again five minutes later.

'Saying what?' Susanna pinned the list to the pantry door.

'Saying David wants to know if his beloved has had a good night and hasn't run away from him or anything.'

'Run away from him?' She felt a silly smile spread across her face and stay there. If she could run *to* him, she would, because the ceremony itself was for her mother's sake, and the wait had been so long!

Mrs Smith emerged from the broom cupboard and gave Sophie a nudge. 'She's in love, that one, look at her.'

Sophie grabbed her arm and they began to dance around the table, crooning the war's most popular song amended by themselves:

> 'She'll be his 'til the stars lose their glory,
> His 'til the birds fail to sing . . .'

Overwhelmed suddenly, *with joy*, Susanna felt she'd never forget this moment of her wedding day – when there was dancing in her kitchen, breakfast waiting for the two longed-for ones who'd very nearly starved to death, and a few words sent by David had just gone straight to her heart, as they always did.